DARING AND UNDAUNTED,
THEY FOLLOWED THEIR VISION
IN A STILL-VIRGIN LAND
OF OPPORTUNITY, TEMPTATION,
AND TREACHERY . . .

PHILIP TRENT—A Medal of Honor was not enough. Against odds and reason he would fight for ideals that could cost him his life . . . and the woman he loved.

LEAH MILES—She was torn between her love for Philip and devotion to her brother, a man whose burning envy and ambition could shatter all her dreams.

LLOYD MILES—His cunning ability to do the dirty work established his place in Washington. Greed and a lust for recognition fed his limitless talent for betrayal.

ROSE PULLIAM—Insinuating herself into the trust of those who couldn't be trusted, she would become as powerful as the men who were addicted to her seductive but deadly favors.

COLLIS HUNTINGTON—Bribery, seduction, and the fine art of the double cross were all weapons in his arsenal. He would destroy whatever stood between him and the power he craved.

THE ROBBER BARONS Volume I

POWER
AND GLORY

Gerald Canfield

 Created by the producers of
The First Americans, The White Indian,
and **The Holts: An American Dynasty.**

Book Creations Inc., Canaan, NY • *Lyle Kenyon Engel, Founder*

A DELL BOOK

Published by
Dell Publishing
a division of
Bantam Doubleday Dell Publishing Group, Inc.
666 Fifth Avenue
New York, New York 10103

The trademark Dell® is registered in the U.S. Patent and Trademark Office.

ISBN: 0-440-20545-X

Printed in the United States of America

Published simultaneously in Canada

August 1992

10 9 8 7 6 5 4 3 2 1

OPM

The progress of evolution from
President Washington to President Grant
was alone evidence enough to upset Darwin.

—*Henry Adams*

BUSINESS BARONS

Dr. Thomas Durant—*Union Pacific's Vice-President*
Collis P. Huntington—*Central Pacific's man in Washington*
George Train—*Durant's publicist*
General Grenville Dodge—*Union Pacific's chief construction engineer*

POLITICIANS

Schuyler Colfax—*Speaker of the House*
John O'Brian—*Representative from Indiana*
Oakes Ames—*Representative from Massachusetts*
Lafayette Baker—*Government and industrial spy*
Gus Trent—*Maryland State Representative*
J. T. Moverly—*Head of Congressional Investigative Committee*
B. F. Butler—*Representative from Massachusetts, Civil War major-general*

THE PLAYERS

Philip Trent—*Congressional investigator*
Lloyd Miles—*Durant aide*
Leah Miles—*Lloyd's sister*
Rosanna Pulliam—*Government and industrial spy*
Julia Grey—*Trent's secretary*
Archibald Edwards—*House Speaker's chief of staff*

R. TOELKE '90

PROLOGUE

October 27, 1864

In the October twilight a small vessel trailing a smudge of black smoke from a single amidships stack edged away from the motherly protection of the Union navy gunboats in Albemarle Sound toward the wide mouth of the Roanoke River. The fifteen sailors aboard the launch, including Lieutenant William B. Cushing, United States Navy, had volunteered for this mission to get relief from the grinding tedium of duty aboard the ships blockading Wilmington, the vital Confederate port that lay to the south of North Carolina's big sounds.

The sixteenth man, Major Lloyd Miles, had his own reasons for being the lone army representative on a venture of doubtful—to say the least—cuimination.

As the launch reached cruising speed, Miles braced himself against the vessel's motion by anchoring his rump against the rail. He had been introduced to Lieutenant Cushing only an hour before, and this was his first opportunity to examine the young officer.

Cushing stood with his legs wide and his arms behind his back. As Miles watched, the lieutenant turned, grinned, and winked at the navy men; but he had only a nod for the army officer who had been rung in on him at the last minute. Cush-

1

ing had made it clear that he considered Major Lloyd Miles to be deadweight, a liability.

Cushing's hard face made him look older than his twenty-one years. The length of his hair pushed naval regulations to their limits, and he seldom blinked, his eyes glaring out defiantly from beneath his heavy eyebrows. His mouth was a straight, morose line.

In talking with members of the volunteer crew while waiting for departure from the mother ship, Miles had been told that Cushing was a firm but fair commander aboard his ship, the Union cruiser *Monticello.* Miles knew from his contacts with higher authorities that many navy officers of Cushing's rank or higher called him—teasingly, fondly, or with overt envy—the navy's own hero.

It was because of Cushing's growing fame that Lloyd Miles was on board the navy steam launch entering the Roanoke River.

Cushing had first gained notoriety—and the grudging respect of Union navy senior officers—in 1862, when he took the steamer *Ellis* up the New River to Jacksonville, to capture two rebel schooners. His reputation for accomplishing the impossible, along with his steely self-confidence, had convinced the navy high command to allow him to undertake this mission, the goal of which was to sink a ship that had altered the naval balance of power in the strategic North Carolina coastal sounds. That ship, the Confederate ram *Albemarle,* was a deadly threat to the unarmored Union gunboats on her occasional excursions away from her moorings at Plymouth, eight miles up the Roanoke.

Of all the men aboard the launch, only Lloyd Miles knew that, oddly enough, Cushing's fame and his past achievements had almost led the Navy Department to turn down his plan to sink the *Albemarle.* The Union badly needed heroes. The war was going well by strategic standards, but the besieged Confederacy was fighting a desperate last stand to save home and country. The casualty lists from north, south, and west were daggers of pain penetrating the heart of the Union. To be able to tell a mourning nation about the great and honorable feats of death-defying daring by a man like Will

Cushing would divert attention from the less glamorous men who were being killed by the thousands. But to lose Cushing in some harebrained stunt would be a severe blow to Union morale.

The discussions of Cushing's proposal to go after the *Albemarle* had extended all the way up to the office of Secretary of War Edwin McMasters Stanton and had involved not only the navy but army generals and certain politicians. The army, fearing that Cushing might succeed, had not wanted to be left out of the heroics. The generals had suggested that the army might help by staging a penetration toward the Roanoake and Plymouth. The navy had politely refused the offer on the grounds that such an action would draw rebel attention to the Plymouth area and put all defense forces on the alert. In the end the navy agreed, reluctantly, to allow a covert army observer to accompany Cushing's party. The action was taken in the name of interservice cooperation. The army officer would be given every courtesy but none of the credit.

So it was that along with Lieutenant Cushing and his fourteen-man crew, Major Lloyd Miles, a staff officer from the Army of the James, was in the launch that was puffing its way up the river.

The night of October 27, 1864, had been selected for the raid because of its protective, moonless gloom. The first seven miles of the journey passed quickly, without incident; but the relaxed atmosphere was suddenly altered as the crewmen realized they were approaching the first point of danger.

Miles, sensing the increased alertness, whispered a question to the man next to him and was answered with a fiercely hissed warning to be silent. Confederate pickets were stationed on the wreck of the *Southfield* just one mile below Plymouth. Fire from the *Southfield* could rake the open deck of the launch. If the raiding party were sighted at the *Southfield* watch point, there'd be no chance of getting close to the *Albemarle* undetected.

Miles held his breath. He had heard enough about Cushing to believe that even if they were spotted by the men on the

Southfield, Cushing would push on. He let out a sigh when the launch was safely past the wreck.

Cushing moved quickly among his crew, patting a shoulder here, shaking a hand there, and whispering words that under less dramatic circumstances might have seemed like bravado. He had a perky little salute for Miles.

"Into the lion's mouth, eh, Major?" Cushing asked.

"Excelsior," Miles said in what he hoped was a light tone. He was well aware of the lieutenant's disdain for him.

"I have to be here, Major," Cushing said. Miles could see the whiteness of his teeth through a tight grin. "I have a certain reputation to live up to. Why in God's name are you here?"

"Mr. Cushing," Miles said, "that is an excellent question, for which I shall try to find an answer at a more convenient time, providing that we both are still interested."

The steam engine of the thirty-foot launch chuckled so quietly that it was not heard by the Confederate infantry on the shore until it was within sight of the wedge-shaped, iron-covered *Albemarle,* moored next to the bank on the Plymouth side of the river. Cushing whispered an order, and the mutter of the launch's engine became a pounding, accelerating roar. The vessel leapt forward toward the menacing silhouette of the Confederate ram.

With blinding flashes and unnerving thunder the Southern infantry opened fire from the riverbank, their rifle balls clanging and reverberating against the launch's stack and sides. A man cried out in pain as he was hit. Responding quickly, the sailors manning the launch's howitzer fired a shell, and after it exploded on shore, shouts of alarm came from the *Albemarle.*

A torpedo had been rigged to extend at an upward angle from the bow, secured there by lines running to a davit forward of the stack. In the flash of gunfire Miles saw Cushing loose the lines, lowering the torpedo to a less acute angle. The bulk of the ironclad loomed over the launch. Cushing let out a yell of excitement, and Miles heard himself screaming, "Go, go, go!" Within seconds the torpedo would smash into the vulnerable hull of the ram below her thick iron armor.

Cushing was motioning his men toward the stern of the launch. "Get ready to jump for it!" he screamed, flinging aside his overcoat and shoes.

Miles rid himself of his cumbersome outer clothing as the launch approached the log boom that floated in a protective perimeter around the ram. Muttering a benediction, he braced himself. A gun aboard the *Albemarle* bellowed just over Cushing's head as he leaned forward to check the angle of the torpedo. The launch hesitated, threatened to stall, and then with a lurch and a mighty splashing of water plunged over the log boom.

In the future Lloyd Miles would say that the impact with the log boom had thrown him overboard. He was not the first to go but among the first. He took one last look forward and saw Cushing lowering the torpedo. In those last few seconds the deadly point of the weapon was inserted under the armored overhang of the ram.

From where he was in the water, Miles wasn't sure whether the explosion of the torpedo or a cannon blast from the *Albemarle* sent a wave of water surging up over the sides of the launch, swamping it. The crew—those who had survived the hail of musket fire—were taking to the water while rebel soldiers and sailors fired at them from a range of mere feet. Miles could hear the distinctive sound made by balls zipping past his ears. Several voices were screaming out to him to surrender, even as the rifle fire continued.

Voices called out from the dark water. The rebels were still yelling for everyone to surrender. Miles stretched out in the dark, frigid water and swam for his life. Behind him the *Albemarle* settled to the bottom of the river, never to fight again.

CHAPTER 1

Major Lloyd Miles reined in his horse to allow the passage of a company of blue-coated infantry marching down toward the transports anchored in Virginia's James River. These were fresh men, alert and straight backed, their youthful élan not yet blunted by contact with the stubborn, exhausted, but still deadly soldiers of the Confederate armies. The pink-cheeked lieutenant marching with the company threw Miles a perfect West Point salute, which the major returned with one lazy, smooth motion.

A stranger looking at Major Lloyd Miles on this November 1864 morning would have seen a man comfortable in his uniform, a man who looked as if he had spent more than a few months with a field unit chasing wily old Bobby Lee or one of Lee's talented generals. The once-pristine blue of the major's tunic was sun bleached, and his wide-brimmed hat, which dipped rakishly over his left eye, showed the effects of rain and wind. He was a trim man, his face clean shaven in a time when bushy beards and sweeping mustaches were the rule.

In army terminology Miles's face would have been described as standard issue: mouth, one—equipped with medium-full lips with a natural set just short of a smile; nose, one—attractively thin and as yet unbroken, just long enough to give it a certain character; eyebrows, two—fuller toward

7

the center and arched upward, giving his blue eyes a slightly quizzical look that made those meeting Miles for the first time mistake his natural expression for one of personal interest.

As he approached the riverfront Miles was challenged not once but three times by the concentric circles of Union guards around the mooring spot of the steamer *Greyhound,* the floating headquarters for Major General Benjamin Franklin Butler, commander of the Army of the James. A wry half-smile made Miles look boyish as he identified himself to the same men who had often seen him enter Butler's headquarters. He couldn't blame the general for his abundant security; if Miles had done some of the things that Butler had, he would have wanted still another ring of armed guards around him.

Southerners were not alone in hating Butler, also known as the "Beast of New Orleans." Miles suspected that it wouldn't be difficult to find men in Butler's own command who would cheerfully send the fat man off to his doubtful reward, for many soldiers had lost friends because of his bungling. Miles could understand the frustration of the men who made up the Army of the James—men who hid their idealism and patriotism behind cynical comments regarding the intelligence and abilities of their officers. Even though Miles had not participated in bloody and futile charges—had not faced Johnny Reb across a muddy, smoke-covered, body-strewn field—he was sick and tired of senior officers who were unable to move their units into battle position in time, who chose exactly the wrong times and places to engage the enemy, and who seemed to be totally oblivious to the tragic fact that their stupidity was being paid for with the blood of the common soldiers under their command.

Before his temporary assignment with the navy on Will Cushing's mission, Miles had repeatedly filed a request for a transfer; but General Butler had denied it every time. Miles was feeling a bit desperate as he dismounted, left his horse in the care of a young private, and saluted the officer of the guard at the gangplank leading to the deck of the *Greyhound.* Only an idiot—or a Southerner—could deny that the war was nearly over. Old Vinegar Face, General William Tecumseh Sherman, had taken Atlanta and was getting down to the serious business of cutting the Confederacy in twain. The Mississippi was closed to Confederate commerce, and Grant had old Bobby Lee penned up behind trenches in Richmond and Petersburg. All the rebel ports except Wilmington, in North Carolina, were closed. Confederate soldiers were going into battle barefoot, ragged, hungry, and short of everything but determination.

It would soon be over, and all Lloyd Miles would have to show for his two years of service would be several letters of commendation from senior officers and the personal knowledge that he had put his life on the line at least once. That was not enough. There would be opportunity aplenty after the war for an ambitious young man. But an ambitious young man who could sport a couple of medals, evidence of military glory, would have a head start on the others.

Lloyd Miles knew that with each passing day his chances of reaping a bit of glory were diminishing. Of course, there was still the upcoming expedition to Fort Fisher, which protected the primary sea entrance to Wilmington, but that would be largely a naval operation. Miles wanted glory, but he wasn't interested in earning it by taking part in another bloody amphibious assault.

Another reason for Miles's reluctance to join in that mission was his total lack of confidence in the general. Butler could be fierce with the ladies—his infamous Order Number 28 had threatened to regard any female insulting a Union soldier in New Orleans as "a woman of the town plying her avocation"—but in battle he was a slow-moving, slow-thinking behemoth easily baffled by almost any reb maneuver. Since being transferred from duty with the occupying forces in North Carolina to General Butler's staff, Lloyd Miles had wished on more than one occasion that he were in a position to claim the reward put on the head of the "outlaw" Butler by President Jefferson Davis of the Confederacy.

Butler's headquarters aboard the steamer *Greyhound* had been made comfortable with furniture and fittings shipped by military transport from Washington. As Lloyd Miles entered the general's office and saluted him with a cheery "Good morning, sir," Butler sat beside his ornate desk, his trunklike legs thrown wide, his gleaming sword resting between his thighs with its tip on the floor. He was almost totally bald and, like many bald men, tried to compensate by letting the fringe of hair at his neck grow untidily long. His corpulence caused his new blue tunic to bulge. A double row of brass buttons gleamed brightly, and the epaulets on his shoulders sported tassels of gold. Hidden behind his walrus mustache was a flaccid mouth. His eyes were hooded so heavily that it seemed that he would have difficulty seeing.

"So, you're back, Miles. I heard you were alive," Butler said. Since the presence of an army observer on Cushing's raid had been kept secret from the public, Butler had lost interest in the mission.

"I suppose, sir," Miles said cheerfully, "that you've seen the latest newspapers."

Butler grunted, his usual response to a question to which he did not know the answer.

"It got rather exciting down south in your old area of command," Miles said. Butler had served as commander of the Department of Virginia and North Carolina before being given command of the Army of the James.

Miles spread a Washington paper on Butler's desk. The fat man moved ponderously, lowered his hooded eyes, read for a few moments, then cursed.

Miles's eyebrows arched as he smiled. He had correctly anticipated Butler's reaction to the adoring, almost worshipful attention that the press was giving to the navy's prime daredevil, Lieutenant William Cushing, for his latest exploit, the sinking of the *Albemarle*.

"Rather good publicity for the navy, isn't it, sir?" Miles asked in a serious tone.

Miles understood his commanding officer well enough to know that Butler's fondest dream was to see his own name in a favorable light in the newspapers, as opposed to the publicity he'd gotten for his stint in New Orleans and for his bungling at Bermuda Hundred, where Miles had been marooned with him. Old P. T. Beauregard had sat across the base of the

peninsula like a stopper in a bottle while an opportunity to
take the Confederate capital was lost. After Butler had allowed the Army of the James to be rendered useless by a
single swift maneuver by Beauregard, one editorial had said,
"If, indeed, President Lincoln's intent is to prolong the war
into the decade of the seventies, it would behoove him to look
for more generals of the caliber of General B. F. Butler."

"Are you being a smart aleck, Miles?" Butler growled.

"Not at all, sir," the major said. "I am as envious as you
are, sir, of this wonderful publicity being given to the navy. I
suspect that many officers of our often-maligned army feel as
you and I do about this."

"And just how do we feel, Major?" Butler asked with a
failing attempt at sarcasm.

"I feel, sir, that it's damned well high time that the army
did something to make them write about us in words like
these." He read from the newspaper article. " 'Once again,
the heroic and daring Lieutenant W. B. Cushing has demonstrated the bravery and dedication to duty of the Union
navy—' "

"Enough," Butler said.

The general's surly silence told Miles that he was expected
to continue. "I have, sir, a plan to counter this attention
being given to the navy."

"Speak, then. You know I'm busy."

"You are aware, sir, that General Lee has said that if the
port at Wilmington falls, he can no longer support an army
in the field."

"That's why I'm sending an expedition to close that
damned port," Butler said impatiently.

"Yes, sir, I know," Miles responded. "But that expedition
isn't going to be ready for a while yet, is it, sir? In the meantime the blockade runners dash in and out of Wilmington
just as if we didn't have a sizable armada in blockading position offshore. And the ordnance and supplies that come into
Wilmington on the blockade runners is off-loaded onto rail-
cars and shipped north to General Lee."

Miles spread a map on Butler's desk. "The matériel that
comes into Wilmington starts north toward Lee's army on

one single-track rail line." He tapped his forefinger on the straight mark on the map that indicated the Wilmington and Weldon Railroad. "One artery, General. One line of rails. That's all that connects Lee with his source of supplies."

Butler's heavy lids lifted for a moment, showing a glitter of eye.

"General, I propose to take a group of volunteers through the enemy lines, starting from our own position in northern North Carolina. I propose to cut the Wilmington and Weldon Railroad near the source of Lee's supplies, just outside Wilmington."

Butler grunted.

"I've made an extensive study of the situation, sir," Miles continued. "There are no troops to speak of guarding the railroad. There's a small garrison at Fort Fisher, but that's miles away to the south of Wilmington. The nearest sizable reb forces are here—facing our occupation troops in the north of the state. With a relatively small number of men I can infiltrate the reb lines, live off the country, rendezvous at a given point—here, there's a bridge here that would take the rebs weeks . . . *months* . . . to replace—and shut off Lee's lifeblood as surely as if the navy had been successful at blockading the port."

"Hmmm," Butler said.

"It would make good press, General. Some of the newspaper boys would be glad to take a good whack at the navy." He spread his hands as if to illustrate a glaring headline, saying, "Army daredevils close port of Wilmington: Where for long years the Union navy has failed to stop the flow of supplies and ordnance through the strategic port on the Cape Fear River, a small and daring group of Union Army volunteers has succeeded in depriving the Confederate Army of northern Virginia of desperately needed matériel." He grinned. "Get the idea?"

Butler grunted.

"May I take that as permission to go ahead, sir?" Miles asked with a grin.

Butler's eyes showed slits of color as he lifted his brows. "Miles, you and I have a lot in common."

"Yes, sir," said Miles, a bit puzzled.

"You're not interested in closing the Wilmington and Weldon Railroad. You know as well as I do that the whole bedamned coast of North Carolina will be closed within a matter of weeks. You know that Sherman will be marching to the coast and sweeping all the way north. If we don't hurry, Sherman will close the port at Wilmington before I can get my expedition to Fort Fisher under way."

"Then why not cancel the expedition and save a lot of lives that will be lost assaulting a fortified position from the sea?" the major asked.

A laugh rumbled deep down in the folds of Butler's massive belly. "For the same reason you want to blow up an insignificant little bridge on a railroad," Butler said. "As I said, you're not interested in blowing up a railroad bridge; you want to come out of this war with a reputation . . . a medal or two."

Lloyd Miles grinned wryly and looked down at his feet for a moment before responding. "Well, sir, you have a point. It won't hurt to have a few medals when we're all back in civilian life. Given a chance to hire a war hero or an ordinary fellow, whom do you think an employer would choose?"

Butler laughed. "Yep, a lot in common. Tell you what, Miles. I'm going to be frank with you. I'm not sure you can succeed in this operation you're suggesting. You have no combat experience. You haven't served in the field since you received your commission in sixty-two. I think I'd be a bit reckless to back you in something in which I have little confidence."

Miles started to speak, but Butler waved his pudgy hand. "On the other hand, if you were successful, I'd have been foolish not to have supported you, wouldn't I?"

Arching his eyebrows, Miles said, "I would be very generous with my praise of a certain superior officer who had opened the way for me to become a hero." He smiled. "And who then recommended me for some not too modest military reward."

"Your praise for that superior officer must come *after* the fact, my boy." Butler raised his eyes in warning.

"I understand. Just in case I fail."

Butler nodded. "Go down to North Carolina. I'll give you a letter—which must be kept absolutely secret—to be destroyed. You can organize your group from men in the North Carolina occupation forces."

"Thank you, sir," Miles said, a genuine smile making him look younger than his twenty-five years. He waited while Butler scribbled the promised letter, then read it and grinned again. Butler had given him a blank check for men and supplies from the North Carolina command.

Before sunrise the next morning Lloyd Miles was aboard a gunship steaming down the James River. Soon the Atlantic extended endlessly on all sides as the gunship headed farther out to sea, giving stormy Cape Hatteras a wide berth.

CHAPTER 2

Union troops had been in New Bern, on the Neuse River, since the middle of March in 1862. Some men serving in the Department of North Carolina had arrived in the state with General A. E. Burnside early in the war, and most of them were perfectly content to wait out the slow months and years in a backwater. The alternative could be deadly. When the huge—and, to the public, glorious—armies met along the Mississippi or in Virginia, men died.

Not that it was all a picnic for the Union occupation forces in North Carolina. Now and then Johnny Reb got a burr in his britches and tried to dislodge the Yankee hold on the coastal waterways, and a few men came to know the real purpose of war—kill or be killed; but Johnny, like old Abe Lincoln, had his main attentions elsewhere and for the most part seemed content to let the status quo continue in northern North Carolina.

Old-timers in the occupation force knew that the worst thing that could happen was for important people from Washington to come into department headquarters. Their arrival usually meant a demand for some sort of action, and action meant that a fellow might get himself killed or, perhaps even worse, find himself in the tender care of army doctors, who made a speed contest of cutting off a man's leg. So it was that the members of the enlisted ranks kept an informal watch on the comings and goings via the Neuse River, and word spread quickly when a new officer arrived. But the arrival of a young captain with the insignia of the Engineer Corps warranted little attention, except to elicit uneasy remarks that he was the second new officer to arrive within a week, the first being a staff-type major named Lloyd Miles.

The newer arrival, Captain Philip Trent, was a tall man, a full five foot eleven. His sandy-blond hair extended untidily from under an unrumpled field cap. At first glance the bored and sometimes slovenly veterans of the years of occupation dismissed him as just another Washington type, but on closer examination they observed that the knees of his blue trousers were threadbare and worn. His tunic, clean and well pressed, was sun faded and clung to his slim form in a way that suggested he was quite accustomed to the uniform. He returned soldierly salutes with a little smile but met slipshod greetings with a hard, cold stare that quickly caused enlisted shoulders to straighten. A few men, those who had seen action on the main battlefronts, recognized in the captain's gray eyes an unsettling light—the quiet, haunting gaze of a man who had been present when rebel artillery was pounding and men were dying.

Philip Trent could easily have avoided army service. He was the son of Gustavus Trent, a member of the Maryland state senate and a Republican party wheelhorse. Gus Trent's ability to raise campaign funds and his almost uncanny knack for delivering the vote in his own Baltimore precincts had for over a decade given him entry to the halls of power in Washington. Although he was not the sort of man who would have suggested it himself, if Philip had asked, Gus Trent would have used his political influence to find his son a safe job in Washington, where he could have contributed to the war effort without having to face shot and shell. But Philip had not consulted his father before joining those men who were the first to don uniforms after the cannonading of Fort Sumter. He had entered the army, along with hundreds of thousands of young men, as an idealist who believed that a

Union put together by men like Washington and Jefferson was worth preserving.

Nor did Philip lose his idealism when it became apparent that there were young men who did not choose to serve in the army or the navy. After the military draft was instituted, it was still possible for a man with means to hire another fellow to wear his uniform, to buy a living body to take his own place in front of the guns. There were, after all, tasks to be performed on the home front, some of them highly lucrative, for war had greatly accelerated the demand for manufactured goods and the produce of the land.

As a lieutenant Philip had seen the carnage of the first battle of Bull Run, and he had run in panic with his men, fleeing the deadly hail of Confederate fire. It was there he had received his first wound, a minor one—if any wound could be considered minor in a war where postwound infections were often more deadly than the injuries themselves. He had spent two weeks convalescing in Baltimore with his father, who had told him, "My boy, you're wasting yourself as an infantry officer."

Gus Trent had been referring to Philip's training as an engineer and his work experience as a railroad builder.

"Damn it, boy," Gus had continued, "why do you think we got our butts kicked so badly at Manassas Junction? Because some mother's son in the South decided that doing his job was more important than being a hero, that's why. Some Southern railroad man did his job and moved an army under conditions that everyone thought impossible. We lost that battle because of good railroading, and there you were, a damned good railroad man, running like a striped-ass ape into reb rifle fire, yelling, 'Follow me, men!' "

With the Army of the Potomac under McClellan, Philip had commanded a company at Williamsburg, where the rearguard divisions of D. H. Hill and James Longstreet had lost almost as many men as had the Federal Army. He had, by God's own miracle, survived still another battle near Manassas Junction on the little creek called Bull Run; and he had wept upon seeing the Union dead before the stone wall below Marye's Heights at Fredericksburg. His company had

been force-marched as a part of John F. Reynolds's Infantry
Corps to another creek, called Willoughby Run, near Gettysburg, and it was there that he fell within a few yards of his
general. Unlike Reynolds, however, he survived, with a
shoulder wound that took a long time to heal.

His new duty, taken up in late 1863, utilized his prewar
education and work experience. At first, while his wound was
still troublesome, he had been a staff planner for the movement of troops and matériel by rail. Later he had inveigled
his superiors into making him a traveling troubleshooter in
railroad matters, and it was in this capacity that he entered
occupied territory in North Carolina, not by rail but by ship.
Soon Sherman would be moving east and then north, and he
would be in need of food and equipment. Philip's job was to
examine the prewar rails that had connected New Bern with
points south and west, with an eye toward resupplying Sherman's army from New Bern or, in the event of the success of
an upcoming expedition, from Wilmington.

One of the first faces Philip Trent saw after debarking from
the steamer that had delivered him to New Bern was that of
an old friend. He met the staff major on a boardwalk that had
been built to keep men from sinking knee deep into the river-
side mud. He began a salute, completing it to the accompani-
ment of "Well, by God. Lloyd Miles."

"Trent?" the major asked. "Yes, it is." He extended his
hand toward Philip, then pulled the taller man into a quick,
comradely embrace. "Philip, what in heaven's name brings
you to New Bern?"

"I was told that New Bern is about as far from any real
action as you can get and still be in the army," Philip said. A
man with his service record and his medals could afford to be
modest and even a bit cynical.

"Well, this calls for a toast," Miles said. "I've got quarters
in the town, and I just happen to have a jar of liberated
contraband there. Come on."

The contraband was a fruit jar half-full of a viscous white
liquid, which coiled within itself in oily swirls when moved.

"Stump juice," Miles said, pouring liberal quantities of the liquid into heavy, thick mugs. "White lightning."

"To old friends." Philip lifted his mug and took a deep drink that left him with a cough and watery eyes. "Good," he croaked as Miles grinned.

"Puts hair on your chest," Miles commented.

"And probably burn it off if spilled thereon."

The two men laughed. Miles, after refilling the mugs, said, "You haven't told me why you're here."

"Tour of inspection. I need to take a look at what's left of the railroads hereabouts, with an eye toward making connections with a certain unsmiling general who is expected near these parts in the coming months."

"Ah," Lloyd Miles said, "and, by God, you've found the right man to take you on a little tour." He laughed, pounding Philip on the shoulder. The old wound sent a twinge of protest, but Philip hid the pain. "As it happens, old son, I'm going on a railroad tour myself. Going to have a look at the Wilmington and Weldon Railroad bridge over the North East Cape Fear River."

Philip cocked his head in question. When Miles merely grinned at him, he said, "That's behind reb lines, isn't it?"

"It is. That's what's going to make it fun."

"Oh, great fun."

For a moment Miles was angered. Philip's tone seemed to him to be that of an old battle veteran speaking to a greenhorn; but he told himself that he was imagining things. Then a new source of resentment boiled up like acid into his throat. *The damned navy. So protective of their hero, the great Cushing.* Miles was under strict orders not to reveal to anyone his part in the *Albemarle* affair. If he could, he was thinking, that would take the superior look off Philip Trent's face. He controlled his emotions well.

"Come along with us, Phil. We need a good railroad man."

"To blow up the North East Cape Fear River bridge?"

"Yep."

Philip shook his head. "Sorry. I *build* railroads, or at least I did before the war. Of late I've advised the army on how best to utilize them to give our boys a chance to kill more of their boys. I don't think I'd enjoy blowing one up."

"Look, Trent," Miles said seriously, "what we're going to do will save lives. If we cut off Bobby Lee's source of munitions, he won't be shooting at us up around Richmond and Petersburg. Hell, man, you can always help to rebuild the bridge after Sherman moves up from the South. You want to be ready to resupply his army, don't you? What could be of more help than a close look at the condition of the railroads to the south of us? We will blow up only one bridge. That'll stop the flow of supplies to the north until General Butler can close the port at Fort Fisher and then at Wilmington permanently by occupying the town." He clasped Philip's arm. "Come along. It'll be a lark."

"Show me your maps," Philip said, and with the maps of the territory south of New Bern spread on a table before them—and with Lloyd Miles waxing more and more enthusiastic about his plan to strike a serious blow at the Confederacy before the war ended—he agreed reluctantly to consider the idea.

"That's my old college chum," Miles said happily, clapping him on the shoulder again. "I knew the minute I saw you that Providence had sent you my way. Hell, Phil, it's going to be fun."

CHAPTER 3

A steam launch, much like the one that Lieutenant William Cushing had used to destroy the *Albemarle,* carried Lloyd Miles, Philip Trent, and twelve enlisted men out of the Neuse River on a day that would have been more seasonable in September than November. The launch traveled the sheltered inland waters around Cedar Island, southwest past Beaufort, and out to sea at the Shackleford Banks. The weather continued to be kind, with a warm sun and a light breeze from the southeast. The Union navy owned the Atlantic coastal waters, so there was no danger of encountering a Confederate war vessel.

Only after putting out to sea did the raiding party abandon their uniforms for a motley collection of civilian clothing, mixed with items of rebel gray. Philip's costume was composed of soiled, ragged homespun trousers; a heavy, faded gray shirt; and a baggy woolen jacket.

It was Lloyd Miles's contention that the group of fourteen men, carrying the usual firearms of the Confederate armies, English-made Enfield rifles, would appear to be a detached unit of rebel militia as they marched south from New Topsail Inlet toward the North East Cape Fear River. Philip, however, had seen reb soldiers close up and thought it unlikely that anyone in his right mind could mistake the well-fed group of disguised Federals for half-starved, hollow-eyed Southerners.

He was, to state it conservatively, dubious about several aspects of Lloyd Miles's plan. His most serious concern was the abandonment of uniform. The war that had begun with chivalrous overtones in Charleston Harbor had become that most bitter of conflicts, a war between brothers, and Philip knew that if he were captured, he wouldn't be the first man to be shot as a Yankee spy after being caught behind enemy lines out of uniform. But he had agreed to accompany Miles, and he was just young enough and just proud enough to conceal his nervousness.

The raiding party landed on the mainland behind Topsail Island in a fine mist during the chill morning hours. By first light the group had located the plank road that led southward toward Wilmington and were slouching along, their rifles propped on their shoulders, trying to look as feckless as local rebel militiamen. The ranking enlisted man, Sergeant Ewell Eades, at only twenty-three a grizzled veteran of occupation duty, commented that any reb with two arms, two legs, and half a brain was with Lee in Virginia or Joe Johnston in Georgia, and therefore the members of the raiding party should act accordingly.

"I don't care what you say, Sergeant," said a dismounted cavalryman who had joined the expedition to get out of stable duty. "I ain't gonna cut off no arm or leg just to improve my disguise."

The little group was startled when they abruptly came upon a party of black slaves supervised by a few men in gray. General Butler had informed Miles that the rebs were fortifying the northern approaches to Wilmington, but the major had not expected to encounter work parties so far from the town. It was too late to avoid them. Sergeant Eades, a Tennessee man, drawled a bit more than usual as he greeted the reb sergeant and allowed that it was "right nice fer November."

"Pert' near like summertime," the reb sergeant responded.

Philip, thinking of the thousands of Confederate infantrymen who would hear the shots if they had to fight their way past the work party, held his rifle with sweaty palms. He was filled with instant gratitude for Sergeant Eades's presence of mind.

"Y'all got any decent drinkin' water?" Eades asked.

The Confederate sergeant gestured toward a barrel, and Philip waited his turn as each man took the dipper and drank —or pretended to drink—the water, which was slightly brackish. While Eades stood beside the water barrel, leaning on his musket and talking with the reb sergeant, Miles motioned the men into a rough formation.

"We'uns come down from Jacksonville," Philip heard Eades say as Miles began to lead the group southward. "Ordered to git ourselves down to Fort Fisher. Reckon we's gonna have any trouble with sentries down thataway?"

"I reckon your officers got papers, ain't they?"

"Yep," Eades said.

"I reckon all they'll have to do is show their orders when you hit the main line of rifle pits 'bout two miles down the road."

Philip was relieved as the raiders moved out of sight of the work party, with Eades at the rear, trying not to give the impression of hurrying. Several minutes later the sergeant caught up with Miles and Philip to give his report.

"Well, damn," Miles said. "I'd hoped to be able to stay on the road until we were past the swamp."

The maps showed a large wet area, Holly Shelter Swamp, to the west of the road, but with Confederate troops in their path, they had no choice but to take to the brush.

The Confederate sergeant who had first encountered the Federal raiding party had a short leg as a result of a wound at Shiloh. He watched Ewell Eades amble off down the plank road to catch up with his unit, then turned to the private who sat with his musket across his knees on the tailgate of a mule wagon. "'Pear to you that them ole boys was right nervous?" he asked.

The private snorted, then said enviously, "Didn't look like they missed many meals recently."

"Listen, boy," the sergeant said. "I want you to take a

little walk. Stay fer 'nuff behind them ole boys so's they don't see you. When they git to the main works and talk to an officer, you come on back, hear?"

The private was back within a half hour. "Sergeant," he said, "I found the place where them ole boys done left the plank road and took off 'cross the swamp itself."

The sergeant looked up at the sun, removed his battered hat, then brushed back his stringy hair. "Reckon you better git on one of them mules, boy, and ride on down and tell Cap'n Smithfield 'bout that."

Within a few hundred yards of where the raiding party left the road was some of the worst country Philip had ever seen, terrain more tangled and overgrown than Virginia's wilderness. All day he and the others fought their way through brush entwined with thorny creepers, wading in water up to their waist at times and learning that even in November, North Carolina mosquitoes could be voracious.

That night they camped on a hummock surrounded by scum-covered water. Miles allowed fires, and the warmth restored the men's spirits some. When Ewell Eades killed a small alligator with his bayonet and roasted the reptile's tail over the fire, there was laughter and good-natured ribbing about eating such an ugly beast; but no man refused his share.

With the morning the men breaking trail burst out onto the right-of-way of the Wilmington and Weldon Railroad—within a hundred yards of the camp where they had lit fires so imprudently and talked and laughed in normal voices. Fortunately, no Confederate soldiers were in sight in either direction along the rails, and the men set out along them, grateful for the cleared path.

The railroad bridge across the North East Cape Fear River north of Wilmington was anchored on each bank by a stone buttress. Tar-soaked pilings supported the rails across the dark water. On the near side of the river two tents and a mud-chinked log shack indicated the presence of a permanent guard force.

On the riverbank upstream from the camp Miles and

Philip lay on their stomachs. The guards had apparently been stationed at the bridge for a long time, for they had rigged comfortable seats under a brush canopy near the approach to the bridge. Two of them lounged there now as a distant whistle signaled the approach of a train. It came puffing mightily from the direction of Wilmington, and its whistle shrieked a greeting to the guards as the engine steamed past, pulling a long, impressive line of cars.

"That's what we're going to stop," Miles said to Philip. "That train's headed for Richmond. You can bet your life on that."

Philip looked to where Miles was stretched out at his side. "I think that's exactly what we're doing," he said wryly.

"Heck, there's no more than six men in that camp," Miles said. "We'll take them and have that bridge blown sky-high before you can spit." He glanced up at the sun. "It's early yet. We can be almost back to the plank road before dark if we get moving."

They got moving. Sergeant Eades handled the attack. The rebel guards, who had probably questioned the wisdom of their officers for having marooned them out in the middle of nowhere watching a blasted railroad bridge, discovered too late why vigilance was important. Four of them died immediately. The other two threw their rifles into the river and ran across the trestle.

"Let 'em go," Eades said. "We'll be long gone before they can raise the alarm."

The dynamite that was to be used to blow up the bridge had been split among four men. Ewell Eades, the demolition expert, gathered it and checked its condition. Some of it was fairly well soaked, but he figured the dry sticks would trigger all the wet ones. Then he began the task of lashing two separate charges to the support timbers at either end of the bridge. Miles positioned the men who were not working with Eades on the southern approach.

Philip walked out onto the bridge and looked down at the swirling dark waters. The sun was nearing its zenith, and the air was pleasantly warm. He walked back to the north end of the bridge, where Eades and the demolition team were working steadily but without haste. The charges there were in place, and Eades was stringing out the long fuses when Philip heard a distant clatter, a muted roar, and then the unmistakable shrill, eerie rebel yell. A flurry of shots came as a force of cavalry stormed around the curve just to the north of the bridge and began to close the distance rapidly. He saw the flashes of pistol and musket fire and saw sparks fly as the horses' iron-shod hooves sent railbed stones flying. Lloyd Miles was yelling orders from the other end of the bridge as his men began to return the fire of the rapidly approaching cavalry—at least thirty of them by Philip's hasty estimation.

"Cap'n!" cried Ewell Eades. "There's too many of them for us."

Eades had seized his musket and took deliberate aim and fired, causing a horseman to fall, then skid limply on the gravel of the railbed. The other two men of the demolition team followed suit. Philip knelt, fired, missed, loaded, and fired again, and then the cavalry were on the flat, wide approach to the bridge. Soon the horsemen would be upon them. Already their sabers were flashing in the sun.

"Cap'n," Ewell said, "there ain't nothing we can do."

"Sergeant, are the charges ready?" Before Eades could answer, Philip felt a dull impact in his left thigh, as if he'd been hit by a sledge. The force of it caused him to step back, and when he put his weight on his left leg, he fell.

"You're hit!" Eades said. "Cap'n, I—"

"Take your men and go." Philip reached for his pistol.

The other men of the demolition team were already running for the southern end of the bridge. One faltered in midstride and fell with a great splash into the river.

"Can't leave you here, Cap'n," Eades said, coming to Philip's side to help him to his feet. "Now you just lean on me, sir."

They took only two steps before a rifle ball smashed into the back of Ewell Eades's head. He fell, taking Philip with him, and as Philip went down he felt the impact of still another ball.

* * *

At the other end of the bridge Lloyd Miles had been stunned when the Confederate cavalry charged. But when he saw that Ewell Eades and his men were also shooting at the enemy, he yelled, "No, fire your charges! The bridge, men, the bridge!" But his voice was lost in the cacophony of battle. He saw the members of Eades's team run, saw Philip Trent fall, then rise with Eades's help, only to fall again.

"They're goners, sir," said a man at his side.

Miles started to dash across the bridge, fully intending to go to the aid of his friend. But two men caught him by the arms and pulled him down. "They're dead, sir. I've seen dead men fall before."

The southern cavalrymen, unable to ride their horses across the bridge, were dismounting, and the rifle fire intensified, making the air above Miles's head sing. Men were beginning to die around him. He had failed; the bridge was intact. The two charges placed by Ewell Eades and his men were on the other side. It would have taken a brigade to storm the bridge in the face of the deadly rebel rifles.

"All right, men," Miles said. "Let's go."

Four men joined him in the dash for the brush along the railroad. One fell. Three men were with him as he ran back into the Holly Shelter Swamp and began to make his way toward the plank road and the coast.

It took Lloyd Miles and his men two days to reach the appointed rendezvous spot, two days of agony and despair. They spent the night on a soggy hummock without the benefit of fire. One man had an arm wound that with each hour grew more and more painful. Nevertheless, they survived, which was sadly not true of the comrades they had left on the bridge.

Since Lloyd Miles could not recommend himself for a medal, he used his creativity to write a recommendation that, with the aid of General Butler, resulted in the posthumous award of the Congressional Medal of Honor, the newest of the United States's military honors, to Captain Philip Trent.

Months later, in April, 1865, Gus Trent attended the awards ceremony, in which the President himself, standing

tall and solemn, handed the blue-ribboned gold medal to Gus
with a brief comment about the courage and the sacrifice of
Captain Philip Trent. Gus spoke briefly with Major Lloyd
Miles, who described Philip's bravery in holding off a force of
over a hundred rebel cavalrymen—Miles felt perfectly justified inflating the number of the enemy just a bit—in order to
allow his comrades to escape.

Gus did not question either Miles or General Butler regarding the wisdom of a raid against a railroad bridge when
both men knew that the Fort Fisher expedition had been
scheduled for Christmas, just a month later. That expedition
had failed, of course—chiefly, Gus thought, because of the
man who had commanded it—but Admiral Porter and General Alfred Terry had done the job properly in mid-January,
securing for the Union the last port open to the Confederacy.
So his son had died in a futile attempt to cut off rail connections to a port that was to fall permanently into Union hands
only two months later.

By the time the President put the Congressional Medal of
Honor into Gus Trent's hands, Grant's men were in Richmond, and Sherman had put down the last resistance in
North Carolina. The little ceremony of the presentation of a
medal to a dead soldier by the tall, glum-faced President
would be crowded out of every newspaper by the headlines
that told of the surrender of Robert E. Lee at Appomattox
Court House.

Ironically, while the newspapers were filled with joyful reports of the death of the Confederacy, Lloyd Miles received a
clipping from the office of General Butler, who was back in
civilian clothes to resume his political career. The article was
from a Raleigh, North Carolina, newspaper, dated November 1864, and it gave a short, unexciting account of a small
incident at the North East River bridge near Wilmington:

The alertness of a veteran Confederate sergeant assigned to
the defenses of Wilmington resulted this week in the death
or capture of a group of Buffaloes making an attempt to
destroy the Wilmington and Weldon Railroad bridge over

the North East Cape Fear. Alerted by two brave soldiers who escaped the brutal initial attack of the renegades, a force of cavalry, under the command of General William Whiting, which happened to be on a training mission just to the north, surprised the Yankee desperadoes in the act of setting charges on the river bridge. At least twenty of the Yankee-sympathizing scum were killed or captured.

Lloyd Miles grinned. *At least twenty* . . . More than his entire force. And he had brought three men out with him, which was more than Cushing had brought out of Plymouth after sinking the *Albemarle.* Cushing's reward had been fame; Lloyd Miles's had been to be classed as a "Buffalo," a Southerner who worked with or for the occupying Yankees— in Southern eyes the lowest of the low. But what the hell, Miles thought. Butler knew that he'd tried and that only bad luck had prevented him from closing down the Wilmington and Weldon. He had his medal—not the Congressional Medal of Honor such as the one Philip had, but a rather respectable medal, the second best available to an army man, the Distinguished Service Medal. It was better to be alive and have the second best than to be a dead hero like poor old Philip.

Miles had made many excellent contacts during his service. Butler, who had been relieved of command of the Army of the James after his failure at Fort Fisher, showed all signs of holding on to his political base in Massachusetts. Even though Miles himself would not have voted for Beast Butler, he realized that Butler, in Congress, would be a good friend to have.

Meanwhile, Miles was running hard just to keep in place, for the competition was going to be severe. Thousands of ex-officers were going back into civilian life, each using all of his army contacts to try to get a leg up on the others in the eternal quest for financial success, position, and power.

CHAPTER 4

For days Philip Trent was unconscious and could not have guessed that he had been reported killed in action by his friend Lloyd Miles. For weeks afterward he was too ill to care.

A Confederate doctor who had ridden with the cavalry to the North East Cape Fear River bridge had found papers that identified the wounded man as Captain Philip Trent of the United States Army Corps of Engineers.

"Reckon I'd best try to save this 'un," the doctor had said, "so we'll have someone left to shoot as a spy."

Philip had been taken by train to Wilmington and placed under guard in a hospital room. He had been in and out of a coma long enough to make the doctors wonder if he could be saved after all. He'd been shot in the left thigh and the right calf.

When he had finally regained consciousness for more than a few hours at a time, Philip had been questioned by two officers from General Whiting's Wilmington command. He had given them his name and rank and told them that he'd been following orders, that his had been a military mission, and that he was not a spy.

"Captain," the senior rebel officer had said, "you may have been under military orders, but you were not in military uniform. You were dressed to pass as a Confederate militiaman, and that makes you a spy. But we're civilized folks. We won't shoot you until you can at least stand on your own two feet to face the firing squad."

Philip had been so near death from shock and loss of blood when he first arrived at the hospital that the doctors had not cut off his legs, although the risk of infection was high and amputation was the usual treatment for severe leg wounds. Later, perhaps, his captors' desire to see him walk to his fate prevented the rebel doctors from whacking off one or both of his lower limbs. A good sawbones could remove a leg at the knee in less than a minute. When General Terry's amphibious forces took Fort Fisher in January of 1865, while Philip was still quite ill, piles of amputated legs and arms grew around the rebel hospitals inside the compound. Indeed, after all major battles, parts of many men were put underground days or weeks before shock, blood loss, and infection sent many of their former owners to the same destination.

"Son, you're a lucky man," Philip was told by the grizzled old doctor who had treated him during the weeks of his slow recovery. "If they had thought you were strong enough when you were brought in, you'd be pushing yourself around the floor on a wheeled dolly now, and you're double lucky that you've escaped gangrene. But since you're shot in both legs and can't limp, you won't get any sympathy at all when you walk out to face the firing squad."

Philip was still too weak to stand, much less walk to face a firing squad, when he—and everyone else in the hospital and the town of Wilmington—heard the fearful and prolonged roar of the most intense naval bombardment in history. Soon after the bombardment ceased, a nurse, her eyes red with weeping, told him that Fort Fisher had fallen. In the days that followed, he heard the passage of troops in the street outside, but his mending bones would not allow him to move to a window to see the color of their uniforms.

The Confederate doctors no longer came to his room— only volunteer nurses appeared and told him that the Yankees were occupying the town. Since he was getting the food, rest, and care he needed and no longer faced the prospect of going before a rebel firing squad, he was content to stay in his

bed and let his wounds heal. Soon, he knew, he would be able
to get word of his whereabouts to his father. He had long
since lost track of the date and the day of the week. He
guessed that more than two weeks had passed following the
bombardment of Fort Fisher when there appeared in his
room a man in blue with the insignia of the Union Medical
Corps.

"Understand you're one of ours," said the doctor, who was
holding Philip's identification. He studied it for a moment,
then broke into a smile. "I guess you're happy to see us."

"You're not too pretty, Doctor," Philip said, grinning
broadly, "but compared to the muzzles of a reb firing squad,
you're a raving beauty."

"Just don't try to kiss me, sir," the doctor said. "That
would be against regulations."

Philip had been given a lot of time to think while he lay in
the Confederate hospital—too much time. Although he was
happy to be alive when the war ended, he could not bring
himself to rejoice in victory. He was a bit wiser than he had
been when he had rushed to the recruiting station after the
shooting began at Fort Sumter; and, he had to admit, he was
just a tad bitter.

The Wilmington hospital was being run by the Union
Army when Sherman marched past Wilmington to fight the
last significant battle of the war at Bentonville. That battle
seemed to Philip just as futile and senseless as his somewhat
juvenile adventure with Lloyd Miles had been. All in all, he
had seen too many men die. From the very beginning, when
the blue army marched off to battle so confidently, the war
had seemed to be nothing more than mistake after mistake by
Union generals and politicians.

The man with whom Lloyd Miles had planned his raid
into Confederate territory, General Benjamin Franklin Butler, was a prime example of the effect of politics on the Union
war effort, for Butler had proven himself worse than ineffec-
tual as a leader of troops. Yet Philip knew Butler was only
one of many high officers in the Union Army who had at-
tained general's stars because of pressure on President Lin-

coln to reward loyal Republicans, to appease powerful war Democrats, or to court influential legislators and their constituents.

When at last Philip was able to hobble aboard a train with the aid of two canes, he did not know whether or not his father knew he was alive. He had been told by his captors that a few men had escaped after the abortive raid on the railroad bridge. The usual procedure would have been for the survivors to have had Captain Trent listed as missing in action, and he hoped that had been the case. He had requested early on that a letter be sent to his father, but in those last weeks of the war it was highly unlikely that any missive had arrived in Baltimore. But even in the confusion of the war's ending, his second letter, written after the Union occupation of Wilmington, would, he felt, surely have reached Gus Trent.

Indeed, both of the letters written by Philip had disappeared from the face of the earth, never to reach their destination. State Representative Gustavus Trent learned of his son's resurrection from the gloriously decorated dead only when a hackney cab stopped in front of the Trent home in Baltimore and a thin, ravaged figure in blue came limping up the cobblestone walk, leaning on a cane in either hand. Gus was stunned into momentary inaction, but then, heedless of his age and bulk, he ran down the stairs and threw open the front door to look down into his son's tired gray eyes.

Those gray eyes were more than slightly damp as Gus enclosed Philip's gaunt frame in a bear hug. Gus smelled of rosewater and cigar smoke, a familiar scent from Philip's childhood, which filled his heart to overflowing. He made no objection as his father helped him up the stairs, into the entry, and then to the formal parlor. There, both men tried to talk at once, paused, laughed, and embraced again before Gus shouted for his manservant and Philip sank down gratefully into a comfortable leather chair.

Gus had his man bring brandy. Then he stood before Philip, a delicate crystal snifter raised in his hand. "To my son," he said.

Philip raised his snifter. "To home."

The glasses clinked.

"Ah, well," Philip breathed after his first sip.

"Something wrong?" Gus asked.

"Not one dad-gummed thing. I was just comparing this to the last drink I had. North Carolina white lightning. Home-made. Had the kick of a mule in it."

"We try," Gus said, "but we're unable to provide all the luxuries."

"When I complain you'll know it," Philip said with a grin.

"Welcome home, Son."

By evening the Trent house was full. Philip was tired and wanted nothing more than to go upstairs to his room and the bed in which he'd slept as he was growing into manhood. But people were an important part of Gus Trent's life; he thrived on them. Gus had built his career on his ability to make the most insignificant man feel important in his presence, and as the center of attention Philip could not disappoint his father by retreating.

At dinner the talk was of the death of the man who had guided the Union to victory and about the Southerner—the word came out sounding like profanity—who had replaced him.

"He's soft in the head," said one of Maryland's members of the House of Representatives. "He wants to make it easy on the South."

"So did Mr. Lincoln, as I understand it," Philip said. "I see no reason to be vindictive. The purpose of the war was to preserve the Union. I fail to see how we can ever hope to be one country again if the radicals are successful in their desire to punish the South. God knows they've been punished enough. There'll be generations of old maids in the South, gentlemen. The flower of their manhood is dead."

"And what of our dead?" asked the congressman. "Half a million of the sons of our nation fell to rebel guns."

"May they all rest in peace," Philip said, "*all* of them— Union and reb. And may their ghosts forgive all of us who participated in the late senselessness, although I myself might have some difficulty forgiving those who failed to talk sensibly during the early days when it might have been possible to prevent the war."

There were murmurs of protest, but Gus Trent halted them by producing a small, velvet-covered box. He opened the case and held it up to show the gleam of gold to the gathering. "Before you criticize my son too severely for his views, gentlemen," he said, "remember that unlike most of us he saw war firsthand, and he holds the highest honor our nation can bestow upon a soldier."

"My God," Philip said, grinning not because he had received the Congressional Medal of Honor but because he remembered how badly Lloyd Miles had wanted a medal.

"Yes, my God," Gus said. "Thank you, Lord God, for proving us wrong when we thought this award was being given posthumously."

Later, when he and Gus were alone, Philip read the citation that went with his medal. There were flowery words of praise for Captain Philip Trent's bravery and for his sacrifice in an effort to save his command from being overrun by superior forces.

"Heck, Dad," he said, grinning again, "there were no more than thirty of the rebs, and all I did was get caught on the wrong end of the bridge. I fired my rifle once or twice, and I missed."

The original recommendation for the medal had come from Major Lloyd Miles, Philip's immediate superior. The first endorsement had come from General B. F. Butler.

Philip held the little gold bauble in his hand. "The nation's highest honor," he mused. "An award for futility."

Gus started to object, but Philip raised his hand to stop him. "Men died there at the bridge, Dad, and there was no real reason for it. Even if we had been successful, even if we had finished setting the charges and had blown up the bridge, I doubt that our action would have had much effect on events. The war was over for all practical purposes."

Gus brought out the brandy again. They sat in the big room and talked as they had done often during the years when Philip was the son of the house. Gus had been a busy man, but he'd always been there when Philip needed him.

"So," Gus asked, "what now?"

Philip patted his weakened, shrunken thigh. "A lot of walking and a lot of Cook's good food. I have to get my legs built back up."

"All the time in the world, Son," Gus said. "You know this is your home as much as mine."

"I know," he answered, moved by his father's words. He remained quiet for a time. When he broke the silence, he spoke softly, musingly. "Want to know a secret? I was relieved—I have to confess that I was almost glad—when we failed to blow up that bridge. I guess I'd seen enough destruction, Dad. I was and am sick of it. I want to go back to work. I want to build, not destroy."

"Well, there is ample opportunity for that," Gus remarked. "If you want to go back to railroading, you'll find yourself in demand. I'd say you can pick and choose."

"I was thinking of California," Philip said.

"Hmmm."

"I suppose it's just that—" He paused, unable to formulate words.

"You want to get as far away from it—the war—as you can, is that it?"

"I guess. I don't really know," Philip muttered. "Yes, I suppose so. But it's not only that. There'll be more challenges out west, what with the Central Pacific having to cross the mountains."

Gus shifted his position in his chair. "Son, there are other opportunities."

"Closer to home?" Philip asked, grinning.

"I was thinking of that. But I was also thinking that railroad building isn't the only possibility for you. I know you're good at it; but you're not going to make your mark working for another man, important as it is to have good engineers out in front of the rail-laying crews. There are so many opportunities, Phil. Money is plentiful. The whole nation, including the South, is going to be hungry for manufactured goods. The raw materials are going to have to be found and mined. The farms of the West produce more food than is consumed there, and it's badly needed in the East. There are fortunes to be made, and not in the manner of the war profiteers. There are ways to make good money, honorable money, and benefit others at the same time, by doing society a service, by creating new job opportunities."

"Dad, isn't there time a little bit later for me to think about making my mark?"

Gus laughed. "Well, hell, yes. How old are you—twenty-five?"

Philip lifted one finger, smiling. "You're behind the times, Dad. I'm coming up on twenty-eight."

"Then there's not as much time as I thought," Gus said.

Day by day Philip grew stronger. His walks became longer and longer. He discarded one cane, then the other. He had to laugh when he remembered the rebel doctor's comment about not being able to limp because both legs were hurt, for his walk was a stiff one. He rocked to one side and then the other as the legs mended and muscles were rebuilt.

During those days in the Trent home with his father he read, ate until his belly was distended, and listened to the talk of the great and powerful who often sat at Gus Trent's table. Their discussion often included names that were becoming household words—Jay Gould, Jim Fisk, J. P. Morgan, Philip Armour, Andrew Carnegie, James Hill, John D. Rockefeller, Collis Huntington, and Leland Stanford. Most of these men had been in their early twenties when the war began, but they had not visited the offices of the army recruiters. Although Philip Trent held his nation's highest military honor, only a few people knew his name; meanwhile the names of those who had profited from the war were spoken with awe, their words quoted in voices filled with something akin to reverence tinged with open envy.

Gus Trent's opinion of the men who had become rich because of the war was not a flattering one, for Gus had never succumbed to the obsession with financial gain that had, it seemed, captured everyone else in the country in its greedy grasp. "There's not a genius among them, Philip. They were just in the right place at the right time to take advantage of the war. Oh, they were wise enough, I guess, to see that the war was going to trigger a second industrial revolution in this country. A lot of them gained credibility by dovetailing their own ambitions with the American ideal of one unified, powerful nation. Thomas Jefferson had that dream back in the calm and easy days when pigs rooted in the White House yard, but he couldn't have foreseen how quickly we'd all be propelled into a new age by this war."

Philip, while not harboring any wish to be fabulously wealthy, was interested by the achievements of the men who, because of their vast fortunes and their control of such vital elements as the nation's railroads, wielded as much power as had the dukes and barons of feudal times. And he was in the right place to hear things that were not public knowledge. From the Maryland congressman he had heard that Pierpont Morgan bought a large lot of defective muskets from the government for $17,486 and had sold them to the Federal Army in the West for $109,912.

"But he had to be aware," Philip said, "that any soldier who fired one of those rifles risked losing a thumb."

The congressman shrugged.

Morgan was not the only man to make a profit from the war. Cornelius Vanderbilt took commissions of ten percent on the lease of obsolete steamships to the U.S. Navy. And Philip himself had encountered—and had eaten when he was hungry enough—the wormy, rotten pork that people like Philip Armour had sold to the army.

In that gathering of men in Gus Trent's house there was grudging but open admiration for Jay Cooke, who had once said, "I shall be rich." That desire had, it seemed to Philip, become the national dream. Cooke had wrapped himself in the red-white-and-blue of the flag, had done his patriotic duty by selling government bonds—and had drawn commissions of over three million dollars a year.

"What you should do, young Philip," Gus Trent suggested, "is establish your own railroad. The rush is on to crisscross this continent with rails. The government has money to lend. Hell, boy, we're handing money to the builders of the transcontinental railroad almost faster than the mint can print it. And we're giving them enough land out there in the great American desert to make a dozen European-sized nations."

"I'm sure that's true, Dad," Philip replied. "But I've made up my mind. I'm going to California to work for the Central Pacific."

In spite of the newly reunited nation's movement into what the editorialists were calling the modern age, there were still just three ways to get to California from the East Coast. The overland route, of course, offered months of travel and hardship to anyone attempting it, and Philip rejected it outright. And the thirteen thousand miles by sea from New York to San Francisco around Cape Horn involved months of sailing through some of the world's most treacherous waters. But by crossing the Isthmus of Panama, which was a part of the Great Republic of Columbia, a traveler could cut off eight thousand miles of sea travel.

Philip Trent chose to go cross-isthmus. He would have an easier time of it than the early forty-niners, who had had to trek through the disease-ridden jungles without the benefit of the Panama Railroad, which was not completed until 1855. He arrived in Colón, the northern terminus of the little railroad, to plunge into Panama's enervating heat. He stayed in Colón just long enough to buy his ticket for the forty-seven-and-a-half-mile ride over the most expensive railroad in the world. It had been the most costly to build—both in money and in lives—and was the dearest to ride. The fare was twenty-five dollars in gold, but the operators of the railroad said that was a bargain, since the Panama Railroad was, after all, the *first* transcontinental line, going from ocean to ocean.

The train plunged immediately into lush, primeval jungle. Flocks of multicolored birds, disturbed by the rattling, chugging passage of the engine, burst into the sky, while swarms of blue butterflies dashed themselves against the moving coaches. The whistle of the locomotive startled troops of monkeys, sending them chattering through the treetops.

Halfway through the journey the train stopped at the little

town of Barbacoas. There would be, the passengers were told, a half-hour delay. After leaving the train, Philip walked the muddy streets to see firsthand the abject misery of the Panamanian natives. Potbellied, hungry-eyed children swarmed around him, begging for coins. An expressionless woman sat on a decaying stoop with one flabby breast exposed as she fed a naked baby.

Philip had arrived in Panama during the rainy season, and he already knew that when it rained in Panama, it was not just rain. As the skies filled with towering clouds the air seemed to condense into liquidity, accompanied by the roar of wind in the jungle. The force of it, the incredible weight of the rain, sent even natives scurrying for cover. When a rainstorm came up as Philip waited in Barbacoas, he ran for a tin-roofed board walkway in front of a store. He was joined there by several grubby children, who bunched themselves up as far from Philip as they could get and still be under shelter. They watched him with huge, limpid eyes around which flies crawled, ignored and undisturbed.

The jungle had vanished, hidden by the curtain of rain. Philip could barely see the brightly colored coaches of the train. The hissings of the locomotive were lost in the roar of the storm. He winked at the huddled urchins, emptied his pockets of coins, and after pointing to the intended recipient, tossed the pennies one at a time. There was a coin for each child, and his generosity prompted huge grins. One boy spoke in Spanish, and Philip shrugged, indicating that he did not understand. The boy fell silent and turned his fly-rimmed eyes to watch the rain.

Gradually Philip became aware of voices from inside the building. A male voice rose in volume so that it was evident, even over the continuing thunder of rain, that a heated argument was going on. Suddenly the door burst open, and a woman fell through, landing on the wet boards of the walk with a thud, her long skirts hiked up to reveal her reedy, dark legs. She tried to scramble away even as she tugged on her skirts to pull them down. But she was not quick enough. A dark-skinned man, large for a Panamanian, leapt through the door and lashed down at her bare legs with an evil-looking braided whip. Philip heard the meaty sound as the whip slashed a red welt.

"Here now!" Philip yelled as the Panamanian's arm rose for another blow.

The small boys were leaping off the boardwalk, dashing away into the rain. The whip sang through the air again, and the woman screamed with the blow.

For long moments Philip hesitated. He was a visitor in a strange land, merely passing through. What was happening was not his business. And yet . . .

Casual cruelty had always sickened him. Violence had always seemed to be so fruitless. He had just lived through four years of the most widespread, destructive violence that the world had ever known, so what did it matter if one ignorant man in a muddy little town in a barbaric country gave pain to one woman? The woman who screamed under the lash would survive. He'd seen men die in all of the inventive, maiming, dehumanizing ways that had come with modern warfare. When a bursting artillery shell shredded the living flesh of a dozen men, the wounds didn't heal; the marks left by the lash on the legs of a Panamanian woman would.

There had been times during the war when he had lost himself totally, had performed actions without being aware. At Fredericksburg he had led his men in a charge into the terrible fire of the well-protected rebs, screaming all the way, he was told, surviving only because two of his sergeants grabbed his arms and pulled him down into a ditch out of the line of fire. There on a covered boardwalk in a steaming town in central Panama, it happened again.

Perhaps his reaction to the beating of the woman was the culmination of years of frustration during which he had watched men die, helpless to aid them. Whatever the reason, he was moving forward before he knew it, his hand closing over the Panamanian man's wrist. The dark, powerful man jerked his hand away. The lash stung Philip's cheek.

A red-black haze of anger blanked out what followed. Philip would never know how the dark man had come to lie on his back in the mud of the street. An observer would have seen the American move swiftly, his left hand slashing out

with the speed of a coiled snake, his right following to send
the Panamanian sprawling off the boardwalk to land heavily
on his back. It was then, while the dark man was trying to
suck wind back into his forcefully emptied lungs, that Philip
regained his awareness. When he saw the dark man's hand
groping under his soiled shirt, Philip held up his own left
hand, saying, "No, don't. . . ." But the dark man's hand
came into view with a gleam of dark metal, and Philip's
instinct for survival, developed during those years when he
had seen enough battle to last a dozen men a lifetime, took
over. His right hand was filled with his own weapon.

He had carried arms for so long that it had become second
nature to him, and the world of the 1860s was one of violence
and danger. He had armed himself for his trip to California
with the New Model Army revolver, the Colt .44, a formida-
ble weapon and one with which he was very familiar. It was
at home in his hand, and his aim was true, unlike that of the
Panamanian. He heard a pistol ball thunk past his ear, saw
the result of his own fire as his round took the dark man in
the chest and knocked him back into the mud. He heard a
sound from his rear and whirled just in time to see another
Panamanian at the door, a shotgun in his hand. Without
conscious thought Philip centered the muzzle of the .44 on
the man's nose. The bark of the pistol was followed in a split
second by the roar of the shotgun. The charge blew a hole in
the tin roof of the overhang as the Panamanian was thrust
backward, his nose gone and his life snuffed out as Philip's
bullet smashed into his brain.

As suddenly as it had begun, the rain ended. In the silence
Philip realized what had happened. Two men were dead, and
the Panamanian woman who had been the victim of the lash
was crawling down the steps and into the mud to lift her
mate's head into her lap. With anguish on her face she
looked up at Philip, and a wail came from her gaping mouth.

A crowd was gathering, their hate-filled faces glaring at
Philip. He knew that his situation was not a good one. He
was a stranger, and he was unable to speak the local language
to explain that he had killed in self-defense. When he saw
two men edging toward him, he waved the muzzle of the .44

at them. They backed away. Gesturing threateningly with the pistol, he made a path through the growing crowd, and when he was at last in the clear, he ran for the train, expecting at any moment to feel the jolting blow of a bullet in his back.

The locomotive's whistle shrilled. A shock ran through the passenger cars as the engineer engaged the drive wheels, and the train jerked forward. Just as it did, Philip leapt onto the steps of his car and stood there on the platform, looking back as the train gained momentum. He caught a glimpse of the woman. She was sitting in the mud with a dead man's head in her lap—and at that instant he knew that what he had done was as senseless as Lloyd Miles's raid on the Wilmington and Weldon Railroad bridge. His impulsive, idealistic defense of a mistreated woman had brought death, just as the impulsive, idealistic reactions of both Southern and Northern firebrands had brought death with the war. Because of his interference in what had probably been a domestic dispute between man and wife, two men were dead and a woman was left alone.

As he made his way to his seat he held the Colt .44 in his hand and looked at it, resisting an urge to throw it into the jungle outside the window of the passenger car. It was not the fault of the pistol; the pistol was an inanimate object, a tool. He reloaded the two spent chambers, put the revolver away, closed his eyes, and prayed that he had seen the last of violence and death.

During the remainder of the trip to California Philip concluded that it was time for him to put away ideals, to doff the suit of uncomfortable, rusting armor, to rid himself of the encumbrances of an errant, would-be knight who had been born too late, long past the age of chivalry.

He was standing at the bow of the ship when it entered the Golden Gate. His days and nights of anguished guilt were behind him. What had happened had happened, and perhaps it had been intended by God. Perhaps he had been nothing more than a divine instrument, an instrument of death for two men whose time—for reasons beyond his understanding

—had come. Just as he would rebuke all memory and thoughts of war and death, he would put the incident behind him.

He looked at the soaring headlands on either side of the Golden Gate, saw the city of San Francisco climbing its hills from the bustling waterfront, and brushed his hand in front of his eyes as if to push away the past.

"Enough," he whispered. "Enough."

CHAPTER 5

The energetic bustle of the City by the Bay did much to take Philip Trent's mind off the past. The ship docked on a day that fell officially in winter, but the weather belied the calendar. He did not have to venture far from the waterfront to find a hotel. The short walk took him into a different world, a world of dark, polished woods and shimmering crystal chandeliers that spoke of the era of extravagance that had come with the discovery of gold.

A polite, neatly dressed desk clerk who spoke with a French accent informed him that he was fortunate, that a room had just been vacated. It was a comfortable place, but the cost, Philip thought wryly, just might interfere with his sleep. He was not a rich man. He had withdrawn all of his savings before leaving Baltimore, and the expenditures required for his journey had made a sizable dent in his fortune. He could not afford to stay long in San Francisco.

He had no difficulty arranging a meeting with the man he wanted to see in San Francisco, ex–territorial governor Leland Stanford. He discovered why when he was ushered quickly into Stanford's inner office, where a distinguished man in his early forties was seated behind a huge desk, which, judging from its English design, had traveled far.

"So you're Gus Trent's boy," Stanford said, coming to his

feet and walking with authority around the ornately carved desk to extend his hand. "How is the old war-horse?"

"Fat and sassy, sir," Philip said, thinking, *It is a small world, after all.* He had had no idea that his father knew Leland Stanford, but he was not surprised. Gus had always believed in letting his son make his own way, and Philip had never tried to use his father's position to advance himself. If anything, he'd gone in the opposite direction, stubbornly insisting on earning his way through college at the University of Maryland, although Gus had been willing to pay his expenses at Yale.

"I met your father at the convention back in sixty," Stanford said. "We've corresponded many times since."

Stanford was a partner and president of the Central Pacific Railroad, and Philip had done a bit of research into the man's life and character. He knew that Stanford had been a delegate to the Republican presidential convention in 1860 and that he was politically powerful not only in California but throughout the nation, the result of having made generous contributions to the Republican party.

Leland Stanford had made his original fortune by operating a store in San Francisco during Gold Rush days. He had had some legal training and was known as a man of "virile power." Stanford had met his three partners, Collis Huntington, Mark Hopkins, and Charles Crocker, before the war and with them had formed the Pacific Association to engage in various business ventures. While Huntington was the apparent leader of the quartet, Stanford was the member with political sagacity, representing the group to government in Sacramento and in Washington.

When Philip shook the hand of Leland Stanford, he knew that he was facing one of those men who was in the process of becoming a legend in his own time, one of the new American nobility, a baron of commerce. That Stanford was a man of imagination and courage was without doubt. He and his associates had begun on speculation what seemed to many an impossible task. The federal government had given them a charter for the Central Pacific Railroad, along with the promise to pay in bonds for work in progress—at a rate ranging from sixteen thousand dollars plus land grants for rails laid in flat country to forty-eight thousand for construction in the mountains.

Construction had begun on the Central Pacific early in 1863, while the war was still raging. Now, with the shooting over, another kind of war was being fought by two competing commercial giants: the Central Pacific, building from the west, and the Union Pacific, laying rails from the east. The future of the nation was at stake, for in its eagerness to have the West welded to the East by a transcontinental railroad, the federal government was granting millions of acres of land to the railroad builders—land whose future value could not be fully imagined.

It took less than an hour for Philip to become an employee of the Central Pacific Railroad. He was flattered but slightly disappointed when his interview with Leland Stanford was over. He had hoped to join the advance crews in the California mountains and had imagined himself in the forefront, surveying and planning the difficult route, then helping to solve the massive problems of laying rails in difficult terrain. Instead, because of his troubleshooting experience with the Union Army, Stanford had asked him to perform a similar service for the Central Pacific.

There were advantages to his new job. He traveled in a private railroad car, his salary was higher than he had dared hope, and he saw a great deal of California. He wrote glowing letters to his father, praising the California climate and describing an area that seemed to be bursting at the seams with growth.

"Dad," he wrote, "I'm sure you've heard it said that California is the land of opportunity, a golden land that will offer unlimited possibilities once the transcontinental is complete. Don't you believe that. Multiply all that optimism by about one hundred and *then* believe it."

The railroad. The railroad. All of California was captivated by the railroad, and the nation itself kept its eyes on the rail builders. Newspapers dutifully reported the completion of every mile of track and competed among themselves in publishing glowing predictions about the prosperity that the railroad would bring to the great American desert—that still-mysterious area between St. Louis and the Pacific Ocean. The railroad was celebrated in song and poem, by word of mouth, and in published stories.

The first dark cloud on Philip's new, rosy horizon had formed at the very beginning of his inspection tour of Central Pacific tracks in California, when he discovered that the railroad was using iron rails, which were soft and would soon need replacement, instead of steel rails made by the Bessemer process. Moreover, the Central Pacific was paying the construction company building the railroad the higher steel prices for the iron rails. This he was able to discover because he carried a letter of authority from Leland Stanford stipulating that he be given access to any railroad employee or official and be allowed to examine records in any office.

The Central Pacific's construction activities were not confined to building the one-track line aimed eastward toward and through the mountains. All over the state of California rails were being laid. Philip enjoyed nothing more than to leave his private car and walk down to the track's end to watch the orderly placing of ties and the alignment of the rails, to hear the ring of the hammers and the shouts of the foremen. He liked talking to the prideful Irishmen, workers who felt a sense of proprietorship because, after all, it was their sweat and blood that was making the railroad. Some of them were railroad gypsies and had traveled far, having worked on rails in the East and with the Union Pacific on the Great Plains, where a man could stand on the tracks and look down the rails so far that the two lines of steel seemed to converge.

"There was this wee town in—where was it? Kansas or Nebraska?" a muscular Irish gandy dancer asked during one of Philip's visits to the railhead. Philip was seated on a stack of ties near a blackened coffeepot simmering over an open fire. "The U.P. front men went to the little town and told the folks there how much it was going to cost them to have the railroad come through. Well, I guess the townspeople thought that whether they paid or not, the railroad would

have to come through since the surveying had already been
done and a lot of the right-of-way had been graded. So they
said they didn't think they'd pay anything at all. Well, the
U.P. built a new depot ten miles to the west, put a little curve
in the track, and now there's a new town at the railroad
station, and the town that wouldn't pay is as dead as if God
Himself had sent a tornado through to kill it.''

"Same way with the Central Pacific," another Irishman
said.

"I don't think so," Philip responded.

His comment was met with laughter. "Go talk to the folks
in Los Angeles," the Irishman said.

Philip took the man's suggestion a few days later, hooking
his car onto a train headed in that direction.

Los Angeles was a budding city with high hopes. When
the train pulled into the little town, which had ambitions of
rivaling San Francisco, Philip noted the raw look to the
sprawl of wooden structures. The fertile fields around the
city, however, offered a winter's bounty of the fruits of
the earth. The nearby port provided Los Angeles with an
ocean outlet for agricultural produce. The railroad linked the
city and the valley to the state as a whole and eventually
would be a way for the valley's produce to be shipped to the
markets of the East.

The Los Angeles terminal of the Central Pacific was operating efficiently in the hands of a railroad veteran who had
worked his way up from the track-laying gang. He greeted
Philip with wary politeness but loosened up a bit after some
friendly chatter. Philip had not lived for years with a master
of winning people over without learning something.

Over dinner that night the stationmaster said, "Well, Mr.
Trent, it's not my affair, really, but both of 'em—the Union
Pacific and the Central Pacific, too—got those little towns
along their rights-of-way by the short hairs, so to speak. It's
nothing but blackmail; but I guess it'll all come out in the
wash, 'cause the towns and cities will get back the money
they pay out in increased trade and growth."

"Do you know definitely, from your own experience, that

the Central Pacific demands payment from towns along its right-of-way?" Philip asked.

The stationmaster laughed. "Well, I was with Mr. Collis P. Huntington when he told the high-muck-a-mucks of Los Angeles that unless the C.P. was given a sum of money equal to five percent of the assessed valuation of all of Los Angeles County, the railroad would bypass the whole area."

"You heard this with your own ears?"

"I wasn't the only one, Mr. Trent."

Philip's first reports to the office of Leland Stanford in San Francisco had concerned the use of iron rails, which were relatively soft and therefore wore out quickly. He had strongly advised the use of Bessemer steel, documenting his advice with statistics from his army and prearmy experience. The first two reports were ignored. When he sent a third, more strongly worded, he received in return a brief note signed by Stanford telling him that the material used in the rails was the business of company planners, not his.

Time and time again Philip saw evidence of waste. Time and time again he sent carefully worded, well-documented reports to Stanford, suggesting ways to save money on construction.

"With some simple economies and more careful supervision of expenditures and purchases," he wrote, "it would be possible to cut the cost of construction from the present sixteen thousand dollars per mile to perhaps half that figure."

"Your job," a subordinate of Leland Stanford's responded, "is to see that the trains are running on time and that the existing network of rails in California is being utilized in the most efficient manner. It is not your job to meddle in construction matters."

When at last Philip wrote requesting urgently that he be relieved of his present duties and assigned to the engineering staff at the transcontinental railhead, Leland Stanford made the decision.

"He's an intelligent young man, so far as it goes," Stanford told his associates, "but he's impractical." He signed the order that sent Philip to the eastern railhead.

* * *

Men like Leland Stanford were well aware of what they stood to gain for their efforts. The rail barons came into ownership of a strip of land extending twenty miles out from the railroad for each mile of track laid. Public money was creating two financial giants, the Central Pacific and the Union Pacific, and every employee of the Central Pacific, from Leland Stanford and his partners down to the foreman at the railhead, knew that a mile of track "stolen" from the Union Pacific represented enormous wealth in the future. The twenty square miles of land granted per railroad-mile could be marketed to the farmers and ranchers who would, with railroad access, begin to people the formerly empty lands.

Although Philip admitted that the rewards for the railroad barons were extravagant, he could rationalize the reasons for the government's generosity. He had seen the West Coast and knew that it was in the nation's interest to connect it to the other states of the Union. The West's mineral and agricultural riches would contribute to a new era of progress and prosperity for the nation. If a few men became fabulously wealthy . . . well, that was the American way.

All men had the right to be rich, Philip reasoned; he himself had that right. He had made a conscious choice to pursue a career that was rewarding not so much in riches as in a sense of accomplishment. He didn't doubt for a minute that if he really wanted to be a rich man, he could be. Perhaps in the future he would feel a need for money, especially when and if he found the right woman and started a family.

Meanwhile, as spring came to the Sierra Nevadas north and east of Sacramento, he was outdoors breathing air that was so pure, so fresh, it was intoxicating. He was part of an effort that would rank with the great engineering feats of all time: with the pyramids, with Ferdinand de Lesseps's project in the Egyptian desert—the Suez Canal—whose completion, it was estimated, would coincide with the joining of the two branches of the transcontinental in three years' time.

* * *

Upon Philip's arrival at the railhead, he learned that the engineer in charge was a Bostonian who had stubbornly refused to, as he put it, "go native." He came from his comfortable home-office-on-wheels each morning dressed as if he were going for a stroll on Boston Commons, complete with derby hat tilted prissily over his left eye. His name was Elton Clemmons. He was just over fifty years old, and he did not know Gus Trent—or if he did, he failed to mention it as he questioned Philip about his experience in railroading.

"We'll give you a try with the grading team," Clemmons said, as if conferring a great largess on Philip.

"Thank you, Mr. Clemmons. I appreciate that," Philip replied quite honestly. He reported to the grading team, a large crew consisting of highly skilled Irish demolition men and small armies of Chinese coolies whose job it was to move the rock and earth blasted off the shoulder of the mountain by the Irishmen. He quickly discovered that he was the only engineer assigned to the team at the moment.

Mick Farrel—every crew seemed to have at least one Irishman named Mick—said, "Y'see, *Mister* Trent, the brain boys already done their jobs here."

Farrel, the foreman of the grading crew, reported directly to Clemmons, the chief engineer. For a day or two Philip made himself unobtrusive, merely watching as the huge charges of explosives sent up titanic showers of dust and particles and precipitated roaring rockslides, which were soon swarming with the energetic Chinese workers. The grade was being cut into difficult terrain, an exposed mountainside, and two hundred feet below it, a switchback had already been blasted out. Quite often the explosions sent rock tumbling down onto the lower roadbed, so the coolie gangs were forced to do the same clearing work over and over. Blasts were sometimes set off without giving warning to the Chinese workers below, and Philip saw more than one narrow escape as rocks tumbled past them. He held his tongue, although his impulse was to order Farrel to be more concerned with the safety of the Chinese workers.

When, after a few days, the roadbed had been cut to a point where there was no switchback below, Philip said,

"Mr. Farrel, I think it would make more sense if we moved the blasting crews up the slope. We'll cut out the grade there and then come back down to this point. That way we won't be knocking loose rock onto an already finished grade. It will save lots of time, and we won't be endangering the Chinese workers down below."

Farrel looked at Philip with a squint. He was a solidly built man, wider than Philip in the chest and shoulders but about three inches shorter. "Have y'taken over the boss's job, then?"

"No, Mr. Farrel," Philip said patiently. "But it's just common sense not to do the same work two or three times when it can be avoided."

"Perhaps y'would like to take that up with Mr. Clemmons," Farrel said. "Now, if you'll excuse me, *Mister* Trent, I have me work to do."

Philip put his hand on Farrel's shoulder as the Irishman turned to walk away. Farrel whirled, snarling. "They pay you more money than they pay me, Mr. Engineer, but that gives you no cause to lay hands on me."

Philip sighed. Farrel was not the first uppity foreman with whom he'd had to deal. Railroad building was man's work, and it attracted its share of egoists. "I think, Farrel, that you and I are going to have to have a serious discussion, if you understand my meaning."

The Irishman's eyes gleamed. He grinned, showing a blackened, dead tooth. "Shall it be before God and everybody, or would y'like to have this, ah, discussion in private?"

"I think it will make more of an impression on you, Mr. Farrel, if we let the whole world listen."

"As y'wish, *sir,*" Farrel said, clenching his fists and hunching his shoulders. He telegraphed his intentions with his tongue, which went to the corner of his mouth, and with his entire torso, so that it was easy for Philip to step aside, avoid the roundhouse right, and with the same motion lace two quick but solid blows to the side of the Irishman's chin.

"Better keep your tongue in your mouth," Philip said as Farrel backed off, his eyes going wide with surprise. "I wouldn't want a foreman who couldn't talk plainly because he'd bitten off the end of his tongue."

"Worry about yer own," Farrel said, moving in a bit more cautiously, only to run into what he later described as a whirlwind of fists.

There are two choices for a man who hates violence but works in a field where men are men and violence is second nature to them. He can avoid all violence, thereby becoming ineffective, or he can become superior in administering violence, as Philip had done during his years as a railroader. He had naturally quick reflexes. To a stolid, plodding man like Farrel it seemed that Philip's fists moved as fast as a flitting dragonfly. The Irishman found himself on the ground and dazed before his own fists could make contact. He shook his head, looked at the engineer with new respect, and gamely came back for more until, his face swollen and blooded, he allowed Philip to help him to his feet.

"You see, Mr. Farrel," Philip said with panting breath, "that's the trouble with you Irishmen. It takes too long to get your attention."

Farrel stomped off away from the watching crew, leaving it in Philip's charge. Philip was in the process of moving the crew up the slope a short time later when Elton Clemmons came up the hill, picking his steps gingerly and brushing dust from his jacket. With him was Mick Farrel, his face displaying the results of his encounter with the superior boxer. But he was grinning . . . as much as his cut lips would allow.

"Just what in blazes do you think you're doing?" Clemmons demanded of Philip.

Philip explained, although he could not believe that an explanation of so logical a notion would be necessary for an engineer of Clemmons's reputation.

The chief engineer snorted. "We've learned from experience that it doesn't pay to get ahead of yourself out here, Trent. Now, you may have been a good railroader back East, where things are simple; but tell me what the hell you'd do if you went up there and cut out a bed and then, when you connected it with the lower switchback, you found that your grade was too steep?"

Philip was genuinely surprised by the question—any surveyor worthy of the name could avoid such a problem. He started to speak.

"Furthermore, I don't appreciate your manhandling one of my finest foremen, Trent," Clemmons said before he could reply. "You'll either learn to control yourself and work with the team, or letters from Mr. Stanford notwithstanding, you'll be riding back down the tracks to Sacramento!"

Philip's immediate impulse was to ask when the next train was heading out, but he swallowed his anger.

During the next two weeks Philip saw the same waste and carelessness that he'd observed while troubleshooting the Central Pacific's tracks in California. In the mountains, however, the lack of safety precautions posed an even greater danger to the crews, primarily the Chinese laborers. It was customary for the engineers and the foremen to push the labor force—whether they were Irish or Chinese—to a point just short of the limits of human endurance.

With each day Philip grew more and more dissatisfied and more incredulous that such wasteful practices could continue. It was almost as if the Central Pacific wanted the railroad to cost twice as much as it should have.

Philip reached the end of his tolerance when Mick Farrel gave orders for a huge blast without bothering to clear the slope below, where a gang of Chinese workers was laboring. In the ensuing landslide ten Chinese men were killed, and many more severely injured.

Philip knew that it would be useless to go to Elton Clemmons to report the cause of the disaster. Instead, he boarded an empty train that had brought ties and rails to the railhead and rode down to the nearest town, where he sent a telegram to Leland Stanford, citing the waste and unnecessary safety hazards at the railhead. He told of the death of the ten Chinese workers, of needlessly having to clear lower switchbacks many times, and of errors in the calculation of the grade—errors that would be expensive to correct in the future when laden trains would be unable to climb the steep grade in winter conditions. He concluded by requesting that Stanford, if he had doubts about Philip's findings, send an investigator.

Philip had to argue with the telegraph operator for a while to get him to send such a long message at company expense. Once it had been sent, he waited for a reply.

The answer was not long in coming. It was signed by Leland Stanford, and it consisted of fewer than ten words: Central Pacific no longer requires services Philip Trent.

CHAPTER 6

"The problem with you, Dad," Philip said, looking at Gus over the rim of his glass, "is simple."

"Glad to hear that," Gus replied. "All you have to do is tell me what it is, and all things will be better. I'll lose twenty pounds and forty years. My knees will no longer be stiff, and my hair will grow back."

Philip was slightly drunk. During his college days at the University of Maryland, his friends—Lloyd Miles among them—had called him a cheap drunk because it took no more than three ounces of any respectable booze to make him giddy. He'd had at least four ounces of Gus Trent's imported brandy this evening, and he felt wonderful. But he had felt pretty chipper even before having his first drink.

After receiving the telegram terminating his employment, Philip had picked up his back pay at the Central Pacific offices in Sacramento. Stanford and the Central Pacific had been quite generous in giving him a full month's salary as severance pay. With what he had accumulated, it proved barely enough to pay his fare back to Baltimore. During the long months of the tedious voyage home from California—he had considered it unwise to return through Panama, lest the authorities there arrest him—Philip had agonized over his situation. The solution to his problems had come to him in a

57

flash of revelation almost the minute he had set foot in his boyhood home.

"Your problem, my amiable and honorable father, is this," he said, grinning widely. "You're always right."

Gus raised an eyebrow.

"Yes," Philip emphasized, nodding vehemently, "you're a fine fellow otherwise. You're a loyal friend, a good companion. You have only a few vices, such as stinking up the house with your cigars, and you're moderately handsome for an old duffer."

Gus gave a grunt of amused protest.

"But, you see, State Representative Gustavus Trent, all those admirable qualities of character are besmirched by your annoying habit of always being right." He tossed off the last drops of brandy in his glass and leaned back, his gray eyes rounded as he gazed with raised eyebrows at his father.

Gus shifted in his chair and after a moment responded, "If that is true, Philip, it is a grievous fault, and I suspect that I'm about to pay for it."

"Not at all," Philip said magnanimously. "Only cost you another shot of this liquid French dynamite."

Gus poured. "What, may I ask, have I been right about lately?"

"You suggested that I defer going to California, that there are opportunities for me other than being out in the field building railroads."

"My, my," Gus crooned. "Am I more intelligent than even I imagined? And what did I suggest as a possible alternative?"

Philip frowned in concentration. "Can't remember," he said, "but every mile of rails laid by the Central Pacific is costing twice what it should cost."

"Ah."

"You want to know why?"

"Well, it's not in my bailiwick," Gus answered, "but I know a few people down the road a piece who are wondering just that. I was talking with Moverly just the other day, as a matter of fact." J. T. Moverly, an old friend of Gus's, was the senior member of Maryland's delegation in the House of

Representatives in Washington. "He said it's beginning to look as if the Union Pacific's cost estimates are going to balloon up from the original forty-four million to over ninety million."

"More than a one-hundred-percent overrun," Philip said. "And I imagine the figures will be very similar with the Central Pacific. Want to know why?"

Gus let out a sigh and grinned. "You asked me that once before."

Philip sat forward in his chair. "Because they *want* it to run high."

" 'They'?"

"I reported case after case of waste and inefficiency and downright fraud to Leland Stanford," Philip said. "You see what it got me."

"Well, it's good for the soul and the ego to be fired from a job at least once in your life."

"Were you?"

"No," Gus said. "Maybe that's my problem."

"They're deliberately running up the cost of construction," Philip continued. "Now the question is, why?"

"I hesitate to make the suggestion that I think I should make lest you accuse me of being right again."

Philip snickered. "Well, hell, I'm used to it."

"If you're really concerned about the things you saw on the Central Pacific, I think it might behoove you to have a talk with Jeb Moverly." He made a mental note to get word to his old friend as quickly as possible to alert him to an upcoming visit from Philip. Gus considered his son to be a chip off the old block, with talents so far not utilized. He would never have presumed to try to direct his son into a political career; but if by a bit of pushing here and a tiny bit of suggestion there he should get Philip interested in public office, then with the two of them working together, young Philip Trent would be unstoppable.

Having finished still another shot of brandy, Philip pushed himself up out of the chair. "Think I'll turn in."

Gus's voice stopped him just as he was about to open the front door. "Plan to sleep outside?"

"Why not?" Philip asked, grinning stupidly.

"More comfortable in bed," Gus said, rising and steering his son toward the stairs.

With Philip lying crosswise on his bed a few minutes later, only half undressed, Gus stood in the doorway of the room and looked musingly at his son. He had no way of knowing what changes had occurred in Philip during the war, but he suspected that his son's overindulgence in alcohol was a symptom of some very serious concern. Although Philip was made of pretty good stuff, he was still just a little too idealistic, Gus felt. If seeing the conditions of construction on the Central Pacific had disturbed Philip, what would happen when and if he became involved in the cynical, self-serving world of the nation's capital?

Gus lowered his head and said in a whisper, "He said I'm always right, Lord. Please let me be right in sending him into that bear's den down in Washington."

J. T. Moverly, a wisp of a man, fragile and silver haired, greeted Philip with genuine warmth. He ushered his friend's son into a conference room, where two members of the press awaited. He introduced Philip to them, stating his former military rank and mentioning that he was one of the winners of the Congressional Medal of Honor. Stories retrospecting incidents that had occurred during the recent war were relegated to back pages in those autumn days of 1866, so the reporters' questions were polite but without enthusiasm, and the interview was over quickly.

Alone in his inner office, the congressman seated himself near Philip in one of a pair of leather club chairs. "Now that I've used you to draw a little bit of attention to the old home state, my boy, what can I do for you?"

"Well, Congressman Moverly, I'm thinking about trying to find a job in Washington."

"Excellent," Moverly said. "You have one as of now. What is it you want to do?"

Philip explained his interest in the cost of the transcontinental railroad.

Moverly was thoughtfully silent. When he finally spoke, he

looked Philip in the eyes. "If you're of a mind to take on the railroads, you're starting down a road that you may very well find to be long and snaky."

"I just think that there's something awry. Eventually the people are going to pay the bills for the transcontinental, aren't they?"

"Taxes do supply the federal money that's being given to the railroads, yes. And the lands being given to them belong to the public." The congressman cleared his throat. "You're serious, then?"

"Quite," Philip said. "I don't know, as yet, just what I can do. That's why I came to see you, sir. I thought the prestige of your office might give me access to information that would otherwise be denied to me."

"It probably would. Then what? Public exposure of waste and fraud?"

The congressman's tone of voice caused Philip to look at him questioningly. "No?"

Moverly shook his head sadly. "I can get you any number of reporters who will write that the railroads are dictatorial, tyrannical, corrupt, and wasteful. The story would even be published. And the next day the paper would be in a stack on a fish-market shelf, waiting for its ultimate destiny."

Philip could find nothing to say.

"Look, Philip," the congressman said. "If you want a job in my office, you've got it. I'll back you in any investigation you want to institute into railroad affairs. But let me tell you this: in spite of the fact that I've been here a long time—too damned long—I'm still small potatoes. Moreover, I'm in my last term. I'm too old to go through the ordeal of another campaign. Oh, I've got my committee chairmanship and my seats on other committees, and I can get the floor in the House anytime I want it; but I'm not the man to tackle the railroads, nor do I have the time left in office. Let me suggest a course of action that may be more productive. I'm going to send you over to a very good friend of mine, Schuyler Colfax."

"Speaker of the House?" Philip asked.

"Yep. You're a man of action, and so's he. You're an honest man, and so is Schuyler, and he has told me himself that he's very seriously concerned about the excesses of the railroad barons."

Moverly took pen and paper and began to write. Finished, he blotted the paper, folded it, and handed it to Philip. "Read it if you like before you give it to Schuyler."

So it was that for the first time in his life Philip called on friendship to achieve a goal. He presented Moverly's letter to a portly man whose wide mouth was always, it seemed, at half-smile. Schuyler Colfax, Speaker of the House of Representatives, wore a beard that protruded downward like an afterthought from clean-shaven temples and cheeks. His three-piece suit was expensively tailored, his linen gleaming white.

Colfax had admitted Philip Trent into his office without waiting. That Philip was Gus Trent's son would have gained him admittance and whatever he wanted, within reason, in most congressional offices since Gus's favor was of great value to the Republican party. Also, the young man held the Medal of Honor. Even before Philip expressed his interest in working for Colfax, the congressman from Indiana had decided that it wouldn't do any harm to have a Medal of Honor winner on his staff, so long as the man wasn't some kind of martial maniac.

In fact, Colfax was very favorably impressed by Philip Trent. He asked a few questions about Philip's military experience and listened with interest as Philip briefed him on his experience in railroading before, during, and after the war. Colfax asked seemingly endless questions about Philip's observations during the months of his employment by the Central Pacific.

"I think, Philip—if I may call you that?"

"Yes, sir."

"I think, Philip, that you are going to be a valuable addition to my staff. Perhaps Congressman Moverly told you that I have supported the building of the transcontinental railroad."

"He did, sir."

"But did he also tell you that of late I have begun to rethink my attitude toward the railroads, while holding forth the possibility of new legislation to control excesses?"

Philip nodded. "He intimated something of the sort."

"Philip?" Colfax's eyes were smiling with his wide mouth. "Will you help me collect the information that Congress must have in order to make the proper decisions regarding this matter?"

"I will do my best, sir," Philip said with relief.

Thus, with surprising ease, Philip became a member of the staff of Congressman Schuyler Colfax. And from that friendly beginning Philip was a staunch Colfax loyalist, despite the fact that the Speaker's hard-line Republican policies toward the defeated South went against Philip's beliefs.

Following that first interview with the Speaker, Philip was hand delivered by Colfax to a balding, overweight man named Archibald Edwards, Colfax's chief of staff.

"You're a lucky young man," Edwards told Philip. "You're in the right place at the right time. If you want to make your mark, you've picked the right star to follow, my boy, for Speaker Colfax is a comer." He clapped Philip on the back. "Yes, if you stick with the Speaker, my boy, you'll go far."

Philip was assigned a surprisingly comfortable office with a view of busy Constitution Avenue. He began to put down on paper all of his observations and conclusions from his employment with the Central Pacific. Days later, when he had finished, he requested a meeting with Colfax.

"The Speaker is a busy man, Phil," Archibald Edwards told him. "If you have anything you'd like to bring to the Speaker's attention, I'll have a look at it."

Philip spent Christmas at his father's house in Baltimore. There was little time for the long father-son talks that were customary with them, for they were rarely alone—the house rang with the laughter and chatter of guests, and carols were bellowed at the maximum output of male lungs. Visiting females left hints of their perfumes in the water closets. Children tittered happily and slid down the well-smoothed banister of the stairway, just as Philip had done many times when he was a child.

"This house likes the sound of a child's laughter," Gus said one evening after the departure of a group of guests, among which had been three little girls. He winked at Philip. "No push, no shove, my boy—"

"But why don't I get married and make you a couple of grandchildren?"

"Well, that is a very common event, a young man's getting married."

"Have you picked out the girl for me, Dad?"

"Off with you," Gus said. "I'm for bed."

Washington, D.C., geographically a southern city, could be cold and raw in January. New snow had made the streets barely passable. It was a time to be at home with a good book, a cheery fire, and a hot toddy, but Philip was standing on the street instead, looking for a hansom cab. Both Schuyler Colfax and his chief of staff were suffering the winter misery of stuffy noses, sore throats, runny eyes, and debilitating exhaustion, and to Philip had fallen the task of representing the Speaker at a reception at the home of an Ohio congressman, who was said by old Washington hands to be a rising star.

Edwards had briefed Philip on the background of Congressman James A. Garfield.

"He had a good war record," Edwards had said, sniffing and wiping his eyes and nose. "Organized a regiment and fought with it at Shiloh. Came out of the war a major general of volunteers and won election from the Nineteenth District in Ohio by a large margin. The Speaker values his friendship, Phil. Pass along regrets for the Speaker and for me as well."

At last Philip found a cabbie who was willing to brave the snow and an icy wind to deliver him to the house of James Garfield. From the moment Philip shook the man's hand, he knew something about Garfield, for he had lived with a man of similar type all his life. Like Gus Trent, Garfield was one of those rare men with a genius for making friends.

"So you're Gus Trent's son," Garfield said, holding on to Philip's hand and pulling him aside.

"I'm proud to say I am," Philip responded—his standard answer to the question. He was no longer surprised by the number of men who knew his father. "I'd like to take this opportunity, sir, to relay the regrets of the Speaker and of Mr. Edwards for being unable to attend."

Garfield brushed off the absence of the Speaker with a wave of his hand. "We're honored to have a winner of the Medal of Honor with us." He winked. "Old Schuyler wouldn't be pleased to hear that I'd said you make a more than pleasing substitute for him."

"You're very kind, sir," Philip said.

"Not at all. I do feel honored. That was a very courageous thing you did down in North Carolina, Captain. Very courageous. Well-conceived plan, bad luck in the execution, eh?"

Philip grinned. "There just happened to be a company of reb cavalry on maneuvers a mile or two north of the bridge." Philip was surprised that Garfield knew the details of the abortive raid on the Wilmington and Weldon.

"Had some bad luck myself at times," Garfield said. "Look, Captain, I'd like nothing better than to spend the evening talking over the war. I guess I'm a soldier at heart, eh?" He shook Philip's hand again. "Let's have dinner one night soon."

"Thank you, sir," Philip said, not bothering to comment on Garfield's suggestion. Such nonspecific invitations were common currency in Washington.

The reception was a large and noisy one, and Philip, relatively new in Washington, was overwhelmed by names and faces. He shook hands with congressmen and senators, bowed to their ladies, and was assessed and discarded rapidly by name-dropping socialites. He was introduced to expensively dressed men whose alert eyes and confident bearing branded them as part of that new breed, the entrepreneurs. And there were, of course, the inevitable lobbyists, who made no secret of their partisan interests. When word got around that Philip was representing the Speaker of the House, he became the center of the lobbyists' attention.

Philip was wondering if he had done his duty and could slip away back to his rooms when he heard a familiar voice.

"Phil, you old son of a gun," Lloyd Miles said, pulling Philip into a bear hug. "I just heard you were in town. I've been meaning to look you up."

Miles was resplendent in a tailored frock coat and silk vest. If anything, he looked younger than he had looked in uniform. He was still clean shaven, and his brown hair was neatly trimmed.

He pulled Philip through an archway into the library. "Phil, when I heard that you were not dead, after all, I kicked myself for having left you there. I hope you believe that. I honestly thought that you had been killed."

"You wouldn't have been able to do anything had you known I was alive," Philip replied. "The Johnnies were too close. Besides, the only thing that saved my life, so I was told, was that a doctor was riding with the rebs. If you had been able to reach me and had tried to carry me away, I'd have bled to death in the swamp."

Lloyd Miles, his brown eyes very serious, took Philip by the shoulders. "Well, I wouldn't have left you, Phil, if I'd known you were alive."

"I know that, Lloyd. But what a talented liar you are," Philip said, laughing. "A hundred cavalry, indeed."

Miles broke into a smile. "From where I was, looking into the muzzles of their rifles, it *seemed* to be a hundred." He laughed and clapped Philip on the shoulder. "Got you the best bauble the army has to offer, didn't I?"

"I'm a little sad about that," Philip stated, grinning, "since you were the one who wanted it so badly."

"You'd have done the same for me," Miles insisted. "I didn't come out empty-handed. Beast Butler got me the Distinguished Service Medal."

"Good for you," Philip said. "You're looking prosperous. The medal must have worked."

"I'm a railroad man. I work for the Union Pacific. I heard that you did some time out west with the C.P."

"I did," Philip confirmed without elaboration. "I didn't

know you had railroad experience . . . other than what little you got down there in North Carolina."

Lloyd Miles tapped his temple knowingly. "They hired me for this, my boy, the old brain. I work directly with Thomas Durant."

Philip raised his eyebrows. Dr. Thomas Durant was the top man in the Union Pacific organization, a New York financier whose name had become widely recognized. "I'm impressed."

"In army talk I'd be called an aide-de-camp, I guess. Right-hand man. Whatever." He winked. "The man doesn't make a move without my advice."

"Oh, ho!" Philip exclaimed.

"And you . . . in politics, no less."

"Not really."

"No? Here you are representing the office of one of the most powerful men in Washington, and you say, 'Politics? Not really.' I'm proud of you, man, *proud*. I could have told you you'd be wasting your talents out there in the Wild West carrying railroad tracks up and down mountainsides. This is where it is, my friend. The power. The money. Think of how many millions of dollars flow through this town." He put his hand on Philip's forearm. "I'm pleased to see that you've finally gotten your priorities aligned."

"I believe I have," Philip agreed, slightly uncomfortable with what he was about to say. "I came down here to work for Schuyler Colfax because I don't think it's right for the federal government to be paying twice as much per mile for track as they should be paying. I think that I might be able to do something, however insignificant, to make things better."

Miles gave him a mock-disapproving look. "Lord, Phil, you? A reformer?"

Philip shrugged.

"Well, we won't let it destroy our mutual admiration, will we?" he asked breezily. "I truly understand how you feel. It would be great if everyone who wields power in this town were an idealist like you, Philip. It really would. Unfortunately they're not. Oh, most of them are as honest as they have to be. No one's looting the Treasury—at least not physically carrying off the gold. But, after all, a man has to look out for himself and his family."

"Materialism above all?" Philip asked.

"I don't read the essays written by the intellectuals," Lloyd Miles stated. "All I know is that this country is on the verge of the greatest expansion in the history of the world, and if I can, I'm going to be a part of it. In short, I'm going to get mine. And in the process, I suspect, some of my good fortune will rub off on others, because financial success is never just one man's reward. In the process of getting rich, I will carry others with me." He took Philip's arm. "Look, I know that things could be run better on the U.P. and, I suspect, on the C.P. But think how many jobs the railroads are creating, man. Think of the opportunity they're giving immigrants, like the Irish."

"And the Chinese?" Philip asked ironically. "Are they to be given equal citizenship like the Irish?"

Miles shrugged, then brightened. "Hey, there's someone I want you to meet." He pulled Philip out of the library and across the floor, excusing himself as he pushed through conversation groups.

Philip saw the woman from halfway across the room. She was petite, straight of back, proud in posture, and not as full in figure as the fashionable beauties of the day. Her hair was a lustrous, golden brown, and when she turned to face Philip, having heard Lloyd call her name, he saw that her eyes were the blue of a western sky, startling in their clarity and brilliance, possessing a power that took his breath away.

"My kid sister, Phil. Leah."

"Leah," Philip whispered to himself.

"My brother has spoken of you often, Mr. Trent," Leah Miles said, extending a white-gloved hand.

"My *maiden* sister, incidentally," Miles added as Philip felt the warmth of the hand within the glove, felt a distinctly shocking discharge of electricity as their hands touched.

"Twenty-four and unmarried, Mr. Trent," Leah said, laughingly going along with her brother's teasing.

"She says it's because all of the *real* men were away at war." Miles smiled at his sister. "Now that the war is over, and all of us real men are back home, what's the excuse, Leah?"

Philip's heart leapt as Leah lifted her sultry lids and gazed at him with those startlingly blue eyes. "Could it be, Lloyd dear, that you simply have not introduced me to the right man as yet?" Her expression was soft and friendly but not exactly a smile of invitation. "My brother is an incorrigible matchmaker. I pray that you will ignore him."

"He is rather easily ignorable, isn't he?" Philip asked with a grin.

"Already we have opinions in common, Mr. Trent. I knew I was going to like you."

"Well enough to dance with me?"

Her eyes sparkled. "Of course."

Philip no longer thought of leaving the reception early. Leah Miles, once in his arms, drew his full attention. She looked up at him as his arm tightened around her, and her eyes widened almost imperceptibly for a moment. Perhaps, he thought, she had read his mind, for as he felt the slimness of her waist and her warmth coming through her sedate, attractive gown, he had decided that this was the woman who was to be his wife.

He could not believe his luck. She liked him. This radiant creature liked him. It was evident in her face, in her blue eyes, in the way she rested her neatly gloved hand on his arm as they walked from the dance floor.

Lloyd Miles was talking with a brigadier general in uniform. Leah joined in the talk, but it was not until she spoke knowledgeably about horse racing that Philip was aware of the subject of the conversation.

"General Emerson's horse has a lineage going back to Diomed, Philip," she explained.

Philip, lost in her eyes, nodded blankly.

"I can see that means nothing to you," the general said. He turned his back on Philip, trying to shoulder him out of the group. For a moment Philip emerged from his daze, put his hand on the general's shoulder, and rather forcibly pulled the man back.

"Excuse me, General," he said, "but you were standing in front of me."

Emerson's face flushed, but he held his tongue.

"The general has little patience with anyone who doesn't know horse racing well enough to know that the legendary Diomed was a winner of the English Derby," Miles explained. He patted Emerson on the shoulder. "Really, General, you must learn a bit of patience. The war is over, you know."

"If you'll excuse me," the general said stiffly, turning to stalk away.

Miles laughed. "Obnoxious bastard. A political general. Earned his rank when his father implanted him in his mother's womb—if, indeed, his father and mother were at home on the same night."

"Lloyd," Leah said in a shocked tone.

"More money than brains," Miles went on, his voice full of resentment. "He's matching his wonderful horse against all comers, no handicap." He brushed his hand through his casually tousled hair. "Well, more's the fun, eh? You must come along with us, Phil. The race is tomorrow."

"I'd be delighted," Philip said, looking at Leah.

"Oh, damn," Miles said. "I forgot. I'm not going to be able to go, after all."

"Lloyd, you promised," Leah said.

"I know, Leah, and I'm terribly sorry. . . . Look, I'm sure that my old friend will fill in for me, won't you, Phil?"

Philip's pulse quickened. "With pleasure."

"Leah knows the spot. It's just outside the Federal District in Virginia. If the snow doesn't get any worse, you can make the drive from our apartment in less than an hour, so will you pick my little sister up around nine?"

"I told you he was a frustrated matchmaker," Leah said, leaning toward Philip. "Do you see how skillfully he has thrown us together? I hope you don't mind."

"Heavens, no," Philip protested.

"For I do so want to see the brigadier get his comeuppance."

"And will he?" Philip asked. "His horse sounds quite impressive."

"Unbeaten, as a matter of fact," Miles stated, "and thought widely to be unbeatable." He withdrew a wallet from inside his coat and began to count out greenbacks of large denominations. "Phil, I'd like you to place this for me in the betting pool, if you don't mind."

"Be glad to." Philip took the money and counted it—ten one-hundred-dollar bills. "A thousand dollars on the descendant of Diomed?"

"Whoa." Lloyd Miles's hand went to Philip's arm. "Wrong horse. Put the thousand on a horse named Empire State."

"Empire State?"

"He belongs to the junior congressman from New York," Miles explained. "And, by the way, if you'd like to pick up some pocket money, bet on the New York horse."

"A thousand dollars is pocket money?" Philip asked.

Miles laughed. "A piddling amount," he said, waving his hand.

Philip gave a wry laugh. "Perhaps I should be working for Thomas Durant."

"You could be," Miles said. "And not out in the wilderness laying rails."

But Philip's eyes were on Leah, and he let the statement pass.

CHAPTER 7

As Philip drove a span of sleek blacks along wintry lanes on a brisk, crystal morning, his entire being was focused on the young woman at his side. She was bundled in furs, her lovely face framed in white ermine, her blue eyes matching the azure of the January sky, washed clean by the recent storm. She sat close to him and shared the heavy bearskin robe that covered their legs.

During the hour and a quarter that it took for the surrey to reach the site of the race, their talk was of the sort that has passed between lovers since the beginning of time—questions about likes and dislikes that attempted to penetrate the outer shell, asked while gazing into the other's eyes, trying to see the core person therein. Philip could not learn enough about Leah quickly enough to satisfy his yearnings; and she had a sweetly burning desire to have known him from his boyhood, to know how he had looked in school and what games he had liked to play.

The shouts of a sizable crowd roused them from their world made for two. Leah's cheeks were pink. Philip realized that his nose was very cold. He wiped it with a kerchief, and when she took the cloth from his hand and touched it daintily to her own nose, he felt a surge of love for this blue-eyed woman. Somehow that act of sharing foretold an intimacy that would surely fulfill his dreams.

Ahead, a few dozen vehicles were tied up around a snow-covered meadow. Some of the horses wore feed bags and were chewing contentedly on oats or corn. A dainty-looking little mare stomped her feet against the chill. A series of loud snorts greeted the new arrivals, along with shouts that came from the crowd. Philip heard the thunder of hooves and saw two bay horses flash past, running on a circular path that had been cleared along the perimeter of the meadow.

"Have we missed it?" he asked.

"I would think that this is a preliminary race. There's too much money riding on the brigadier's horse to have them run the race before the appointed time."

Leah was right; they had arrived with time to spare. Philip recognized a few men in the crowd, the inevitable lobbyists, two senators, and Congressman James Garfield. Leah, who had been in Washington longer than Philip, pointed out members of the executive staff, a Supreme Court judge, and other politicians.

"Where do I go to wager Lloyd's money?" he asked her. When Leah pointed to a cluster of men around a closed wagon, he added, "It's rather a lot to risk on a horse race, isn't it?"

"Well, Lloyd has always been a bit, ah, flamboyant."

"Can he afford to lose a thousand dollars?"

She looked away quickly, then back, and there was something on her face that told him of her discomfort. Her voice was faint. "I don't think he plans to lose, you see."

The brigadier's horse was by far the favorite in the betting. A slate beside the closed wagon showed that if Lloyd Miles won his bet, his return would be three for one.

The look on Leah's face confirmed for Philip what he had suspected. Somehow the race was predetermined . . . *fixed*. He felt uneasy as he edged his way up to a sleekly dressed man who was taking the bets, calling them out to be entered into a leather-bound book by a heavily bundled young man who touched his pen to his tongue before dipping it into the inkwell.

After Philip placed the bet, the younger man with the pen repeated, "One thousand dollars on Empire State."

"Well, here's a generous fellow," said a dapper gentleman.

"Do you know something we don't, sir?" asked another bystander.

"They breed some fine horses in New York State," Philip said. He grinned at the general laughter. Men pushed forward to wager more money on the horse with the blood of Diomed, for the thousand that Philip had bet added greatly to the betting pool, giving supporters of the English-bred horse more to win.

Philip returned to the spot where he'd left Leah, only to find her missing. He heard a male voice calling his name and looked around to see Leah sitting with James Garfield on the front seat of a surrey.

"We've saved a place for you, Mr. Trent!" Garfield called.

Philip walked over to the surrey, and as he climbed into the back of it, he said, "You must have arrived early to get such a choice spot."

"Lovely morning," Garfield declared expansively. "I'm not that keen on horse racing, but any excuse to get one out into such bracing weather, eh?" He extended his hand to Philip. "So, did you get your bet down?"

Philip shook the congressman's hand and said, "Yes," although he had an urge to tell Garfield that he had been placing the money for a friend.

"On?" Garfield asked, looking at him intently.

"Empire State," Philip answered, watching Garfield's reaction closely. The congressman merely nodded.

A shout went up, and onto the beaten track pranced the brigadier's horse—tall, beautiful, full of life, and eager to run. Empire State was a bit more sedate but a lot of horse nevertheless. Lloyd's choice was shorter than the son of Diomed by half a hand but strong in the flank and withers. There were few preliminaries. All those who had wanted to wager money had done so, and now everyone crowded close to the unfenced track.

A single line of men stood just in front of the horses harnessed to Garfield's surrey, careful not to obstruct the view of its occupants. They were discussing the footing, which was, they claimed, a bit slippery on the dirt track, although most of the snow had been swept aside or beaten away by horses' hooves.

"What do you think, Mr. Trent?" Garfield asked.

"I bow to the experts," Philip answered.

"This expert says that the footing will favor Empire State," Leah added over her shoulder. "Being a New York State horse, he's seen snow before."

"Let us say that's one reason why some few are betting on Empire State," Garfield observed.

Accompanied by a great shout, the two horses leapt into motion as one, a start that could not have been more equal; but from the first seconds it was apparent that the New York horse was the superior one. Empire State won going away, won convincingly by at least six lengths. A moan of disbelief came from the crowd. A half-dozen men moved quickly toward the betting wagon, where the bet taker, a look of shock on his face, began to count out money.

"I suppose I should go cash in the bet I placed," Philip said. "Care to accompany me, Mr. Garfield?"

"Mr. Trent, I don't bet on fixed races," Garfield said with a cold little smile.

Philip felt his face flush. He was in an awkward position, but his loyalty to his friend prevented him from explaining to Garfield that he had merely been doing someone a service by placing the bet. He had come to like Garfield during their brief acquaintance and was impressed by the man's open friendliness. Although he told himself that if Garfield had been a real friend, he would have given him the benefit of the doubt before openly condemning him in front of Leah, it didn't help a great deal.

He went to the money wagon, and when he returned, Lloyd Miles's winnings made a bulky packet in his inside coat pocket. Garfield was helping Leah down from his surrey.

"Congressman, we appreciate the trackside seat," Philip said.

"My pleasure. Trent, keep in touch, will you? Let's remember that we're going to have dinner one night." But there was a chill in the congressman's eye and a lack of sincerity in his tone.

A cry from behind them drew their attention. The brigadier's horse was on the ground, its legs twitching weakly for a few moments before it was still. A man with a black bag in his hand rushed to kneel beside the horse, then looked into the dead eyes and into the mouth. "This horse has been heavily drugged!" he shouted.

There were shocked cries, followed by demands that the money lost on bets be given back. A stern-faced man climbed to the top of the money wagon and shouted for attention. "It is evident," he said, "that there has been foul play. Now, gentlemen, money has been paid out to those who bet on Empire State. As the gentlemen you are, you will, of course, return this money, since it is obvious that Empire State won dishonorably."

A buggy was wheeling out onto the road, its driver lashing the horses to greater speed. Philip recognized the driver as one of the men who had been in front of him at the money wagon, collecting his bet on Empire State.

"I'll be back in a moment," Philip said to Leah. He pushed his way through the agitated crowd around the betting wagon and handed back Lloyd's winnings.

"At least there is one honest man among us," the money changer said.

The race and its disturbing aftermath were heavy on Philip's mind as Leah and he began the drive back to the city. They rode in silence for a long while until finally she said, "You could have told Mr. Garfield that you were placing the bet for Lloyd."

"Yes," Philip answered somberly.

"But you didn't." She put her mittened hand on his arm. "Thank you."

Soon they were chattering away again, a man and a woman getting to know each other, driven by those mysterious biological forces that make for that most happy and most sorrowful of human emotions, love.

* * *

Lloyd Miles stopped in at the offices of Schuyler Colfax at midmorning the next day. Without returning Miles's greeting Philip handed him his original thousand dollars. Miles flipped through the bills. "Didn't have a chance to collect before the brigadier's horse died?"

"As a matter of fact, I did."

Miles looked at him questioningly.

"I returned the money."

"Good Lord. You simply gave away thousands?"

Philip looked at his old friend coldly. "I'm not going to ask you how you knew that the race was fixed."

"You gave back my winnings?"

"Lloyd, I think we'd better drop this," Philip said.

Lloyd Miles shrugged. "Well, easy come and all. Lord, Philip, you are the blushing innocent, aren't you?"

"I have work to do," Philip said, turning away.

Miles followed, and taking Philip's arm, he laughed. "All right, my friend, I hereby apologize. But you're never going to make it in this town unless you develop some toughness."

"If it is a requirement to cheat, then I don't want to, as you say, make it in this town." He looked into Lloyd Miles's smiling face. "That was a beautiful horse. He was vibrant and full of life, and now he's dead. Someone poisoned him, Lloyd."

"I didn't know how it was going to be done," Miles said in a subdued voice. "I only knew that Empire State was going to win."

"How did you know?"

"How many congressmen did you see at the race?"

"A few."

"Well, there you are."

"You're saying that members of the House of Representatives of the United States conspired to fix a horse race?"

"Far be it from me to accuse the honorable men who are in a position to decide the future of our nation." Miles gave a cynical smile. "But as I recall, Empire State is owned by a New York congressman."

"I saw no one that I recognized place a bet on Empire State."

Miles shrugged. "The gentlemen of the national legislature had their bets laid on by hired hands."

"So you asked me to place your bet." Philip looked Lloyd Miles in the eyes. "Was I being used in place of a hired hand?"

"You know better than that, Phil," Miles said sincerely. "You know I'd have placed the bet myself if Durant hadn't needed my services yesterday morning. And I'd have placed money for you, if you'd asked. You and I are small potatoes, old friend. There are certain advantages to such a condition. Sometimes a small potato can get away with things that the big ones can't."

"Lloyd, I really do have work to do."

"Hell's bells, you're making me feel guilty," Miles said with evident frustration. "I get a good tip on how to pick up a quick dollar, I share it with you, and all of a sudden I'm a criminal." He reached for Philip's hand. "All right, Phil. I've learned something about you. Actually, I'm pleased. Don't write me off your list just yet. Leah thinks you're a good influence on me. Who knows, you and my sister might even reform me and turn me into a pure and honest citizen."

"Lloyd," Philip said, laughing, "get out of here and let me get to work."

The knowledge that Lloyd Miles had taken advantage of a fixed race continued to bother Philip, but he found it impossible to be angry with Miles for long—especially since he intended to be the man's brother-in-law.

For the balance of January and into a dreary, frigid February, Philip's assignment was to compile all the information he could about the planning, building, and financing of the transcontinental railroad. He spent time with Schuyler Colfax's top man, Archibald Edwards, who said that Philip was on the right track and "getting to know the territory."

Philip had stopped asking for an appointment with Colfax after being put off several times. He resolved that when he was ready, he would, if necessary, simply walk into the Speaker's office unannounced and present his conclusions regarding waste and corruption on the transcontinental.

He had acquired a copy of the Pacific Railroad Bill of 1862, which had given both the Union Pacific and the Central Pacific their charters. He had the legalistic prose of the bill well planted in his memory. Moreover, he had discovered one source of information outside the office, his friend Lloyd Miles.

"Of course there's graft involved in the operation of the C.P.," Miles had told him one shivery night as Philip, Leah, and Miles sat before a roaring coal fire in the apartment that Leah shared with her brother. "Way back in the early sixties old Elton Clemmons—I think you know him—"

"Yes," Philip said, remembering the Bostonian who refused to adopt the more practical, rugged mode of dress prevalent at the Central Pacific railhead.

"Well, Clemmons told Collis Huntington that the average cost per mile of building the C.P. would be thirty thousand dollars. Huntington told him to double that estimate to sixty thousand."

"But why?" Leah asked. "Why inflate the cost of his own railroad?"

"My child," Miles teased, "such things are too much for you, and trying to understand them would strain your tiny feminine brain."

Leah threw a pillow at her brother and stuck out her tongue. "That's just a way of saying that you don't understand it yourself."

Miles laughed. "Well, you can bet Collis P. Huntington understands it." He tapped Philip on the knee with his forefinger, a habit he had of calling attention in advance to a statement he considered particularly interesting. "When Huntington first came to Washington, he was carrying two hundred thousand dollars, all the capital of the company he had formed with Stanford, Hopkins, and Crocker. The inside word is that he used every dollar of it to grease the wheels on Capitol Hill, meaning to buy the support of senators and representatives."

"This inside word, just what is it inside of?" Philip asked. "Would there be any way to document Huntington's spending so much money on bribes?"

Lloyd Miles shrugged. "I doubt it. But you can believe me."

Philip was learning from experience that the "inside" rumors that flitted around Washington usually were based on truth. He made a note to look into the known facts about Collis P. Huntington, who lived in Washington—the better, Philip thought with his growing cynicism, to influence railroad legislation.

During those winter months Philip and Leah were often together, and at such times railroads and his work were far from his mind. They spoke frequently of things they would do together in the future, as if there was a mutual understanding that they would be married.

Lloyd did all he could to encourage their relationship. "If you two lovebirds can tear your eyes off each other for a moment," he said one night, "I have a suggestion. We've all been cooped up for too long. I think it's time we all went to a big blowout."

Leah moaned in mock pain. She was sitting next to Philip, her hand in his.

"My boss, Thomas Durant, knows how to throw a party," Miles said. "Saturday night." He held up his hand. "No discussion, youngsters. We're going. That's it."

CHAPTER 8

Lloyd Miles had been on duty at the Washington home of Thomas Durant for an hour before Philip and Leah arrived. When he saw them enter, he made his way toward them, nodding and speaking to a half-dozen men before he reached them.

"My, my, doesn't my big brother look handsome?" Leah said. She gave him a society peck on the cheek.

"Look, you two, just make yourselves at home. Circulate." Miles nudged Philip and grinned. "Lots of brass here tonight, Captain. On your toes." He patted Leah's arm. "Got to run. Duty calls."

It was a glittering gathering. Among the notables were two Cabinet members and numerous senators and representatives, including Philip's boss, Speaker of the House Schuyler Colfax. Philip introduced Leah to Colfax, who took her hand and leered at her, his mouth a pink moistness hiding in the bush of his beard.

"Ah, my dear," Colfax said, "your youthful charm ornaments this staid gathering." He turned to Philip. "What a lucky fellow you are, Philip."

"I think so, sir. Luckier still when she agrees to marry me."

"Splendid," Colfax remarked. "And will the lady say yes?"

"The lady does not recall being asked," Leah teased.

"Why, Philip," Colfax commented, beaming in a fatherly way, "I had no idea you were shy. Shall I, then, be your John Alden?"

"No, thank you, sir," Philip replied. "I remember what happened in that case, and I wouldn't want to take a chance that such a charming gentleman as you might decide to speak for yourself." No harm, he thought, in buttering up the boss a bit.

Colfax roared with laughter. "Arrant flattery, my boy, but thank you." He bent low and brought his lips to within an inch of Leah's gloved hand. "If you say yes, young lady, I vow to you that I'll help you smooth the rough edges off this young scoundrel."

When Colfax had gone off to glad-hand more influential persons, Philip steered Leah to a quiet corner. "What do you mean, I haven't asked?" he demanded.

"Are you saying that you have?" Her eyes were wide, her face a caricature of innocence.

"Perhaps not in so many words, but—"

"Perhaps I'd like to hear the words." Her look had altered to one of adoration as he held her eyes with his. Her beauty, her sultry warmth, and the knowledge that she returned his love made his throat constrict.

"Leah," he began, and it came out a croak. He cleared his throat. "Leah, I don't want to continue my life without you at my side. In all sincerity, in all humbleness, I beseech you to be my wife."

"Oh, all right, if you insist," she said lightly, smiling in a teasing way. She quickly became intense, pressing against him and whispering, "I *must* be kissed, this minute."

He held her away from him, his hands on her arms. "Not until I've had a decent answer to my proposal."

"Yes," she said, leaning forward, her lips moist and her eyes filled with him. "Yes, yes, yes. But only if you'll kiss me right now."

"Not before God and everybody," he said, looking around.

He led her across the ballroom and pushed open two doors before he found the one to the library. They entered, and he closed the door behind them. One lamp was burning low, its light absorbed by the shelves of books and the dark wood of the paneling. He guided her to privacy, behind a tall, free-standing bookshelf.

She came into his arms gladly, lifting her mouth to his. Time stopped. The world spun on, but neither of them turned with it, for they had found a universe of their own, a place where there was only the warmth of the kiss, the pressing of their bodies, and the sweet whisper of the promise of things to come. Words of love were given and returned, and always the kiss until she gently pushed him away with a sighing intake of breath. She was about to speak when the door opened and two men entered.

Philip and Leah were hidden from view. His eyes were even with an opening above a row of books, and he could see that the two men were Thomas Durant and Archibald Edwards, Philip's immediate superior in the office of the Speaker of the House. The two men exchanged no words. Thomas Durant reached inside his coat and withdrew an envelope. He handed it to Archibald Edwards. Edwards opened the flap, thumbed the contents—obviously green-backs—and then made the envelope disappear under his coat. The event happened with a swiftness that seemed quite odd. They left the library one at a time, a full minute apart, clearly not wanting to be seen together.

Philip felt a surge of anger, an emotion engendered by the sudden conviction that he had been betrayed. He had placed his trust in Schuyler Colfax, and for that long moment as he stood in silence with his arms around Leah, it seemed obvious that the money Durant had given to the Speaker's right-hand man could be destined only for the pockets of the Speaker.

Leah stirred and looked up at him. "Is something wrong?" she asked.

He shook his head. There could be, after all, many explanations for that exchange of money that did not involve a man whom everyone thought to be honorable. He smiled down at Leah.

"We, too, should go," she said.

"One more kiss," he whispered.

"You are overwhelmingly persuasive," she said, lifting her lips to his.

He sank into the wonder of the kiss, and then it was his turn to sigh and push her away. "How can I wait?" he whispered.

"As I do, with great difficulty."

"Then we must be married soon."

"I have no mother to fret and delay things with her desire to make a perfect wedding," Leah declared.

"We'll have to tell old Lloyd."

She smiled. "I think he'll be pleased."

"I hope so."

She was clinging to his arm as they walked out of the library. She pulled him to a halt and whispered, "Everyone can *see.*"

He laughed. "I have the same feeling, as if everyone knows what we were doing. But, after all, we're betrothed now."

"Ummm," she said.

He had eyes only for her. He did not notice that Archibald Edwards was standing in a group of men near the library door. He did not see Edwards knit his brow and worry his lower lip with his teeth for a moment when he saw Philip and Leah emerge.

Lloyd Miles was an artist's idealized portrait of the virile, up-and-coming young man that night at Thomas Durant's social affair. He wore evening dress, and his brown hair was long but neat. His blue eyes could transmit a sincerity that warmed the object of his attention into thinking that Miles was truly a friend.

Miles was good at his job, for which Thomas Durant and the Union Pacific Railroad paid him what would have seemed to most Americans a princely salary. As the evening passed, it was his responsibility to see that certain important politicians were steered into the conversation group that surrounded Thomas Durant.

Durant was a big man. His face and head, although he affected a scraggly beard and heavy, down-turned mustache, seemed slightly too small for his body. His wide-set eyes had something of the look of a raptor. His thinning hair was beginning to show streaks of gray. He worked smoothly with Lloyd Miles, ready to dismiss politely one contact in order to turn his full attention to the next senator or representative that Miles had corralled for the Durant treatment.

Throughout the early part of the evening Lloyd Miles had been especially solicitous of Indiana Congressman John O'Brian. The portly legislator was a bit unsteady on his feet, and his expensively tailored evening wear appeared slightly rumpled. When Miles snared a full glass from the tray of a passing waiter and put it into O'Brian's hands, he noticed that Philip was watching, lifting one eyebrow. Miles winked and made a drinking motion with his hand to indicate that O'Brian was a man who believed in hoisting a few.

Lloyd Miles was careful to arrange things so that Philip and Leah were nowhere near when he nodded to a fashionably shapely, flamboyantly dressed blond woman who had been awaiting his signal. "John," Miles said, holding out his hand and gathering the blond woman in to stand face to face with the congressman, "I want you to meet a lovely lady. Miss Renee Proctor, may I present Congressman John O'Brian."

O'Brian's lips were moist as he touched them to the young woman's hand.

"Oh, my, I do so love to talk with really important men," she cooed so ingenuously that Miles gave her a warning look. O'Brian, however, had eyes only for her chest, where her low-cut gown gave a creamy-skinned hint of other wonders. "The processes of our government just fascinate me," she went on, hooking her arm around O'Brian's. "I'd just love it if we could find some quiet place to have a really *intimate* conversation."

Miles rolled his eyes. Rosanna Pulliam—for that was Renee Proctor's real name—was laying it on thick, but O'Brian was looking down at her, his eyes showing the glaze that marks a man about to reach his limit of drink.

O'Brian was a married man, but his wife was at home in Indiana. He was egotistical enough, Miles knew, to believe that this attractive young woman's invitation was for something other than talk. Miles also was aware that O'Brian kept an apartment near the Capitol but was prudent enough, drunk or not, to avoid being seen there with a woman the likes of Rosanna. Yet John O'Brian's glassy eyes gave a clear indication of how eager he was to spend some time alone with her.

When Miles offered a suggestion, O'Brian leapt at it.

"John," he whispered into the congressman's ear, "I hate to be the one to tell you this, but you're just a little bit intoxicated."

O'Brian laughed. "How can you tell?"

"It might be a good idea, John, if you found yourself a bed."

O'Brian winked. "'Zackly what I'm thinking."

"And it wouldn't do, would it, to have you gallivanting around by yourself in this condition?"

"No, sir," O'Brian said, clutching Rosanna's hand.

"Renee would be happy to accompany you, wouldn't you, dear?"

"I'd just love to," Rosanna simpered.

Miles slipped a key into O'Brian's hand. "This is the key to a quiet little place not far from here," he whispered. "Take my word for it. It's absolutely private." He handed the congressman a card with an address written on it.

"Lloyd, boy, I owe you one," John O'Brian said as Rosanna tugged on his arm and steered him toward the front door.

Miles watched them leave, the portly man being steadied by the woman. "That's what I'm counting on, John, old boy," he said under his breath.

John O'Brian looked back at Miles, who was standing there so tall, so handsome, so debonair. *Well, old Lloyd's nothing more than a pimp,* he thought, and he grinned to himself. Old Lloyd wanted something from him, and it wasn't difficult to guess what. Sooner or later there'd be legislation before the House that would affect the Union Pacific Railroad in some way, and when the vote came, Lloyd Miles would expect him to vote the way that would most benefit the railroad. But it would take more than a willing woman, thrust into his hands without much subtlety, to bribe John O'Brian.

He felt the woman's soft, warm young body press against his, felt the heat of her hand on his arm, and a sense of desperate need began to rise in him. Ordinarily he was a careful man. This enticing young blond tart would not be the first Washington woman he had bedded, for there always seemed to be a ready supply of willing lollipops who collected moments with men of influence and power the way others collected stamps or butterflies. But he had never *needed* a woman the way he needed this Renee Proctor.

John O'Brian was the product of a small town. His experience in Washington had made him more urbane, but there was still, as his friends in Congress were wont to say, a lot of the country in the boy. For example, he disdained hired cabs. Although it strained his salary as a congressman, he kept his own team of matched blacks in a stable near his apartment and had his own surrey.

The woman laughed as he tried to help her into the surrey. "I can make it, thank you," she said. She seated herself and watched him reel around in front of the horses to untie them. His foot slipped as he tried to climb into the driver's seat.

"Love, would you like me to drive?" she asked, sliding across the seat to press against him after he had made it up.

"No," O'Brian said harshly. "Nobody drives these horses but me."

Twice he had to ask her for directions. It didn't occur to him to question how she knew the way to the apartment to which Lloyd Miles had given him the key. She stayed close at his side, her hands on his arm, her voice a warm purr in his ear. In his eagerness he clucked his horses to a smooth trot.

The night was mild and moonless. They had passed through the regal area of mansions and were traversing a stretch of woods when she said, "There's a narrow bridge ahead, love. Best slow down."

He pulled the horses to a walk. Their hooves clattered onto the plank bridge, and at that moment she pulled his head toward her and put her wet mouth on his. He felt a surge of desire and clutched at her with his free arm.

"Careful," she whispered, her lips making little butterfly flutterings against his.

She was tracing his lips with her tongue when he felt the reins being tugged. Suddenly the right rear wheel of the vehicle slipped off the edge of the bridge, and the surrey dropped sickeningly. He was trying to hang on to the seat and hold the woman while yelling at the horses. The team of blacks was struggling, panicking as the surrey's weight pulled them backward. The strain suddenly broke the tongue of the surrey with a sound like a pistol shot, and the remaining harness and gear could not hold the weight. The surrey toppled, turning upside down as it fell. One horse ripped free and neighed in terror as it dashed away; the other was dragged after the surrey and hit the black water of the creek with a huge splash.

The shock of the icy water cleared O'Brian's head instantly. He was underwater, and he was being drawn down. He felt a tug around his wrist from the reins, finally freed his hand, and surfaced to gasp air into his lungs. The creek was no more than fifty feet wide, and the surrey had gone off the exact center of the bridge. He struck out for the bank and then remembered. . . .

Treading water, he looked around. He wanted to call out, but he had forgotten the blond woman's name. "Hey!" he yelled. "Hey, where are you?"

He heard a mighty splashing downstream. He could see a dark form reach the bank and scramble up. It was one of the horses. The current was carrying O'Brian away from the bridge, his heavy coat, boots, and clothing dragging him down. It was almost too late when he started swimming for the bank again, but he made it, struggled up through the mud, and fell on his face. The mud seemed more frigid than the water. A light wind bit at him painfully as he struggled to his feet. His cheeks burned with the cold. He trudged up and down the bank, desperately trying to see the blond woman on the surface of the dark water. An owl was hooting from a tree across the stream, and the running water made chuckling sounds. Fighting the underbrush, he walked down the creek . . . and then he knew that she was gone. He was shivering uncontrollably.

His mind began to function despite the cold and the shock. He could not appear at his own apartment in such a condition. The doorman, if no one else, would see him. He couldn't go back to the Durant house to seek the help of Lloyd Miles. But he still had the key in his pocket, and the apartment was not far away.

He walked and ran the remaining distance. He was worried not only about the woman but about his beloved horses. No doorman was present at the apartment house, he was relieved to see, and he rushed in and up a flight of stairs, dripping water behind him. Then he was inside, the door shut behind him.

A fire was banked in the stove. He kindled it and added wood, and when it was crackling, he peeled off his wet clothing, dried himself, and wrapped up in a blanket. Gradually his shivering subsided. He yearned for a drink, and after a few minutes of looking he found a bottle. Not bothering with a glass, he turned it up and swallowed.

The whiskey cleared his head. He had to do something and do it quickly. In a wardrobe he found clothing, and letting the blanket fall to the floor, he pulled on the trousers. They would not button, but he could hide that by wearing a heavy overcoat. Fully attired, he left the apartment, locking the door behind him, and went down into the street, looking in both directions. Nobody was in sight. He began to walk, his pulse growing more rapid from the exertion as well as the excitement, until he encountered two young boys. Giving them greenbacks, he instructed them to deliver a message to Lloyd Miles. Satisfied that they would do what he wished, he returned to the apartment and steadied his nerves with more of the whiskey.

Miles arrived almost an hour later. "What is it, John?" he asked as he closed the door. O'Brian tried to explain, but the words apparently were too incoherent for Miles to understand, for he put his hands on the congressman's shoulders and shook him. "What's wrong?"

Gradually O'Brian got the story across to Miles, who said with horror in his voice, "My God, man, you just let her drown?"

"Nothing I could do." O'Brian shrugged. "Almost drowned myself. Looked for her."

"You *looked* for her," Miles repeated. "You didn't call for help?"

"No one near," O'Brian said. "Guess not too many people use that little lane."

"You just let her drown," Miles said sadly.

"Lloyd, ole boy, you've gotta help me."

Miles stood silent for a moment, his chin cupped thoughtfully in his hand. "I guess the first thing we should do is notify the police."

"God, no!" O'Brian exclaimed. "Now, let's think this over, Lloyd. Let's look at it from all angles."

"A woman is dead," Lloyd Miles stated flatly.

"But it wasn't my fault!" O'Brian insisted. "She was messing round with me as we crossed the bridge. She thought we were too close to the edge and grabbed the reins . . . pulled 'em the wrong way, and the wheels went off the edge. It wasn't my fault, Lloyd!"

Miles rubbed his chin. "Well, she *was* drinking."

"She was very drunk," O'Brian said excitedly, beginning to see a way out. He stood up. "I couldn't help what happened. Look, Lloyd, think of what's at stake here. I know you want my vote in matters pertaining to the Union Pacific. I guess you're really my friend. But I'm not stupid enough to think that friendship is all that's between us—it's your job to lobby me. I know that." He put his hands on Miles's shoulders and pulled him around to face him. "If this got out I wouldn't be able to stay in Congress. You wouldn't have a chance to lobby me for my vote, would you?"

Miles frowned. "That seems of little importance at the moment."

"Hey, Lloyd, who was this woman? Lemme tell you, she was no lady. She was all over me . . . couldn't wait to get to the apartment."

"She was not a whore," Miles said stonily, looking at the floor.

"No . . . I didn't say that."

"Not your ordinary, streetwalking whore," Miles added.

O'Brian's expression brightened. "What, then? One of those women who's available at a fee at the right place and the right time? That's a whore, boy."

Lloyd Miles looked at O'Brian's bloodshot eyes. "Well, I'll grant you that she did make herself available, but only to men like you, men of position . . . gentlemen."

"A *courtesan,* then, to use a kinder word," O'Brian said. "Lloyd, is my career, my position, to be ruined by the death of a courtesan?"

Miles stared at O'Brian a moment and then said, "John, maybe we'd better be sure she's dead before we decide."

Lloyd Miles led the way back to the creek, walking swiftly and not talking. He steered O'Brian away from the bridge to a bend in the creek. To Lloyd's relief O'Brian asked no questions. Miles found the huddled bundle lying in the shallow water exactly where he had expected to find it. He waded into the water, amazed at how cold it was, and bent over.

"Is it the woman?" O'Brian asked from behind him.

"Yes," Miles said.

"And she's—"

"Dead." He was surprised to hear the congressman begin to sob violently. He stood up, pulled his pocket flask out, and forced a swallow of brandy into O'Brian's mouth.

"Help me, Lloyd," the congressman begged.

"I will," Miles said. "I think you're right. She's not worth it."

"Who knows that you hired her for me tonight?" O'Brian asked.

"No one." Miles saw O'Brian's doughy face light up.

"Are you sure? No book entries for the cost?"

"Do I look stupid?"

"No, Lloyd, you don't look stupid," O'Brian said. "Help me, boy. You won't regret it."

Miles was elated. Everything had gone as planned, and

now John O'Brian was right where he wanted him. But Miles contained his excitement. "All right," he said. "Listen to me. You go on back into town. I'll have your clothes cleaned and send them to you."

"My horses—"

"Damn your horses," Miles said. "You can worry about your horses later. You'd better have a good story ready about how you lost your surrey in the creek. Now, I doubt that anyone noticed your leaving with this Proctor woman. If so, I'll cover for you. As far as anyone else is concerned, if they ask, she tried to latch on to you and you told her to leave you alone. I saw her leave the party myself. She said she was sick of Washington and its prim, blue-nosed men, and she was going home to Philadelphia."

O'Brian gripped Miles's hand in both of his. "You won't be sorry, Lloyd."

"Go on. Get back to town."

"All right."

Miles heard movement behind him even before O'Brian was out of sight. Rosanna Pulliam waded out of the shallow water, her heavy clothing dripping water. Her wet hair hung limply, streaming down over her shoulders. Miles pulled off his topcoat and put it around her.

"Did you have to stand there talking all night?" she asked with an involuntary shudder that made her teeth chatter. "I'm freezing."

He walked her quickly to a closed carriage hidden in a nearby clump of trees. She had needed the vehicle as a place to wait, to be at least half warm, until Miles could arrange to bring O'Brian back to the creek for what they had called, laughingly, the death scene. She climbed into the carriage ahead of him and began to strip off her heavy, wet clothing. Miles helped her bundle into a flannel robe, then wrapped blankets around her.

"Better?" he asked.

"I don't think I'll ever thaw out."

"You did well, little Rose."

For a moment she was off guard. Her voice was sharp. "Don't call me that."

He put his hands under the blankets and robe and cupped her breasts. "I'll call you anything I damn well please, Rose."

His hands were cold. She shivered in spite of the quick heat of anger that flared up in her. The words she wanted to say remained on her tongue, for she had long ago learned to command her somewhat volatile emotions. She laughed, and she was laughing at herself for letting a little man like Lloyd Miles disturb her, even momentarily. She had handled men whose manhood and importance could be measured in multiples of Lloyd Miles.

"Always the bastard," she said teasingly.

"My, my," he said. "Now the girl tries flattery."

He climbed into the driver's seat and guided the carriage back to the hideaway apartment to which he had given John O'Brian the key. Miles sipped brandy and waited while Rosanna had a hot bath. She came back into the room swaddled in flannel, a towel wrapped around her head, her face and neck pink from the bath.

"Need some help?" Miles asked, removing the towel from her head and taking a dry towel from her hand. She had discarded the heavy wheat-colored wig she'd worn earlier in the evening. Her hair was dark and gleaming wet. She sank down in front of his chair and leaned her head back to let him dry her hair. Without the heavy makeup she had worn to Durant's reception her face was smooth and taut. Only the most perceptive observer would have recognized in this youthful, vibrant young woman the brazen blond hussy of the early evening.

"You did a remarkable job of disguise," Miles remarked.

"Thank you. You see, no experience is ever wasted. I learned how to alter my appearance during my brief theatrical career."

Miles put aside the towel and bent to press his nose into her fragrant hair. "It went well," he said.

"He was so drunk, he didn't know that I was pulling on the reins."

"Oh, yes he did. But no matter."

She turned her face up to him. Her mouth was large, her lips full. "Then only two things are needed now."

He lifted an eyebrow in question.

"First, some of that brandy. Second, a bit of money, my love."

He chuckled, then pushed her away from his knees. She accepted a glass of brandy with a smile and watched him as he went to the closet and brought back an envelope from his coat pocket. "We're very much alike, you and I," he mused.

"I'm not sure I'm flattered by that," she said as she counted the money.

"We both have a desire to possess a great deal of that which you now hold in your hand."

She nodded. "In that way we are alike."

"And in other ways," he said, reaching for her. She made no objection as he removed the flannel robe. Her eyes studied his face as he led her toward the bedroom. Men. They thought that they alone knew how to wield power; but in her smooth-skinned, svelte limbs, in her firm, protruding breasts, she had weapons of persuasion that no man had ever owned. Against the white sheets of the bed she was pink, soft, and receptive. . . .

When she awoke later, her arm was across Miles's chest, her face nestled on his shoulder. He was a comfortable man, a passionate man, and, surprisingly, quite considerate in bed. She felt pleasantly used. A glance at the clock told her the hour was quite late—or early, depending upon one's point of view. She stirred and found that Miles was awake.

"Rose, I think you'd make a good household servant," he said.

The odd remark dispelled her drowsiness. In the short time since she'd convinced Lloyd Miles that he needed her in his office at the Union Pacific suite in Durant's Washington headquarters, she'd come to know that his mind could take devious turns.

"Perhaps," she said, curious.

"You like money. So do I. And there's so much of it floating around, little Rose, just waiting for someone like you or me to stake a claim to it. I'm going to get mine. You stick with me, and I'll see to it that you get yours."

"But not quite as much as you'll get, I warrant," she said.

He chuckled. "Where true wealth is concerned it's only a matter of degree. I, of course, have not reached that stage of development yet, but I'm told that after a certain point money becomes nothing more than a method of keeping score."

"I'm listening," she said, snuggling back to his shoulder.

"Do you know Collis P. Huntington?"

"He's one of the important men of the Central Pacific, isn't he?"

"In Washington he *is* the Central Pacific. He happens to be looking for a household servant, a combination of upstairs maid and dining attendant."

"I don't think I'd like being a maid." She had accomplished exactly what she had set out to do, to establish herself in the Union Pacific offices with access to a variety of information through Lloyd Miles. At the moment she saw nothing to gain by leaving that position to play whatever game Lloyd had in mind.

"You'd look fetching in livery."

"Go to hell," she whispered.

"It's important to me, Rose. Think of the enormous sums of money that change hands in Washington. Think of the millions involved in building the transcontinental."

"I don't see how my becoming Collis Huntington's maid would put any of that in my purse."

"You see, that's your trouble," he taunted. "No imagination. Let me explain it. At the moment my paycheck depends on the goodwill of Dr. Thomas Durant. My advancement, meaning my chances at increasing my income, depend on Durant. If I please Durant, if I produce for him, then I am advanced, and my income increases. When my income increases, your income increases." He stroked her back. "I think that Thomas Durant would be very pleased to have an ear"—he lifted his head and nibbled at her left ear—"and such a delicious ear, in the Central Pacific camp. I think he'd be very generous to the man who arranged it." He leaned over her on one elbow. "It's important to me, Rose."

She sighed, trying to think of it as another role, another challenge. It could be interesting, at that, and maybe even informative. The day-to-day office work at the Union Pacific hadn't been either exciting or rewarding.

"Soon you'll be hiring maids for yourself," he told her.

"Of course."

"And wearing ermine and silk."

"Only for you," she teased, doing naughty things with her hand.

"Huntington will hire you. Just be respectable little Rose from the Lower East Side of New York and you'll get the job. You Irish people are known as hard workers. Then, once you're established in the house, I think you'll know how to take the best advantage of your position." He caressed one full breast. "You might even decide on a way to become more than just a maid."

"If I do it, it will cost you dearly, love," she said, her hand still busy.

"I'll want any little tidbit of information regarding the business of the Central Pacific," he said. "I'll want to know the name of everyone who visits the Huntington house. I'll want to know what they talk about."

"I haven't said I'd do it." She wasn't sure, not yet, if going along with Lloyd's latest scheme was compatible with her overall design. She would have to do some thinking, perhaps even some consultation, before deciding.

"But you will, for me," he said. "Won't you?"

"We'll talk about it later," she murmured, lifting herself to him.

"Good Lord, woman," he said. "Aren't you ready to go to sleep?"

"Are you?"

His body trembled in anticipation. "No, I think not," he said, pulling her atop him.

It was not until late that night, when Philip was alone and falling asleep, that he remembered the incident in the library of the Durant house. He bunched the feather pillow, clasped his hands behind his head, and stared at the dark ceiling. He had no doubt that he'd seen the passing of a goodly amount of money from Durant to Edwards. His first conclusion had been that he'd witnessed a bribe, a payoff designed to buy political favor for the Union Pacific Railroad. Now, in retrospect, he was still suspicious, for this was Washington, and it was well-known that corruption had come to the nation's capital. But he knew Archibald Edwards, had talked with him many times, and he had accepted Edwards as a man of honesty. Even though he'd seen the passing of money with his own eyes, he was not ready to believe that Edwards had accepted an overt bribe from Durant, for to believe that would necessarily lead to the conclusion that Schuyler Colfax was on the take. Surely Edwards was not corrupt; surely the Speaker of the United States House of Representatives was above bribery.

He turned onto his side, sighed deeply, and let his thoughts turn to a far more pleasant subject, Leah. He would not, he decided, let himself become infected with the disease of suspicion that was epidemic in Washington.

CHAPTER 9

At the beginning of a new week, on a splendid winter day of blue skies and invigorating breezes, Philip whistled his way to the office of the Speaker of the House. The affairs of the transcontinental railroad and the corruptive effect of the vast sums of money involved were far from his mind, for his consciousness was filled with memories of a blue-eyed lady with whom he'd spent the bulk of the day before, a wintry Sunday. The world intruded into his state of bliss when he passed the open door of Archibald Edwards's office, glanced in, and voiced a greeting.

Edwards stood behind his desk, facing the door, and called, "Just a minute, Trent."

Philip stopped and took a step back to the doorway. Edwards opened an envelope and removed a thick stack of greenbacks. He riffled the bills and looked at Philip with a challenging little smile. The envelope from which he had removed the money was large and brown, the same as the envelope that Thomas Durant had handed Edwards in Durant's library on Saturday evening.

"Come in, Trent," Edwards said. "Let me show you something interesting."

Philip faced Edwards across the desk. Edwards slapped the thick sheaf of bills against the palm of his hand. "Here, Trent, is the lifeblood of politics."

Philip nodded.

"Your father would understand," Edwards went on.

Philip felt his face coloring. Edwards was openly bracing him on the matter of the money, daring him to think anything other than what Edwards wanted him to think: that the money was a legitimate campaign contribution from a loyal party member.

"Gus Trent is one of the best fund-raisers in the party," Edward said, "but even he would say that I've done well with this." Again he slapped the bills against his palm, then turned, bent down, and put them on an empty shelf in his open safe. He slammed the door to the safe and straightened. "I'm not at liberty to name the donor, but that money goes into the Speaker's campaign chest. And you'll learn, if you stay with us—"

Philip searched Edwards's face, wondering if he'd just heard a veiled threat.

"—that the Speaker is very generous. In his position as one of the most powerful men in the party and, therefore, one of the more efficient money raisers, he shares his campaign funds with others who face Democratic challenges."

"Quite admirable of him," Philip said.

Edwards changed his tone. "How is your work going, Trent?"

"So-so," Philip said. "I will need to have a conference with the Speaker soon."

"Of course, of course," Edwards said, waving one hand. "By the by, I know you haven't been assigned a personal secretary, but if you need any help in transcribing material or in preparing new papers, feel free to call on one of the office secretaries. You'll find that they're quite efficient." He put his hand on an odd-looking device perched on the corner of his desk. "Soon, perhaps, they'll be even more so. Are you familiar with this machine?"

"No, sir, I'm not."

"It's a new invention by a Mr. Christopher Latham Sholes. It's called a typewriter." He pecked on the keys, and the machine clattered. He pulled the paper from it and showed it to Philip. "Astounding, isn't it? As if the letters had been

made by a printing press. Mind you, I'm not sure that it will
see widespread use—it makes a dreadful racket, and I fear
that it will intimidate our gentle members of the opposite sex
with its complexity. But I've promised Sholes that I'll give it
a try here in the office."

"Interesting," Philip said.

"Yes, well. I know you have work to do, my boy."

Thus dismissed, Philip went to his own office, sat down,
and put his feet on the desk. He was sure that Edwards had
deliberately flaunted the money. He tried to reconstruct the
events of Saturday night. At the time he had been sure that
neither Edwards nor Durant had been aware of the presence
of two young lovers in the dimly lit room. It was possible
that one of them had seen Leah and him leave the library. He
couldn't remember seeing either Edwards or Durant, but
then he had come fresh from Leah's kiss and his attention
was all for her. If, however, Edwards had somehow found
out that the transfer of greenbacks had been witnessed, his
almost too obvious display of the money would be explained,
leaving Philip to continue to wonder if the money had really
been a bribe. Ironically, if the money had been intended to
enrich Edwards or Colfax—or both—Leah and Philip had
done those gentlemen out of a nice piece of pocket change.
Now the sum would have to be entered into Edwards's books
as a political contribution to be used by Colfax or other legislators who were favorable to the aims of the Union Pacific.

Gus Trent was in Washington that day and treated his son
to lunch. After an easy chat, during which each man brought
the other up to date on his affairs, Philip told his father that
Gus might have a chance at being a grandfather sooner than
later. Then, for a good half an hour, Philip talked about Leah
Miles, much to the amusement and pleasure of his father.

"Well, my boy," Gus said, looking at his watch, "I'd like
to stay and hear more about this goddess come to earth, but I
have an appointment."

Philip flushed. "I do tend to run on when I'm talking
about Leah."

"Enjoy," Gus said. "I envy you. I felt the same way about your mother when I was courting her."

"She's a lot like Mother in some ways," Philip said, fondly remembering his mother, who had died of consumption when he was twelve. "You're going to like Leah, Dad."

Gus patted his son on the shoulder as he rose. "If she's your choice, then I like her already."

Philip followed Gus out onto the sidewalk and strolled beside him toward the Capitol building. "Dad, there's something I'd like to present to you for comment."

"Fire away."

He told Gus about seeing Edwards accept money from Thomas Durant and how Edwards had explained the transaction.

"So, you've caught the Washington disease," Gus said. "Suspicion." He looked at Philip seriously. "We know there's corruption in Washington. In a country like this, where the voters are not quite as well-informed as we'd like them to be, where any clown with a good personality and a fine speaking style can be elected to national office, we're bound to get some bad seeds in the fields where the Republic is cultivated —as witness the fact that the voters of Massachusetts have elected B. J. Butler to the House of Representatives again. But in general, Philip, I like to think that our national legislature, the two houses of Congress, represents the flower of democracy." He shrugged. "If an occasional weed gets into the bouquet, then we just have to pluck it out."

"And who does the plucking?" Philip asked.

"You. Men like Schuyler Colfax. There are always honest men about."

"And you're sure Colfax is one of them?"

"I've known Schuyler since he first came to Washington," Gus said. "If I knew for sure that there was only one honorable man in this city, and I had to pick him out, Schuyler would have to be one of the three or four men that I'd name."

"And Archibald Edwards?"

Gus frowned. "He seems to be a good man. I don't think he could get away with too much, working for Schuyler, even if he was one of the bad seeds. A man of integrity can often be fooled by a scoundrel, but not for long. I'd say, Philip, that Edwards was telling you the truth, that the money from Durant was a political contribution, not a personal bribe."

"When does it stop being one and become the other?"

"When it's put to personal use," Gus answered quickly. "Look, if it's bothering you that much, I suggest you have a talk with Schuyler."

Philip had the unexpected opportunity to put his father's suggestion into action immediately after lunch. Schuyler Colfax was entering the office just as Philip returned, and Philip matched the Speaker's stride. "I need a few minutes with you, sir," he said.

"Have to wait, my boy," Colfax replied. "Busy, busy."

"Sir," Philip said resolutely, "I'm afraid this can't wait."

Colfax jerked to a stop and looked challengingly at Philip. "Come into my office." He led the way and, sitting down at his desk, told Philip, "You'll have to make it quick."

"Sir, for weeks I've been trying to report to you. I came to work for you with a specific purpose in mind. I know beyond a doubt that the federal government is being cheated by both transcontinental railroad companies. Simple arithmetic and common sense tell one that."

When Colfax, looking impatient, started to speak, Philip raised a hand. "But that's not why I'm here. I'm here because your top man in this office took a sizable amount of money from Thomas Durant."

Colfax furrowed his brow and then smiled. "And you want to know if this office is in the pay of the Union Pacific, is that it?"

Philip stared at Colfax for a few seconds and answered with a nod, "If you want to put it that bluntly, sir, then so be it."

"We are not," Colfax stated. He rose from his chair, came around the desk, and when Philip also stood up, slung a fatherly arm around his shoulders. "Look, my boy, Thomas Durant is a loyal Republican. Oh, he would like to influence the vote of the Speaker of the House. Of course he would, and he'd advance much more money to do that than he gives to the coffers of the party." He withdrew his arm and faced Philip. "Actually, I should be angry that you would suspect such a thing, but in this cynical age I can see why a young idealist such as yourself—and thank God there are still men like you in this country—would wonder." He raised his right hand. "The money you saw Mr. Edwards put into his safe has already been delivered by special messenger to the chairman of the Republican party and will be distributed to congressmen who face Democratic challenges in the next election. You may, if you like, consult the ledger in Mr. Edwards's office."

"That won't be necessary," Philip said, impressed by the Speaker's sincerity.

"Good, good. Look, Philip, since we haven't been able to find a time to get together, perhaps it would be best if you put your latest findings regarding waste and graft on the transcontinental on paper, just as you did with your Central Pacific findings." He was escorting Philip toward the door with a hand on his shoulder. "When you are finished, give your report to Mr. Edwards, if you please."

Philip was smiling as he left the Speaker's office, not because he was pleased with what the Speaker had said but rather in mild amusement. Colfax had demonstrated all the qualities of a successful politician. He had made himself believable with sincerity and flattery, and the way he'd escorted Philip out of the office, hand on his shoulder, talking with evident candor, had been a masterpiece of dismissal without prejudice. But Gus trusted Colfax, and Philip trusted his father's political knowledge and instincts.

Philip went to his office and worked on his report. He finished it before five o'clock and took it to the office of Archibald Edwards, who assured him that it would be placed on Colfax's desk the next morning.

Lloyd Miles, on that brilliant Monday morning, refilled his employer's delicate bone-china cup from a sterling-silver coffee warmer, then put the server back on its heavy, ornate tray. Dr. Thomas Durant sat with one leg crossed over the

other in a fine leather chair in his library. Miles sipped coffee
and waited for Durant to speak.

"A rather successful party Saturday night, don't you
think?" the railroad baron asked.

"Very successful," Miles confirmed.

"I saw you spending time with O'Brian."

"Yes, sir." He paused, choosing his words carefully. "I can
tell you, sir, that in any matter that touches on the affairs of
the Union Pacific, Mr. O'Brian's vote will please you."

"Very good," Durant said. He did not ask Miles how this
remarkable feat had been accomplished. Miles knew that Durant did not want to know how he had changed the opinions
of a man who had been—as many in the Congress were—
leaning toward legislation that would be unfavorable for the
railroads. Nor did he ask Miles for assurance that John
O'Brian would no longer be antirailroad. When a man in
Durant's employ told him something, he accepted it at face
value unless events proved it to be a lie. In that case the
gentleman who had told the falsehood did not remain on
Durant's staff and, in fact, had difficulty finding a job in
railroading anywhere on the North American continent.

"Miles," Durant said, "I think the time has come for you
to assume a greater share of responsibility."

"Thank you, sir," the younger man said. He waited respectfully, although he was burning inside to know what Durant had in mind.

Durant emptied his cup. Miles poured again, this time refilling his own. The china and silver were English, and together they represented enough money for Lloyd Miles to
purchase a new carriage and a team of matching bays, something that had been on his mind for months.

When Durant spoke, his tone was soft and musing. "Miles,
had I a choice, I wouldn't be living in Washington. Don't like
the city. Don't like the climate. Winter one day, balmy the
next. Unhealthy."

"Well, I'm a Maryland man myself," Miles said. "I'm accustomed to the weather."

"And I'm far from home," Durant continued, "away from
my friends." He looked up and seemed to brighten. "But in a

good cause, eh?" He leaned forward. "We must give them something to lose, Miles. As I've heard it said, there's no difficulty getting men to look after their own property."

"Yes, sir."

"There is too much at stake here to allow a few petty politicians to spoil the stew by mucking around. When the tracks meet and the transcontinental is finished, the names of the men who built the railroad will be a part of history. Then all these small harassments will not matter. But for the moment we must take steps to assure that the antirailroad clique in Washington is kept in its place, that it is not allowed to grow."

"Give them something to lose," Miles said, knowing that Durant liked to be quoted.

"Exactly." Durant rose, went to his desk, and came back to hand Miles a packet. Miles opened the large envelope and saw the gilt edges of stock certificates. He examined one certificate. In ornate script the name Crédit Mobilier was emblazoned in gold across the top. Miles's heart pumped, for he was holding in his hand a small fortune. Crédit Mobilier was the privately owned holding company that had been formed to handle the acquisition of material for the Union Pacific. Though he was not yet privy to all the secrets of Thomas Durant and the Union Pacific, he did know that the men who owned the Union Pacific also owned Crédit Mobilier, and that Durant was the manager of Crédit Mobilier's funds. It was through Crédit Mobilier that immediate profits were being realized.

The process was a simple one: the Union Pacific awarded its construction contracts to Crédit Mobilier. Crédit Mobilier charged the railroad more than twice the actual cost of materials and labor. Since Durant and the other barons of the Union Pacific owned Crédit Mobilier, the profits went into their pockets immediately. Crédit Mobilier had already made Durant a financial power, although years would pass before the railroad itself showed a profit.

The shares of Crédit Mobilier that Lloyd Miles held in his hand represented instant wealth. He looked at Durant and waited, knowing that instructions were forthcoming.

"Distribute them wisely, at a price that cannot be refused, to members of the House and the Senate," Durant said.

"Ah," Miles said. "Yes. I think I can *persuade*—"

"I don't want to hear names," Durant protested.

"I understand. Except perhaps one, Mr. Durant."

Durant raised his brows.

"So that these certificates can never be tracked back to this office, I think it might be wise to allow our new friend, John O'Brian, to place them."

Durant nodded and after a few moments said, "Excellent. But remember, they are to be sold, not presented as a gift." He winked. "Of course, you have full discretion to place a value on the merchandise yourself, for the stock market is not always right and is, to say the least, unpredictable, is it not?"

Miles rose, but Durant motioned him back into his chair. "Sit, sit," he said. "We have so little opportunity to chat. Your sister, is she well?"

Miles laughed. "Marvelously well. She's in the throes of first love."

"Ah," Durant said. "I envy the lucky man."

"Perhaps you've heard of him. An old college friend of mine, Philip Trent."

"Gus Trent's boy?"

"The same."

"Medal of Honor?"

"For which I wrote the citation," Miles said.

"Works in Schuyler Colfax's office."

"I was keeping that as a surprise, sir." Miles grinned.

"He is, then, a true friend?"

"Yes, sir. And he's going to be my brother-in-law."

Durant mused for a moment. "Tread easily, Miles. Easily."

Miles had not caught the quick, odd look that Durant had given him. "I will, sir. You can be assured of that. But an ear in the office of the Speaker of the House . . ."

"Mr. Miles," Durant said softly, "by all means keep Philip Trent as your friend if that pleases you. Let him marry your sister if that pleases both you and her. But do not, and I repeat, do *not,* make it obvious that you are trying to get him to talk about the affairs of the Speaker. Am I understood?"

"You are," Miles said, more than slightly puzzled. He had thought that Durant would have welcomed a friendly contact in Colfax's office.

Durant rose, went to his desk again, and came back with another envelope, identical to the first. "I was going to hold off on this," he said, "although you will note the name on the certificates."

Miles's hands trembled ever so slightly as he opened the envelope, lifted a stock certificate, saw the golden words, and, miraculously, read his name.

"One hundred shares, my boy," Durant said magnanimously. "Call it a sort of bonus."

"You already had my loyalty, sir," Miles said. "Now you have my gratitude." He rose, shook Durant's hand, and left the office, holding his breath from excitement. In one instant he had become a man of substance.

Enough of the morning was left for Lloyd Miles to call at the office of Congressman John O'Brian. O'Brian greeted him warily, his eyes questioning.

"All is well, friend," Miles assured him.

O'Brian, obviously thinking about the woman he believed to be dead, looked relieved.

"In fact," Miles said, "I have come bearing gifts."

It took him a while to explain. O'Brian's first reaction was marked reluctance. His obvious distaste for the plan began to fade, however, when Miles set aside one little sheaf of stock certificates and said, "These have your name on them, John."

O'Brian picked up the certificates and read the amounts printed in ornate letters on the rich, thick paper. "I believe," he said, "that we can discuss the possibilities."

Lloyd Miles smiled. "It's a simple matter of passing along a good investment opportunity to a selected group of your friends," he said.

"What does Oakes think of this?" O'Brian asked.

Miles decided on his answer quickly. The name of Oakes Ames, congressman from Massachusetts, was, of course, familiar to him, as it was to everyone who worked for the Union Pacific. "It won't be necessary to offer Oakes any of the stock," he said. "After all, he put a million dollars' worth of his shovel company's money into the U.P."

Oliver Ames & Sons, a company founded by Oakes and Oliver Ames's father, was known primarily for its manufacture of shovels and had flourished during the California Gold Rush.

"I'm not stupid, Miles," O'Brian said.

"Perhaps I didn't follow your meaning," Miles replied.

"Everyone knows that Oakes is heavy into U.P. stock and that he and his brother, Oliver, own enough of Crédit Mobilier to control it if they care to. I asked about Oakes because he would recognize the fact that he has a vested interest in this little affair. He might be of some help."

Lloyd Miles was in an awkward position. He had not anticipated O'Brian's bringing Oakes Ames into the situation. He did not know whether Thomas Durant had consulted the Ames brothers before deciding to distribute shares in the holding company at a fraction of their cost to selected lawmakers, but he suspected not. There was no love lost between Thomas Durant and Oakes Ames. In fact, there existed between them a state of undeclared war, in which the weapons were shareholders' votes, stock options, and the power that comes with money. Their private war promised the victor control not only of the Union Pacific Railroad but of what could very well be the most promising money-making business organization ever assembled, Crédit Mobilier.

Miles made his decision. The behind-the-scenes battle between Durant and Oakes Ames need not concern John O'Brian, who had a specific job to do. "I'll leave it up to you to talk to Oakes," he said. "I think you know the object of this little exercise, John. When you're finished, please send me a list of stockholders, the number of shares owned by each, and the amount paid. I'm sure you'll make good choices regarding those to whom you sell the stock." He laughed. "At least I hope so. I'm a stockholder, too, you know, just as you are. What you do with the other shares will have a direct bearing on the worth of our own holdings."

"Thank you for explaining that to me, Miles," O'Brian said with rich sarcasm.

When Oakes and Oliver Ames were both in Washington, they shared an office at Crédit Mobilier. Oakes Ames had his congressional offices, of course, but in those inspiring days when the rails were being extended westward at record-breaking speeds, when money was pouring into the accounts of the company that acted as contractor and purchasing agent for the railroad, he spent more time at Crédit Mobilier than in his Capitol Hill suite.

The relationship between the Ames brothers had been established for many years, long before the father for whom Oliver Ames was named retired and left the management of Oliver Ames & Sons to Oakes, the elder by three years, and to his namesake. To the world Oakes was the big brother, the hand shaker, the taciturn, simple man of temperance who could relate to everyone. Although Oliver, too, had once entered politics and served in the Massachusetts State Senate, he was the thinker, the silent presence in the background of his older brother's hail-fellow-well-met friendliness, the brains, some said, of the Ames financial empire.

When a secretary announced that Congressman John O'Brian was in the anteroom asking to see Congressman Ames, Oliver nodded, picked up the accounting sheets he'd been discussing with Oakes, and disappeared behind a little partition, which gave him some privacy in his cubbyhole.

"Oakes, damned glad to see you," John O'Brian gushed, his hand thrust forward.

"And you," Oakes returned. "Always a pleasure to see my fellow committee member. What can I do for you, John?"

"Well, I smelled coffee brewing as I came through the outer office. . . ."

Oakes rang for his secretary. Soon each man had a steaming mug in his hands, and the conversation touched lightly on things pending before Congress. Oakes was waiting for O'Brian to get to the subject that had brought him to the office. He stiffened with interest when O'Brian opened his case and withdrew a stack of stock certificates, for he recognized Crédit Mobilier stock immediately.

"This is why I'm here, Oakes," O'Brian said, putting the sheaf of certificates on the desk in front of Ames.

"Ummm," Oakes said, fingering the expensive-looking papers.

"I've been assigned to place these stock certificates where they will do the most good."

"You've become a stockbroker?" Oakes asked mildly.

"Of one stock." O'Brian chuckled. "And I think even I can sell it, because the price is—" He named a figure that caused Oakes Ames to freeze for a moment.

"Durant," Oakes muttered.

"Well, I don't know," O'Brian replied. "Actually, I wondered if you had a hand in it."

"With whom did you talk?"

"Young fellow who works for Durant, all right. Name's Lloyd Miles."

"Yes . . . Durant." Oakes put his chin in his hand and mused. After a long time he broke into laughter.

"Glad you find it funny," O'Brian said.

"So even Thomas Durant can come up with a good idea once in a while," Oakes murmured. "Look, John, I think you're doing a tremendous service for the Union Pacific, and I hope that you're being very well rewarded."

"There are a few shares for me."

Oakes chuckled again. "Yes, by God, even Durant can come up with a good idea now and then. I'll be glad to give you a hand with this, John, if you'd care to have my help."

"That's why I'm here," O'Brian said. "I'd be grateful."

Oakes was counting. When he was finished, he whistled. His mind was racing as he voiced his thoughts. "If Durant took this many shares from his own holdings, he's damaged his position severely."

"I didn't ask where they came from," O'Brian said, frowning. "So how do you want to do this?"

"Tell me whom you have in mind," Oakes said, and for some minutes they passed names back and forth. Finally they divided the list, unequally, with the greater number of men in the House and Senate to be contacted by Oakes Ames.

Oliver Ames did not show his face around the partition until the door had closed behind John O'Brian. He came then to sit in the chair that O'Brian had vacated. "Unwise, Oakes," he said softly. "Very unwise."

There was no resentment in Oakes's surprised look. As he propped his feet up on the desk he explained, "There's nothing wrong with what I'm going to do. It's been done many times before. One interests leading businessmen in the community in a venture by giving them stock or by selling it to them cheaply."

"Congress is not exactly a business community," Oliver pointed out.

"But it is," Oakes insisted. "Look, only fools—men like John O'Brian—can live on a congressman's salary. If a man isn't a good businessman, if he can't make his mark in the competitive world, I don't think I'd want him as my representative in Washington, handling billions of dollars of the taxpayers' money."

Oliver Ames was shaking his head, and a little smile played on his lips. "Oakes, where did Durant get the shares?"

Oakes cocked his head in thought. "That's what I was going to ask you."

"With a battle for control coming up, he certainly didn't take them from his own holdings," Oliver said.

"Where, then?"

"From me, Oakes."

"You?" He let his feet fall to the floor with a bang. "By God, you?"

"From me. And why, Oakes, didn't I come to you with the distribution plan in the first place?"

"I don't know," Oakes said, his face clouded with bewilderment. "You should have."

"I didn't come to you to distribute the stock because I think that certain people would make rather nasty accusations—such as bribery, corruption, venality—if it ever became known that stock had been sold to members of the government at a fraction of its worth. If word leaked out I wouldn't want my brother and Oliver Ames and Sons to be associated with the distribution of the stock. I asked Durant to handle the matter so that he could take the blame, if the need ever arose. And now, Brother, you've opened your sometimes foolish mouth at the wrong time again."

"Then I'll tell John to do it himself," Oakes said quickly.

Oliver shook his head. "Too late for that now. O'Brian knows that you know. Soon everyone that O'Brian knows will *know* that you know. So go ahead and help distribute the stock. At least you'll be able to pick the best hands into which to put it." He rose and leaned over the desk, his weight on his hands. "Oakes, when you came to me and asked me to join you in building the Easton Branch Railroad back in Massachusetts, I expressed my misgivings then. If you'll remember, I told you that Oliver Ames and Sons had done pretty well selling shovels."

"Lord, we did sell some shovels, didn't we, Oliver?"

"And we had to swallow a loss of one million dollars when the West Coast merchants to whom you'd extended credit failed," Oliver said coldly. "You're not much of a business-man, Brother. I helped you build the Easton Branch Rail-road because it benefited Oliver Ames and Sons by bringing a branch of the railroad right to the factory.

"When you came to me and said, 'Oliver, let's put a million or two into the Union Pacific,' I thought about it for a long time. I finally agreed to do it not because I believed in you, Brother, but because I believed that the railroads are the future of this country. I went along with you even though I knew that it would be decades before the railroad would begin to show a profit, and I pulled our chestnuts out of the fire by forming Crédit Mobilier in order to get our investment back before we bankrupted the goose that lays the golden eggs—the home firm, Oliver Ames and Sons.

"Now you're rocking the boat again, Brother, and I'm a little tired of that. If you go down this time, you will go down alone. I will not let you drag me and Oliver Ames and Sons down with you. Do I make myself clear?"

Oakes had shifted his eyes away from the calm face, the steady stare. "You do, Oliver," he said. "Look, there's nothing to worry about." He laughed uncomfortably. "I didn't really think that Thomas Durant would have been smart enough to dream up this stock sale. It has your brand on it, Oliver. Yes, sir . . ." He lapsed into silence.

Oliver Ames shook his head and disappeared around the partition into his cubbyhole. He had meant every word he'd said to his brother. He had an abiding interest in seeing the transcontinental built, but not at the expense of Oliver Ames & Sons, the home company.

Oliver, in his forties, was bearded and somewhat slimmer than his brother. Nevertheless, he gave the impression of wielding great power. He had never been poor, for he was the second son of a man of influence. Because he had apprenticed himself in the family shovel factory to learn the business from the ground up, he knew work, and he'd seen poverty, and he had long before decided that wealth was better. It was not glory that interested Oliver Ames.

It would be nice for his children and grandchildren to know that their ancestor had been, as his father had been before him, a man of substance, that Oliver Ames may have had some little part in building the first railroad to connect east and west. But posthumous fame would be, he felt, of no great comfort to him. The things he wanted were here and now. For example, he wanted Thomas Durant out as manager of Crédit Mobilier. And he wanted General John A. Dix out as president of the Union Pacific. Both companies needed a stronger, firmer hand at the helm.

Oakes would do very well as manager of Crédit Mobilier, Oliver believed, because Oliver himself would be on hand, constantly looking over his brother's shoulder. Oakes didn't understand the magic of numbers. He would not interest himself in the bookkeeping and day-to-day drudgery but would leave that instead to Oliver. So Oakes could have the title of manager of Crédit Mobilier.

As for heading the railroad? That was another story. The man who was to be president of the Union Pacific after General Dix would have to contend with the greed and hunger for power of men like Thomas Durant, with idealists like that young man who worked in Schuyler Colfax's office, with finicky engineers at the railhead, and with the politicians.

He knew, as he sat in his cubbyhole and listened to his brother glad-hand still another visiting fellow member of the House of Representatives, as he heard Oakes close a "sale" of a block of Crédit Mobilier shares, that he'd have a real battle on his hands before he himself could be named president of the Union Pacific. But it would come.

First he had to get Thomas Durant out of Crédit Mobilier.

The Washington Breakfast Club met once a week, if possible, but not always for the first meal of the day. The four members of the club were not, as yet, their own bosses, so it was often necessary to arrange the meeting for lunchtime or in the evening. No formality was attached to the meeting; no minutes, resolutions, or motions were made. The four men, almost of an age, had been drawn together by a common dream. Each of them wanted to be rich. And each of them worked for one of the men whose names were becoming more and more familiar to the nation and the world. On that Monday in February, Lloyd Miles joined the other three at a quiet restaurant not favored by the great and powerful of the capital city.

Harold Berman, who wore wire-rimmed spectacles and had curly dark hair, was on the payroll of the speculator Jay Gould. Geoffrey Lancaster, with sandy-blond hair and blue eyes, was an assistant to the glum sage of New York, John D. Rockefeller. Paul Jennings, urbane, always impeccably dressed, had the trust of Andrew Carnegie. With Lloyd Miles, who considered himself the right-hand man of Thomas Durant, the other three shared a desire to analyze, study, and pore over the successes of their various employers in order to determine how great fortunes were made. During the months of their friendship they had come to trust one another more and more; thus, more and more knowledge was pooled with each meeting. Each of them had vowed to share any information that might prove to be of profit to the others. At a recent meeting, for example, stock tips came from Geoffrey Lancaster; for when John D. Rockefeller moved, the market moved with him.

This Monday it was Miles's turn. He brought up the subject of Crédit Mobilier.

"But that is a private company," Harold Berman protested. "Crédit Mobilier stock is not offered on the open market."

"Only on Lloyd Miles's private exchange," Miles said, smiling. "And at—" The price he named brought a hush to the table, and even Lancaster, who considered himself a gourmand, left off eating.

Miles continued. "Geoffrey, you made each of us a tidy little sum when we bought into that odd stock that had interested Mr. Rockefeller. Each of you has brought something valuable to the group. This is my first contribution. You will each have fifty shares at the price I named."

"I don't know how you're going to manage it, Lloyd," Jennings said, "but we're grateful, of course."

They were not quite so grateful when Miles told them the conditions. He would indeed sell each of them fifty shares of Crédit Mobilier stock at the shockingly low price that he had named. He did not tell them, however, that the one hundred and fifty shares had been taken from the lot assigned to members of Congress, nor did he tell them why the stock was available. While Miles intended to follow Durant's instructions and have the shares distributed among members of Congress, he also had some plans of his own . . . which included seeing that his friends in the Breakfast Club were ultimately loyal to him. They would have fifty shares each, but they would split the dividends with Lloyd Miles.

"Hey!" Lancaster protested.

Harold Berman, associate of the man who was becoming known as the shark of American finance, chuckled. "Lloyd, one would think you'd been taking lessons from my boss. I suppose that you want control of the stock in our possession at voting time as well."

"As a matter of fact, yes," Miles said.

Lancaster was glowering.

"Cheer up, Geoffrey," Harold Berman said. "Half a loaf is better than none."

Jennings laughed. "Our friend is learning his lessons well," he said. "Share the wealth, but don't be too generous. I think we've just been hitched to the wagon of Mr. Lloyd Miles, at least for the ride involving Crédit Mobilier."

"I hope to have access to additional shares in the future," Miles continued.

"Well, Lloyd," Geoffrey said, "I suppose we can be half grateful, after all."

"I have one other item for discussion," Miles said. "We have talked about expanding our membership. I remember that at least three names have been advanced, all of which were rejected for one reason or another. I advance a fourth name. I vouch for this man. He is an old friend and will be a valuable addition to our group, for he works at the very heart of government and will be able to keep us abreast of events in Congress *before* they happen."

"That could prove to be quite worthwhile," Berman agreed.

"His name is Philip Trent. He works in the office of the Speaker of the House."

"We will, of course, have to discuss this among ourselves," Lancaster said.

"Of course," Miles replied. "I want you to meet Philip and talk with him. Durant is sponsoring a charity ball soon, and that would be an excellent opportunity for you to meet Philip. I'll have invitations delivered to each of you."

"And how much will we be expected to contribute to charity?" Berman asked.

"I'll handle that," Miles told him. "I'll be keeping the books. I'll put you down for a sum compatible with your positions."

"Considering what Gould pays me," Berman said, laughing, "that will be a very small amount."

"Don't worry," Miles said. "Your contribution will not come from your pocket, Harold, lest charity end up with nothing but lint. I'll simply transfer a sum from some other contributor to your name."

"I told you all along that our Lloyd was a creative man," Jennings said.

When Gus Trent met his son and Leah Miles at the Baltimore depot, Leah's face was flushed with the cold and with the excitement of meeting her future father-in-law. Gus examined her and showed his approval with a bear hug and a kiss on the cheek.

"I wanted you and Leah to meet, Dad, before we made a formal announcement of our engagement," Philip said during the ride to the Trent home. Leah sat between the two men on the seat.

"When will the ceremony take place?" Gus asked.

"Soon," Philip said. "After we get the engagement announcement made, we'll talk about the wedding date."

"He has been very coy so far, Mr. Trent, about setting a date," Leah confided.

Gus put his arm around her shoulders and gave her a squeeze. "We'll see that he gets on with it, my dear."

"Dad wants a grandchild," Philip said teasingly, but the thought of making a child with Leah sent a surge of pleasure through him.

"I was afraid he was going to wait until I was too old to be able to move my knees and bounce a grandchild," Gus said to Leah.

"Well, before we talk too much of children," she commented airily, "I think we *will* set a wedding date."

"Next Saturday," Philip said.

"Splendid," Gus said.

"Wait!" Leah wailed. "When I said soon, I didn't mean in five days."

"Now who's dragging her feet?" Philip asked.

"I have a dress to make, after all," she said.

"The Saturday after next?" Philip asked.

"If you like," Gus suggested, "we can have the wedding here, Leah, since you have no family other than your brother."

"I think I'd like that," Leah said. "But not so soon."

"Then you choose a date," Philip said.

"April. When the new leaves begin to show."

"April it is," Philip agreed, leaning to kiss her lightly.

"I think that's wonderful, you two," Lloyd Miles said when Philip and Leah, back in Washington after a pleasant visit in Baltimore, told him of their plans for an April wedding. He shook Philip's hand and kissed his sister. "I do approve, you know. I don't think you could have chosen a better man, Leah, and now I know that you're a smart fellow, Phil, for loving my sister."

Leah went off to the kitchen. Miles poured brandy, handed a glass to Philip, and swirled the dark liquid in his glass. "Well, Brother-in-law . . ."

Philip held up his glass and said, "Well?"

"Here's to family, and to a new level of association between the two of us."

"To old friends," Philip said, and he took a sip of the brandy.

"There's a wedding present I'd like to give to you early," Miles said.

"Ummm?"

"Actually, it's a unique opportunity that can't wait."

"I'm listening."

"As it happens, I have fifty shares in a very solid company that can be made available to you at a fraction of their value."

"Lloyd, I'm not really prepared to gamble on stocks."

"Gamble? Heaven forbid. It's simply that we're making available to certain, uh, *friends* small blocks of stock in"—he paused and glued his eyes on Philip's face before continuing "—the Union Pacific contractor, Crédit Mobilier."

Philip said nothing for a moment, then echoed, "To certain friends?"

"What it means is instant profit," Miles explained. "I wouldn't advise it, but if you choose to sell your block of stock, you can multiply your money immediately."

"But you'd advise me to hold it and take my profit from the grossly inflated markups that Crédit Mobilier puts on its work and materials, is that it?"

Miles heard the sarcasm in Philip's voice. "It's just basic good business."

"Lloyd, you know and I know that it's fraud." Philip, his face grim, got to his feet. "You're offering me a bribe, damn it, and I must say that I am both surprised and angered."

"No, no," Miles protested. "Not a bribe at all, Philip! Just a favor for our friends."

"I am no friend of men who bleed the public coffers," Philip stated in a calmer tone. "Lloyd, did you really expect me to go along with you, to repay the Union Pacific's generosity with information from the office of the Speaker of the House? If so, you misjudge me severely."

Miles had learned that sometimes it pays to be able to hide one's feelings. His primary emotion at that moment was fury. No man could be so lily-white, so pure. Philip had no right to look down his nose at him because he was competitive, because he was so well versed in the ways of the world of high finance that he recognized the difference between outright fraud and sharp management.

Lloyd had no qualms about his part in building the transcontinental, for the railroad was being constructed for the greater good of the United States and would, if the visionaries were right—and in his opinion they were absolutely right —expand the nation enormously. Thomas Durant had said that the completion of the transcontinental would do more for the advancement of the United States as a world power than any single event since Bunker Hill. And now this man, this *friend,* this man who was to become his brother-in-law, had the audacity to censure *him,* Lloyd Miles, a man who was contributing to the completion of the transcontinental.

But he swallowed his anger and his pride. He made no reply when Philip said, "For Leah's sake, and for the sake of our future relationship, I'm going to forget you mentioned Crédit Mobilier stock to me, Lloyd."

"No harm done, then," Miles agreed. And that was as large a lie as he had ever told.

Over dinner, Leah noticed the strain that had suddenly developed between the man she loved and her brother, and when Philip took his leave early, she heard Miles speak slightingly of Philip for the first time.

"What went on between you two?" she asked.

"Why do you think anything went on?"

"It isn't like Philip to leave so early." It was Saturday night. They had made no specific plans, but both of them had been looking forward to spending a quiet, pleasant evening at home.

"It's just that the great and pure Philip Trent must arise early on the Sabbath to read his Bible and pray, I suppose," Miles fumed, not trying to hide his bitterness.

Leah, hurt to the quick, chose to say nothing. Perhaps the two men had had a minor disagreement. She knew her brother, knew that he did not like to have his opinions questioned, and knew that he was quite sensitive. She put his comment down to a momentary mood and prayed that there would never be any serious disagreements between Philip and her brother.

It did not occur to her that one day she might have to choose between her family ties and her love.

CHAPTER 10

"Look," Leah said. *"He's* here."

"He" was Andrew Johnson, seventeenth President of the United States. A small man with receding hair, a prominent nose, and a down-turned mouth, the President was dressed in a somber gray vest and frock coat. His hair was long over his ears. Around him stood a group of men that included the gala's host, Thomas Durant.

Philip and Leah had arrived late at the charity affair, for which Durant and the Union Pacific Railroad had hired the finest and largest hall in Washington. A ten-piece orchestra was playing a waltz. On the dance floor gentlemen in evening dress whirled hoopskirted ladies to the swishing sounds of crinoline and silk. Here and there among the uniformly drab suits of the men and the predominantly dark fabrics worn by the ladies, a gleam of color shone forth as if in affirmation that the sad, dreary days of war were truly in the past. Cigar smoke feathered upward, bluish in the light of the gas jets. A low murmur of conversation, like distant surf, provided background to the music.

Leah turned her gaze back to the President. "Poor man," she said. "You'd think he'd want to avoid public appearances since everyone in Washington seems to be against him. At least two of those men near him who are smiling and nodding are among the radicals who call Mr. Johnson a traitor for

121

wanting to carry out the policy Lincoln had planned for the South."

"He's from Tennessee," Philip remarked. "In my experience Tennessee men were good fighters. But I'm afraid General Grant was right when he said that Mr. Johnson is a man making speeches on the way to his own funeral."

"General Grant will surely be chosen President in the next election," Leah commented. "Don't you think so?"

"Probably," Philip said, "and there'll be some high old times in the White House then." He nudged Leah and pointed to a bulky man who stood apart from the group around the President. "Look who else is here."

"Mr. Secretary of War Stanton," Leah murmured as both of them peered at the round-faced man with a high dome of a forehead and coarse black chin whiskers at least ten inches long. His large nose and eyes gave him a fierce look, which complemented his reputation.

"My, my," Philip said. "I'm surprised that Stanton and Johnson are appearing at the same function."

Leah nodded in agreement. "This could be a most interesting evening."

In fact, Andrew Johnson's presence was the only reason that Edwin Stanton had come to the Durant reception. But Stanton hadn't come to see the President; he had come to *be seen* by Johnson. Stanton intended to make no effort to speak to the man.

When at last Johnson's eyes caught his across the room, Stanton stared back with no change in expression and bobbed his head a fraction of an inch in acknowledgment.

Yes, Copperhead, Stanton thought, using the popular term for those who sympathized with the South. *Yes, I am here.*

Stanton was more than capable of confronting Andrew Johnson if a need arose. He had disputed issues with better men than the one who had become President because of an assassin's bullet. Just being near Johnson made Stanton irate and consequently aggravated his asthma. But if a small oral barb or two would make the President aware that Stanton was there, watching his every move, then Stanton would gladly risk the unpleasant side effect such a confrontation would no doubt bring.

Edwin Stanton had been serving his country since December of 1860 when, at the request of President James Buchanan, he had joined the Cabinet as attorney general, leaving his lucrative Washington law practice. When Abe Lincoln was elected, Stanton, who had supported Lincoln's opponent, had almost immediately become one of the new President's most caustic critics. He had therefore been as surprised as anyone when Lincoln appointed him legal adviser to Secretary of War Simon Cameron, but not surprised at all when, after Cameron's resignation in 1862, he was made secretary. Lincoln, in spite of his faults, knew men, and he had recognized in Stanton an able and tireless patriot who could yell just as loudly and be just as cranky as the self-involved generals of the Union army. Looking back, Stanton had to admit that in spite of their differences, he and Abe Lincoln had worked well together to win the war.

But Andrew Johnson! It was an insult to everything that was good, everything that was sacred and holy to the nation, to have Andrew Johnson sitting in Abe Lincoln's chair. From the very beginning—after Stanton had exercised his authority to keep the government together when the news of Lincoln's death was announced, after he had reluctantly agreed to stay on in the Johnson Cabinet—Johnson had done everything but turn handsprings in an effort to make life easier for the very traitors who had tried to destroy the Union. With each passing week it was more and more evident that Johnson was soft on the issue of punishing the South.

Fortunately, there were still good men in Washington who remembered the bad times—when the beaten men in blue straggled back into the city over the long bridge, bloodied and cowed by the rebel sharpshooters; when one could stand in Washington and look out to see Jubal Early's tattered but tough cavalrymen studying the capital city with covetous eyes; when the government all the way to the White House trembled under the impact of the casualty lists. There were enough of those men—be they radicals, Republicans, or war

Democrats—who agreed that the villains of the South should continue to pay the price of treason and fratricide; and those who held that belief included members of both houses of Congress who felt that less power should reside in the executive office.

This coalition had prepared two measures that were, in effect, a declaration of war between the legislative and executive branches of government: the Command of the Army Act —written almost in its entirety by Edwin Stanton—and the Tenure of Office Act. The Command of the Army Act stated that the President could issue orders to the army only through the general of the army, who—because of the Tenure of Office Act—could only be fired by the President with the permission of the Senate.

Stanton knew that now that the war was over, the Command of the Army Act would have little effect other than to chafe the President and continue Congress's efforts to nibble away at executive powers. It was the Tenure of Office Act that was going to be Johnson's downfall.

With each passing week the opposition grew. Even now a House committee was gathering evidence that would sooner or later rid the government of Johnson. But Stanton, not content with the efforts of the House investigators, had his own small investigative staff, his own little secret service— paid, incidentally, with War Department contingency funds —headed by a man who had proven himself to be expert at uncovering treason, a man who had his own reasons to hate the President.

Yes, Copperhead, Stanton thought, glowering at Johnson as the President smiled and simpered at the rich and powerful men gathered around him. *I am going to get you. It's only a matter of time.*

Lloyd Miles found Leah and Philip near a table laden with refreshments. They were alone and seemed pleased with that condition, gazing into each other's eyes and oblivious to the swirl of well-dressed humanity on the dance floor. Miles gave a little smirk at the couple's obvious self-absorption as he approached them.

"Glad you could come, Phil," Miles said, seizing Philip's hand. He winked at Leah and leaned to kiss her on the cheek. Straightening, he put his hands behind his back and rocked on his toes. "Good turnout."

"All of Washington seems to be here, Lloyd," Leah said.

Miles felt a bit uneasy. He hadn't spoken to Philip since he had offered him the Crédit Mobilier stock, only to have Philip reject it and suggest that Miles was somehow beneath him for dealing in it. Miles still bristled over that. He still felt angry that Philip Trent dared act as if he were too good to be influenced by the driving force behind the American system of government—simple human competitiveness and the desire to better one's standing in the world.

But as much as Miles loathed Philip's holier-than-thou stance, he wanted to be on good terms with his sister's future husband. Taking Philip's arm, he said, "Leah, excuse us for a moment?" He led Philip to an archway. "I've been doing a lot of thinking since I last talked with you. Phil, you're right. It's a bad business, trying to buy friends by selling them stock at a ridiculously low price. I told the boss I wanted nothing more to do with it."

"Good for you, Lloyd," Philip said, smiling.

"That doesn't mean that someone else won't do it," Miles added with a wry smile and a shrug. He hadn't really lied. His part of the distribution of the Crédit Mobilier stock was complete. Now it was being handled by John O'Brian, with the unexpected but welcome help of the honorable Oakes Ames of Massachusetts.

"I'd love to have a list of Washington gentlemen who own Crédit Mobilier stock," Philip said.

"Now, now," Miles said, wagging a finger. "You can't blame a man for wanting to make a dollar, can you? After all, it's a very good investment."

"You sound like George Train talking about Union Pacific stock," Philip said with a chuckle, referring to the railroad's promoter and avoiding the issue of ethics.

"Friends?" Miles asked, extending his hand.

Philip took it, and the two went to rejoin Leah.

Much later in the evening, while his sister was in the ladies' room, Miles seized the opportunity to talk a bit about the Breakfast Club and introduce Philip to the other members. "We're very informal," he told Philip, who was flanked by Harold Berman, Paul Jennings, and Geoffrey Lancaster. "Our main purpose is companionship and the sharing of information that might be mutually advantageous."

"I fear that I would have no good information to contribute," Philip said, though Miles could tell that he was favorably impressed by the three personable young men. "You see, I don't work for a wealthy man, only a humble, poorly paid public servant."

Harold Berman laughed. "Yes, I guess old Schuyler does fall into that category."

"One of the few," Geoffrey Lancaster said, sipping his drink. "Most of them supplement their poor government salary in rather . . . inventive ways."

"You'd be a valuable addition to our group, Mr. Trent," Paul Jennings said, "for the actions of Congress can often have drastic effects on business."

"I would not, of course, be able to violate any confidences," Philip quickly stated.

Miles was pleased when Berman retorted, "Nor are we ourselves free to betray our employers. But when it comes to the actions of Congress, one is often at a loss. Legislation under consideration may seem to have one clear purpose; but after it is passed, some obscure provision within the law allows action that can be diametrically opposed to its original intent—for example, the Fourteenth Amendment."

"God help us," Lancaster muttered good-naturedly. "Berman the lawyer takes the floor again."

"I predict, and you can mark my words, that the *lasting* effect of the Fourteenth Amendment will have nothing at all to do with the franchise for Negroes. There is, you see, a little clause in it that reads, 'nor shall any state deprive any person of life, liberty, or property, without due process of law.' Does that sound important?"

Philip shrugged. The others were silent.

Berman paused, laying one finger vertically across his lips for a moment. "Already attorneys for large corporations, such as your railroad, Lloyd, are studying this due-process clause. You see, it will take only one judge who agrees that a corporation is a *person* or an individual entity, and the protection afforded to a human individual suddenly becomes a legal stand for corporations in a sweeping variety of actions."

"It would seem that there are possibilities," Jennings mused.

"Legal niceties are a bit over my head," Philip said.

"But perhaps men like the Speaker of the House envisioned in advance that the due-process clause was something more than an afterthought, something more than an idealistic little tidbit added to a statement of voting rights for ex-slaves who can neither read nor write," Berman said. "That's what I mean, Mr. Trent, when I say that you might be able to bring valuable information to our group without betraying a confidence. You might have an inkling, from listening to the people in your office, of some obscure effect of legislation under consideration that would give one interested in speculation and business a bit of a running start."

"Of course, Phil," Miles interjected, "the group must vote unanimously to admit you."

"I wasn't aware that I had applied," Philip said with a smile.

"I believe we can assure Mr. Trent that should he be interested in joining us, the vote will be favorable," Berman said.

"Thank you," Philip said. "I will think about it."

But Miles could see that Philip promptly forgot everything in the world when Leah returned to his side.

Philip was ready to abandon the party and spend some time alone with his fiancée. When the song they were dancing to ended, he whispered in her ear a suggestion that they leave, and she answered him with a quick kiss. As they left the dance floor, however, Lloyd Miles appeared, as if out of nowhere. Philip nodded to him as Miles bowed and said to Leah, "A duty dance, Sister?"

"Not necessary, Brother," she said. Philip knew he was harking back to a time when Leah, a skinny teenager, would tell him that it was his sibling duty to dance with her, since others would not. She put her hand on Miles's arm and leaned toward him. "Not for duty but for the sake of old times?"

Miles smiled. "Come along, then, my dear."

They danced well together, but at each turn Leah's eyes sought out Philip. She was looking his way when he was approached by a heavyset man who looked as if he'd been stuffed into his evening wear and then starched.

"Captain Trent?" the man asked.

Philip looked into a face whose main feature was a colorfully crooked nose, which had obviously been broken more than once. A half-smoked cigar distorted one side of the man's thin-lipped mouth. His brown eyes showed the squint wrinkles of a man who had spent a lot of time in the open, and his close-cropped hair and stiff bearing made Philip think of him as an army man or an ex-army man.

"Yes, I'm Philip Trent."

"Victor Flanagan, Captain," the man said, extending his hand. "May I have a word with you?"

"It seems you already are," Philip said, irritated by the repeated use of his old rank.

Undeterred, Flanagan directed him to a relatively isolated corner. "If you'd be kind enough to step this way?"

Philip made no indication of compliance, asking instead, "May I ask the nature of your business with me?"

The man puffed on his stubby cigar and withdrew it from his lips as he exhaled clouds of smoke. Holding the cigar in front of his eyes as if to examine it, he said, "There are those, Captain Trent, who feel that you can do the army and your country a great service."

"For example?" Philip asked.

"Men you know. Important men who know you and your abilities."

Philip was growing annoyed with Flanagan's vagueness. Testily, he stated, "I'd still like to hear a name."

Flanagan replaced the cigar between his lips. "I could name several, and they'd be the names of men you know, or know of."

"Please do," Philip urged.

"Only two at the moment. General B. J. Butler and Lafe Baker."

The names were indeed familiar to Philip. His feelings about Butler were mixed. It was natural that he would have a soft spot for the man who had recommended him for the Congressional Medal of Honor, but he had to balance that against Butler's bungling during the war. The other man, General Lafayette C. Baker, was largely a figure of mystery. Baker had gone to work for the War Department early in the war to fill the vacuum left by Allan Pinkerton of the Pinkerton Detective Agency, who had ceased in a huff to do the Union army's intelligence work after his old friend, General George McClellan, was relieved of command of the army.

Washington was a town that loved its gossip, and Lafe Baker had come in for his share of discussion after being dismissed under a cloud from the government service. Some said that Baker had been fired because of his involvement in the capture and quick death of the man who had killed President Lincoln, John Wilkes Booth. The best that was said of Baker in that affair was that he had shown "wonderful perspicacity" in deducing the whereabouts of Booth when every law enforcement agency in the country had failed—although he had shown bad judgment in disposing of Booth's corpse after supervising the identification of the body himself.

A newspaper columnist, a man who had access to the center of events in Washington, had called Baker "one of the worst rapscallions in an age in which rascality has paid high dividends." The same columnist had hinted that Baker had committed fraud, at best, in the John Wilkes Booth matter, for Baker shared in the reward that had been offered for the assassin. This theory raised the dire specter that somewhere the man who had killed Lincoln was alive and well, that another victim's body had been substituted for Booth's by Baker, and that the deed had been done with Baker's knowledge, either because of Baker's involvement in the assassination itself or because Baker simply wanted to collect the reward money. Although it was difficult to believe that even "one of the worst rapscallions" would connive to let Booth go unpunished, Baker's reputation was still tainted.

"If either General Butler or General Baker has anything to say to me," Philip said, "let him come forward."

Flanagan shifted his eyes from side to side, then whispered, "Now, it wouldn't be too smart for General Baker to show his face in such a gathering, would it?"

"I think I shall have to bid you good night, sir," Philip said stiffly. He wanted nothing to do with Lafe Baker—and if General Butler was connected with Baker, the same was true for him.

As he turned away from Flanagan, he felt a hand on his arm and whirled around in irritation.

"General Butler is right over there, Captain Trent," Flanagan said.

Philip jerked his arm away from Flanagan's hand. He detected a bulky shadow in a darkened alcove and saw the glow of a cigar.

"The army needs you, Captain Trent," Flanagan said. "The general will tell you why."

It was Philip's feeling of obligation to Butler more than his curiosity that took him to the alcove where Butler waited.

Butler put out a pudgy, soft hand. "Good to see you, Trent. I was damned pleased to discover that I had not given the Medal of Honor to a dead man." He nodded toward Flanagan. "This is Sergeant Victor Flanagan. Thank you, Sergeant." He was silent as Flanagan walked away. "Good man. Career in the old army. Lived through most of the major battles of the war."

Butler seemed to be looking into Philip's face, but his crossed eyes made it difficult for Philip to meet his gaze. "What was it you wanted to say to me, General?"

"I don't think it's wise to talk here, Trent. Victor Flanagan will contact you at a later date. You can trust him implicitly. He'll give you some of the details." Butler shifted his odd eyes and bent closer. "That is, if you're interested in doing your country a service."

"I've never shirked my duty," Philip stated. "But I reserve the right to decide exactly what service I am to perform."

"Of course, of course," Butler agreed.

"And I will tell you in advance that I want nothing to do with General Baker."

Butler nodded. "I understand how you feel. I felt the same way myself. But then I listened to Lafe and heard who he was working for and what he wanted to accomplish. I wouldn't draw conclusions without hearing the facts. All I can say now is that you will not be contacted by Lafe Baker."

"And whom is Baker working for?" Philip asked.

"All I am empowered to tell you is that our orders come from the highest level."

Philip knew that Butler never hesitated to tell a lie when a lie was necessary. Furthermore, practice no doubt made the general convincing, so Philip remained skeptical. Although his orders from Baker might come down from the highest level of an organization, that organization might not be the government of the United States, as Butler obviously wanted Philip Trent to believe.

"Flanagan kept saying that the army needs me," Philip said. "Is this a War Department operation of some sort?"

"Well," Butler said with a fat little smile, "General Baker did work with the War Department, didn't he?" He held up a hand quickly. "But I didn't say that it was the department, you know."

"If the army needs me," Philip said, "I'd like to hear it from the army."

Butler put his hand on Philip's shoulder. "If the army were involved—and I'm not saying it is, mind you—wouldn't your value be damaged in certain areas if it was openly known that you were working for the War Department? What is at stake here, Trent, is no small matter. I believe that you, like myself, were an admirer of our late President and his proposed postwar policies for the South, were you not?"

Philip nodded.

"And you know, I assume, that I have been reelected to the House?"

"Yes. My belated congratulations."

"Good. Now. When I got back to Washington, it quickly became evident to me that there was a sort of war going on in the city. It is a three-way struggle for power, with the Congress pitted against the executive branch and the Court. The off-year election gave the radicals control of Congress, and they're intent on using that control to void all of Mr. Lincoln's eminently sensible proposals for the reconstruction of the war-ravaged South. I suppose you are aware that blood has already been shed there in renewed violence—violence that is the direct result of the radicals' repressive policies."

The violence to which Butler referred had occurred in New Orleans, a place Butler knew well. Forty people, mostly Negroes, had been killed in a riot in the Louisiana city.

"I fear that my colleagues in both houses of Congress are interested in only three things," Butler continued. "In punishing the South, in making Congress the dominant branch of government, and in building personal wealth. In pursuit of the second goal they are preparing a final, conclusive attack on the executive branch. At this very moment members of the House are amassing so-called evidence of high crimes and misdemeanors against the man who is the legal President of this great nation, a man duly elected to high office by the people."

"General, I'm not following you," Philip said.

"Patience," Butler said, lifting a finger. "There are men, thank God, honest, patriotic men, who want to preserve the form of government set forth in the Constitution by our founding fathers. To do so, they must break the stranglehold of power that the radicals have on this nation. You are in a position to help in that, Trent."

"In what way?"

"By helping to expose the bribery, vote selling, fraud, and corruption of the radicals in Congress. In this way, by exposing many of them for what they are, we will break their power."

"You're asking me to use my position to spy on members of the Congress, is that it?"

"Don't go high-and-mighty on me, young man," Butler warned. "You look down on Lafe Baker and say you don't want anything to do with him. But let me tell you this: I happen to know that Lafe Baker is a man of honor. I know his record. He served this country well during the war, and his wartime experience makes him eminently qualified to seek out those who are dishonoring the great institution that is the Congress, those whose corruption is costing the taxpayers millions of dollars. Lafe Baker has the intelligence and the patriotism to realize that good men must stand against evil and that it is vital to prevent the radical members of Congress from seizing power. If they succeed in their effort to drive Andrew Johnson out of office, the system of checks and balances that has made this country great will be destroyed forever, and Congress will be the preeminent power in government. Do you want that to happen?"

"General," Philip said, "I find that what you are saying to me doesn't exactly jibe with your speeches on the floor of the House." In fact, Butler was one of the more vociferous radicals in the lower branch of Congress.

Butler laughed. "Don't listen to what I say—check the way I vote."

Philip was not familiar with Butler's voting record; as far as Philip knew, however, the general hadn't been back in office long enough to vote on any measures that might prove that he was indeed on the side of the radicals.

"By making them think that I am one of them," Butler continued, "I am privy to their plots and plans." He paused to puff on his cigar and blow smoke. "From your position on the staff of the Speaker of the House, you can gather invaluable information. We know that you are well suited for the job because you have been thorough in gathering information about graft on the transcontinental railroad. That work, incidentally, parallels our own objectives. Show me men in the Congress who are taking money from the railroads, and I'll show you radicals who are trying to alter our form of government."

"I am not a spy," Philip insisted.

"Damn it, Trent, we have come to you because your military record proves that you are a man of honor and great integrity. Have we been wrong in thinking that you are a patriot?"

At that moment a pair of congressmen, espying Butler, lifted their hands in greeting and started toward the alcove.

"We will talk later," Butler said quickly, putting out his hand. "It was pleasant to meet you again, Captain."

Troubled, Philip went to find Leah and Lloyd. Although he took pleasure in Leah's company in any circumstance, the evening had gone sour for him. The hum of conversation, the strains of music, the swaying of dancers on the floor—all seemed to be part of a false façade thrown up by Washington, a pretty front to cover the rot underneath. Leah quickly agreed when he suggested that they leave the gathering.

Later, alone with her in the Miles apartment, with her kisses hot on his lips, he pushed the things that Butler had said to the back of his mind.

General Ben Butler left the glittering ballroom shortly after talking with Philip Trent. He was quite sure that Trent would come around. He'd known many boys like Trent during the war. All one had had to do was call upon flag, honor, and country, and they went rushing forward into the muzzle flashes of reb cannon and musketry. Yes, Trent would come around. What good it would do, Butler wasn't sure.

Lafe Baker had told him that the "client" was concerned about Trent's investigation of the railroads and therefore wanted to enlist Trent into their organization. The reasoning was that Trent's effectiveness would thus be neutralized, since Baker—and, presumably, the client—would have advance knowledge of any discovery Trent might make in his continuing efforts to discredit the railroads. As a bonus, they would also get information originating in the Speaker's office regarding possible congressional actions that would affect the railroads.

General Butler, as usual, had told some half-truths while talking with Philip Trent, in order to persuade him that they were all working for the same goal. But Butler did not want Trent to join their organization for the same reason as Baker and the client did. In fact, Butler believed that Philip Trent was a troublesome gnat who wasn't worth the worry.

The general's reason for wanting Trent's participation was to get information about crooked congressmen. He wanted damaging evidence against members of Congress for one simple reason: If a fellow knew enough about another fellow to hang the blackguard, that was power. If an enterprising congressman from Massachusetts had the goods on, say, a dozen or so well-placed men in Congress, that congressman would be in an excellent position to get any legislation he desired passed out of committee and onto the floor—and quite possibly made into law.

Butler had some specific plans along that line. While it was true that he was well paid by Lafe Baker on behalf of a client who was, supposedly, unknown to Butler—a client whose interests, by the by, coincided surprisingly with the interests of the Union Pacific Railroad—Butler had not come out of the war a rich man, as some had. Some men had been lucky during the war, men like General Grant's brother-in-law, who had traded in southern cotton and accrued a fortune. Butler had been just a simple officer, doing his job as best he could and accepting the meager stipend paid to him by the War Department. It was time, he thought, that his service to his country began to pay off. So if he could influence Philip Trent to turn over evidence of wrongdoing by members of Congress, or if he could use the little organization put together by Lafe Baker for that purpose, he'd be in a position to begin to collect on his long service.

Butler needed only a few more votes to put forward a simple little scheme that he'd hatched after being reelected. Congress was long overdue a raise in pay. He had almost all the votes he needed not only to approve the raise but to make it retroactive, thus putting a neat little cash bonus into the pockets of every member of Congress, himself included.

A new week, a new month. Time passed, but so pleasantly because of Leah, that Philip felt no sense of urgency beyond finding a way to be with her for lunch, for dinner, for the evening, or for afternoon walks as the weather moderated and false spring came to the city on the Potomac. He spent his time in the office doing make-work, going over and over the figures he had compiled to show the reasons for the doubled cost of the railroad. He had not come to a decision on two matters—his invitation to join Lloyd Miles's Breakfast

Club and his invitation from General Ben Butler to join a less defined, more arcane group—nor had he been contacted again by either organization.

One afternoon he asked Archibald Edwards if Schuyler Colfax had read his report. It was not the first time he had asked that question in recent weeks, and he feared he would get the same answer. His fears were confirmed.

"We're getting to that, Philip," Edwards said as usual. "We realize the importance of your work. It's just that matters in the House are—"

The door to Schuyler Colfax's door opened just then, and suddenly Philip was face to face with a man he recognized from newspaper photographs, Collis P. Huntington. The strongman of the Central Pacific Railroad was emerging from Schuyler Colfax's office. The Speaker was escorting the railroad baron out, a smile on his face and his hand on Huntington's shoulder.

Philip felt his stomach churn. This presented yet another new element in the increasingly complex set of facts from which he was trying to draw out the truth. Was Schuyler Colfax the man he presented himself as being—or was he under the Central Pacific's influence and as full of deceit as the others?

"Dad, I usually trust your opinions," Philip said that evening when he and Leah joined Gus Trent for dinner. Gus was finding reasons to take the short train ride from Baltimore quite often. Like his son, he had fallen in love with Leah Miles, although his love was of a different nature. He yearned for the day when Leah would become the daughter he had never had, and he chided both of them mercilessly about their slow progress in marrying and providing him with a grandchild.

"Nice of you to say so," Gus replied.

"Collis Huntington has bragged openly that he can get any bill he wants through Congress for two hundred thousand dollars," Philip said. It was probably no coincidence that the figure picked by Huntington was the same as the amount of cash he had brought from California in a carpetbag back during the war, when Congress was considering the Pacific Railroad Bill.

"He's probably right," Gus said.

"He spent an hour in the Speaker's office today."

Gus rubbed his chin. "Well, Son, Schuyler was always a railroad congressman in that he favored construction of the transcontinental. He worked for passage of the original bill. But that doesn't necessarily mean that he's in Huntington's hip pocket, does it?"

Philip wanted to believe that his employer was an honest man. Since Colfax believed in the transcontinental, it was natural that there should be contact between his office and the rail barons'. And, Philip told himself, Colfax was already in favor of the railroad, so it would be unnecessary to bribe him. Yet there was the matter of the money that he'd seen Thomas Durant give to Archibald Edwards and the frequent visits to the Speaker's office by important men from both the Union Pacific and the Central Pacific.

Leah, not feeling well that evening, asked the men to bring her home after dinner. "Nothing serious, Gus," she said when her future father-in-law expressed his concern. "Sniffles and a headache. It's probably just the change in the weather."

Philip and Gus saw her safely to the Miles apartment, then they went to the hotel where Gus stayed when he was in town. They had a drink in the bar off the lobby.

When Gus yawned, Philip said, "Looks as if you could use an early night too."

"Hate to admit it, but I could."

Philip decided to walk to his apartment. The route took him past the building that housed Speaker Colfax's offices. Without giving it much thought, he went in, greeting the doorman who stayed on duty as long as anyone was working in the building.

It was not the first time Philip had come back to the office to work in the evening, but it had been some time since he'd been motivated to do so. His labors no longer seemed important, and this fact bothered him. He seemed to be caught up in futility. The report he had compiled for Colfax would not, of course, stand up in a court of law, for there was no documented proof of his allegations that the railroads were bleeding the U.S. Treasury; but the detailed statement certainly contained sufficient evidence to warrant consideration, perhaps enough even to instigate a congressional investigation. By ignoring his report, Colfax and Edwards had, Philip felt, relegated it to unimportance.

So it was out of a sense of futility and resentment that Philip found himself alone in Colfax's suite of offices. He lit the gas lamp in his own office, sat at his desk with his chin in his hand, his eyes unblinking, and stared at the wall for several minutes. Then with sudden resolve he rose and went down the hall to the office of Archibald Edwards. The door was not locked. He entered, closed the door behind him, and struck a match so he could locate the lamp. The gas jet sputtered, fired, and gave light.

The drawers of Edwards's desk were neatly arranged and contained nothing of real interest. He sat in Edwards's chair, asking himself what he had hoped to find, and then he turned his head and saw the safe. The safe had a combination lock. Combinations consist of a series of numbers, which busy men sometimes forget. He searched the center drawer of the desk carefully, returning each item to its place as he looked for a slip of paper on which the combination might be written. Then he removed the drawer, ran his fingers over the underside, and felt something tacked to the wood. Being careful not to shuffle the drawer's contents by tilting it, he lifted it over his head. There was the combination to the safe, written in Edwards's hand on a small piece of paper.

After taking a glance down the hall to reassure himself that he was alone, Philip lost no time opening the safe. Inside were three shelves. A fat envelope had the top shelf all to itself, and Philip took it out and counted its contents: ten thousand dollars. Nothing was written on the envelope to explain whence the money had come.

Replacing the envelope, Philip took a leather-bound ledger from the second shelf. Inside was a long list of political contributions with notations of their sources. He whistled. Just about every major company he had ever heard of and some that he hadn't had contributed to the Speaker's campaign chest. Beside the date on which he'd kissed Leah in Durant's library he found a notation of the receipt of the money from Thomas Durant, verifying what Edwards had told him. Sliding his finger along the dates, he brought it up to the present but found no new entry, no recently recorded amount of ten thousand dollars to correspond to the envelope's contents. He closed the ledger and replaced it.

The third shelf of the safe held personal papers, Edwards's will, a few stock certificates, and, touchingly, letters from a nephew who had been killed while marching toward the sea with Sherman.

Philip checked the contents of the safe to make sure everything was in its original place. He quietly closed the heavy door until it clicked shut, then spun the dial, extinguished the light, and returned to his office.

He had no proof that the money in the plain envelope had come from Collis P. Huntington during his visit to the office that day. But Philip knew that Archibald Edwards was a meticulous man, proud of his ability to handle detail.

It was not at all like Edwards to have received a political contribution without having immediately recorded it in the ledger.

CHAPTER 11

Like most men in these postwar times Collis P. Huntington was bearded. He was also typical in that his heft suggested that he did not push himself away from the table hungry. His most prominent feature was a well-shaped bald dome sweeping upward from his dark eyebrows, which contrasted with the dignity of his graying beard and mustache. At forty-six he felt as youthful and virile as he had at twenty-eight, when he had set out for the California goldfields to find his fortune.

Huntington did not particularly like Washington. Compared to San Francisco it was provincial, despite its being the capital city of a young nation that was beginning to be a force in the world. The climate was trying and the people generally tiresome. Huntington often wondered if he was forever doomed to deal with grubbing, greedy little men who lacked the ability to make their mark in business or industry but who had a minor talent for convincing people to vote for them. He would have much preferred to be at home in California, with his entire family together again. But he knew his own strengths and abilities as well as he knew those of the other three members of the Big Four of the Central Pacific.

Explaining the character of the Central Pacific leadership, Huntington had said, "We are successful, we four, because of our teamwork. Each man complements the others in something they lack. Stanford loves to deal with people, and he has the prestige of having been a governor. Moreover, he is a good lawyer. Mark Hopkins is a fine accountant who understands the value of everything, a very thrifty man who keeps us on the straight and narrow. Crocker is the organizer, the driver of men."

And Huntington? He was a quiet man; but when he spoke, his words carried import. Insiders said that he was the real force behind the Central Pacific. He was capable of getting his hands dirty by throwing tidbits to Washington politicians who were lying sideways in the public trough. Crocker, for instance, had no such patience with public officials. When he took over as construction boss at the railhead, he took gold with him in his saddlebags to reward good workers. Both men dispensed rewards, but Huntington's were not given for hard labor. He was the link to the Congress, the man who did the behind-the-scenes dirty work in the East. His quiet, assured manner was very effective at putting out little brushfires of suspicion regarding Central Pacific affairs.

Huntington was a lonely man, despite his being surrounded by throngs of people who finagled endlessly to get their hands on some of the railroad's money. His Washington home was not as impressive as that of his counterpart in the Union Pacific, Dr. Thomas Durant, but ninety-nine percent of Americans would have been happy to trade domiciles with him. His staff consisted of his business secretary, a young man dedicated to making columns of figures balance; a black cook who had introduced Huntington to southern cooking; and until recently an upstairs maid–dining attendant, who had married his coachman and now was happily pregnant. It was this woman's condition that led to an advertisement in the newspaper and brought to Huntington's door an auburn-haired young woman dressed in somber gray.

Jeff Davis, Huntington's secretary, greeted the tall, conservatively dressed woman, whose dark red hair was neatly tucked under a sensible hat. Her coat was unbuttoned, allowing Davis to see that she was well formed.

"Good day to you, sir," she said in a lilting voice. "I am Rose Delany, and I've come about the position you have open. Would you be Mr. Huntington?"

"Hardly, ma'am. I am Mr. Davis, Mr. Huntington's personal secretary."

"Good for you, sir," the woman said seriously. "Any relation to old Jeff Davis himself?"

Davis sniffed, raising his chin a bit. "Hardly," he repeated coldly. The woman's initial good impression had been eroded by this impudence. Asking stiff, short questions he took down her vital statistics: Rose Delany, formerly of New York, twenty-four years old, experienced in service, unmarried, no deformities, and no noxious diseases.

"And why, Miss Delany, did you leave New York City?"

She paused a moment before replying. "The cold, you know, sir? It gets frightfully cold there. I have my references, sir, if you'll just have a look at them."

Davis opened the envelope. His eyes blinked when he saw the signature on her most recent reference—Mr. Jay Gould. "If you don't mind waiting, Miss Delany, I'll ask Mr. Huntington if he can see you now."

Rosanna Pulliam smoothed the dress over her primly positioned legs, smiled, and watched him prance out of the room. He was back within minutes, motioning her to follow him.

Huntington was in his office, his desktop strewn with papers. He glanced up as she entered, looked back down, then lifted his head quickly, his strong eyes examining her minutely. Rosanna had left her coat in the other room. Her sedate gray dress was long sleeved, of course, and high necked, but it clearly displayed her well-endowed torso.

"Miss Delany, sir," Davis said as he backed toward the door.

"Thank you, Jeff. Have a seat, Miss Delany," Huntington said.

Rosanna was having trouble getting accustomed to being called Delany, although it had been her mother's maiden name. As she sat, she noticed that Huntington was examining her musingly. Before speaking, he looked at her letters of reference—letters that had been prepared by Lloyd Miles, with the aid of the members of his Breakfast Club.

"Your last position was in the household of Mr. Jay Gould, Miss Delany?" Huntington asked.

"That is correct, sir," Rosanna said demurely. He had no way of guessing that Jay Gould's name had been forged by Harold Berman, who knew Gould's signature well.

While Huntington continued to examine her letters of reference, she studied him through lowered lashes. She had not missed his interested scrutiny of her. She knew men. This one might be richer than most, but he was the same underneath his fine clothing. With some men the flash of a bold eye was effective. She read Huntington differently. With him she would have to be demure and modest, leaving any advance to be made by him.

"Your reason for leaving?"

"Sir, I told your secretary, Mr. Davis, that I left New York City because of the weather. That is partially true."

Huntington looked up. "And the remainder of the truth?"

"It is a personal matter, sir, which gives me some pain." She lifted a hand and dabbed at her eyes with a lace-edged hanky.

"I do not mean to pry, Miss Delany, but you would be working in my home, you know, in contact with members of my family when they come to visit."

"Yes, sir. I know, sir. It's just that—well, there was a boy, sir." She paused, her face flushing. It was a trick that she had perfected during her brief attempt at becoming an actress. Her performance now was inspired by Huntington's obvious approval of her as a woman. Most men were intrigued by females who were slightly—but not seriously—tainted by past associations. If a man had reason to believe that a girl had been just a little naughty, it quickened his responses and often initiated swift action on his part. "Not that there was anything—I mean, I'm a good girl, sir—" She fell silent as if in confusion.

Huntington waited.

"He was a gardener, sir, and he said he wanted to marry me. And then he ran away with a"—she was weeping quietly, another of her small talents—"a barmaid, sir."

"I see," Huntington said.

Rosanna wiped her eyes and straightened her back. "That's neither here nor there, sir, no more it isn't. He led me on, but I didn't listen to his blandishments, sir. I told him, I said, 'Look, Dennis, I am a decent Christian girl, I am, and it will be marriage or nothing, and furthermore—' "

"Yes, well," Huntington interrupted. "I think, Miss Delany, that you'll do quite well for the position. I must warn you, however, that I won't tolerate young men hanging about the place." The way his eyes played over her face and then fell to her bosom told her that she had gotten his attention not only because of her documented ability as a maid.

"Oh, no, sir," she said, shaking her head vehemently. "No worry there, sir. It'll be a blue moon before I listen to another man's blarney, sir."

"Good, good. When can you report for work?"

"All I have to do, sir, is get my things from the boardinghouse where I am staying."

Huntington rose but remained standing behind his desk. "Tell Jeff to have the carriage made ready for you. The coachman will take you to your boardinghouse and bring you back."

Rosanna also stood up. "Thank you, sir. Thank you very much. It's not a pleasant day to be walking outside, is it?"

"No, it isn't," Huntington agreed, his eyes following the lush curve of her bosom to her small waist. "And, Rose—"

"Yes, sir?"

"I'll be alone in the house for some time yet, just me and Jeff Davis. We keep regular hours. Jeff will brief you on mealtimes and your duties, among which will be serving at the table."

Rosanna smiled gratefully. "Yes, sir."

"Good day to you. I hope that you will happy with us."

"I'm sure I will be, sir," she said with a little curtsy. As she left the room, she could feel Huntington's eyes examining her backside.

She found Davis waiting outside Huntington's office. After relaying Huntington's instructions to him, she followed Davis to a drawing room near the entrance, where he told her to make herself comfortable. He left her to find the coachman, and several minutes later he returned with the news that the carriage would be ready in a quarter of an hour.

"Is your name really Jeff?" she asked, giving him a bold eye and smiling to show her pretty, even white teeth.

"I have heard just about everything that can be said about that unfortunate coincidence," Davis said tightly.

"But I think it's marvelous," she cooed. "Between you and me, Mr. Jeff, I always rather admired old Jeff Davis. Had pluck, he did." She beamed at the secretary, her eyes seeking his. "Of course, had I a name like that, I would bloody well change it."

Davis's face went red. He seemed to be searching for words but could not speak. Rosanna continued to smile at him. She knew his type well: a fancy boy who aspired to be a man of importance and was arrogant beyond his position. Jeff Davis might be the one who ran Huntington's household, but she had let him know quickly that she was not one to be bullied.

"I think we can be friends, Mr. Jeff," she said, still beaming that blazing smile at him. "It's a small staff here, and we working folk should stick together, shouldn't we?"

"Miss Delany," Davis said, "the carriage will be out front in just a few minutes. When you return with your belongings, I will show you to your quarters."

"Maybe we can have a friendly cup of tea and get better acquainted, Mr. Jeff," she said, her voice full of suggestion. She was enjoying this little game with the secretary.

Without answering, Davis stalked away, and she was left sitting in Collis P. Huntington's drawing room, smiling gleefully. *So far so good,* she thought.

Rosanna Pulliam quickly learned the routine of the Huntington household. With the mistress of the house in California, there was not much work to be done, just the ordinary dusting and straightening. The place had a feeling of impermanence about it, for it was almost devoid of those things that show a house is lived in, the knickknacks and decorative objects that catch the eye. It was a good house, well built and luxuriously furnished, but it seemed empty.

To counteract the surroundings, Rosanna made it a point to be highly visible whenever possible. She had been furnished with livery, a neat uniform that she had altered to cling to her figure without seeming vulgar.

The first evening that she had Huntington's favorite drink ready when he came home, he looked at her questioningly. "I know that you're an intelligent girl, Rose," he said with a small smile, "but how did you know?"

"Elementary, sir," she answered. "I merely inquired of Mr. Davis."

On another occasion she discovered that Huntington was very fond of the rich, honey-filled baked goods prepared by people of Middle Eastern origin. The next day she located a bakery owned by a friendly couple from Syria and purchased a selection of cakes.

That night she brought in the small plate of cakes with the after-dinner coffee. Sampling one, Huntington smiled with pleasure, rubbed his large stomach, and said, "Rose, I must tell you that Mrs. Huntington would not approve."

"I like to see a man enjoy his food," she commented.

"Have one, Jeff," Huntington said, passing the plate.

Jeff Davis was looking at Rosanna, his lips pursed in thought.

"There are plenty, Mr. Jeff," she encouraged.

"Thank you, no," Davis said dryly. Making a slight bow, he added, "If you'll excuse me, Mr. Huntington."

Huntington made contented sounds as he ate the honeyed cakes. "Mustn't do this too often, Rose. I have to watch my manly figure, you know."

"I like a man with some girth to him," she responded. "Makes him look prosperous and dignified."

Huntington looked at her with a wide grin. "You like your men prosperous, eh?"

"Well, sir," she said seriously, "I have always felt that a gent who is very successful must have something a bit more . . . well, vital than most. Do you know what I mean?"

Collis Huntington knew very well what she meant. He had encountered such women before, women who felt it desirable to bed rich and powerful men as if that purely temporary condition somehow enhanced their position in the world. If this Irish housemaid were indeed of that type, she would be highly insulted if he offered her money.

Huntington had never so much as flirted with a household servant in the past; he'd never been that much in need of a woman. But this Rose from New York was a different sort of female. She was so unique—and so obviously eager to please him—that a tiny little sense of wrongness began to whisper to him from some deeply hidden area in his consciousness.

That whisper went almost unnoticed until, just ten days after she had come to work in his house, he commented, "Rose, you're spoiling me shamelessly. You look after me so very well." She was always at his elbow during the evening meal, which was often the only meal Huntington ate at home. She had, in fact, usurped duties that once had been relegated to Jeff Davis, who doubled as part-time valet. Now Rose was the one who selected his clothes, laying them out in advance of his retirement for the night. Her taste was good, and not once did he dispute her selection of linen and accessories.

"I like doing things for you, sir," she said with her radiant smile. "I know that you're doing work that is very important, that will help the whole country. When I please you, when I can help you, it makes me feel as if I, too, am accomplishing some little worthwhile something."

Huntington, actually flattered by the words of a housemaid, caught himself beaming back at the young woman. It was a pleasure just to look at her. She always seemed so clean and was always so neat. He had become accustomed to having her around—something that just might present a little problem when Mrs. Huntington rejoined him.

"You do please me, girl," he said, his voice low and his posture indicating the stirring that he felt.

"Well, that's why I'm here, sir," she said rather suggestively. "Whatever it takes to please you, sir."

For a moment Rosanna was afraid that it was too soon to have made such a bold statement. But the look in Huntington's eyes had told her to go ahead. She knew from the way that he leaned toward her that he would soon make a move to become intimate with her. And she was right, for that night it happened. . . .

Dressed in a comfortable flannel nightgown, she had just finished washing herself in the basin in her little room when she heard a soft knock at the door. She drew a dressing gown around her shoulders, leaving it open, and went to the door. There was Huntington, wearing a rust-colored robe, his stockingless feet in opera slippers.

"Rose?" he whispered.

Huntington looked a bit odd to her, somehow much younger and quite unsure of himself, until she reached out, took his hands, and pulled him into her room, closing the door behind him. Then she was in his arms . . . and any trace of uncertainty disappeared.

Huntington had never been a man to devote more time to a job than it demanded. He left Rosanna's bed quickly, pulled on his robe, and looked down at her as she lay only partly covered. She was a beautiful woman. At first she had been shy and modest, but quickly—perhaps too quickly, he realized—she had been lifted to enjoyment by his efforts.

"Girl, you're almost too good to be true," he told her as he prepared to leave.

"Ummm," Rosanna purred.

He had not become one of the world's most powerful and influential men by being a fool. He knew that he was exposed as he'd never allowed himself to be exposed before, that this servant girl with her alabaster skin and heated softnesses could cause him damage both in his personal and business life.

"Why are you working as a domestic?" he asked the next night, when he had come to her again. She abruptly opened her eyes, in alarm.

"Sir?"

He sat on the edge of the bed. "You have the ability to be more than a housemaid."

"Thank you, sir, but it's all I know."

"I am not your first man," he stated.

She opened her mouth to protest, but she said nothing.

"Have you been in trouble with the authorities?"

"No," she said quickly. Pulling the sheet up to cover her breasts, she sat up.

"I suspect, girl, that your avowed admiration for men of wealth and power has more purpose than you might want me to suspect."

"I'm sorry, sir, but I don't know what you mean," she said. Rose was beginning to be a bit concerned. She had allowed herself to show him that she was enjoying his virile attentions, for he had proven to be almost as gifted in that direction as Lloyd Miles, and that had aroused his suspicions.

"I'm sorry, sir," she repeated, "I don't know what you mean." She was buying time, time to think.

"You are more than you pretend to be," Huntington said. "Is there something you'd like to tell me?"

She had done so well, she realized, until she had allowed him to bed her. Now she was on dangerous ground, for she had given free rein to her sensuous nature too soon. She didn't think the situation was past salvaging, although she wasn't sure it was worth the bother. Her time in the Huntington household had not produced any startling information regarding the affairs of the Central Pacific Railroad. Huntington did not entertain at home, and in all the time she had been in the house no visitor had called. She was beginning to feel that she was wasting her time and her client's money.

She had to tell Huntington something, and she knew that when lying it was best to parallel the truth as closely as possible.

"This is my first job in domestic service," she said tentatively, watching his face closely for his reaction.

"Ah." He moved beside her, took her hand, and squeezed it. His other hand found its way to her stomach and rubbed gently. "And the letters of recommendation?"

She lowered her eyes like a schoolgirl caught in an impropriety. "They're not real."

"But you had help in preparing them, didn't you?"

"I did," she replied. "A newspaper reporter friend of mine did them for me."

"And what are you supposed to do for your newspaper-man in return?"

"Well, sir, the Central Pacific Railroad is news, isn't it? I'm supposed to tip him off if I learn of anything that might make a good story."

He cupped his hand over her warm mound, and she couldn't keep from inhaling sharply. "And you'd do any-thing, even go to bed with me, to worm information out of me that might make a good news story?"

Rosanna pouted and looked hurt. "If you think that—"

"What am I to think?" he cut her off.

She turned her head away and managed to squeeze out a few tears. "Think what you must, sir, but the truth of the matter is that I took you into my bed because"—she looked at him defiantly—"because I—I wanted you."

She examined his eyes for a hint of surprise but saw noth-ing.

"I think you are an ambitious girl," he commented. "I think that you not only admire men of power and position, as you claim, but that you aspire to such position yourself."

"And if I do?" she asked.

He gave a throaty laugh. "It is very difficult for a woman to amass a fortune alone."

She put her hand on his arm. "You're not angry that I came here under false pretenses?"

"No."

"Even though I came to spy on you, to relate to my friend anything that might be newsworthy?"

He shrugged. "Have you garnered any worthwhile infor-mation for your friend?"

She laughed, then traced a path on his chest with her fin-ger as she answered, "I know that Collis P. Huntington has a sweet tooth." She paused, then said, "I have learned nothing else. Since I came here, no visitor has called, and you have done no entertaining at home."

He grabbed her hand. "You didn't think, did you, that you

could lure me into your bed and, like the female spies of the Confederacy, loosen my tongue with your charms?"

She looked steadily into his eyes with what she hoped was sincerity. "I would never underestimate you, Mr. Huntington, especially now that—that I've come to know you a little better."

"Well, I'm pleased that you did not have so low an opinion of me." He was caressing her body in a manner that had begun to stir her again. "Assuming, Rose, that what you've told me is true—"

"Do you doubt me?" she asked.

He laughed. "Whatever your friend has agreed to pay you for spying on me and my business affairs is, I'd guess, an insignificant amount."

"I shan't be rich through it."

"Perhaps you should join the Huntington team."

She held her breath for a moment. This presented a new possibility, and Rosanna was always interested in new opportunities.

"There are times, my dear, when I require information from others. I'm not sure that you are suited for such a job, for you're too sweet, too straightforward, to make a good spy."

She was so amused by his perception of her that she laughed aloud. Of course she appeared to be an unlikely spy. She had seemed even more implausible in the role that she had played—quite well, thank you—during the war years when she had lived in Richmond as the wife of a Confederate officer while relaying information to the Union. The very fact that she hadn't looked the part had made her ideal for it. She covered her laugh by seizing his hand, which was doing impudent things to her. "Please, I have a one-track mind."

He chuckled and withdrew his hand.

"Exactly what are you suggesting?" she asked.

"I'm suggesting that perhaps you can be rich. That is, if you would be willing to use your abundant charms as directed . . . upon a subject of my choosing."

"I'm to be a prostitute for you, serving not you but men from whom you wish to extract information, is that right?"

"I would prefer to call the position that of a . . . oh, a woman of business."

It was, she knew, a proposition worthy of consideration. Lloyd had told her once that for the moment his income depended upon the goodwill of Thomas Durant. Until she achieved her goals, one of which was to be a woman of independent wealth, her financial well-being would depend on men like Huntington, not on someone like Lloyd Miles, who was as far down the totem pole as she. It was up to her to make the right choice of employers, and she was tempted by Huntington's offer.

She spent some few seconds considering what he would think if she told him all of the truth; but before taking such a rash step, she would need to know more about Huntington. In those few flashing seconds of thought, her conclusion was to delay any permanent decision about her own loyalties until she had all the information.

"A woman of business," she mused. "I see."

Huntington, thinking that her musing indicated hesitation, said, "First of all, we would have to define your position. Secretary?" He shook his head. "No, I think not. Mrs. Huntington wouldn't abide that. I think that you must be C. P. Huntington's mistress, and as such you will be ensconced in a flat befitting your position. Your wardrobe must be fashionable. Now and again we will go places together, quite discreetly, of course. I will introduce you to certain men, most of whom will be the type to enjoy putting one over on old C. P. Huntington behind his back. Their satisfaction at deceiving me by having my mistress will make them so eager to impress you that their tongues will be loosened, I would think."

Again her mind was working rapidly. The barons, men like Huntington, were opening up new areas of opportunity, creating a field of professionalism that had not yet been given a name. In the past those who had chosen her odd and exciting way of earning money had been dependent on wars and rumors of wars, on employment by governments or governmental agencies. In the new and modern America, the barons were building little empires of their own. Some of these men possessed assets greater than those of a small European country. They were beginning to realize the benefits of knowing in advance the plans of other business organizations. Thus she was being offered a position much like the one she already held.

She liked the idea of having a flat of her own, of having almost unlimited money to buy clothing. She had not known true comfort since the war had made Richmond a city under siege, with not only the luxuries but the necessities in short supply. Perhaps, she decided, she could have what Huntington was offering while deferring any final decision about her immediate future. She could explain to Lloyd Miles that she had, as he'd suggested, insinuated herself more intimately into the life of Collis P. Huntington. To the client she would say that she had been forced to make a decision on short notice and that she had considered the move to be in his best interests, since by becoming more intimate with Collis Huntington, the potential for gathering significant information about the Central Pacific was enhanced.

To test Huntington's intentions she said, "I would need money of my own. I couldn't come to you every time I needed a dollar."

"Of course, my dear," he said soothingly. "There will be an account set up in your name. You'll find the amount ample. And there will be a bit of help from me toward investing portions of your earnings so that they will multiply." His hand was busy again. He let his robe slide off his shoulders. "I take it you have decided?"

"I don't know," she said, closing her eyes.

"Let's give it a rest, then," he whispered, pulling the sheet away from her torso. . . .

Hours later, Huntington still lay beside Rosanna, her head resting on his shoulder. "We should keep your friend wondering for a time," he said.

"My friend?" she said sleepily.

Huntington looked down at her. "Your newspaper friend."

"Oh, yes."

"We must see to it that he gets a little tidbit of information, something worthy of publication."

Rosanna said nothing but raised herself up on one elbow.

"Tell him that the Central Pacific has become dissatisfied with its present supplier of rails, that the line is going to switch to another supplier. The name of the mill from which we will be buying our rails, beginning in a few months, is Banting Iron and Steel of Pennsylvania."

"Banting Iron and Steel," Rosanna echoed.

"When will you see him?"

"Monday is my day off," she said.

"Good," Huntington replied. "We don't want him to suspect that you've changed alliances, lest the word get around that you are working for me."

"I understand."

"I suspected you would," he said. He kissed her perfunctorily, left her room, and went to his chambers to bathe.

His visit with Rose Delany had been a pleasant interlude, one that he wouldn't mind repeating. But he had to be sure of her.

Before he retired for the night, he went to his desk and wrote a memo to Jeff Davis:

Contact Pinkerton's. Have them run a thorough check on Rose Delany as quickly as they can. Give them copies of her references but tell them they need not check with the Jay Gould household, since she never worked there.

Upon reading the memo the next morning, Jeff Davis smiled grimly. It pleased him to know that Mr. Huntington did not believe all was primroses and violets with the uppity Miss Delany.

Ten days later he had to force himself to keep from smiling when he delivered the Pinkerton Detective Agency's report to Huntington. The woman had lied. Not only had she never worked for Jay Gould, but she had never been in household service before. Moreover, the only record of employment that Pinkerton's could find was a job in the office of Lloyd Miles at the Union Pacific.

Now, Davis was thinking, *we will soon see the end of Rose*

Delany. He waited with ill-concealed glee while Huntington read the report.

ROSANNA PULLIAM, alias ROSE DELANY, was born January 12, 1842, in Brooklyn, New York. Her parents, Frank and Eileen Pulliam, are deceased, and she has no known surviving relatives. Miss Delany attended Brooklyn Heights Normal School. Her teachers and former neighbors recall her as being a lively girl, often in trouble with her parents—perhaps, it was hinted, just a bit "fast." At the age of fifteen she ran away from home and for a period of perhaps three years worked in various places of entertainment as a dancer, singer, and actress. From 1860, when she appeared in a supporting role in a melodrama touring the major cities of the East, to late 1865, when she went to work for Lloyd Miles in the Union Pacific's Washington offices, her whereabouts and activities have not at this point been discovered. She was known to have made a liaison with an actor of the touring company; but other members of that group said that although she consorted with the actor openly, she was not considered to be promiscuous.

There was an unsupported allegation from a former member of the touring company that she spent the war years in the South. We emphasize, however, that this suggestion is not confirmed by evidence.

Jeff Davis was trying to hide a smirk of satisfaction. "You noted, sir, that the woman was last working for the Union Pacific Railroad?"

Huntington had, of course, noticed. But there was more to Miss Rose Delany Pulliam than was revealed by the Pinkerton report. Certainly her employment by the Union Pacific had to be more than just coincidence. In all probability the "newspaperman" who had paid Rose to go to work in the Huntington house was Lloyd Miles, but there was something about the whole affair that did not quite ring true. Something was missing.

"That explanation is too simple, Jeff," Huntington said. "Tell Pinkerton's man to continue his investigations. If, as it seems on the surface, this woman has been placed here by someone whose name I won't mention, someone who is high in the councils of the Union Pacific Railroad, no harm has been done, and we might possibly turn the situation to our advantage. What most interests me at the moment is where our little Rose spent the war years."

After looking at the problem from all angles, it just didn't make sense to him to think that Thomas Durant would go to the trouble of planting a spy in his house. Durant knew him better than that, knew that a domestic spy would not gain access to the business affairs of the Central Pacific. On the other hand, a mere employee of Durant's, this Lloyd Miles, seemed an unlikely candidate to engage the services of a woman as talented as Rose. Things just didn't fit.

Davis, who appeared to be disappointed, had obviously been expecting an irate outburst from Huntington. He stood there indecisively.

"Yes," Huntington said, "on second thought, Jeff, just pay Pinkerton's fee and thank him for his good work."

Davis, puzzled, did not move.

"Thank you, Jeff," Huntington said in dismissal. He would find out for himself if Thomas Durant had planted a spy in his own household. And he would discover for himself where Miss Rose Delany Pulliam had spent the war years. In doing so he would learn more about the character of an intriguing woman.

Huntington waited only until the evening. "Where were you during the war?" he asked Rosanna as they rested side by side.

She made a protesting sound. She'd almost been asleep.

"Where, Rose?" he insisted.

"Here. Philadelphia. New York."

"You left the touring company you were with in 1860," Huntington said. "What did you do until you went to work for Lloyd Miles?"

She sat up and brushed back her hair, and for a moment her eyes had the fixed stare of a big cat. "So you thought it was necessary to have someone look into my background."

"To be expected, isn't it? After all—"

"Did you find out anything that titillated you?" she asked archly. "My leading man in the touring company was quite handsome."

"Good for him," Huntington said. "What I want to know is where you were and what you did from 1860 to 1865."

She continued to stare at him for several long moments. Then she sighed. "I was in Richmond."

"Oh."

"I met a man named Brett Roberts when we played there, just before the war started. We were there when they started shooting at Fort Sumter. Our manager said that with conditions so unsettled we would have to abandon our tour of the South. Brett asked me to stay with him. I did. We were married. He was wounded during the siege, when the war was almost over. I watched him die of his wounds in a hospital so crowded that even as I held his head in my lap, there were men in various stages of dying all around me." She sniffed. "When the Union army took Richmond, I came here."

Huntington, in spite of his natural cynicism, was touched by Rose's soft, almost emotionless recital, for her eyes conveyed deep sadness. "I'm so sorry, my dear," he said. "Where did you learn the secretarial skills that enabled you to get a job with Lloyd Miles at the Union Pacific?"

She licked her full lips, laughed deep in her throat, and bent to kiss him. "I think, my dear employer, that I was *born* with the skills that enabled me to get that position. As for the work . . . well, I'm a fast study."

Huntington took one more precaution. It required another week, but Pinkerton's man confirmed that Confederate records showed a Captain Brett Roberts had served with the forces defending Richmond and had died of wounds received in action.

CHAPTER 12

Lloyd Miles had had the interests of his employer in mind when he had placed Rosanna Pulliam in Collis P. Huntington's household. Because each mile of track laid represented future wealth, he knew that any tidbit of information that might benefit the Union Pacific would be greatly appreciated by Thomas Durant, and for the moment Miles's fortunes depended entirely on Durant and the Union Pacific.

When Rosanna came to his apartment on the evening of her day off, he knew from her smug look and saucy movements that she had some information for him. She was coy, demanding payment not in money but in attention, and Miles heard himself whispering words of love. And they were true, for while she was in his arms, he did love her. It was easy to love a woman with long supple legs, arms that clung fiercely, and lips that could transport a man into paradise.

When Rosanna told him after their lovemaking that the Central Pacific was going to change to a new supplier of rails, Miles's heart leapt. Although the information would not be of immediate use to the Union Pacific, it presented exciting possibilities that would benefit him and his friends in the Breakfast Club.

After Rose and he had finished for the night, Miles sent her back to her place of employment and went out in search of Harold Berman. It was late on a Monday night, so Miles was fairly confident that his friend would be at home.

Berman, who explained that he had worked late, was just finishing dinner when Miles arrived at his apartment. Accepting his friend's offer of coffee, Miles sank into a winged chair opposite him and told him the information he had received from Rosanna.

Berman nodded, his white teeth showing in a sharklike grin. "I know Banting Iron and Steel," he said. "To meet the demand, they'll have to expand production."

"Can they do it?"

"I think so," Berman said. "They'll have access to unlimited credit when word gets out."

Miles sat back and smiled. "Banting stock will skyrocket."

"Carrying the Famous Four with it," Berman commented, rubbing his hands together.

"I've got most of my working capital in that stock you recommended. The money I'd be putting into Banting would be borrowed, so we'll need to be sure that the Central Pacific truly intends to make the switch."

"I'll do some checking," Berman said. "If what you've learned is indeed true, I'd be highly surprised if Huntington and his associates did not start discreetly buying up Banting stock."

Gus Trent was in Washington again. He stopped by Philip's office just before quitting time, and together they walked to the young man's apartment. Philip used the occasion to ask his father's advice about whether or not to join Lloyd Miles and his Breakfast Club.

"They sound like up-and-coming young men," Gus said after hearing the whole story. "I wouldn't want to make enemies of them."

Philip was surprised by his father's approach to the matter, but he remained silent as they continued walking.

"Then, too, it could be advantageous to have friends who have access to men of vast wealth and power. It's been my observation in the past few years that those men who are reaping so profusely the bounty of our capitalist system do not advance in a vacuum. For example, while Mr. Carnegie was becoming a billionaire, he carried others to millionaire status. So it stands to reason that one day Lloyd Miles and his friends, through their association with the rich and influential, could very well become wealthy themselves."

He paused to watch a young family walking on the Mall. The children were running ahead of their mother and father and tumbling on the grass.

"I'd say, my boy, that your decision depends on what you want for yourself," he said at last. "If you have ambitions to be wealthy, to be a captain of industry or a baron of business, then perhaps you should become a member." He looked at Philip. "But if you think there is even a possibility of your following in your poor old father's footsteps, of becoming a public servant, then there are other considerations."

Philip laughed. "My poor old father hasn't done so badly."

"Ah, but when I die there will be no grand estate to be handed on to you or my grandchildren—if I *ever* have any grandchildren. Only a tired old house and a few pennies saved."

"I wouldn't complain if life gave me the opportunity to be like you, Dad."

Gus blinked, feeling a surge of pride that made his eyes sting. He started walking again. "If that is the case, you have to realize that a politician has to be careful. I have a feeling that as time goes on, those in office whose names are linked with men such as Gould and Rockefeller will be rejected by the voters. We decry the ignorance of the electorate, Philip, but it's surprising how often the so-called unwashed masses rise up and rid the government of true scoundrels. That old saying that if you lie down with dogs, you can expect to get fleas applies doubly to a would-be politician. It's been my observation that it doesn't hurt for a man running for office to have money. It only hurts if he has flaunted it. If it's widely known that he is quite wealthy, people are going to say, 'Oh, well, you know a man has to be crooked to have that much.'"

"I don't have any plans at the moment to run for office,

Dad," Philip said. "But I appreciate hearing your thoughts on the matter."

That night Gus treated Philip and Leah to dinner but left them immediately afterward. When Philip took Leah home rather early, he found Lloyd Miles there, seated in front of the fireplace with a book. Leah went off to freshen up.

"Have a good dinner?" Miles asked idly, gesturing for Philip to take a chair.

"Very nice. Especially since my father picked up the bill," Philip replied as he sat down.

"How is Gus?"

"Fit." Philip laughed. "He keeps needling us about our slowness in getting married and giving him a grandchild."

"Well," Miles commented amiably, "I wouldn't mind bouncing a little niece or nephew on my knee myself."

Philip grinned and shook his head.

"Phil—"

Philip stiffened, alerted by Miles's change of tone.

"There's no formal initiation ceremony or anything like that, but when you've made your decision, we would like to have a special breakfast to welcome you to our little group."

Philip cleared his throat. He had dreaded this moment, but the problem had to be confronted. After considering his father's comments about the Breakfast Club, Philip had decided to decline the invitation. He didn't know what direction his future would take and consequently decided that it would be imprudent to shut the door on a life in politics by allying himself with Lloyd and his friends right now. "Lloyd, I think you would agree that we have different aims in life, would you not?"

Miles cocked his head and looked at him. "I don't know, Philip. Do we? I want to be successful, don't you?"

Philip took a deep breath. "There are different sorts and different degrees of success. You can't measure it all in money."

"Oh?" Miles laughed. "Have you devised another yardstick?"

"There are such things as satisfaction at a job well done, a regard for one's fellows, a knowledge that what one does is for the benefit of the country and the people in general—"

"God, you sound like a politician."

"Well, Lloyd, maybe that's the direction I will take in the future. If I had to say right now what I want out of life, I might have trouble defining it; but I think I might be leaning toward public service."

Miles looked glum. "So?"

"Suppose I ran for Congress and was elected," Philip said. "I would not want to be known as a railroad congressman, or as any kind of congressman except a good one, a representative of the voters who gave me the office, not of some powerful corporation or a group of wealthy and influential men."

"But it is corporations and wealthy men who make campaign donations. Hell, Phil, it isn't the voters who run this country; men like my boss pull the strings. They make good friends."

Philip was uncomfortable, but his decision had to be communicated. "Lloyd, wouldn't you agree that in the eyes of most people, Jay Gould is regarded just about on a level with Blackbeard the Pirate?"

"I see," Miles said, his expression sullen and his blue eyes cold and squinted. "You think you're too pure to be associated with men who work for Gould or Rockefeller or Thomas Durant."

"I think it would be wise for me to proceed slowly in such matters, Lloyd," Philip said. "I know you'll understand that it's nothing personal between you and me and your friends when I respectfully decline your invitation."

"It's your choice," Miles said, spreading his hands and smiling. He remained genial, and when Leah joined them in front of the fire, he entered into the conversation and laughed good-naturedly at the jokes. But soon he left the couple, saying, "Well, I know you young lovers want to be alone."

Miles had learned long ago to control his emotions and hide his true feelings. But from the moment that Philip had said that he would not join the Breakfast Club, Miles, seething, began a campaign to turn his sister against the man she loved. After all he had done for Philip in the past . . . He had not exactly lied, but he had certainly gilded the lily a bit, so that Philip Trent could hold something Miles would have given his right arm for—the Congressional Medal of Honor —and would probably have earned if his presence on Cushing's raid could have been publicized. He had wanted this man as his brother-in-law, and now Philip was telling him that he chose not to be associated with him, with old money-grubbing Lloyd Miles.

The change was not immediately apparent to Leah. She noticed that Miles didn't talk about Philip as much as he had and changed the subject when she brought up his name. And there were small, often sly comments that nibbled insidiously at Philip's character. Nevertheless, several days had gone by before Leah realized that something serious had come between the two men who were most important to her and that some terrible friction was eating at Lloyd Miles.

Although Miles was not all that much older than Leah, he had been father and mother to her from the time she was a young girl. When he was only sixteen, he had taken her out of the home of an aunt who had made life unbearable for both of them. While attending college, he almost miraculously supported her as best he could with his talent for pleasing people and handling details—a talent that brought him better and better jobs until he entered the army with a commission. The aunt, whose stern religious convictions had made life an earthly trial for both of them, now was dead, and there were no other relatives. Miles—brother, friend, surrogate father—was all Leah had had in her life until she'd met Philip.

Because of what her brother had done for her, Leah's love and gratitude for him were deeply ingrained in her. So she could only weep and wonder when she realized that Miles no longer wanted her to marry Philip.

She yearned to discuss the situation with Philip, but she could think of no way to bring up the subject without its seeming that she was accusing one man or the other. She was more successful at getting Miles to talk about it. When he arrived at their apartment one evening, she simply asked, "What has Philip done to make you so angry with him?"

"Angry?" Miles responded, hanging his coat in the closet. "Am I angry?"

"Lloyd, something has happened," she said, "and it's tearing my heart out. I love Philip. And you know how I feel about you. To have the two men who mean the world to me at odds—"

"What has *he* said?" Miles demanded.

At that moment Leah realized that the rancor was all on her brother's part. Philip had never said an unkind word about Miles. "He has said nothing. That's one reason why I'm so puzzled by your attitude toward him. Has he inadvertently done something to upset you?"

"Oh, he's aware of what he's done, all right." Miles walked across the room to the liquor cabinet and pulled out a bottle of whiskey and a glass.

"What is it, then? I'm sure that if he knew he'd hurt you, he would make amends."

"Oh, yes, Saint Philip would try to make amends."

"Lloyd, please." She went to him, turned him to face her, and looked up at him. "Tell me."

"He's just not the sort of man I'd like to see you marry."

"But only days ago you were best friends."

"And a friend does not shun the company of his friend." He moved her away from him and poured his drink. "Or have I been so foolish that I haven't noticed that it's all right for a friend to stab a friend in the back?"

"What has he done?" she asked with intense emotion.

"Ask him," Miles said, and picking up his drink, he stalked off toward his bedroom.

When Philip picked up Leah for dinner that night, he could tell that something was troubling her. They had just set out on foot for a nearby restaurant when she asked, "What has happened between you and Lloyd, Philip?"

Philip had thought that he was prepared to answer that question, a question that had become more and more inevitable as the days passed and it became obvious that Lloyd

Miles was avoiding him. Whenever he did happen to encounter Miles—when he was calling for Leah or bringing her home or spending time with her in the apartment—Miles's greetings were breezy but brief, his comments limited to such subjects as the weather. Now, with Leah at his side, as Philip felt her womanly warmth against his shoulder and smelled her perfume and that undefinable little undertone of scent that was Leah herself, he experienced a moment of sheer terror when she voiced the query that had to be answered.

"I'm afraid that I have, at best, disappointed him," he said. "At worst, and I pray not, I have hurt him."

"I'm sure that whatever you did, you intended no malice," she said.

"In all truth, I did not," he said, putting his arm around her shoulders. The night air was damp and bone chilling. "He asked me to be a member of his investment group."

"The Breakfast Club?" She looked down at the sidewalk. "Lloyd values his association with the other men in his club highly."

"I know. I had to refuse him."

For the first time there was something akin to reproach in her voice as she spoke to him. "Whatever for?"

"Leah, I work for a very important man. You know that. You know that the Speaker of the House must be above suspicion."

Before he could gather his thoughts to continue, she said, "Association with my brother is going to soil you somehow?"

"No, not association with Lloyd. But the implied association with his employer, with Thomas Durant and the Union Pacific, might cause some suspicion to fall on Colfax, since I work for him. The same can be said about the connection, however tenuous all this might seem to you, between the other men in Lloyd's group and Jay Gould, Rockefeller, and Carnegie."

In a defensive tone Leah stated, "My brother would never do anything dishonorable or dishonest."

"I know that, Leah. I said that it wasn't Lloyd I was avoiding. Please understand."

"I understand why Lloyd is upset." She pulled her arm away from his and started walking faster.

Philip closed the gap between them and put his arms around her from behind. They stopped, and he turned her toward him. "It's been bothering me as well. I would never do anything to hurt you."

"When you hurt my brother, you hurt me," she said through quiet tears.

"Please, my darling," he whispered, his heart aching. "Please don't weep. I can't stand to think that I've made you cry."

Philip determined at that moment to do his utmost to repair the breach between Lloyd Miles and him. He thought about it all during dinner and decided the best thing to do was to talk to Miles that night when he took Leah home.

But Lloyd was out, obviously avoiding him, Philip realized. He stayed with Leah that night until they heard Miles's key in the door sometime after eleven.

Miles had been drinking. He halted just inside the door and, swaying on his feet, stared at the pair. "It's late," he said, addressing Leah.

"We've been waiting for you, Lloyd," Philip explained. "It's been a long time since the three of us were together. Why don't we have dinner tomorrow night?"

"Aren't you afraid being seen with me will soil your reputation?" Miles asked, not even looking at Philip.

"Hey," Philip said, advancing to put his hands on Miles's shoulders, "I had no intention of hurting you, Lloyd. I'm sorry."

"Little late for that." Miles pulled away.

"Lloyd, please?" Leah begged. "Let's have an evening together and talk this thing out."

Miles pulled himself up and smiled widely. "I could never refuse you anything, Sister." He directed his smile at Philip. "When she was just a toddler, this high"—he bent and held his hand two feet from the floor—"she knew how to wrap me around her little finger and get exactly what she wanted." His smile faded. "All right. Tomorrow night, then."

"Tomorrow night," Philip repeated. He wanted to kiss

Leah good night, but she was standing next to her brother, whose arm was around her. And Lloyd Miles showed no intention of going to his room. Giving Leah's arm a squeeze, Philip said, "Until tomorrow night, then," and left.

When the door had closed behind Philip, Leah told her brother, "Thank you, Lloyd. I just can't bear to have you two angry at each other."

"I'll let him buy me dinner," Miles said with a crooked grin. "But he's lost his chance to advance himself." He turned Leah toward him and looked into her eyes. His breath smelled of whiskey. "He's a small man, Leah. He'll always be a small man. You deserve better."

And all she could do, knowing that it would be very unwise to try to discuss the matter when he had been drinking, was to smile and pray.

Lloyd Miles's mind was working rapidly. He thought of having Philip Trent around for the rest of his life, of having to listen to Philip's moral platitudes, of having to pretend to respect his naive views of life, of having to swallow his pride and be pleasant to a man who thought that he was so superior that he had refused to accept what was actually an honor and, even more importantly, a personal favor.

He knew he had lied about his being wrapped around Leah's little finger. In truth, she had always been subjugated to his wishes. But Lloyd doubted that he could wean Leah away from Philip merely by being disapproving of him. No, it would take something more, something in the way of a shock to reveal to Leah the man's true, hypocritical self. A simple solution to his problem came to him in a flash of brilliance. It would require a bit of planning and preparation and the cooperation of a certain person.

At dinner the next night in one of Washington's finest restaurants, Lloyd was by turns brilliantly brittle in his comments and then moody and withdrawn. Leah was silent for the most part as they waited for the meal to be served. Twice Philip tried to bring up the subject that had become a barrier between Miles and him; twice Miles changed the subject quickly.

Then, in spite of Leah's pleading looks, Philip gave up. After all, he had done nothing more than exercise freedom of choice in who his associates would be. He had not rejected Lloyd Miles, as witness the fact that they were seated across the table from each other; he had rejected Miles's companions and his association with the princes of capitalism. Philip had offered. He had held out the peace pipe to Miles, and it had been pushed back in his face. He was young, and he, too, had his pride.

The meal was eaten in near silence. The food, usually very good, tasted like straw to Philip. Leah tried once or twice to make conversation, but soon she, too, was moodily silent. When Philip saw Victor Flanagan, the square-shouldered, broken-nosed contact man for General Benjamin Butler, he found himself welcoming what ordinarily would have been an intrusion, for Flanagan motioned with his head and turned toward the gentlemen's room.

Philip excused himself. He entered the room seconds after Flanagan to see the sergeant accepting a brushing from the black attendant. A short cigar was clenched between Flanagan's teeth.

"That's fine," Flanagan told the attendant. He handed the man a greenback. "Now, go buy yourself a drink or something."

When they were alone, Flanagan pulled the cigar out of his mouth and stated, "The general hasn't heard from you."

"No."

"He wants to know if he's to take that as a negative answer."

"He should take it as an indication that I haven't made up my mind," Philip replied.

"As a member of Congress, the general is in a position to do something about the widespread corruption, the malfeasance in office, and the acceptance of bribes, especially from the railroad interests. We're going to move ahead with or without you, Trent."

As happy as Philip had been to get away from the stalled

dinner conversation, his mind had returned to Leah. Since he'd refused Miles's invitation, she had changed. It was as if a small wedge had been driven between them. With each day the void seemed to grow, and this evening wasn't helping.

"It's a damned shame, Captain," Flanagan commented, raising the cigar to his lips. "You've done some important work gathering all the information you have on the excesses of the railroad builders, but you're not the only one who has details. I'd think you'd see that you and the general are working toward the same end. Seems to me you'd want to cooperate with us, so we could combine our information and get something done about the raid that's being made on the Treasury."

"Tell me, Flanagan, as clearly as you can, exactly what you want of me."

"Not me," Flanagan said, "the group. They'd want your papers . . . your information. They'd want you to expand your association with members of the staff of other congressmen, keep your eyes and ears open, and prime the pump a little with leading comments. Most staff members know whether or not their boss is on the take."

Philip was reminded of the stack of greenbacks he had seen in Archibald Edwards's safe. That would be the sort of information Butler's group would want from him, but he was reluctant to voice suspicion or to cast doubt on Schuyler Colfax without definite proof.

On the other hand, if there was a possibility that Colfax was in the pay of the railroad interests but Philip kept that suspicion to himself, he might as well give up, join Miles's Breakfast Club, and start chasing the dollar like the rest of them. He sighed. If Schuyler Colfax was not an honest man, it was unlikely that there was one in Washington.

"Sergeant," Philip ventured, "it does sound as if the general and I have interests in common. Perhaps we could meet and talk about it."

Flanagan quickly shook his head. "Not a good idea. Captain, we're bucking some of the most powerful men in this country. Until we've got all the facts and are ready to take them to the nation as a whole, we have to be very careful. It's almost as if we're working behind enemy lines, sir." He grinned. "You know that feeling, don't you? Well, that's how it is. I'm not saying that you'd be shot if it became known what you're trying to do, but . . ."

Again Philip thought of Leah. The information he had regarding the practices of the Union Pacific would have an effect on Lloyd Miles if it became general knowledge, or if there were a legitimate congressional investigation by men other than railroad congressmen. What effect would that have, he wondered, on his relationship with Leah?

Flanagan puffed on his cigar. "No push, Captain, but have you an answer?"

Philip raised his head and looked at him. "I want to know more."

"Good. Name the time and the place, and we'll talk just as long as you want to talk. But for the moment I think it's time you showed a little faith in us."

"How do I do that?"

The sergeant dropped the cigar on the floor and ground it out with his shoe. "Information."

"My information is all contained in the report I have given to the Speaker and, as of now, is confidential."

"There's one thing that you haven't put into your report," Flanagan said. "Think about it. Tell me about it."

"I don't know what you mean."

Flanagan's eyes were hard. "Have you forgotten that large amount of Union Pacific money that you saw Archibald Edwards putting into his safe?"

There was a popular saying that described the prickly little chill that now ran up and down Philip's spine, causing him to shiver. He'd heard his father say it many times: "A dog just trotted over my grave." It was a grim saying, conveying the feeling of oddness, of threat.

"Are you going to ask how I know that?"

"Yes," Philip said.

"Let me answer your question with a question. What one name, if associated with our group, would convince you to trust us?"

Philip felt that little shiver again. "I have a feeling you're going to say you're talking about Schuyler Colfax?" It came out as a question.

"To that I am not at liberty to say either yes or no," Flanagan answered. "But I can tell you to have a word with your immediate superior when you go into the office tomorrow."

Philip furrowed his brow. "Edwards?"

Flanagan nodded. "Now, Captain, I've given you a lot more information than you've given me. I've done so at Mr. Edwards's suggestion. He's vouched for you; he's sure you'll do the right thing."

"I will speak with Mr. Edwards," Philip said. He left Flanagan with nothing more than a parting nod.

Leah was at the table alone. She looked up at him with a strained set look that was not familiar to him.

"You were gone a very long time," she said. It was the nearest thing to criticism that he'd ever heard from her.

"I'm sorry," he said, taking his seat.

Miles returned to the table with fresh cigars in his pocket, his mood jovial. "I'm for some fresh air," he said, rubbing his stomach, "and perhaps a little nightcap at your place, Philip."

"My pleasure," Philip said. He had hoped to have some time alone with Leah, but he was so pleased by Lloyd's affability that he made no objection to an arrangement that would leave him behind at his apartment while Miles and Leah rode home together in a cab.

Miles insisted on paying the tab at the restaurant, and he paid the cabbie who took them to Philip's apartment. Leah's momentary disapproval of Philip had passed. She clung to his arm during the cab ride, her body soft and warm as it pressed against him.

The wind had picked up during the ride to Philip's building. It clawed at their clothing, chilling their cheeks so that they hurried to the private entrance to Philip's flat. As the foyer door closed behind them, Leah sighed in relief at being out of the wind. Philip unlocked the inner door and bowed sweepingly, motioning her to go up the stairs first.

After stirring up the banked fire in the fireplace, he served white wine and sat beside Leah, holding her hand. Miles entertained, relating anecdotes about the foibles of the rich and famous, particularly those men who paid the salaries of the four members of his investment group. On the surface his gay banter was just that, but Philip suspected an underlying motive. It was as if Miles were saying to him, *These are my friends. This is what you have rejected.*

It happened as Philip had anticipated. Leah insisted that the weather was far too inclement for him to make the trip to the Miles apartment only to have to turn around immediately and come home. He kissed her quickly while Miles was getting their coats, and then he was alone.

As he prepared for bed his thoughts were all of Leah. It was not until he was ready to retire that his mind went back to the unexpected meeting with Victor Flanagan. He walked to the window and looked out. The street was deserted. The frigid wind shook the tops of shrubbery and the trees along the curbs. It wasn't in his nature to sneak around spying on others, but if Butler and his group could indeed help bring the excesses of the railroads to the scrutiny of Congress, could he, in all conscience, refuse to work with the general?

Still undecided, he turned off the light and went to bed.

Upon leaving the apartment, Miles had allowed the cab to rattle along for only two blocks before he had said, "Oh, bosh, I left my hat in Philip's apartment."

"You'd lose your head if it weren't attached," Leah teased.

Miles ordered the cabbie to turn around. The driver pulled to the curb across the street from the building just as a woman in a fur coat walked around the corner and headed for the entrance to Philip's apartment. She was walking swiftly, bending her blond, bare head into the chill wind. Lloyd could scarcely refrain from laughing in delight. The timing was perfect.

"What's this?" he asked in bemusement as the woman opened the outer door and disappeared into the inner darkness. He cleared his throat and mumbled, "Look, I don't think my hat will be going anywhere."

Leah had seen. When Miles bent forward to tell the driver to go, she said, "Wait."

"It's nothing, Leah," he said. "Let's get on home."

"Maybe she's in trouble," Leah said. "Or she's just chosen Philip's doorway as a shelter from the wind."

"Yes, perhaps."

"Go and see if she needs help," Leah said.

"Leah, damn it—"

"Just go, please," Leah said. Her voice was strained, as if she was fighting the doubt, the fear that her world was crumbling.

Miles ran across the street. The wind bit at his face, and he tugged at his coat. He opened the door and put his head inside. "Hello, love," he said to Rosanna Pulliam, who was crouched down in one corner.

"Why are your escapades always scheduled on cold nights?" Rosanna asked.

"Courage," Miles said. "We'll be gone in a minute."

He ran back to the carriage and clambered in, saying, "Brrrrr." And at that blessed moment Philip's light went out.

"Leah," he said mournfully, "I'm sorry."

She fought her tears.

"I'm sure he'll have some explanation," Miles said.

"Let's go home." Leah's voice was muffled. "I am not interested in his explanations."

"Damn, damn, damn," Miles said. "The scoundrel. The out-and-out cad. Just wait. Just wait until I get him—"

"Please," she implored, "can we just go home?"

CHAPTER 13

When Collis P. Huntington received word from his broker in New York that small investors had been nibbling around the edges of Banting Iron and Steel, he nodded in satisfaction. Rose had obeyed his order to pass the false information about a change in the Union Pacific's source of rails.

His broker had been good enough to provide Huntington with the names of those who had purchased the stock, and Huntington lost no time in calling on Pinkerton's to learn which one was the young man with whom Rose was collaborating.

It took the Pinkerton man only a day to get the information, which brought an instant frown to Huntington's face. He had been told by Rose that one man was involved. Now he knew there were four participants, each of them buying Banting stock in his own name, a rather naive way of doing things. Lloyd Miles's name was included, as Huntington had known it would be. And as he had suspected, no newspaperman was on the list. The report disclosed instead that each of the four worked for a financial titan.

Huntington did not believe for a minute that Jay Gould, Andrew Carnegie, Thomas Durant, or John D. Rockefeller would be working through Rose's friends. If men of the caliber of Gould or Rockefeller—even Thomas Durant—had been interested, the purchases of Banting stock would have been in multiples of the amounts that had recently changed hands. Such men did not stoop to petty plundering.

That night Rosanna serviced him well, with a skill that left him quite partial to her. He was truly sorry when he had to ruffle her just a bit.

"Ah, that was well done, indeed," he told her as she snuggled to his side. "Too bad there won't be more of it."

Rose tensed and lifted her head. "What do you mean?"

He sat up and swung his legs over the side of the bed. "Girl, people have simply disappeared from the face of the earth for smaller treacheries than yours."

He saw her face go pale.

"I don't understand," she said.

"Which of the young studs of the so-called Breakfast Club was last in this soft saddle?" he asked. "Which? Berman? Jennings?" He knew from the tic that developed in one of her eyes that he was hitting her hard. "No, I think not. More likely Lancaster. He's the handsome one. Or was it Thomas Durant's man, Lloyd Miles? Or, perhaps, all of them? How many of them know you've been placed in my household as a spy?"

Rose widened her eyes and waited.

"I would advise you not to lie to me again."

He had told her by his questions about Miles and his friends what he had learned. She decided to play the role of the helpless little woman. "I . . . don't . . . know what to say," she stammered, as she crawled to the edge of the bed and began to pull on her undergarments.

"I didn't think you were a stupid girl, Rose." He buried his hand in her thick auburn-tinted hair and yanked her backward. She gasped but did not scream. "Listen to me," he hissed. "I liked having you around. I thought you could be useful to me, and I was prepared to be generous; but you have lied to me once too often."

The pain of having her hair pulled had turned to a cold, crystalline anger. Her quavering voice belied her inner hardness. "Only one man knows. I didn't lie to you about that. The others are his friends, not mine. I thought I was just going to earn a few dollars by reporting the things I saw and heard in your house. When you offered to make me a part of your organization, I didn't know how to tell you that I hadn't been truthful." She looked up at him, having willed tears into her eyes. "I do want to work for you, Mr. Huntington."

He looked at her, wanting to believe her. "The man you worked for at the U.P., Lloyd Miles, was he the one who put you up to this?"

She nodded.

"Be very careful in your answer to this one," he said threateningly. "Did Thomas Durant know that Miles was planting a spy in my house?"

"No," she said. "I'm reasonably sure that he didn't. Lloyd gave me the impression that he wanted to be able to surprise Dr. Durant if I came up with any important information."

Huntington was deep in thought. It still seemed too simple to believe that Lloyd Miles alone had conceived the plan of putting Rose into his house. But he was influenced by the sweet, pink, exposed flesh that was so near him. She had seemed so frightened. He accepted her story. He laughed. "What is Lloyd Miles to you other than your employer?"

"He promised to marry me," she whispered, letting her eyes fall. "I don't think he ever had any intention of doing so."

"Would it bother you if we taught Miles and his friends a painful little lesson?"

She looked up, blinked away the tears. "I—I don't think so." Then, in a stronger voice, she added, "No, it would not bother me."

"They were rather stupid to jump onto the first financial tidbit you fed them," Huntington said. "Yes, I think we'll teach your greedy little friends a lesson." He put his hand on her bare shoulder. "You're sure you don't mind seeing Lloyd Miles hurt?"

"I'm sure."

"I hope so," he said. "To be truly successful in this world, Rose, you have to be able to control your emotions. You have to learn to use love and lust for your own pleasure without letting them interfere with your overall aims."

"Yes," she whispered.

"Then I'm going to tell you what I have in mind. I'm going to buy Banting stock, enough to drive the price higher slowly. I'm sure your friends will ride along, buying as the price goes up, certain that the new activity indicates the truth of what you have told them. Then, when they are in as deeply as they can get—and their greed will make that very deep—I will pump all the stock I have purchased onto the market at once. Do you know what that means?"

"It means they'll lose everything," she said.

"You will have a chance to warn them," he pointed out meaningfully. "Perhaps you would be tempted to warn just one of them, making him promise faithfully that he would not tell the others. . . ."

"You're testing me," she said. "I won't warn anyone."

"We shall see." He caressed her bare breasts. "I trust that your lover will not be putting any of your money into Banting stock, will he?"

"I have none for him to use, and if I had, I wouldn't trust him with it."

"In your work with Miles were you privy to information exchanged between Durant and him?"

"Not really." She smiled. "I'm afraid that Lloyd considered me more ornamental than useful."

He seemed to be interested in her smooth shoulder. He bent to touch it with his lips, but there was a look in his eyes that told her his mind was still at work. It was time to cement her new position with him, to give him something of value.

"There was one thing," she said.

"Yes?"

"Durant gave Lloyd a large block of stock in Crédit Mobilier to distribute to members of Congress at a fraction of its cost."

"Ah," he said. "And do you know the names of the gentlemen who were to receive this largess?"

"I heard just two names," she said. "Oakes Ames and John O'Brian."

"That's very good," he said, as if speaking to a child. He

was thinking that this sweet little morsel might have more than one use after all. "I've changed my mind—you must continue your relationship with Lloyd Miles," he said as he positioned her to his liking. "I think it best that we do nothing that might make Mr. Miles think that I'm onto his little game. I won't buy up Banting stock and dump it. Here's what we shall do instead: tomorrow you will contact your friend and tell him that the Central Pacific has changed its mind, that it is not going to buy rails from Banting Iron and Steel. Tell him to sell his stock as quickly as he can without loss. Since the activity has driven the price up, he and his friends will make a small profit. Does that please you?"

"I—I don't hate him," she said. "I guess I'm pleased that he won't lose all his money."

"That is one small by-product of the decision," he said. "The main reason I want you to get that message to Miles is to keep him ignorant of the fact that I'm aware of his little scheme. Continue your relationship with Miles as if nothing has happened." He chuckled. "And when you're with him, show a vast interest in the affairs of Dr. Thomas Durant and the Union Pacific."

"Just as if *nothing* has happened?" Rose asked, gasping with pleasure as Huntington took her.

"Control your emotions, my dear. Mustn't do anything to arouse his suspicions," Huntington said. "In fact, from time to time, I will give you information to pass along to him."

It was, he thought, almost belittling to match wits with amateurs. Already Lloyd Miles's spy in his bosom had given *him* information that could be very valuable in the future. If the need ever arose to cause confusion in the Union Pacific ranks, all he had to do was leak the word that various members of Congress had been bribed with Crédit Mobilier stock. He filed the thought for future use and concentrated on the pleasant task at hand.

"You want me to keep my relationship with him the same?" she asked as she clung fiercely.

"Exactly," Huntington told her.

So it was rather exciting for Rose, on her next day off, to be in bed with Lloyd Miles. There seemed to be an extra little fillip of pleasure in making love to a man whom she was actively betraying.

During Philip's first weeks of loneliness in the Confederate hospital, pain had dulled his senses. As he had healed, the pain lessened to a dull red awareness that permeated his entire being; he had learned, however, to isolate the discomfort in one part of his mind while the greater part of his awareness found ways to pass the long, agonizing months. During that period, self-analysis had given him insights into the complex of mind, soul, and body that was Philip Trent.

Since his hospitalization he had not given up this pattern of introspection. Understanding himself as he did, he knew full well why he had decided to hear out the men of General Butler's group: Philip was driven by the frustration he experienced in Schuyler Colfax's office because of the inaction on his report about the corruption on the railroad.

On the morning following his unsuccessful attempt to mend the damaged relationship between Lloyd Miles and himself, he sought out Archibald Edwards at his first opportunity. Philip was in no mood to be circumspect and said right off, "I talked with a man named Victor Flanagan last night."

"Did you?" Edwards said.

"I won't play games with you," Philip told him. "Does Victor Flanagan represent you?"

Edwards looked around the office and lowered his voice. "Let me say that we have the same friends."

"If your friends are to become my friends," Philip declared, "I'm going to have to be shown more action than I've seen so far. For example, if we're on the same side, Mr. Edwards, why has my report been buried here in the office?"

"As a matter of fact, it has not," Edwards replied. "It has been read by some very important men who are at this moment preparing to do something about the situation."

"Am I to know the names of these very important men?"

"You're with us, then?" Edwards asked.

"Yes, at least in wanting to clean up the graft on the railroad."

"Good." Edwards extended his hand. "You already have one contact that could be valuable to us. Your friend Lloyd Miles could supply information regarding his employer."

"Anything Lloyd could tell me is, I believe, already in my report." He did not state his feeling of revulsion at being asked to spy on a friend.

"That's just it, Trent," Edwards said. "You're so all-fired sure that you know everything there is to know. You think that because you can add two and two and come up with the conclusion that the Central Pacific is paying too much for rails that we can take it to court or before Congress. Well, my young friend, it's going to take much more than that. You're not dealing with the corner hardware store operator here. You're nipping at the heels of some of the most powerful men in this country. If you doubt that money buys power, then you'd best be careful lest you be crushed. Now if you're serious about wanting to do something, you'll take orders."

"I'm listening," Philip said.

"You're a personable young man. You get invitations to all the affairs in this city because of your position. Circulate. Get to know the staff members of as many elected officials as you can. Learn how Washington operates before you start to try to change it."

Philip was silent.

Edwards took the edge off his voice. "In fact, progress has been made. A man I think you know has been named to head a committee that will soon begin an investigation of waste. He's asked the Speaker to have you come to see him, with the possibility of your being assigned to the committee's staff for the duration of the inquiry."

"I'm interested," Philip said.

"Then I suggest you visit the office of J. T. Moverly, the representative from your congressional district in Maryland. You have the Speaker's permission to pass along any information you may have. We have already supplied Representative Moverly with a copy of your report."

"Let me see if I understand," Philip said. "The Speaker wants me to work with J. T. Moverly now?"

"That's correct," Edwards said.

"You must know that it was Congressman Moverly who sent me to see the Speaker when I first came to Washington. He told me at that time that his health was failing, that as a lame-duck congressman he could do little to fight such powerful interests as the railroads. Now, suddenly, all that has changed?"

"There'll be some good men on the committee," Edwards said.

Philip said no more, although he had other questions. Why would Colfax himself not get involved in the effort to investigate the railroads? If, as Flanagan and Edwards intimated, Colfax was in the forefront of the effort to eliminate dishonesty in government, why did the Speaker want to keep his participation so secret? Not once since Philip had joined the Colfax staff had he been given the opportunity to present his case fully to the Speaker. And now he was being shunted aside—or so it seemed—to work with a man whose power was on the wane in Washington. Unfortunately, he had no choice in the matter.

"We'll keep in touch," Edwards said, extending his hand.

Alone in his office, Edwards leaned back in his chair and cupped his hands behind his head. If it had been left up to him, he would have ignored Philip Trent. He had been against trying to make Trent a part of the network and had told Lafe Baker so from the beginning. Trent offered no threat. Now the matter was academic, for when Trent went to work for J. T. Moverly's pitiful little committee, he would be rendered as powerless as Moverly himself.

The lame-duck congressman from Maryland had been letting what influence he had dwindle away because of his ill health and imminent retirement. If Moverly had a small resurgence of ambition to exert influence in the railroad investigation, there were two good men on the majority side on Moverly's committee to keep him under control.

Edwards inhaled deeply, sighed, and lit a cigar that he'd taken from the box on Schuyler Colfax's desk. He rolled the cigar in his fingers as he savored the first acrid penetration of smoke into his lungs, then smiled wryly. It was about the only bonus he was going to get. He'd worked for the Speaker ever since Colfax had come to Washington, and he'd seen hundreds of thousands of dollars come into the office and disappear into campaign funds. He had heard once that it was a bank's busiest teller, the man who felt the weight of the largest amount of money in his hands each day, who was most likely to embezzle. Edwards could understand how a man who counted the other fellow's money all day long would experience the pangs of avarice. He, too, had handled large sums of money. He, too, had seen the money pass him by. Thus he felt no shame for taking the Union Pacific's gold on the third day of each month without Schuyler Colfax's knowledge. Everyone else in Washington was getting a slice of the cake, and now it was the turn of Mr. Archibald Edwards, congressional aide.

He took up pen and paper and began to compose his thoughts for relay through Victor Flanagan to Baker. *It is my opinion,* he wrote, *that the report prepared by Philip Trent will never be put before the Congress by the Speaker. It will get some brief notoriety, perhaps, when it is aired by the Moverly committee, but the majority spokesmen on the committee will quickly discredit it.*

J. T. Moverly looked older and more fragile than when Philip had last seen him. He was in what he had said would be his last term in Congress. Seeing the effort it took for the congressman to rise from his chair and come forward to shake his hand, Philip wondered why such a feeble old man had been chosen for such an important inquiry.

Moverly's mind, however, was still quite active. He handed documents to Philip, which Philip had never seen, that included invoices for materials on the business forms of the Crédit Mobilier company.

"These invoices illustrate my greatest concern," Moverly said, "the soaring costs of the transcontinental."

"How did you get them?" Philip asked.

"Almost by accident. There was a train wreck. A commercial traveler picked up a few loose sheets of paper and turned them over to a sheriff's deputy from a town that had been blackmailed by the Union Pacific into making heavy payments in exchange for a depot. The deputy mailed them to his congressman, wanting to know why a nine-pound sledge cost the Union Pacific twice as much as the same hammer cost in the hardware store in his town."

Philip looked at the papers. "Mr. Moverly—"

"We've been friends long enough for you to call me J.T. I like that better."

"Thank you. Have you any indication how many members of Congress own stock in Crédit Mobilier?"

"I have heard a rumor or two, that's all."

"You've received a copy of a report that I did for Colfax, I believe."

Moverly nodded. "Excellent material, Philip. In fact, that's why I asked Schuyler if I could borrow you for a few months. I want you—that is, the committee wants you—to follow up on some of your conclusions or findings, as the case may be. You'll be doing a lot of traveling."

Thoughts of Leah flashed through Philip's mind. The last thing he wanted was to be apart from her now, especially since his refusal to join her brother's club had created a barrier between them. But he could not turn down the opportunity to be sure that his findings about the railroad graft were known. He nodded. "I'll be happy to do whatever you think is helpful."

"Good. You'll be leaving the day after tomorrow."

Leah Miles had asked herself a thousand agonizing questions on that day after she had witnessed the blond woman entering Philip's flat. She had wept; her eyes were puffy and red. She had let her anger flow and once had actually thrown a book across the room, only to run after it and lift it tenderly and be thankful she had not broken the spine.

But how had the blond woman known that Philip was at home alone? Leah had wondered. There were several possibilities. Perhaps the woman lived nearby and had watched from a window, waiting for Leah and Lloyd to depart. On the other hand, the timing might have been sheer accident. Perhaps the woman was accustomed to entering Philip's apartment late at night. Perhaps there was a prearranged signal, a lowering of a blind, the placement of a light . . . something. Whatever the answer, Leah had, with her own eyes, seen the woman go into the building, and speculating about why caused her great anguish. When, in the early evening, she opened the door to see Philip standing there, she felt dizzy.

Philip's smile faded quickly as he looked at her. "My dear," he whispered, reaching for her. She stepped back and motioned him into the room with her hand. "Is something wrong?" he asked.

"A touch of the winter malady," she said.

He reached for her again, and once again she avoided him, saying, "No, don't kiss me. You'll catch it."

He grinned. "A fate I'll gladly risk."

"No," she said sharply. She moved to stand near the fireplace. "It's nothing, really. It will pass. How was your day?"

"Leah?" he asked, moving toward her once again.

"Please don't touch me," she said.

"Is something wrong?"

"No. I'm just not feeling well."

"I'll fix you a hot whiskey," he offered.

"No." She turned her face away, unable to look at him without weeping. "I think I must rest now."

"Yes, all right," he said. "I'll go in a minute. But I have something to tell you."

She jerked her head to look at him, thinking, *Are you going to tell me about the woman, Philip?*

"I'll be leaving tomorrow morning," he said.

Her face became even paler.

"I'm working for the Moverly committee now, and J.T. has asked me to go west to take a look, with full congressional authority, at the construction methods of the Union Pacific."

"Oh," she said softly, and suddenly the hurt she had been suffering all day lost its significance and was replaced by the knowledge that she wouldn't be seeing him for ever so long. Moreover, there was still a certain amount of peril at the railhead in the West—Indians, violent storms, the unknown. "How long—"

"It's sort of indefinite," he said. "Until I consider the job done. I'd say at least two months."

The words that she uttered next sounded as if they were coming from someone else's lips. "Take me with you." She wanted instantly to retract the words and felt a deep shame to be begging this man who had hurt her so profoundly; but the words were said, and they seemed to hang in the air for an eternity before he answered.

"If I only could . . ." he said.

All the pain Leah had been feeling was now nothing more than a minor, half-remembered irritation. This was Philip who stood before her, tall, dapper, so handsome that just to look at his eyes and his little smile made her melt inside. No, the thought of two months without him was not the only reason she had begged. "Take me with you," she repeated. "You can."

"Leah, you have no idea of the conditions at the railhead. There's a movable town that follows the construction. They call it Hell-on-Wheels. It's peopled with the dregs of humanity—gamblers, killers, thieves, and women like Hooker's girls. I'll be staying mostly with the work crews. There would be no place for you there, and I couldn't leave you in Hell-on-Wheels."

A feeling of desperation grew in her. Even though the hurt of knowing he had betrayed her was submerged for the moment, it was still there, and she feared what it would grow into during his absence. Lloyd, who had turned against Philip for reasons she did not fully understand, would use her fiancé's absence to try to convince her that Philip was not the man for her.

But he was. *He was.* "I want to be with you," she said, her voice soft but urgent. "I want you to delay your departure until we can be married. I want to share your life. I don't want to have to live without you for two months, two weeks, or even two days."

"Oh, my darling girl," he said, and this time he overcame her weak protest to enfold her in his arms.

"Please take me with you."

"It's impossible, darling. I'm sorry."

She pushed away from him, her mouth sagging. She wondered if he would take the blond woman with him if she asked. She wanted to blurt out to him that if he left her behind, she would be forced to choose between him and her brother. But there was in her enough pride to prevent her total subjection to Philip, regardless of the strength of the love. Most human misunderstandings come about from lack of communication, and so the endless cycle took one more turn as she concluded that she had humbled herself enough. She had begged him to marry her, to take her with him. She had known when she asked him that by marrying him she would alienate her brother. She had, in that intense moment, made her choice, and the choice was her love for Philip. He had refused her. She had made a desperate effort to overcome her hurt and to bind herself to him—and he had refused her.

She lifted her shoulders and composed herself. "I really must rest now."

"I'll drop by for a few minutes tomorrow, before my train," he said.

"I think it best that we say good-bye now."

"Please. I will want one more look at you before I go."

She said nothing. The decision had been made. Nothing else mattered.

"I'll write to you," Philip said, reluctant to leave her, feeling that something was awry between them but unable to understand. "I'll do my best to get back for that certain event we have planned, though it will have to be put off until May."

She did not speak. She allowed his kiss. He attributed her lack of response to the fact that she was ill.

At the door he turned.

"Be careful," she said.

"I will."

"I would have gone with you," she said.

* * *

Late that night, when Lloyd Miles returned to the apartment, Leah, wrapped in a knitted shawl, was sitting in front of the fireplace.

"To what do I owe the pleasure of having my sister all to myself for once?" he asked.

"Philip is going west, to the railhead."

"Is he, now?" Miles asked. "I heard just today that he's now a member of the staff of the Moverly committee. That's an excellent spot for him, the saint and the walking mummy, working together."

"He'll be gone for months," Leah stated.

"Good," Miles said. "That will give us time to resolve a situation that has become intolerable."

"Please, Lloyd."

"The time has come, Sister, for you to make a decision. You've allowed your lover to insult me. He has stated that he considers himself to be too good for me and my friends. Even if you can accept this, I can't. I can't let you make the mistake of marrying a prude, a pretender, a hypocrite who tells me that I am so unacceptable in civilized society that he doesn't want to be seen in my company."

"I think you overstate what Philip meant."

"And now he is actively attacking me. When he accuses the Union Pacific of corruption, he accuses me, for I am loyal to the Union Pacific."

"He's a fair man," Leah said. "He will do his job, nothing more."

"Well, I have a job to do too. And as it happens, I think my job is more vital to the future of this nation than his. I am a part of the effort to link the two separate sections of this continent together for the first time. I am doing something constructive, something that will benefit the nation as a whole. He is trying to tear apart what we are building." He moved to stand in front of her and looked down into her face.

"Leah, he is trying to blacken the names of good and loyal Americans whose contributions to the railroad will become a part of history." He bent, lifted her chin, and looked into her eyes. "I can't allow the relationship between you and Trent to continue."

"Lloyd, don't."

"I don't want him in my home. I don't want to see his face again. I don't want you seeing him."

"Lloyd, don't do this to me."

"I can say the same thing. Don't you do this to *me*. Don't throw away the years of mutual support we've shared, Leah." He smiled. "Remember when I came and kidnapped you from the old dragon and you laughed all the way to the railway station because you'd never have to listen to Auntie's belittlement again?"

"I remember," she whispered.

"We've been a good team, Leah." He held up his hand. "Look, I'm not advocating that we become an old-maid old-bachelor brother-sister act. One day, perhaps, I'll marry, and I'm sure you will too. You'll find another man, my girl. Take my word for it."

"I don't want another man," she said.

His face hardened. "There is no room for Philip Trent in my life. If you must have him in yours, then you will have to make a choice. Or, to put it tritely, you must choose him or me. You can't have both."

She was trembling. She had suffered two severe blows to her love and her pride. First she'd been convinced that Philip was carrying on with another woman, even as he swore undying love for her. Then she had humbled herself before him, only to be rejected.

"I love you, Leah," Miles said. "You know that I do. You know that you can always count on me. I haven't asked much from you in return, but now I do ask that you forget Philip Trent."

"I can never forget him," she whispered as Miles turned away, not hearing her last remark. The feeling of deadness came back to her, the feeling she'd experienced when she'd seen the blond woman go into Philip's apartment and Philip's light go out.

She suspected that she would live with that feeling for the duration of her time on earth.

CHAPTER 14

Unlike those who had profited from the blood and misery of the war years, Oakes Ames had been a rich man before the hostilities began. Oliver Ames & Sons, his family's shovel factory in Massachusetts, had been valued at four million dollars in 1862, when Oakes was first elected to the House of Representatives. Success had not been handed to Oakes on the blade of a silver shovel, however. Like his brother, Oliver, he had gone to work in their father's factory as a boy, learning the business from the handle down. He was given, and he deserved, the credit for transforming a small plant into a nationally known entity. Physical labor had developed his body so that he looked more like a gandy dancer in dress clothing than a wealthy congressman. His shoulders were broad, his body brawny, and he carried himself with a certain dignity and spoke unhesitatingly. Overall, he gave the impression of being a man of worth.

Oakes and Oliver Ames had been passionately in favor of a transcontinental railroad from the beginning. After all, had there been a direct cross-country link to the California goldfields in forty-nine and the years immediately afterward, Oliver Ames & Sons could have sold implements in multiples of their actual sales, and if communications between East and West had been better developed, the loss of a million dollars in bad debts to California merchants might have been avoided.

In 1867, with twenty thousand men toiling to link the two coasts with rails, Oakes Ames was in his third term of office as a representative of the great state of Massachusetts, and he was proud of the service he had given his country. When Abe Lincoln himself was little more than a greenhorn in Washington, he had called Oakes in to ask his support regarding the transcontinental.

In those early, grim days of war, when the federal armies seemed to be nothing more than a cat's-paw for the rebel generals, Oakes had wondered if the tall, somber man in the White House had doubts about taking the country into civil conflict. If so, Lincoln had not shown it, although he was obviously concerned with the progress of the war and with that other terrible conflict, the Indian war—the clash of cultures that had persisted from the early days of white settlement in North America—and the problems that it now presented for the transcontinental railroad.

"Mr. Lincoln said to me," Oakes told his brother, "he said, 'Oakes, I didn't call you over to talk about the Indian wars, except for their effect on the building of the Union Pacific.' He said, 'Oakes, we need that railroad.'"

Oliver listened without comment. He had agreed that it was desirable to build a transcontinental railroad. He had put up his share of a million dollars to buy controlling interest in a company that he himself had organized, Crédit Mobilier. He also put up his share of the six hundred thousand dollars that Oakes wanted to lend to the Union Pacific. Oliver was content to let the Union Pacific people think that most of the six hundred thousand had come from Oakes. He was content to let Oakes be the spokesman.

"Mr. Lincoln leaned toward me, Oliver," Oakes went on. "He said, 'My friend, you are a member of the Pacific Railroad Committee of the House of Representatives. I want you to take a greater interest in the matter. I want you to find out why things are moving so slowly out west. See that the Union Pacific gets built and you will be one of the remembered men of your generation.' I realized the great importance that Mr.

Lincoln put on the railroad when he said to me, 'Oakes, we have offered generous subsidies to the railroad builders, but perhaps not enough. If you must, ask the Congress to double the subsidies.' He said, *'This railroad must be built.'*"

To Oakes Ames, who felt that he had been given a sacred mission by the man he had admired most in his life, Abe Lincoln dead was a greater spur to action than Abe Lincoln alive. The tragic loss of the great man had left, Oakes felt, only himself to bring to fruition Lincoln's dream of making the separate parts of the nation one. He saw no conflict in doing his duty, in keeping his promise to the dead President, while at the same time making a dollar from his investments in the railroad and Crédit Mobilier. After all, the profit motive was what had made America a great and growing nation.

For some time the Ames brothers had limited their support for the transcontinental railroad to backing it to the hilt in Washington and assisting it financially. What brought them to decide to be active in the management of the Union Pacific and its holding company, Crédit Mobilier, were money problems. Thomas Durant, in spite of the help of an enthusiastic publicity man, George Francis Train, was having difficulty selling Union Pacific stock.

"He's rather a little man, this Dr. Thomas Durant," Oakes told his brother. "I told him that his plans for the Union Pacific Railroad were not in agreement with ours."

Oliver nodded.

"I said, 'Dr. Durant, to me and my brother the Union Pacific is more than a get-rich-quick scheme.' He bristled at this, I assure you, Oliver, but the fellow can add. He knows that we control Crédit Mobilier. When I told him that we were going to take charge, that we were going to finance the construction through Crédit Mobilier, he went absolutely pale. Says he, 'But I am the manager of Crédit Mobilier.'"

At that point Oakes paused dramatically, thrusting his large chin forward. "Says I, 'No, Dr. Durant, you *were* the manager of Crédit Mobilier. Please note the past tense.'"

Lloyd Miles had never seen Thomas Durant in such a foul mood. The dapper Californian looked as if he could snap a railroad spike in two. Miles soon learned why when Durant told him that he had been removed as manager of the Crédit Mobilier. "But I am still vice president of the Union Pacific, by God. Oakes Ames and his brother, the sons of bitches, can't take that away from me, not even with their Crédit Mobilier stock and their connections."

Lloyd Miles was wisely silent. He had been aware of a growing disagreement between his employer and Oakes Ames. Oakes and his brother, Oliver, owned controlling shares in Crédit Mobilier and could therefore appoint whomever they pleased to be manager. It appeared from what Durant said that they had been pleased to take the reins themselves.

"Well," Durant finally said, a philosophical smile forming on his face, "perhaps it's all for the good. Oakes Ames has drawn up a contract stating that Crédit Mobilier is to be paid between forty-two and ninety-six thousand dollars in construction money for each mile of track, depending on the terrain." His smile became wider. "Cherish the Crédit Mobilier stock you have, Miles. The dividends will be, to say the least, worthwhile."

"Yes, I will," Miles said. He waited for a moment to see if his employer had finished talking. Durant was looking down at papers on his desk.

"Dr. Durant," Miles began, "J. T. Moverly's little committee has sent a man west."

Durant looked up quickly.

"I don't think there's anything to worry about, really," Miles added hurriedly. "Congressman Ames has seen to it that many senators and representatives have a stake in the transcontinental, and they won't do anything to hinder its progress. And even if Congressman Ames isn't chairman of the Moverly committee, he'll have John O'Brian on his side."

"Who is the man they've sent west?"

Miles cleared his throat, thinking angry thoughts about his onetime friend. "Philip Trent."

"The one who wrote the report for Schuyler Colfax?"

"Yes, sir."

Durant leaned back in his chair. "Friend of yours, isn't he?"

"He was, yes."

"Do I take it," Durant asked, "that he is no longer a friend?"

"Yes, you may take it that way," Miles answered.

Durant quickly sat forward and folded his hands in front of him on the desk. "And is he still engaged to your sister, Lloyd?"

Miles swallowed. "I believe she is coming to her senses at last, sir."

Durant looked at the ceiling for several moments as he tapped his fingernails on the desk. "So far this Trent has been only a minor irritation," he said. "But there may come a time when we will be forced to deal with him." He looked directly at Miles. "If it becomes necessary to ruffle this young cock's feathers, would that be of concern to you?"

"Not in the slightest," Miles said immediately. But as the words seemed to hang in the air he felt an uneasiness in the pit of his stomach.

General Lafayette C. Baker, known to friends, enemies, and the press as Lafe, was sitting alone in a closed carriage in the cold and the dark out in the countryside. He was freezing, for the Washington area was paying for the pleasant days of premature spring by suffering a wintry incursion of frigid air from the northwest.

Damn, how he hated being forced to deal with amateurs, and especially with a man such as Thomas Durant, who, having been successful in the field of business and accumulating more money than most, felt that he was an authority in all arenas.

While Lafe appreciated the generosity with which Durant rewarded him for reporting everything said by Durant's private little Washington network, he also acknowledged that Durant was a worrisome sort. It had been Durant's idea to try to enlist Trent into the network in the first place, reasoning that Trent's effectiveness could better be controlled that way. When Lafe had reported Archibald Edwards's contention that Durant was seeing Philip Trent as more of a threat than he really was, Durant had been furious.

Lately Lafe had been thinking of the glory days when he had worked for the Old Man, as he'd called Secretary of War Edwin Stanton, when Lafe Baker had been almost a law unto himself. Back then he had commanded a hard-nosed troop of cavalry to patrol the Washington area, and he'd had the power to arrest and question any man who'd looked at him with crossed eyes. Then, at least, he'd been a professional working for a professional. The Old Man knew the ropes.

Now Lafe was being forced by circumstances to work for a rich man who wanted to play at spies, and even though Lafe could remember the good days, he tended to blame Edwin Stanton for his present circumstances.

As Lafe sat in the closed carriage, shivering from the cold and waiting for Durant to arrive, he felt no fondness or respect for Edwin Stanton. When Stanton had suggested that he continue to work for the War Department, even though the war had ended and military intelligence was no longer needed, Lafe had agreed. He had entered into the secretary's campaign against President Andrew Johnson eagerly—too eagerly, as it turned out. Stanton had ordered him to collect evidence against President Johnson, and then, when the very activity that Stanton had ordered got Johnson's dander up, Stanton had backed down, deserting Lafe and leaving him to be ignominiously kicked out of government service.

Just thinking of Andrew Johnson stirred Lafe's blood with righteous anger and made him feel warmer. He knew that Johnson was a raving Southern sympathizer, a Copperhead in the nation's very bosom. He'd known that Andrew Johnson was a hypocrite even before the end of the war and the death of Abraham Lincoln.

Washington was Lafe Baker's town. He'd been building his network of contacts in the city since before the war, and at one time he'd had informants from the shantytowns on the outskirts to the halls of Congress. It was no secret that Andrew Johnson often had certain visitors at night, after working hours. It was a simple matter for Lafe to bide his time until the man in the White House got lonely. Lafe himself had arrested the woman as she came out of the President's living quarters. He hadn't wanted to make things difficult for her; she was only an instrument to show the low state of Andrew Johnson's morality. He was more surprised than anyone when the woman brought charges of false imprisonment and extortion against him, and he was flabbergasted when the courts took her seriously.

By sheer bad luck he'd picked the one nighttime female visitor to the White House who had a legitimate reason for being there, and when Johnson took the opportunity to fire him, Lafe was left out in the cold by Stanton and the War Department.

Johnson had said that he, the President, would not tolerate anyone spying on him, not even the man who had brought the assassin John Wilkes Booth to his deserved end.

During the war Lafe had learned a few things, patience among them. A man who was traveling through enemy territory counting guns, trains, soldiers, and the stars on the uniforms of rebel generals couldn't afford to be testy and inclined to rash actions. He hadn't successfully managed one of the prime coups of the war—getting an interview with the President of the Confederacy, old Jeff Davis himself—by being impatient. Now he was determined to bide his time until he could prove himself to all those who had wronged him.

He had a few things going to accomplish that end. One of them was the writing of a book, which would tell the world once and for all that Lafe Baker had done one hell of a fine job supplying the Union with intelligence during the war. The book would jack a few jaws wide open. He'd tell everyone how he had exposed and arrested Southern spies and would-be assassins. After all, it was Lafe Baker who had nabbed the steel magnolia, Belle Boyd, one of the most dangerous rebel spies. He had also exposed and captured Wat Bowie, not to mention dozens of others.

In short, the book would prove that Lafe Baker was not a man who could be brushed aside like a summer blowfly by a man who was not worthy of being President of the United States. He would even a few scores with his book. Intelligent people would be able to read between the lines and understand that whatever he had done, he'd done for patriotic reasons.

His musings were cut short by the snort of a horse, followed by the squeak of an axle in need of grease. He waited until the approaching carriage had pulled to a halt before walking over to it. He opened the door, climbed in, and sat down opposite Thomas Durant.

"You're late," Lafe said.

"If I'm not paying you enough to ask you to wait for a few minutes—"

"I don't like waiting, not even for you," Lafe said harshly.

Durant puffed on his cigar furiously. "I do apologize, General Baker," he minced. "The delay, however, was unavoidable."

"You asked for this meeting," Lafe said. "What's on your mind?"

"Philip Trent."

"For God's sake—" Lafe began.

Durant cut him off. "The Moverly committee has sent him west with congressional authority to look at the books of the Union Pacific."

"I would hope," Lafe said, "that you have men who know how to present two different pictures with a set of books."

"Yes."

"Then how can he do any harm?"

"I don't know," Durant said. "I just don't like having a congressional investigator running around out at the railhead."

"Is someone out there going to say, 'Mr. Trent, the Union Pacific is cheating the hell out of the government'?"

"Damn it, I don't think so. Look, I didn't come here to argue with you, Baker. I told you to talk with Trent. You didn't obey my orders."

"Because I learned that Trent thinks I'm poison," Lafe said mildly. "I've explained that to you. I took what I felt to be the next best method, using that fool Butler. At least there was a common thread between them. Butler was the one who pushed through Trent's Medal of Honor."

Durant snorted. "You were wrong."

"Perhaps. I'm not right all of the time, only most of the time." Lafe smiled widely. "That makes me try harder." He leaned to get a breath of fresh air. The cigar was making it rather aromatic in the closed vehicle. "What do you want me to do?"

"Trent's a railroad man. He might see some things that other congressional people haven't during their visits. We cannot risk having him stir up trouble. I want him watched the entire time he's on U.P. property. If he discovers anything, however harmless it seems, I don't want evidence of any of the U.P.'s business dealings getting back to the Moverly committee in Washington."

"How far am I authorized to go?" Lafe asked.

A chilly silence filled the carriage until Thomas Durant finally spoke. "You have told me to leave the details up to you, Mr. Baker. You have told me that you are a professional in these clandestine matters."

"That far, huh?" Lafe said softly.

When the meeting broke off, Lafe Baker drove back into town to the little house where he hid out like a bat during the daylight hours. He knew what Thomas Durant had instructed him to do—see that Philip Trent met with a fatal "accident." Yet Durant had not said the words and would, with a clear conscience, Lafe knew, be riding off and puffing away on his noxious cigar. Durant was a businessman, all right, Lafe thought with disdain. He was not above sharpening a point of law in order to increase profits, but he would never stoop to calling himself a murderer, no matter what intent lay hidden behind his words.

He was wondering if Durant's gold was worth his staying in Washington. Phineas Headley, a newspaperman, was ready to begin serious work on the book, aiding him in organization and polishing his style. Why not chuck it all, find a quiet place, and go to work on the book?

The answer to that was simple, for Lafe Baker had never been one to save money. He was broke, and he needed Thomas Durant's Union Pacific gold to build a nest egg. Well, the job that Durant had asked him to do now went above and beyond the gathering of intelligence about antirailroad activities. Before he would arrange Trent's murder, he'd ask for a bonus that, when collected after the job was finished, would give him enough to hole up with Phineas Headley and write the book.

In spite of his extensive experience, travel by train was still an adventure for Philip Trent. He shamelessly used his congressional credentials and his past associations to gain admittance to the great repair shops and roundhouses of the East as he slowly made his way westward on the railroads that had been built before the war. He was still a boy in that the hissing, thrumming power of a locomotive thrilled him. For half a day he rode in the cab of a steam engine with the engineer and fireman, emerging at the end of the run with his grinning face darkened by soot and smoke.

As he traveled northwest to Chicago he let himself revel in the romance of the rails, the magic of covering distance so quickly. The things about rail travel that bothered others— the reek of coal smoke, the grainy soot that accumulated on one's skin and soiled one's white linen, the vibration and rattle, the swaying, the constant click-clack of the wheels— for him were the stuff of legend. True, the cars did not offer passengers the height of luxury, and one hour the car was too hot and the next too cold; but he was conquering distance at a pace that would have astounded people who had lived only a score of years before.

With his head stuck out a window Philip admired the great bridge that crossed the broad stretch of the Mississippi River. In Iowa, he boarded one of the first Chicago and Northwestern trains to traverse the tracks from Davenport to Council Bluffs, on the western edge of the state. From there he crossed the Missouri River and at the eastern terminus of the Union Pacific began the last leg of his journey.

As the train pulled out of Omaha, he began to get the feel of the plains that reached westward, that flat reach of fertile soil that was mistakenly called by many the Great American Desert. He noted Thomas Durant's "Ox-bow Route," a southern turn that had added nine unnecessary miles to the track and put an additional $144,000 in government subsidies into the hands of the Union Pacific in the early going when money had been quite scarce.

Philip was just getting settled in his seat when he felt a hand on his shoulder. He looked up into a face of Mephistophelian darkness. The man had piercing black eyes, a tiny swirled black mustache, and tightly trimmed chin whiskers.

"I believe, sir, that you are Philip Trent," he stated.

"I am," Philip answered.

"May I present myself?" With a flourish the stranger extended a card that read, *George Francis Train, Esquire. Representing the Union Pacific Railroad.*

Philip rose and extended his hand. "I've heard of you, Mr. Train. Pleased to meet you."

The aptly named George Francis Train was Thomas Durant's drumbeater and advance man. Engaging and charming in spite of his sinister look, Train was equally at home speaking to New York stockbrokers about the future of Union Pacific stock as he was convincing the residents of a small prairie town to mortgage their future in order to pay the Union Pacific, lest the tracks pass them by and leave them to sink back into the deep sod of the plains.

"I understand, Mr. Trent, that you are here on behalf of the House of Representatives," Train said.

"I wouldn't go quite that far," Philip replied. He was interested and a bit surprised that word of his fact-finding tour had already reached the Union Pacific organization.

"If I may join you," Train proposed, making a slight bow.

"Certainly," Philip answered, sitting next to the open window and gesturing for Train to take the seat on the aisle.

"I have been instructed by my superiors to be of help to you whenever possible," Train explained. "In spite of the ugly rumors one hears around Washington, you will find, Mr. Trent, that the Union Pacific Railroad has nothing to hide from the Congress."

Philip decided that it was best not to respond to that statement with anything but civility. "Thank you," he said.

"In fact," Train continued, "I believe you will see, Mr. Trent, that the Pacific Railroad is the nation, and the nation is the Pacific Railroad! I think I can demonstrate to you that this magnificent feat of engineering and extraordinary accomplishment in the face of terrible dangers represents not only the present but also the future of our great nation."

Philip could see why the man had been given the job of promoting the Union Pacific, and he had to admit that Train was good—so good, in fact, that Train seemed to have convinced even himself. "I appreciate your offer of help."

"If you'll allow me to do so, Mr. Trent, I will show you the true magnificence of our endeavor. Ahead of us, fighting the Indian, the elements, time itself, and the enmity of many, are two thousand and fifty dedicated men at work on the grades. Behind them, four hundred and fifty tracklayers labor from light to light in an effort to complete this grand and glorious work ahead of schedule."

Philip was beginning to be just a bit put off by Train's pomposity and by the way that he was trying to impress him with numbers. "Yes, I have heard it said that if indeed the railroad is not completed well before the target date in 1874, the interest on loans will bankrupt both the Union Pacific and the Central Pacific."

Train smoothed his mustache with one finger and smiled with one side of his mouth. "I will admit that a certain amount of urgency exists." He brightened. "Look, just there. That site, sir, illustrates the sacrifices that have been made to push the rails westward. There, at Plum Creek, Chief Turkey Leg of the Cheyenne ambushed a repair party, killed three, and scalped one man alive. The Cheyenne then wrecked a freight train and committed hideous mutilations upon the bodies of the train's crew. And only the courageous action of a conductor who fled from the plundered train prevented a second freighter from plowing into the wreckage."

Apart from such gruesome incidents, Philip could see that the first few hundred miles of track west of Omaha had been relatively easy going for the Union Pacific. The puffing locomotive snaked its way through seas of grass studded here and there with farmsteads. The scar of the railbed and the patches of plowed land were intrusions into the otherwise virgin prairie. It seemed almost unfair for the Union Pacific to have had such easy terrain—any engineer worthy of the name could have laid out the almost gradeless tracks through the Great Plains—while the Central Pacific had entered the foothills of the Sierra Nevada range to fight deep snow, rock-slides, and sheer rock faces almost immediately.

Philip had long known that his country was one of vast distances. He had covered not a few miles of countryside on foot while marching with the army, so he was aware that the United States east of the Mississippi was in itself an impressive sweep of country. In traveling by clipper to Central America down the Atlantic seaboard, he had experienced a feeling of ever greater distances. He realized now, however, that one could not appreciate the true vastness of the nation except by crossing it on land. The undulating grassland seemed to go on forever, even though the smoking iron horse covered more miles in a few days than the Oregon pioneers had been able to cross in months.

To realize the true importance of the transcontinental railroad, one had to ride it, to watch mile after mile after countless, empty mile pass the windows, to see the vast expanses, the little streams with their gracefully curving lines of trees along the banks. The railroad would bind the thirteen original colonies and the states that had been admitted to the Union in the first half of the century with the sweeping grandeur of the West and California, potentially the richest state of all. The land that had been purchased by Jefferson would be consolidated more firmly into the nation. The natural resources of the great West would be within easy shipment of the industrial East. The United States had emerged from the war a military power, possessor of the world's most modern army. The transcontinental railroad would enhance the new stature of the country and would help to make the United States the most powerful nation in the world.

Musing thus, Philip listened to the enthusiastic chatter of George Francis Train. Perhaps, he had to admit, the transcontinental railroad was *almost* as important to the United States as Train represented it.

The grading and tracklaying crews were being pushed hard to reach Cheyenne before winter. To the east of the railhead little settlements were already springing up along the tracks; but there were still empty stretches where the track and the telegraph lines seemed to be swallowed up by unfathomable distance, dwarfed into insignificance by the towering dome of sky. There the wind whined through the wire, and a Cheyenne warrior could place his ear against the post that supported the wire and hear the white man's babble, odd little sounds that traveled by magic from station to station.

Wolf's Tooth, a young, powerfully built Cheyenne, was the son of a chief. He was a proud warrior, and bitter toward his elders, who had allowed the white man to despoil the land and to kill or drive away the buffalo. He resented the intrusion of the iron rails, but he hated most of all the magic wire that swayed in the winds and sang a song of loneliness and spied on the Cheyenne, notifying the white men at some distant station when a hunting party or a war party of Cheyenne rode under it. But Wolf's Tooth knew that it was the iron horse itself that was the reason for the tracks and the wire.

"We will kill the iron horse," Wolf's Tooth told his followers, forty-plus young Cheyenne warriors who were keen for glory. "First we must stop him, for he runs faster than our horses. Here is how we will do it."

Wolf's Tooth's plan required the cooperation of many women, who fashioned six stout ropes of rawhide, braided so strongly that one rope would have halted a bull buffalo at full gallop. The women followed their men to the railroad and stood between the rails to marvel at the way they came together in the distance. When, by pressing an ear to the sun-heated iron, a warrior heard the first warning of the approach of the iron horse, Wolf's Tooth ordered the women into hiding in a nearby swale and prepared his forces.

The six strong rawhide ropes were stretched across the tracks. At each end of each rope four warriors secured the rawhide to the pommels of their saddles and prepared for the struggle by chanting prayers of war to the sky. Six ropes of rawhide, four warriors on each rope end, forty-eight Indians altogether—more than a match, thought Wolf's Tooth, for one iron horse.

* * *

George Francis Train had fallen silent for the moment. Philip was watching the rush of landscape past the window, mesmerized into drowsiness by the movement. Train was nodding, his chin on his chest, when a man burst into the car shouting, "Indians ahead!"

Philip leaned out the window and saw groups of mounted Indians positioned in six precise lines alongside the track.

"I'd pull in my head if I were you," Train suggested.

"They're not showing weapons."

Train looked over Philip's shoulder. "Cheyenne," he said. "They've been giving us some trouble."

The locomotive was now almost even with the Indians, who kicked their horses into a gallop and whooped as their movement took the slack out of the rawhide ropes.

The locomotive slammed into the six ropes, one after another, the rawhide stretching, then jerking. Horses were sent tumbling, and saddles were ripped away. Whooping Indians who hit the ground bounced, then lay still. A few of the horses were running full out, their speed increased by the hard pull on the rawhide tied to the saddles. Inexorably the horses and their riders were pulled toward the swaying, rattling train.

"Oh, my God," Philip breathed in horror as rider after rider was jerked into the side of the train, moving at twenty-five miles per hour. A horse screamed as its legs went under the wheels, and blood burst in a crimson flower from the crushed head of a Cheyenne. Then the moment was past, and behind the train the Cheyenne women sent up a wail of shocked grief.

Wolf's Tooth, who had aspired to halt and destroy the iron horse, was not among the survivors.

After one look at Hell-on-Wheels, the mobile settlement that followed the railhead, Philip was convinced to accept the Union Pacific's hospitality for accommodations. He was shown to the boarding train, the rolling living quarters that housed the tracklayers, and after depositing his luggage and

George Train's, the two men went to explore the temporary town called Hell-on-Wheels.

It was nothing more than two lines of board shanties on either side of a sandy street, inhabited by the lower elements of humanity. More saloons lined the street than stores selling provisions, and there were gambling houses and, of course, a brothel. The business ladies stood outside their wooden quarters, openly soliciting potential customers. A land huckster stood in front of a tent, shouting, "Get the buy of the year right here!"

"Most likely he's selling a lot in some town that has not even been surveyed yet," Train said.

"Will he get many takers?" Philip asked.

"Oh, enough to make it worth his being here," Train answered.

The two men continued walking until a commotion in one saloon caught their attention, and they stopped for a moment. The next instant a man flew headfirst through the air into the dust of the street after being tossed from the doorway. The man lay still. Philip was about to go check on his condition after a moment when the redheaded man stirred, got to his knees, pushed himself to his feet, and went staggering off.

"Irishman," Train observed. "Probably came into town with a full week's wages in his pocket. It only takes a few hours for Hell-on-Wheels to clean a man out and then toss him away."

The entire Union Pacific operation was to move westward the next day, following along the newly laid track until it reached the railhead, which was almost across Nebraska now. George Train assured Philip that Hell-on-Wheels would follow. Indeed, as they prepared to leave that morning, Philip noticed that the brothel was being dismantled board by board and stacked into open wagons.

Philip, still accompanied by George Train, rode a work train to the railhead in advance of the boarding train. He was as far west as one could go on the Union Pacific. The pellucid air was filled with the ring of hammer on steel and marked by the plume of smoke from the work-train locomotive. From over a hill came the boom of an explosion as the grading crew blasted its way toward increasingly difficult terrain.

"Well, Mr. Train," Philip said as the work train pulled to a halt, "I have enjoyed your company."

"You haven't seen the last of me," the promoter said jovially. "Remember, I'll be happy to assist you in any way during your stay here."

Philip took the opportunity to get away on his own. His first task, he had decided during the long hours on the train, would be to pay a visit to the field office of Crédit Mobilier and examine their books. Wanting to do so before George Francis Train or anyone else could warn them that a government-sanctioned inspector had arrived, Philip hastily made his way through the bustle of the work camp to a resplendently painted car, identified by a gilt-edged sign as the field office of Crédit Mobilier.

Philip climbed up the few stairs and, after giving the door two sharp knocks, opened it and stepped inside. The interior of the parlor car was handsomely appointed with rich, carved mahogany trim and plush velvet upholstery and curtains. From behind a huge claw-foot desk a neatly dressed young man looked up and nodded at Philip.

"Good morning," Philip greeted him. "I'd like to see the purchasing agent."

The young man rose and said from behind his desk, "I'm sorry, Mr. Trent. The purchasing agent is in Omaha. My name is Sanford Hughes. How may I help you?"

Despite his precautions, Philip was not too surprised to find that he was expected. "Perhaps you can allow me to examine your books, Mr. Hughes." His last few words were lost in the thunder of a nearby blast. Through a window he saw smoke and dust billowing up from behind the hill to the west.

"The lads are hard at it this morning," Hughes said. "I'm afraid I didn't hear what you said."

"I said I want to see your books," Philip repeated with a smile.

"By what authority, sir?"

Philip handed the young man letters drafted on the letterhead of J. T. Moverly, authorizing him to use congressional privilege in any manner necessary to ascertain the financial costs of building the Union Pacific.

"This is unreasonable," the young man protested, but there was no conviction in his voice.

"Well, when you accept money from the government, the government has the right to see how it is spent," Philip responded.

"Of course. Right this way, then, Mr. Trent." Hughes showed Philip to an unoccupied desk even more elaborate than Hughes's own. "This is where our purchasing agent usually sits, but since he's not in, you are free to make yourself comfortable at it. I'll get the materials you asked to see."

Soon Philip was going over a neatly kept set of books whose author had gone to extraordinary lengths to justify every penny of the cost of construction. Philip spent several hours poring over them but could find nothing incriminating.

Having made a few notes, he finished, then handed the large ledger to Sanford Hughes. "Now let me see the books that show the true cost of materials," he said.

There was something approaching contempt in the young man's smile. "I'm sure, Mr. Trent, that I have no idea what you mean by that remark."

CHAPTER 15

Balmy days gave Leah Miles the opportunity to shed the cumbersome clothing of winter and, with only a light shawl thrown over the shoulders of her dark dress, walk along the river. She used such occasions to read the letters that arrived regularly from Philip. They were coming all the way from Wyoming Territory, covering half the distance across the continent in just over a week.

The letters were uniformly tender, expressing Philip's loneliness and his desire to be with her.

She had not yet answered any of them.

Lloyd had taken delivery of the first letters, three of them having arrived at once. He had given her time to read them and then had asked, "So, how is the saint faring out there among the ruffians of the West?"

The second time he mentioned the letters from Philip, he picked up an envelope from the table beside her chair. "Did you notice the date on this? There was a time, and not long ago, when it took months to deliver mail from Wyoming Territory to Washington."

"We live in a marvelous age," Leah commented.

"It's the railroad, Leah," he replied. "The transcontinental. The Union Pacific. We're cutting through the empty wilderness out there, changing the face of the country. The mail's traveling almost two thousand miles in just over a

week will be only one minor benefit brought by the railroad."
He looked into her eyes. "Consider that when you think of
Trent and men like him who are doing everything in their
power to discredit the pioneers of this vast change. Imagine
what would happen if Trent and his kind have their way."

"I don't believe Philip wants to stop construction of the
railroad, Lloyd," she said. She prayed silently that he was
not going to launch another attack on Philip.

In the weeks since Philip had left Washington, there had
been an incessant strain between Lloyd and her. As for
Leah's state of mind, she was an aching mass of indecision.
There had been a time, immediately after she had experienced the indignity of being rejected after begging Philip to
marry her, when she had agreed with Lloyd that it would be
wise to return the diamond ring he had given to her and end
their engagement. More than once she'd seated herself at her
desk to compose the letter telling Philip so, but each time she
had succeeded in putting only a few words on paper. Then,
realizing the finality of saying, *I have reluctantly come to the*
conclusion that it would be impossible for me to marry you,
she had thrown the incomplete letters away.

Lloyd's face darkened. It seemed that the mere mention of
Philip was enough to infuriate him. "You damned well can't
tell from his actions that he doesn't want to stop construction, or at best slow it while those idiots in Congress pore
over every account and ask questions about each penny that
the railroad has spent. It doesn't matter to him that the men
who are building the transcontinental have the best interests
of the country at heart. The antirailroad congressmen who
have hired him to do their work of blackguarding the railroad are out to discredit true patriots in any way possible,
and if they're allowed to do so, they'll use the power of Congress to back up Trent's lies."

The willow trees along the Potomac, encouraged by the
false spring, were beginning to bud. Leah hoped that it would
turn cold again before the fruit trees and flowers began to
bud lest they later be killed by the frosts that were sure to
return. She saw in the show of pink in the buds of a peach
tree a parallel to her relationship with Philip. Her love for

him had burst into flower prematurely, and now her brother's opposition was a return of winter, and the blossom of her love was endangered. The pain of remembering the fair-haired woman who had gone into Philip's apartment was the frost that would, it seemed, wither the exposed petals of her emotion for Philip.

She spent hours walking alone, going over and over every moment she'd spent with him, asking herself how he possibly could have been so callous as to consort with another woman after having promised to marry her. Then she tried to rationalize her brother's unreasoning resentment against Philip, for in truth it did not seem to her that her beloved's transgression against Lloyd had been serious enough to warrant Lloyd's extreme reaction.

On a gentle day as she strolled along the river, she pushed all doubt out of her mind, for there was no denying that she loved Philip and would love him always. It was time to resolve the issue. She would face Lloyd squarely and ask him to review once more exactly what Philip had done to alienate him. She loved her brother, of course. Their attachment to each other had been strengthened by the hardships of their childhood, by the unpleasantness of having been forced to live with the aunt who had mistreated both of them. She could not believe that Lloyd really understood how much she loved Philip, for if he knew, he would not ask her to give up that love.

Lloyd came home late that night. Reason told Leah to postpone talking with him, but so great was her desire to convince him that he was wrong about Philip that she followed him into the kitchen. It was his wont to have a light snack after a social evening when he had been drinking. She cut bread that she'd baked only that morning, topped it with chunks of yellow cheese, and sliced ham over it all. He sat down at the table, winked at her happily, and began to eat.

"Lloyd, we must talk," she began, taking a seat across from him.

"You talk," he mumbled through a mouthful of food.

"I am being torn apart." Leah had not intended to open

the conversation so dramatically, but the words had come spontaneously, along with tears in her eyes.

"Ummm," he murmured.

"I don't really understand why you have come to hate Philip, but I simply cannot go on any longer being torn between the two of you."

Lloyd swallowed and put down his fork. "The man is not our kind of people, Leah."

"He was your friend."

"And he is now my enemy. If he can't find discrepancies in the books of the construction company out west, he'll manufacture them. He's supposed to be a railroad engineer. He should be able to understand why construction costs are running so high. He's on a witch-hunt."

"I can't believe that."

"He tells you that he spends all his nights on the work train," Lloyd said. "But I wonder—"

She had not mentioned Philip's comments on his accommodations aboard the work train to her brother. "You've been reading my letters?" she asked, shocked.

Lloyd shrugged. "He has allied himself with powerful men who want to, at best, take over the railroad or, at worst, stop construction."

"You've been reading my mail?" she asked, still incredulous.

"Yes, blast it, I've read your precious letters," he said, coming to his feet. "I consider it my duty to know as much as possible about the actions of that scoundrel. And my knowledge of the way he thinks might just enable me to better protect my only sister from the designs of a man who has no honor."

Leah was shaking her head in disbelief that Lloyd would invade her privacy to the extent of going into her correspondence box.

"I have noticed, Leah, that he is being quite evasive about whether or not he'll be back in Washington in time for the April date you have set for your wedding. And I noted that he fails to mention going into the construction town at all, although, knowing him as I do, I'm sure that he does. The railroad, you see, does not permit the women of the town on railroad property."

"No!" she said in denial of the implied accusation.

"I haven't told you," Lloyd pressed on, "but I did some checking on that woman we saw going into his apartment. She's not quite a common woman of the town. She deals with a more exclusive clientele, but her profession is the same as a woman of the streets."

Leah was still shaking her head vehemently.

"I've told you more than once that Philip Trent is not the man for you. The choice I gave you is still here for you to make." He reached for her hand. She accepted his touch numbly. "Sis, you know that I'm thinking of you and your welfare. That's all I'm concerned with. If Trent were a man of honor, I could swallow my pride."

He talked on, but the words had a hollow ring in her ears. He had put the entire weight of their sibling relationship upon her, leaving her no choice. She was not capable of deserting the brother who had been everything to her—brother, friend, father, and mother.

"Yes," she heard herself saying. "Yes, I will do as you wish."

Lloyd Miles would never know how deeply the words seared her heart. She left him sitting at the kitchen table.

He nibbled at his sandwich, then pushed it away in disgust and found a bottle of whiskey under the cabinet. Tilting the bottle, he drank deeply . . . and past events raced through Lloyd's mind. The taste became the raw, medicinal tang of North Carolina moonshine, and there was Philip across the table making a face at the taste, laughing, reaching for his glass to drink more.

Lloyd remembered college, those carefree moments he'd been able to steal when he wasn't studying or working to support Leah and himself—those happy-go-lucky, wild nights he had spent with old Phil, in mostly unsuccessful pursuit of the town girls. Old Phil, always ready to do anything for a laugh as long as things didn't get out of hand, ready for fun but always a steadying influence, applying the brakes if Lloyd, releasing the tension of his horrendous work

schedule, tended to travel too fast toward trouble. Then he
saw Philip at the bridge over the North East Cape Fear and
for a moment remembered the jolt of sorrow he'd felt when
he saw Philip fall, presumably dead.

Leah had made her decision, but he still had one to make.

He reviewed another, more recent scene in his mind. In
this case the man across the table from him was Thomas
Durant. . . .

"All Trent has done so far," Lloyd was telling Durant, "is
to use his congressional authority to look at the Crédit Mobilier records on site."

"I know that from the telegraphs sent by the office manager," Durant said.

"I don't think he represents any real problem," Lloyd said.

"Miles," Durant said, "right now Oakes Ames and John
O'Brian are distributing Crédit Mobilier stock to a list of
selected members of both the House and the Senate. That
information must not be made public. Now, I know that
there's no way Trent can stumble onto the stock distribution
out west, but he can be bothersome. He knows his railroading. I've learned that from the report he wrote for Colfax."

"George Train will keep him out of our hair," Lloyd said.

Durant laughed. "Well, George is a splendid fellow, isn't
he? Worth his weight in gold. But he's too eager to please. He
wants to be liked—by anybody and everybody. I wouldn't
put it past George to steer Trent into places where he has no
business just to get Trent's approval." He turned solemn.
"Miles, we've come too far to allow one man to endanger our
future plans. I told you that it was up to you to see to it that
Trent didn't cause any real problems. You seem to be either
unwilling or unable to do anything about him."

"Dr. Durant—"

"So you're not to concern yourself anymore about Mr.
Philip Trent," Durant said. "The matter is now out of your
hands. . . ."

* * *

Remembering the cold look in Durant's eyes and the hardness of his voice, Lloyd Miles felt an ominous chill run up his spine to the back of his neck.

As he sat in the kitchen sipping from the bottle, Lloyd could not be certain that Durant's words had meant danger for Philip. But when Durant had said that the matter was no longer Lloyd's concern, he had felt an ominous sense of finality.

He shook his head and put the stopper back in the bottle. Durant was not a criminal, he assured himself, not the sort of man to order sinister measures.

He put the matter out of his mind. At least he had finally convinced Leah to forget Philip Trent.

In the foothills of the Laramie Mountains, Philip was standing atop an impressive cut with George Train and the man in charge of the actual building of the Union Pacific, General Grenville Dodge. Their horses were nearby. Dodge had been the one to persuade President Abraham Lincoln that the eastern terminus of the Union Pacific should be in Omaha, right across the Missouri River from Council Bluffs, Iowa.

Appointed the railroad's chief engineer just the year before, in January of 1866, the thirty-five-year-old Dodge had accepted the job as if it were a mission from above. The Railroad Act of 1862 had become his bible, for he knew that much of the wording in the legislation was Lincoln's own:

> The track upon the entire line of railroad shall be of uniform width, to be determined by the President of the United States, so that, when completed, cars can be run from the Missouri River to the Pacific Coast; the grades and curves shall not exceed the maximum grades and curves of the Baltimore and Ohio Railroad, i.e., 116 feet to the mile and a radius of 400 feet to the mile; the whole line of said railroad and branches and telegraph shall be operated as one continuous line.

By the spring of 1867, Grenville Dodge had pushed the Union Pacific through drought and storm and winter to the eastern slope of the Rocky Mountains, despite hostile Indians and the interference of the authorities and politicians back east.

The men who built railroads formed a loose fraternity. Dodge was undertaking the greatest feat of railroading to date, and Philip Trent was well aware of the man and his accomplishments. And it was not unusual that Dodge had heard of Philip, who had cut his railroading teeth on the Baltimore and Ohio. Dodge also knew of Philip by the reputation he'd earned during his army career. So they stood side by side with Train, members of a rather exclusive, unchartered club, and watched a puffing work engine creep into the cut below, where men swarmed about the train that had just arrived from the East and began to off-load rails and ties.

Dodge, a bearded man with dark, sunken eyes, was talking of the future, one of his favorite subjects. "Captain Trent, we opened up two million acres of farmland for settlement within two hundred miles of Omaha. And that was just the beginning. There's a million acres of arable land behind us along the North Platte. There's timber here." He waved his hand to indicate the Laramie Plains. "Limestone ahead of us west of Cheyenne; coal everywhere, easily available, lignite coal, which burns with a clean red flame that makes it good for home use. We've laid tracks right over huge deposits of iron ore. One day, because of its mineral wealth, this area will be as prosperous as Pennsylvania."

Dodge paused and looked at Philip. "I know that you're here as a representative of Congress," he said. "And I know why."

"General, I'm as much in favor of the transcontinental as you are," Philip said.

"There are those who think you're here to make trouble," Dodge declared.

"I'm here to be sure that the federal government is getting its money's worth."

Dodge nodded. "That concerns me as well."

George Train, who until this point had remained uncharacteristically silent, now commented, "General, we're all

concerned about doing the job as economically as possible—
and as quickly as possible."

Philip could tell from Grenville Dodge's reaction to
George Train's comment that Dodge had little use for the
dark-faced publicity man. Dodge turned to Philip and asked,
"Are you getting the cooperation you need for your inquiry,
Captain?"

Philip hesitated.

"Everything is open to him," Train spoke up.

"I was addressing Captain Trent," Dodge told Train frost-
ily.

Philip took the opportunity to speak. "Mr. Train has been
very helpful."

Dodge mused for long moments, looking from under his
bushy eyebrows at the nattily dressed Train. "Mr. Train, if
you don't mind, I'd like a few words with Captain Trent
alone."

Train sniffed, but he turned without protest, mounted his
horse, and rode away toward a path leading down into the
cut.

"Captain," Dodge stated, "I've done my best to eliminate
waste. It is a national shame that so great an undertaking as
this railroad, which will bind East and West together forever,
should be tainted by waste and greed; but the task is being
undertaken by men, and men, after all, are fallible. Nor must
we forget that the builders are entitled to a generous profit
because of the high risk involved."

"General, I agree," Philip replied. "And so do the members of the investigative committee. But when we see the
Union Pacific paying steel prices for iron rails, when we see a
simple pickax purchased at more than double the price it
would bring in Omaha, then we begin to wonder if there are
not deceptive business practices involved."

"Captain, I assure you that if you uncover the slightest
evidence that the federal government is being cheated, I will
stand behind you all the way." He turned to face Philip. "In
fact, if you experience any difficulties obtaining the information you seek, please come to me quickly."

"Thank you, sir," Philip said. He was about to mention

the false Crédit Mobilier ledger he had been shown when a
warning whistle sounded from the cut below. The Irish work
crews began to pull back. Then a section of rock seemed to
lift and shatter. The sound of a mighty blast reached Philip
and Dodge a second later, followed by the rumble of falling
rock. The crews moved forward to attack the loose debris
even before the dust of the explosion began to settle.

Philip folded his arms across his chest. "Looks as if you
have some good men on the blasting crew."

"The best," Dodge agreed. "I understand that you were
once very good at directing the placement of charges."

"Well . . ." Philip shrugged.

"By the by, Captain, I'm going to ride out to check on the
advance survey just after lunch. Glad to have your company
if you'd care to ride along."

"I'd like that," Philip answered.

George Train was already in the supervisors' dining car
when Philip and Dodge entered. He rose, inviting them to
join him. The conversation during the meal was light. Afterward, Train expressed an interest in joining Philip and
Dodge, and the three of them rode up the cut, out the far end
and into a grassy swale lined with fine fir trees, then on toward the next ridge to the west.

It was a pleasant and uneventful trip to where the survey
party was marking the lines of the cut to be blasted through
the ridge. Someone had just shot a deer, and from the cook
tent came the pleasant aroma of meat being seared.

"Venison stew, Gen'ral," the cook called out as he approached Dodge and the others. "Ready 'bout dark."

With a grin, Dodge nodded to the cook and, turning to
Philip and Dodge, proclaimed, "Gentlemen, until you've
eaten this man's venison stew, you haven't lived. Shall we
stay the night?"

"I'm afraid I have to get back, General," Train said.

"I think I, too, will pass on the stew, General," Philip said.
He was hoping for a letter from Leah, although weeks had
gone by and still he had not received one. Each day that
passed with no word from her caused his concern to grow.

After an inspection of the surveying work in progress and a look westward from the top of the ridge toward ever more difficult country, Philip and George Train took their leave of General Dodge and rode slowly toward the railhead. They could have found their way back by the clouds of dust and the occasional distant boom of blasting as the cut was widened to the desired measurements. As they approached the site a blasting foreman came to meet them.

"Lose the general?" the foreman asked.

"Staying with the surveying party to eat venison stew," Train explained.

"Yep, that man likes his stew," the foreman commented.

"Safe to ride on through?" Train asked him.

"Yep. Be maybe a half hour before we have the next one ready."

Philip's horse led the way into the narrow cut, between rough rock walls that rose steeply on either side. The area where the cut was being widened ran for a distance of about two hundred feet. The sound of hammers on steel rang in the narrow confines as the blasting crews drilled holes for more charges.

Soon Philip and Train were past the drillers and into the deepest area of the cut. Rock towered above them on both sides to a height of over fifty feet. The bottom of the cut was in deep shadow, and Philip glanced back to see Train's horse only a few feet behind. Train nodded, smiled, and yelled out, "I'm going to be ready for a drink, Trent. How about you?"

Philip's affirmative answer was lost in a roaring thunderclap of sound. His head jerked up to see the southern wall of the cut swell outward, then begin to fragment. His ears were numbed by the sound, but he put the heel to his horse and yelled, leaning forward as the animal leapt into a gallop. He turned and shouted an unnecessary warning to Train, who was kicking his own frightened horse to greater efforts. Above them countless tons of rock obeyed the law of gravity, death in dun-gray masses falling toward them. Behind Train's galloping horse the first of the falling rock smashed onto the granite floor of the cut, sending up a new wave of thunder. Philip could just hear Train yelling encouragement to his horse.

The frantic pounding of Philip's heart began to ease when he saw that he had ridden clear of the explosion-born avalanche. He turned in the saddle just in time to see a single bouncing stone plummet through the air and smash into the neck of George Train's horse. The animal's legs folded, and it hit the ground neck first, then flipped over completely. Train flew from the saddle, landed on his feet, and ran a few giant steps before losing his balance and skidding on his stomach. Directly over him a shelf of granite slowly peeled away from the side of the cut, a huge slab of rock that began to topple even as Philip reined in his horse, turned him, and went galloping back toward Train.

Train, dazed by his tumble, was getting to his hands and knees when Philip steered his horse alongside, reached his arm out, and called for him to climb on. He grasped Philip's arm with both hands and pulled himself up, managing to fling one leg over the horse behind the saddle as Philip spurred the animal away.

The horse and its two riders were in a race against crushing death. The rumble of it was in their ears, and they felt the sting of small pebbles that bounced off the rock floor of the cut. Behind them came the smashing impact, and then there was only the dust as the horse raced on and Train, jolting up and down on the horse's rump, cursed like a maniac.

When Philip was able to communicate to his horse that they were out of danger and finally pulled it to a stop, Train slid off the animal and stood unsteadily. His expensive suit was filthy, one sleeve ripped at the shoulder and the knees of his trousers torn and bloodied. He was still spouting inventive profanity as he dusted himself, then looked up at Philip. His hat was gone. His hair, wet with perspiration, clung to his head.

"I thought I was a goner," he said. "I owe you one, Philip."

"Next time we're caught in a blast zone, it will be your turn," Philip said with a casualness that belied his churning insides. He knew that they had come very close to death.

"I am very grateful."

"Get up behind me," Philip instructed. "It looks as if you have some cuts that need attention."

Train examined his elbows and knees. "Skin burns," he said. "More harm done to the suit than to me. Let's ride back and see that foreman," he suggested, climbing up behind Philip

"I was thinking the same thing," Philip agreed.

They met a swearing, livid foreman in the cut. As the man ran toward them, Philip halted the horse.

"I don't know how it happened, Mr. Train," the supervisor apologized before either of them could speak. "We had those charges set for one last blast once we had the cut widened, but the charges weren't fused. Didn't even have any blasting caps in place!"

"But it did happen, didn't it?" Train said angrily. "Who set the charges?"

"Ewell Sullivan," the foreman said. "Best dynamite man I've got."

"It would please me mightily if you'd find Mr. Sullivan," Train said.

While he and Philip waited, Train pulled up his trousers and again examined his knees. They were badly skinned, as were his elbows.

At last Ewell Sullivan, a big Irishman with a devil-take-you grin and eyes the green of the old country, and the foreman walked toward Philip and Train from the western end of the cut.

"All I can say is that things happen for which there can be no explanation," Sullivan contended. "Now, the thing that really puzzles me is not that one charge went off without having a fuse lighted and without a blasting cap, but that all of them in that pattern went off."

"Do you have any idea at all how it could have happened?" Train asked.

"Well, I heard tell once how lightning set off a blast before it was supposed to go," Sullivan remarked.

"Lightning out of a clear sky?" Train asked.

Sullivan nodded emphatically. "The good Lord can do miracles and odd things."

Philip had been examining the Irishman closely. The strong, green eyes showed a reluctance to meet his or to look directly at Train.

"When was the last time you checked the charges?" Philip asked him.

"Two hours ago, right after I finished setting 'em," Sullivan answered. "Good drilling. Way the shelf came down almost in one piece showed that it was good drilling and positioning."

"Just lovely positioning," Train added sarcastically.

Philip glanced appreciatively at Train and then asked Sullivan, "Who could have gone back up there and fused the charges?"

"Oh, no, sir," Sullivan burst out. "You're so wrong there, to think that any man on this job would try to do harm to Mr. Train. Why, he's one of the best-liked men on the railroad."

"You see," Train said, winking at Philip. "They love me. Why, none of them would try to smash me under a few thousand tons of Wyoming stone. None, indeed."

"Let's go see to those scrapes," Philip said.

When they were out of the hearing of the foreman and Sullivan, Philip told Train, "I don't doubt that they do love you, George; but you and I have been together almost from the minute I arrived at the railhead. Maybe they gave up trying to get me alone and decided that, love you or not, it was time to get rid of the congressional investigator."

"Philip," Train said, "I'm having trouble writing off this incident as one of those inexplicable miracles that Sullivan was talking about."

Philip nodded in agreement. "Six or eight separate charges would detonate spontaneously at the same instant only if they had been set and fused by an expert."

"That makes me both angry and sad because it leaves me with the same conclusion that you reached—that someone didn't care if I died with you, if, indeed, you were the target —or that someone tried to kill me. I think we must assume that you were the target. What does that make me? An accessory to dying. A nothing who just happened to be in the way."

"It makes me angry myself," Philip pointed out. "And not a little bit scared."

Train laughed. "Only a little bit scared? When I looked up and saw that whole wall coming down on top of me, I thought I was going to have to look for new drawers if I got out of that cut alive."

Philip accompanied Train to the hospital car, where Train's abrasions were treated with something that burned so badly, the dark-faced man closed his eyes and inhaled hissingly through his teeth. Philip had drinks ready in the sitting area of Train's car when the man came out of the sleeping quarters in fresh clothing.

"It's no wonder we were ambushed. You came here to nail the Union Pacific to the wall," Train said, "like a wolf skin on the side of a barn."

"I came here to put a stop to overcharging," Philip corrected. "If we are right in thinking that such practices exist."

"They exist."

Philip, surprised by his companion's blunt honesty, handed Train his drink and lifted his own glass silently. Train returned the gesture, and they drank deeply.

Philip sighed with relief, then remarked, "And I suspect that your orders were to show the city slicker around, let him see some book entries that make the U.P. look angelically clean, and steer him away from anyone who might give incriminating evidence. In general, to see to it that I went back to Washington without firm proof that there is fraud against the government."

Train grinned sheepishly at him. "I've been wondering, my friend, if the same man who gave me my orders—and you're right on the mark in your supposition—also gave the orders to drop half of Wyoming on your head regardless of who was with you."

"And?"

"I will not name names, Philip," Train asserted. "Not at this time. God help me, I *believe* in this railroad. I still think it's America at its best. I don't want to see construction stopped or delayed. But there comes a time—"

"George, there are two sets of books. Let me see the real figures."

George Train was silent for a moment. Then, holding out his glass for a refill, he said, "I think I just might do that."

CHAPTER 16

George Francis Train had always considered himself to be an honest fellow. He had never stolen so much as a nickel, and he had never cheated at cards. He would have said that his morality was as strongly intact as the next man's. The only times he lied were for the purposes of business, and that was not only permissible but expected in an age of grab and hold. He was an *homme d'affaires,* a business agent, and his business was the promotion of the Union Pacific Railroad. That he had been telling lies of omission to Philip Trent—and, through Trent, to the Congress of the United States—bothered him not at all, for what business did the federal government have trying to tell entrepreneurs how much profit they deserved on a high-risk project? Had the federal government been capable of building a transcontinental railroad, it would have done so.

Train had dealt with many government slugs—which was his designation for federal employees, because in his experience the only time a government man broke out in a sweat of exertion was when he strained himself reaching for a bribe— and he had a low opinion of any man who would forsake the golden opportunities of the open marketplace. At first he had placed Philip Trent in that category. But that perception had begun to change even before Trent risked his life by riding directly into the path of a cascade of boulders to save the

223

publicist's hide. That act had a profound effect on Train's thinking, as did the certain knowledge that a would-be murderer, following orders, considered Train's life to be expendable.

He told himself that he had almost been killed because some hireling, some railroad thug who would kill for a ten-dollar gold piece, had not realized who he, Train, was. He told himself that his good friend Dr. Thomas Durant would not sacrifice him so carelessly, nor would Durant allow others to do so, especially when the congressional spy had not gathered any damaging information.

But Train had looked up to see death hurtling down on him, and if it hadn't been for Philip Trent, the Irishmen would be digging down through the shattered rocks, looking for Train's mangled body.

He did indeed owe a debt to Philip Trent. And he owed the Union Pacific—or to be more specific, he owed whoever had given the order to kill Philip Trent and, not incidentally, himself—something that would hit them where it would hurt most, in the pocketbook. He had given all he could to the railroad, for he believed it when he said, "The Pacific Railroad is the nation, and the nation is the Pacific Railroad." It was like being thrown over by a long-term lover without the hint of a reason. In short, George Francis Train was upset. He was riled, angered, insulted, and shamed—for when one is so callously betrayed, one wonders about one's own failings.

He had to move slowly, slowly, with infinite care and precise timing.

"I'm going to give you what you came for," he told Philip, "but I'm not going to risk my hide doing it. If you want proof that the U.P. is bleeding the federal subsidies white, then you have to accept my pace."

Philip Trent was eager to get back to Washington to learn why Leah had not been writing to him; he feared that she was upset because their wedding would have to be postponed. Unfortunately, he had no choice but to agree to Train's conditions. The flamboyant publicity man toured him up and down the Union Pacific lines, all the way from Omaha to the Laramie Hills, visiting the facilities, roundhouses, repair sheds, and offices. Slowly Philip began to accumulate irrefutable proof of the Union Pacific's policy of cheating the federal government and its own investors to gain immediate profit for Crédit Mobilier stockholders.

Trent had proof in writing that in many cases Union Pacific payments for materials were inflated to cover twice the value of what was actually delivered. He discovered that while the railroad paid the price for top-quality goods, the cheapest and shoddiest were substituted. Being an old railroad man himself, Philip was astounded by the arrogance of the management when he was given receipts showing that the Union Pacific had paid Crédit Mobilier for enough lubricating oil to maintain a thousand locomotives for a hundred years; not surprisingly though, only the normal supply of oil was housed in the storage sheds.

Much of the evidence, which was either given to him by Train or came into his hands as the result of a quiet tip from the Union Pacific promoter, involved relatively small amounts of graft; but the total, he estimated, would add up to close to a one-hundred-percent overrun on original cost estimates. He was again astounded, for it was clear the entire scheme had been engineered with great effort and scrupulous planning.

Philip was almost ready to return to Washington. He had enough solid evidence to give the Moverly committee reason to recommend a reexamination of the federal subsidy program for the transcontinental railroad.

After George Train and Philip had ridden the promoter's private car back to the railhead, Philip was invited to dine with General Grenville Dodge. The general was expansive, for the work crews had been very productive during the spring months, and it was clear that the rails would reach Cheyenne before winter. The meal was almost over before Dodge inquired about Philip's progress in his inquiry.

"General," Philip said, "I think you'll understand when I say that I am not at liberty to discuss my findings with anyone other than Congressman Moverly and his committee."

Dodge nodded. "That sounds as if you've found what you came for."

Philip was silent.

"Well, what will come will come," Dodge mused. "I do not concern myself with the financing of this task. I only see to it that the rails are laid at a pace just short of breaking the backs of my Irishmen." Lighting a cigar, he put his booted feet on the corner of the table. "And speaking of my Irishmen, Captain, I'm getting sick and tired of seeing them fleeced and abused by the parasites in Hell-on-Wheels."

"I can understand why," Philip said, remembering his first visit to the portable railhead town when he had seen a railroad worker being tossed bodily into the street.

"A man is going to act like a man," Dodge said. "He's bound to go where there are women, and a laborer likes his whiskey and his gambling. I can understand that, and I can see that where there is a need, someone will step in and fill it. So we have Hell-on-Wheels, and we have the whores and the saloons and the gambling houses. But the parasites are not content with taking my Irishmen's money in exchange for sex or whiskey or in an honest card game. They serve my men raw whiskey that would choke a buzzard, and then they take what's left of his money and throw him into the street. And there isn't an honest card game to be found."

Philip nodded. "I've been in the town once or twice. Each time I felt as if I was taking my life in my hands."

"Because you were," Dodge said. "I've considered declaring martial law, but quite frankly, I don't have the men to enforce it. After all, I need my troops to keep the thieving Indians from carrying off everything they can lift." He puffed, then grinned around his big cigar. "But there's always more than one way to skin a cat."

Dodge let his feet fall to the floor with a thump. "How would you like to go to a little Irish party, Captain?"

"That depends on what sort of party it's going to be," Philip replied.

"I'd suggest you bring that old army revolver I saw you carrying one day."

"Where's this party going to be, General?"

"In town," Dodge answered. "We'll be in good company, Captain. My toughest Irishmen are going to see what can be done about cleaning up that hellhole."

Hell-on-Wheels was operating at its evening peak when Philip stood with Grenville Dodge on a little hill looking down at the muddy street, the ramshackle wooden buildings, and the glow of lamplight from the windows of the saloons and the brothel.

"I think you and I should find a good place from which to watch these proceedings," Dodge suggested to Philip.

"You've talked me into it," Philip said.

The streets of the mobile town were crawling with soldiers, railroad workers, teamsters, cowboys, and sheepmen from the surrounding countryside. Piano music was coming from a saloon, and a woman's shrill, almost hysterical laugh cut through the night. The Irish railroad workers—at least fifty of them—whom Dodge had brought Philip along to see were quiet and serious. They carried all sorts of weapons—knives, clubs, guns, and heavy iron bars. One man, a foreman who had a pistol strapped to his hip, was giving the orders.

"All right, boys," the foreman said, "you know what's what. Remember what they did to Fallon last night."

"Man named Fallon was killed," Dodge told Philip. "He wasn't quite as drunk as they thought he was when they tried to steal his money."

"I remember what that bouncer in the California Saloon done to me," a voice called out. "He's mine."

The Irishmen moved as a solid front into the town. Shouts of alarm came from men on the street as the line of railroad workers surged forward, penetrating the first of the gambling houses. Two shots came from inside, followed by shouts and a scream of pain. Bodies began to fly out the door, and then more shots were heard. The Irishmen moved on to the brothel, where shrill feminine shrieks could be heard. A moment later women in various stages of undress ran out the back and front doors.

The railroad men met organized resistance at the California Saloon. A hail of gunshots scattered the advancing line of

Irishmen. Here and there among the Irishmen the fire was being answered.

"They've got a little war on their hands down there, General," Philip said.

"I think, Captain, if we made a flanking movement—" Dodge started moving without waiting for Philip to answer. Philip, having come this far with Dodge, had no choice but to follow. They ran behind the brothel, keeping to the shadows, and approached the California Saloon from the western side. There were windows there. Dodge lashed out with his pistol, and glass shattered. He began shooting into the saloon. Philip peered in through a window and saw that most of the men inside were fighting to get out the back door. Only a few were at the front, firing on the Irishmen.

Dodge began to shoot out the hanging lamps. One smashed to the floor, and fire spread quickly over the spilled oil. There were shouts of warning . . . and then the men who had been firing at the Irishmen turned their guns toward the window.

Philip had not intended to take part in the battle, for he had no desire to kill. But when he saw the fiery blast of gun muzzles pointing at him, he experienced that odd departure from self that he'd known at Fredericksburg and Barbacoas; he felt, rather than heard or saw, his own pistol begin to fire. When he again noticed the chill of the night, smelled the stench of burned gunpowder, and felt the heavy pistol in his hands, there was light in the eastern sky . . . and Hell-on-Wheels was very, very quiet.

Philip stood beside a cook tent. Someone had built a fire to ward off the morning coolness. A supply train would be at the railhead shortly after dawn. When it went east, he would be on it.

George Train, with two mugs of coffee in his hand, came out of the cook tent. "Our breakfast will be ready in a few minutes."

The Irishmen had wolfed down their breakfast of salty ham, potatoes, and sourdough bread before the sun was up.

Already their hammers were ringing. Some of the men within Philip's view sported bruises and bandages.

"Heard you and the general had a little outing last night," Train said.

Philip nodded grimly.

"Speak of the devil," Train said, motioning with his coffee mug.

Grenville Dodge walked toward them, trailing cigar smoke. He threw Philip a cocky little salute and grinned hugely. "Mornin', Captain. You look none the worse for wear."

"You're looking perky yourself, General," Train said.

"What are the chances of getting a bit of chow?" Dodge asked.

Train chuckled. "Much better, now that you're here."

Hell-on-Wheels was not mentioned during breakfast. It was only when they were finished and Dodge stood that he said, "I'm going on a little inspection tour. I think you'll both find it interesting."

Philip and George joined Grenville. It was not necessary for them to go into Hell-on-Wheels to see the results of the night's work. The little cemetery had undergone a sudden expansion. A score of new graves were marked only by plain wooden crosses.

"Quick work," Train commented.

Philip felt a bit queasy. He knew that at least three of the men who lay in the Wyoming earth had died by his gun.

"We believe in cleaning up our own mess," Dodge said. "Here, gentlemen, lie the gun-toting scum of Hell-on-Wheels."

"And ours?" Philip asked.

"Not here," Dodge said. "We bury our own on U.P. land, on the right-of-way, so they can hear the trains go by and know that they were a part of something grand."

"Well, the gamblers are honest now," Train observed, kicking dust onto a fresh mound of earth.

Hunting Wolf, war chief of the Laramie Cheyenne, had lost two sons in the continuing struggle with the white man.

His elder son had died with honor, taking no fewer than three long-knifed blue soldiers with him. His younger boy, Wolf's Tooth, had been dragged to his death by the iron horse, his head crushed by the passage of that smoking, rattling intruder. For a long time Hunting Wolf had pondered revenge but had resisted the urge to take white scalps until he had gathered a force of warriors superior to any war party that had been assembled in recent memory.

Since Hunting Wolf did not spend his time idly watching the comings and goings of the iron horse, he was operating on the assumption that if he could kill the evil thing, all would be well. The land would be free of the stinking smoke and the clatter, and the white man would give up his effort to divide the land with a barrier of iron rails.

He carefully made his plans. His younger son had tried to lasso the iron horse and had learned of the thing's power. But the iron horse had to have the slick, bright rails, or it could not run over the prairie.

Hunting Wolf waited until the iron horse had rattled its way west. He sent young braves up the telegraph poles to hack at the wires with their blades until loose copper strands lay twisted on the ground. Meanwhile, other braves tumbled stones down onto the track from the top of a cut, for since the iron horse had to have the shiny rails to run, it was reasonable to conclude that if the rails were blocked by a pile of heavy boulders, the beast would be brought to a halt.

At the Sidney station the telegraph wire went dead in the middle of a morning exchange of pleasantries with the railhead. The operator rolled his eyes and said, "Damn. The Indians are at it again." He called for a station clerk and told him to get over to the office and tell them that something was going on between Sidney and the railhead.

George Train's private car had been placed just in front of the caboose for the trip away from the railhead. Since the supply train was moving backward, heading eastward toward the Sidney yards, Train's car was second in line.

Train and Philip Trent were the only ones in the private

car when it suddenly jerked, pitching both of them forward, almost out of their seats. Metal screeched on metal as the engineer set all brakes. Philip lunged to a window and peered out beyond the caboose. The train was entering a cut.

"The track up ahead is blocked," he told Train. "Rockslide."

Train lurched out of his seat and jerked a rifle from its rack on the wall, then moved to a window. The train was slowing. Philip, half hypnotized, watched as the distance between the caboose and the rockslide dwindled. If the train were moving with any speed when it plowed into the rocks, the fragile caboose would crumble into kindling wood, and the private car would take the brunt of the collision.

Behind him George Train's rifle blasted. The wheels of the caboose hit loose rock, and the caboose lifted but ground to a halt. The private car was still on the rails. Train was not the only man firing as fast as he could; from the cars behind them the rifles of the train guards were blasting. A slug whined through the window and took out a chunk of polished wood.

"It might help a mite if you'd use that pistol," Train barked.

Philip looked out to see painted Indians jumping down the pile of rocks toward the tilted caboose. Drawing his pistol, he began firing and saw two warriors go down.

"What's the matter with that damned engineer?" Train yelled. "He should be getting us out of here!"

Just as he spoke the train shuddered in an attempt to move in the other direction. The wheels of the caboose slid off the rocks, then off the rails, digging into the shoulder on one side and bouncing over the ties on the other. The derailed car was acting as an effective brake.

An Indian leapt down from the side of the cut and fired an arrow directly at Philip, who ducked just in time. The arrow thudded into the ceiling of the car. Philip fired at the Indian's face and saw it dissolve into a bloody pulp even as he lifted his pistol and prepared to fire at still another Cheyenne, who was running down the side of the cut.

The next arrow to enter the car was flaming. Train

stomped out the fire and quickly returned to the window. The train jerked and shuddered as the engineer tried to pull it away from the ambush. The sound of rifle fire from the direction of the engine grew louder.

"The soldiers are moving toward us," Train said. "We'll just have to hold on until they get here."

Philip's pistol was out of ammunition. He was reloading when a Cheyenne brave lunged up through the window and slashed at him with a wicked-looking tomahawk. Philip struck out instinctively, smashing the barrel of the pistol into the Indian's face.

There were running footsteps on the roof of the car and then the bark of rifles.

"The boys in blue," Train said, flashing a quick grin.

Philip saw Indians climbing the sides of the cut in an effort to escape the rifle fire coming from the top of the train. Several tumbled down the rocks, one screaming in agony until he struck the bottom, and then a blue-clad body fell to the shoulder of the roadbed. Philip smelled smoke coming from the rear of the car, the sleeping quarters. While Train remained intent on getting in a few last shots, Philip ran to the rear and threw open the door. A large man was standing with his back to Philip—feeding Philip's papers into a fire that had been started by a flaming Indian arrow.

"Hold it!" Philip yelled. He lunged forward. He wanted the man alive to find out why he was destroying the evidence of Union Pacific cheating that Train and he had gathered with so much difficulty. Just as he aimed a blow at the man's head, the train jerked, and Philip fell. Before he could recover, the blunt, iron-tipped toe of the man's boot crashed into his temple. With fading awareness, Philip saw a face that he recognized, the face of Ewell Sullivan—the dynamite man who had disclaimed any responsibility for the blast that had almost killed George Train and him.

The world was hazy, but Philip managed to get to his feet. He couldn't figure out what had happened to his pistol, for when he lifted his hand to shoot, it was empty. He aimed his fist at Sullivan's nose; but he was moving in slow motion, and Sullivan's big fist smashed into his chin instead. As Philip was falling he heard a gunshot nearby, thunderous in the enclosed confines of the sleeping quarters. He didn't know whether or not he'd been hit. But as light came to his eyes again, he saw George Train bending over the huge, fallen man. Smoke was wisping up from the barrel of Train's pistol.

Train's weapon was an old .44, the muzzle loader that had been the principal handgun in the war until it was made obsolete by the New Model Army Colt. The old .44 had done an efficient job on Ewell Sullivan, however. He had only half a face.

"Wish I hadn't done that," Train muttered. "It would have been interesting to have a talk with that fellow."

Philip climbed to his feet, steadying himself by holding on to a bunk. The fire on the other bunk was blazing well. Philip's briefcase was totally empty.

There were no more gunshots from outside. The surviving braves had withdrawn, leaving many of their dead behind them.

George Train was beating out the fire in his bunk with a blanket while Philip gingerly rubbed his bruised temple. The acrid smoke made him cough. As Train pushed him forward into the clearer air of the parlor, he said, "You recognized the man, I assume."

"Sullivan."

"He tried to kill us. Now he's burned everything we gathered." Train took Philip's arm. "Are you all right?"

"My head is the size of a bushel basket, that's all." Philip tried to smile. "Turnabout, George? You just saved my life, you know."

"So we're even on that score," Train said. "Look, we can reconstruct from memory most of what was lost."

Philip shook his head. "As evidence that would be worthless."

"Then we'll go back and do it all over again."

The empty supply train sat in the heat of the sun. A work train would come out from Sidney to remove the rocks from the tracks. Train asked some soldiers to remove Ewell Sullivan's body from the sleeping quarters. On its right-of-way the Union Pacific made its own law; there would be no investigation about Sullivan's death. Train told the soldiers that the Irishman had died fighting the Indians, and no one questioned him. Ewell Sullivan was buried beside the tracks.

When the train arrived at the Sidney yards, the young publicist was moody and silent. Philip shook Train's hand and told him good-bye.

"George, you're a railroad man," Philip said. "You believe in the transcontinental railroad. Well, so do I. And I think you've done enough that could jeopardize your job. I think if we went back and tried, as you suggested, to do it all over again, we'd both be buried out there on the right-of-way, and I don't really want to spend eternity listening to trains go by. What I would like for you to do is help me to write down as much as you can remember—not to be used as evidence but for my own information, as a guide for future investigation."

"What will you do, my friend?" Train asked.

Philip let out a long sigh. "Go at it from the other end, I suppose. I know now what they're doing out here. Maybe we can pin it down at the source, in the main U.P. offices, with the manufacturers from whom the U.P. is buying its materials."

"There's one other thing we can do," Train broke in. "And it's as much for my information as for yours. I'd like to know who gave the orders that sent half a Wyoming mountain down on our heads."

At first the chief telegraph operator in the Sidney station protested. But when George Train asked him if he'd like to wire the home office to see if Train's orders were to be followed, the man gave in and opened his file of messages. It took the two men hours to go through them, for Train began checking the ones that had been received before Philip's arrival. At last their search turned up two pertinent messages.

The earlier one had originated in New York and had not been signed. It had been sent to the comptroller at the railhead and read: *Open public books congressional investigator.* Train said he knew of no way to trace the order back to an individual in the New York Union Pacific office.

"By public I would guess they meant the doctored books," he observed.

The other message, only days old, had been sent from Washington. Since it, too, had been transmitted unsigned, there was no indication of its source. It had, however, been sent and delivered to Ewell Sullivan. *Stop Washington shipment by any means necessary.*

"That doesn't leave much doubt about their intentions, does it?" George Train asked grimly.

A sense of indignation so powerful that it made Philip dizzy clouded his thinking. He had known it previously, of course, but the six words on paper—and the way the death order referred to him as something inanimate—forced a realization of what might have occurred to burst in his mind like an exploding shell. He, Philip Trent, a fairly normal, healthy American who had survived the years of slaughter during the Civil War, could very well have met his death at the hands of men whose only motive for killing him was avarice.

Dark anger replaced his indignation. They had tried to take his future, the future that included Leah. That fact alone was enough to alter forever his attitude toward life. He could imagine the loss . . . never to hold her again, never to kiss her. Never to marry her and know her as a man knows his wife.

With a burning clarity he saw himself anew. Since the day he had fallen across one rail of the Wilmington and Weldon Railroad on the banks of the North East Cape Fear River with two rebel minié balls in him, he had been a reed blowing in the wind, allowing events to take him where they would. With only a vague purpose motivated by the desire to put the war years behind him, he had wandered to California. Then he had drifted back to Baltimore. He had not chosen to work in Washington—at least not after careful consideration and comparison of all alternative possibilities. He had let the winds of chance and association blow him into the offices of Schuyler Colfax. He had condemned the wasteful and larcenous practices of the builders of the railroad, but his efforts to expose them had been the actions of a man merely going through the motions. And he had wasted a lot of time waiting for Colfax to do something.

He would wait no longer. His resolve was strengthened by the ache in his head and the vivid image of his own body crushed under tons of falling rock or lying on the floor of George Train's private car with blood oozing from a head wound.

It was time to fight.

CHAPTER 17

The trip eastward was an uneasy one for Philip. It was an odd feeling to have been targeted for death. Of course, during the war men had killed other men; but even though hundreds of thousands of rebs would have done him bodily harm had they been offered the opportunity in battle, not one of them had been told, "Kill Philip Trent." When Ewell Sullivan had set off the charges that sent half a mountainside tumbling down toward George Train and Philip, the Irishman had undoubtedly been acting on specific orders to murder the investigator . . . and not even in the name of some lofty cause—as in the war—but for pure and simple personal gain.

George Train traveled east with Philip, though his private car was left in North Platte, Nebraska. The yard there was given instructions to repair the smoke and fire damage, to replace the paneling and ceiling, both of which had been punctured by Cheyenne arrows and bullets, and to clean away every trace of Ewell Sullivan's blood.

When Philip and Train reached Omaha, they parted company.

"I don't think I have to tell you to be careful," Train said.

Philip patted his side, where he carried the pistol in his waistband. "You, too, George," he said. "Some of the people you work for play rough."

"I'll keep my head down," Train replied. "And I'll be

waiting to see what comes next." They shook hands warmly, and then Train walked away.

A moment later he stopped and turned around. Philip was standing with one hand in his pocket, watching a locomotive puff its way toward the station. Train had noted a new sense of purpose in Trent since the incident in his private car.

"Philip, my friend," he said under his breath, "I wish you well. I just hope they don't chew you up and spit you out."

For once in his life Philip had had enough of trains. He did not engage in sightseeing on the trip from Chicago to Washington and made no effort to examine the yards and facilities at the various stops. He arrived in Washington just before dark, tired, grimy and red-eyed, reeking of soot and coal smoke. After hailing a cab, he went directly to see Leah, whom he had not heard from for too long a time. He knocked on the apartment door and heard heavy footsteps from inside. When the door opened, he was looking into the face of Lloyd Miles.

"Hello, Lloyd," Philip said.

Miles's face was stony. "You're back."

"I know I'm a mess," Philip apologized, looking down at himself and brushing off his pants, "but I want to see her, just for a few minutes, before I go home and clean up."

"My sister is not at home to callers," Miles stated.

For a moment the words did not penetrate Philip's exhaustion. He opened his mouth and managed to say, "What? What do you mean?"

"Trent, I believe we share a common language, but if you don't understand me, perhaps you will be able to comprehend this." He handed Philip a sealed letter and abruptly closed the door.

Philip looked at the envelope in his hand as if it had fangs. On it was his full name, written in large letters. It was Leah's handwriting. He opened the letter, and as he scanned her words quickly, he felt icy needles of pain. He reread them, unwilling to believe his own eyes.

My Dear Philip,

For some reason known only to God, or perhaps to the demons that have tormented me into making this decision, you have seen fit to place yourself in antagonistic opposition to the aims of my brother and the host of loyal Americans who believe in the transcontinental railroad. And yet it is not that, not your attempts to abort construction of the railroad, that prompts me to write this letter to you.

I could not live with the two men in my life at odds with each other, and if it becomes a question of loyalties, I find that I must choose my blood kin, the man who has been more than a brother to me.

Knowing you, Philip, I am certain you will want to discuss the matter, but I assure you that such a course would be unproductive and painful for both of us. So with this I bid you best wishes. If you can bring yourself to do me one last kindness, let it be the consideration of my wish that you do not contact me further.

The letter was signed with her full name. The words carried such a sense of finality that Philip was stunned. He raised his hand to knock on the door, then reconsidered. Exhausted as he was, he was in no condition to think clearly, and now anger was building in him. He knew that if he knocked and Lloyd Miles opened the door again, violence could very well result. He would not be able to hold himself back, and fisticuffs with Leah's brother would do nothing but complicate the situation.

Downstairs, Philip found another cab and instructed the driver to take him to his apartment. It was growing dark when he reached his building. The spring evening was made fragrant by blooming flowers in the gardens along the street, and the air was soft and pleasantly warm; but the beauty of it was lost on him as he carried his luggage up the stairs and put the key in the lock to enter his apartment.

The stench of cigar smoke drove the fuzziness of exhaustion out of his brain. Someone was in the dark room, but if that someone had intended him harm, he reasoned, it would already have happened. Philip put down his bag, walked calmly to a table, and lit a lamp, which he lifted as he turned.

"Evenin', Captain," Victor Flanagan said. He had made himself quite comfortable.

"You son of a bitch," Philip growled. "What are you doing here?"

"Now, Captain, you wouldn't have wanted me to wait for you outside in the dampness of evening, would you?"

"All right, Flanagan, what do you want?" Philip said. "I've been traveling for over a week. I'm dirty, and I'm tired."

"Won't take much of your time, Captain," Flanagan said, removing the cigar from his thin lips. "I came for the information you picked up out west."

"The hell you say." Philip sat down and stared at the stocky man. He had determined that he was going to fight, that he was actively going to seek the identity of the man or men who had given Ewell Sullivan orders to kill him. But he was extremely reluctant to work with the likes of Victor Flanagan and his associates—partly because he found the man so loathsome. For a split second he wondered if by rejecting the association with the group represented by Flanagan, Butler, and Edwards, he was losing possible allies.

"I don't mean that you have to give me the originals," Flanagan explained. "Just brief me on the important points of what you found."

Apparently Flanagan knew nothing of the fire in George Train's car that had destroyed all of the evidence. "Sergeant Flanagan," Philip said evenly, "the first man who will see my notes is Congressman J. T. Moverly."

The sergeant stood and leaned over to put his face inches away from Philip's. "You're refusing to cooperate?"

Flanagan had been eating onions, Philip discovered. "I have refused only to give to you any information that is the property of the Moverly committee."

"Well, now, maybe I'll just take what I want," he said.

Philip moved quickly, drawing his pistol from the waistband of his trousers. "Don't try it," he warned. He put the muzzle on Flanagan's nose, and the big man tensed. "Now back off."

Flanagan retreated slowly. Philip rose, moving far enough from Flanagan to discourage any attempt to disarm him.

"You wouldn't shoot me," Flanagan said, leaning forward.

"Don't bet your life on it." The sound of Philip's voice caused Flanagan to step back. Philip motioned with the barrel of the .44 toward the door and said, "Out."

"They're not going to like this," Flanagan warned, but he was moving toward the door.

"Flanagan, you may tell General Butler that I would be interested in having a talk with him."

"The general has to be careful. After all, he's a member of Congress."

"I'm impressed," Philip uttered with sarcasm. "Just tell him what I said."

When Flanagan was gone, Philip bolted the door and put the pistol down on a table. He didn't want to have to think about Flanagan and the men he represented, not at that moment. His first concern was the reason for Leah's letter. Obviously, someone—Miles—had misinformed her. He was not opposed to the construction of the transcontinental railroad. He was not at odds with Lloyd Miles, not so far as he knew. But, as he thought about it, he felt a sinking sensation in the pit of his stomach. Miles had always been extremely sensitive to slights. Had his refusal to join Miles's little club caused such enmity? No. The reason had to go deeper than Miles's sensitivity to disapproval.

Once he was bathed and in bed, the same tired thoughts kept going in circles in Philip's brain until he fell asleep.

He was awakened at daylight by a banging on his door. He checked his clock; it was just past dawn, much too early for visitors. He pulled on a robe, opened the door, and took a note from a uniformed messenger. It was from Archibald Edwards: *Imperative that you stop by my office first thing this morning. I will be there from seven A.M.*

It was seven-thirty when Philip arrived at the Colfax offices. The outer door was open, though the office workers had not yet arrived. He walked through the reception area into the corridor, then stopped in front of the open door to Edwards's office.

"Come in," Edwards called. A flickering gas lamp cast shadows on his face, giving it a sinister look. "First of all, Philip, I want to apologize for Victor Flanagan's behavior. He had no business entering your apartment without your permission."

Philip nodded and waited for Edwards to continue.

"Sergeant Flanagan is a man eager to perform his duty," Edwards said, motioning to Philip to sit down. "A good man, but perhaps too willing to overstep his authority." He leaned forward. "It was not, however, just a whim of the sergeant's that placed him in your apartment, Philip. He had been instructed to request a summary of your findings to be passed along to me, and then to others."

"As I told Flanagan," Philip said, "the information I have gathered is the property of Mr. Moverly's committee."

Edwards shook his head sadly. "I had thought, Philip, that you agreed to work with us."

Philip remained silent.

"I admire your integrity, of course. But you don't understand how things work in this town. You are placing your loyalty with a man who will be gone from Washington with the next election, possibly even sooner if his health continues to deteriorate."

"I believe he'll last out his term."

"Perhaps," Edwards allowed, "but you had the right idea in the first place, my boy, to hitch your wagon to a rising star. It was the Speaker's intention that you were merely, as the army says, on detached service with the Moverly committee. Shouldn't your primary loyalty be to Schuyler Colfax?"

"Mr. Edwards," Philip said, "it's been months now since I put my first report in your hands to be delivered to the Speaker. In those months the artificially high cost of building the railroad has continued to cheat the government and the citizens of this country."

"Ah, well, still the young idealist," Edwards said. His

voice hardened. "Let's cut the horse manure, Trent. You were not all that damned idealistic when you murdered two Colombian nationals in the town of Barbacoas in Panama in 1865."

Philip had to exercise iron control to keep from showing his surprise. Edwards lifted a sheaf of papers from his desk. "Here in my hand is a copy of an official request from the Colombian government for the extradition of one Philip Trent. If complied with, this order will send you back to Panama to stand trial for murder. Of course, if you are a true idealist, you might be eager to prove your innocence."

"Edwards, you can take your extradition order and go to hell," Philip grated, standing. "Or perhaps you'd like to explain why a rather large sum of money delivered directly into the hands of the Speaker of the House by a principal of the Central Pacific Railroad did not appear on the party's campaign contribution books."

Edwards laughed indulgently. "Oh, come now. I deny your allegation, of course, but even if it were true and this office had accepted money without notation in the ledger, how difficult would it be for me to go back to the books and ink in the contribution on the proper date?" He pointed to Philip's case. "Do you have your report in there?"

"What is in my case is my business," Philip said, turning away.

"Trent," Edwards called out, "I'm going to give you a day or so to reconsider."

"Thank you very much," Philip said under his breath.

He felt uneasy as he left the Colfax suite. He was not surprised to learn that the Colombian government wanted him returned to Panama to stand trial for the killing of the two men in Barbacoas. Nor was it remarkable that a man in Edwards's position as chief of staff to the most powerful man in the House of Representatives had obtained documents pertaining to the extradition request. What had surprised him was the threat from Edwards and the apparent malice with which the threat was voiced.

It was not the possibility of being extradited to Panama that concerned him the most at the moment. What made him very nervous was the intensity of Edwards's desire to see the information that he'd brought back from the West. Philip was merely an ex–army captain. In the Washington arena he had no personal clout. His only power was derived from his position with Moverly's committee, and as Edwards had pointed out, Moverly was a lame-duck congressman. What influence the congressman held was fading with each day that brought the elections of 1868 nearer.

And Gus? His father wielded a certain amount of clout, but he was, after all, a state, not federal, representative. Men like Schuyler Colfax would call Gus Trent a party hack, damning him with the faint praise of being a good fund-raiser.

There was a messenger service in the building where Colfax kept his offices. Feeling just a bit silly—after all, it was broad daylight on a pleasant spring day in the nation's capital—Philip removed the notes that George Train and he had reconstructed, placed them in a large envelope, and sent them by messenger to the office of the Moverly committee. His case was not much lighter, for the sheaf of notes was pitifully thin, not a worthy showing for his months in the West.

He decided to walk to Moverly's office. The day promised to be pleasantly mild and warm with plentiful sun, and he had some thinking to do. A few early-bird sightseers strolled in front of the White House. Government clerks hurrying to work dodged in and out among delivery drays, carriages, and smartly moving surreys on the busy street; but when Philip turned off Pennsylvania Avenue onto a side street, he found the road empty. It was as if he'd entered another world. He felt grateful for the lack of distractions.

He reviewed again the scene with Flanagan in his apartment, and then the interview with Edwards. Flanagan and Edwards were supposedly on the side of the angels, his allies, but neither of them had acted the part in the latest encounters. If anything, Edwards had conducted himself as if he were a dangerous enemy, threatening him and oddly intent on knowing what Philip had in his case. If there had ever been any real possibility that Philip would have cooperated with them and given them information, that possibility was now gone forever. Perhaps, Philip mused, it was for the best. Edwards's actions had served to warn him not to trust anyone and to be on his guard at all times. The chief of staff's words also made him wonder anew about the purity—or lack of it—of the Speaker of the House.

Most of the houses that lined the residential street were still closed up for the night, with shades and drapery tightly drawn. Philip's mind wandered away from the enigma of Edwards's motivation as he imagined the families inside the houses, man and wife still asleep, perhaps touching, warm and secure. Such thoughts, of course, put Leah's face before him, and an intense loneliness enveloped him.

Since it was still quite early, he walked at a leisurely pace, preoccupied with speculation as to Leah's state of mind when she had written the letter telling him that it was all over between them. He was altogether unwilling to accept that letter as final. He knew that he would fret his way through the day, waiting impatiently for a chance to go to her, to ask her face to face how she could possibly believe that differences between Miles and him could affect the love they had for each other.

Hearing the sound of brisk footsteps behind him, Philip turned his head to see two men in work clothing walking up the street, lunch pails in hand, hats pushed back, and hobnailed boots ringing out on the pavement. They laughed and talked in the manner of old friends. He smiled to himself and remembered nostalgically how it had once been the same for Lloyd and him. When the tread of their boots apprised him that they were overtaking him, he slowed, and the men split up and started to pass him on either side.

"Morning," he said.

"And to you, sir," one of the men said, smiling and touching the visor of his hat.

When they were three or four steps ahead of him, they drew together again. One was a large man, the other weedy and frail looking; both of them were quite ordinary of face.

Philip lagged a bit to let them get well ahead, hoping to

regain the privacy he'd been enjoying before the two men overtook him.

Stopping as one, they suddenly turned to face him. Philip felt their threat.

"I'll take that," the large man said, lunging for Philip's case.

But Philip was too fast for the big man. He jerked the case out of reach and danced away. The thin man moved swiftly to block him.

When the big man moved toward him, Philip caught him coming in with a left to the chin. He saw movement from his left side, ducked, and took a heavy blow on the back of his neck from the thin man's lunch box. Philip, stunned, saw the big man looming over him, and in his large, upraised hand was a leather-covered billy club. The moment stretched out in time as Philip tried desperately to pick up his case to block the blow that was coming inexorably toward his head. But he could not move swiftly enough.

The lead-filled billy connected almost gently with Philip's skull, just behind the left ear. Fortunately for him the big man was not a killer. . . .

He raised his head. His left cheek was pressed against a smooth cobblestone in the pavement. A rumbling sound came to him from what seemed to be stellar distances, and trying to lift his torso, he fell back. Flashes of white appeared before his eyes, blurring his vision. He could see the texture and color of a cobblestone that protruded above the others near his face.

His head hurt dreadfully. He could not organize his thoughts enough to understand why he was lying in the middle of the street, his cheek pressed onto the stones. He could not understand why the rumbling sound in his head seemed to be getting closer.

When, at last, he was able to lift his head again, he saw elongated legs and iron-rimmed wheels. He scrambled to his hands and knees. To his distorted vision it seemed that a milk wagon was about to run him down. The horses appeared to tower over him. He cried out but heard only a strangled moan, and then he felt hands on his shoulders and heard someone say, "Are you drunk, mister?"

Philip looked up into the concerned face of a boy in his teens.

"Not . . . drunk," he managed to grunt.

"Hey, you're all bloody!"

He heard running feet and the shrill sound of a police whistle. And then there was only blackness.

A cadaverous-looking man in a wrinkled black suit stood beside the hospital bed. "Mr. Trent, I'm Lieutenant Tom Jensen, Washington Police. How do you feel?"

"I see two of you," Philip said. He had been surprised to find himself in a strange room when he regained consciousness, and it had taken him some time to get his bearings.

The lieutenant chuckled. "Aside from that?"

"Headache."

"It's no picnic, being hit on the head," Jensen said. "Happened to me once in the war. Tree limb fell on me during an artillery duel. I had a headache for a week."

"You're a regular little bundle of cheer," Philip said.

Jensen laughed. "Well, if you've still got your sense of humor, you're going to live." He cleared his throat. "Wanta tell me what happened, Mr. Trent?"

"Two men tried to rob me. One of them must have turned and hit me in the head after they had passed me. They wanted my case. That's all I know. I understand that a milk-wagon driver called for help when he found me bleeding in the street."

"Did they demand money?" Jensen had pulled out a pad and pencil and was taking notes.

"No, just the case."

"What was in the case?"

Philip shook his head and sighed. "Nothing, it was empty."

"Empty?"

"They were after something I'd sent on by messenger."

"Ah," Jensen said. "And what was that something?"

"Papers that were the property of the Moverly investigating committee."

"Ah."

"I don't suppose the two men were apprehended."

"No. We were hoping, Mr. Trent, that you might give us some positive identification of the culprits."

"Didn't look at them that closely," Philip explained. "Just two men on the street—working types, work clothing. Clean. Blue cloth caps." He paused. "I couldn't even begin to describe their faces. One was a large man, my height, and muscular. The other was shorter and thin. That's it, I'm afraid."

Jensen sighed. "Not much to go on, Mr. Trent. But you believe they were after something specific, not just money?"

"That would be my guess."

"They ripped the lining out of your case and emptied your pockets but left your wallet with your identification lying on the street. How much money were you carrying, incidentally?"

"Oh, no more than ten dollars. I can't say exactly. One five-dollar bill, a couple of ones, a silver dollar. Probably some change."

"Would you examine your personal possessions for me, please?"

Philip looked over at the small table next to his bed where his clothes were folded.

"Anything else missing?"

"No, not that I can remember."

Jensen sighed again. "Well, Mr. Trent, if anything more occurs to you about your attackers, you know where to find me. And if anything turns up, I'll be in touch."

"I don't expect it will," Philip said.

"To be truthful, I think you're right," the policeman said. "Your description of the men who robbed you would fit a thousand workers in our fair city."

Philip spent the night in the hospital and left the next day at midmorning against the advice of the doctor who had treated him. He took a cab to the Miles apartment.

* * *

Leah answered the knock. Her face went pale when she saw Philip standing in the doorway. When her eyes darted to the bandage on his head, her hand went to her mouth.

"Hello, Leah," he said, pushing into the room without waiting for an invitation. "I must talk with you."

She turned away, her heart pounding, for the sight of Philip's bandaged head had given her a start, generating a quick concern for him that was almost painful in its intensity. She knew that she was vulnerable at that moment, so she walked away from him into the sitting room, hoping to give herself time to regain her composure. She had known that this moment would come sooner or later, and she had steeled herself against it, only to have her defenses penetrated by the sudden shock of seeing that he had been injured.

"Leah, whatever it is that is bothering Lloyd can be resolved," he said. "Good Lord, if he was so upset by my declining to join his little investment group—"

"Little?" she asked, for his denigrating tone when speaking of the Breakfast Club seemed to indicate that Lloyd had been correct in calling Philip a snob.

He held up a hand. "A figure of speech. Small in number. If that's the reason—"

"I don't care to discuss this, Philip. I thought I had made myself clear in my letter to you."

"It was your handwriting," he said, his gray eyes gazing at her intently, "but not the voice of my Leah."

"Nevertheless," she said after taking a deep breath, "you must accept it." She could not have believed that she could suffer so much agony and continue to live. The pained expression on his face, the pleading way that he was looking at her, cut through her resolve like freshly stropped razors. "There is nothing left for us, Philip."

"I hear your words, but I also see your eyes," he said. "Your eyes are calling you a liar."

"I fear that you imagine things, Mr. Trent."

"Leah, we set a date."

"And you seemed to think that it was not important to keep that date," she flared, the hurt swelling up in her.

"I thought you understood the importance of the work I was doing."

"Oh, I did, thoroughly. I understand that you were trying to prove that my brother's employers were criminals and thus, by association, that my brother was a man without morals."

"You know me better than that, Leah."

His impatient tone gave her the strength she needed. "Do I? Perhaps you have me mixed up with another woman, a woman with blond hair."

"I don't know what you're talking about," he said.

She made a wry face. It was too belittling to continue in that vein. "I asked you, Philip, not to initiate this uncomfortable scene. Your total disregard of my wishes is, to me, simply another indication of your character. There is nothing to be gained by continuing this confrontation."

She walked past him to the front door and opened it. "Good-bye."

He did not move at first, and Leah began to panic, wondering just what she would do if he refused to leave. But then his back seemed to stiffen, and he walked to the door.

"Yes," he said, "I'll go. I'll go when I hear from these lips" —he touched her full lips with the tip of his forefinger— "that you no longer love me."

She felt her face flush. The realization of what would happen if she spoke sent visions of the future flashing through her mind: She was sitting alone and lonely in front of the fire . . . knitting, mending, cooking meals for Lloyd. . . . Lloyd himself had said that he would find the right woman someday and get married. Would she live with Lloyd and his bride? *Spinster.* For there was in her the sure knowledge that she would never love again and, therefore, never accept another man into her arms.

The force of old hurt, of Philip's pretended ignorance of the blond woman, and of her duty to her brother gave her the momentary strength to say, "If that will satisfy you, then I say it. I don't love you, Philip. I don't think I ever did, really."

She steeled herself against the shock in his face. "Leah—" Then he sagged and walked, resigned, into the hallway.

"Good-bye, Mr. Trent," she said, closing the door.

If Philip could have seen through the solid oak, if he could have heard the agony she underwent trying to hold back her scream of despair, her sobs, he would have known the truth. For she closed the door by leaning against it, the strength gone from her limbs. And as the finality of it penetrated and her throat ached from the sobs that shook her body, she sank helplessly to the floor, to huddle there in abject misery.

Philip stood head down, fighting the childish urge to weep. He lifted his chin, forced his mouth into firm lines, and turned from her door. He did not understand her behavior, and he was sure that he'd never understand it; but she'd made her position clear. She had made the choice. The one woman that he'd ever truly loved, the woman he'd chosen to be his wife and the mother of his children, had turned him out with cold, steel-hard words. And it was the last that hurt most. *I don't think I ever did, really.*

Three days later, with only a scabbed wound under his ear to remind him of his encounter on the side street, Philip sat before J. T. Moverly's committee and spoke of his investigations of the Union Pacific, his findings, and how all physical evidence had been deliberately destroyed. He did not mention George Train's name.

Congressman John O'Brian was interested in the shooting of the man who had burned Philip's papers. "You have neglected to tell us who came to your assistance, Captain Trent."

"Yes, sir, I have done so on purpose," Philip replied. "The man who came to my aid is a loyal employee of the Union Pacific Railroad. He is vitally interested in seeing the railroad completed, even though he would like to see the graft and waste eliminated. I promised him that his name would not be linked with this congressional investigation."

"I'm sure he's an exemplary fellow," O'Brian remarked, "and a quick hand with a pistol. He didn't hesitate to kill this

Ewell Sullivan. But I wonder, Captain Trent, why he wasn't called upon to make a statement, at least to go through the motions of proving that his shooting of this man was justified."

"Mr. O'Brian," Philip said, "one reason I included that incident in my recitation of events was to show this committee just how all-powerful the Union Pacific is along its right-of-way. The Union Pacific is the law once one passes Omaha. Ewell Sullivan was buried by U.P. employees on U.P. land. Those who were killed in the cleanup of Hell-on-Wheels were buried the same way. The attempt to kill me and my friend occurred on U.P. property, and the only investigation of any of those events was made by U.P. personnel."

"Be that as it may," said Congressman Oakes Ames, millionaire, politician, and railroad man, "you're asking us to believe that you and this man who so quickly murdered Ewell Sullivan—"

"It wasn't murder, Congressman," Philip said heatedly.

"Please do not interrupt," Ames said harshly. "You're asking us to take your word, supported only by hearsay from a man whose name you will not reveal, that the builders of the Union Pacific are blackguards, thieves, defrauders, and murderers."

"Those are your words, Mr. Ames," Philip said, "not mine."

Ames lifted his head and looked toward the ceiling. "Gentlemen," he said, "isn't this a waste of time?"

"Mr. Ames," Moverly broke in, "I dispute your attack on the integrity of Mr. Trent. I assure you that I have the greatest confidence in this young man, and—"

"Granted, Mr. Moverly," Ames said. "I do not overlook the fact that Mr. Trent is the holder of the Congressional Medal of Honor. I point out only that the so-called evidence he has presented here, in the form of handwritten notes purportedly taken from conveniently lost documents, would not hold up in a court of law."

"This is not a court of law," Moverly said.

"But, my dear sir," Ames thundered, "as long as I am a member of Congress, neither this committee nor any other will be used to blacken the names of great Americans without solid proof! Some members of this committee might not be dedicated to justice, but I assure you that I am."

"I myself wonder," said John O'Brian, "just what private grudge this young man might hold against the Union Pacific Railroad, or perhaps the transcontinental as a dual entity, since he once was in the employ of the Central Pacific and left, according to Mr. Leland Stanford himself, without a great feeling of loss on the part of the railroad." He coughed as a cacophony of voices rose throughout the room at his revelation. "That last is a paraphrasing of Mr. Stanford's words to lessen the severity of his comment to me regarding Mr. Trent."

"Gentlemen," Moverly said, pounding his gavel, "this hearing is not concerned with Mr. Trent's past employment."

"Mr. Chairman," Oakes Ames boomed, "in view of the very doubtful worth of the testimony of this otherwise admirable young man, I move that this investigation be terminated."

"I second that motion," John O'Brian called out.

"You are out of order!" Moverly shouted, pounding the gavel. "Only the chairman of this committee can decide when the committee's investigation is completed."

"I move, Mr. Chairman," Ames said with a sardonic grin, "that in that event I be excused from further futile hours on this witch-hunt. I will leave any forthcoming disclosures of unsubstantiated testimony to you, Mr. Chairman." And with that he rose and stalked out of the hearing room, followed by John O'Brian and two other "railroad" congressmen.

"Mr. Trent," Moverly said, "if you'll be so kind as to leave your notes with the committee council . . ."

"Yes, sir."

"This committee stands in adjournment until further notice," Moverly said, with one final bang of his gavel.

CHAPTER 18

In the dog days of August, President Andrew Johnson asked Secretary of War Edwin Stanton for his resignation. To those who were aware of the intense animosity between the two men, Johnson's action came as an anticlimax, for it had long been expected.

Lafe Baker experienced mixed emotions as he read the news of Stanton's apparent defeat. It was ironic justice for Stanton to be treated just as Lafe had by the man in the White House. Lafe realized, however, that he had never quite given up hope that Stanton would remember the unequaled service Lafe had performed for him during the war. The former spy also realized that he had always felt that if worse came to worst, he could go to Stanton for some covert help. Now, with Stanton out, he felt like a picket caught in an open meadow between two advancing armies—exposed on all sides, without official protection and without a powerful friend in Washington. When he read that Stanton had no intention of resigning and was asking for Senate support under the Tenure of Office Act, he felt relief.

Meanwhile, the President had appointed General U. S. Grant to replace Stanton as secretary of war. Congress was in recess and would not reconvene until December.

* * *

J. T. Moverly died at dinnertime on the day of Philip's testimony before the Moverly committee. He went to sleep in his chair while waiting for the meal to be served, and when his wife tried to awaken him, he was gone. He had not called out to her or even moaned.

"A good way to go," Gus Trent said the next day. He had located his son at his temporary office in Moverly's suite. "I'm not being trite, Philip, when I say that J.T.'s death is a loss to our state and to our country."

Philip nodded. "He seemed very tired during the committee hearings."

"Well, the good Lord decided it was time for him to get plenty of rest," Gus observed. "When it comes my time, I could ask no more. A good day's work, a good chair, and then Judgment Day."

"If it's all right with you," Philip said, "I'd like to have you around for a few more years."

"I'll do my best. But it's said that a boy is never truly a man until his father is dead."

Philip grinned and said, "I'll chance it."

He had been gathering his papers and a few personal items from the desk he'd been using since returning from the West. Once everything was in his case, he closed it and looked around. "Well, we didn't accomplish much, Dad. And now that J.T. is dead, I'm not sure quite which way to turn."

"Can't win 'em all."

"I was never even in the running," Philip said. "Oakes Ames and John O'Brian all but called me a liar."

"Congressional privilege, my boy."

Philip led the way to the street. They walked to Gus's favorite restaurant, where they were greeted familiarly and ushered to Gus's usual table. "Better let me treat today, Dad," Philip said after they had ordered, adding, "while I can."

"Do I detect a note of self-pity?"

"Well, I'm not sure I have a job. Since I went to work for the Moverly committee, my salary has come from there."

"You haven't been in touch with Schuyler?"

"Haven't had time, really," Philip explained. "I spent

most of the evening with Mrs. Moverly. Then first thing this morning I helped make the arrangements to send J.T. home for burial." He shrugged. "There's something else I have to do before I concern myself too much about whether or not I have a job."

Gus nodded but did not pry. That "something else" of Philip's sounded as if it was personal, reminding Gus that he hadn't seen Leah on his last two visits and had not even heard his son mention her name.

Over lunch Philip talked about the demise of the Moverly committee and what it meant for him. "I'm not sure I want to go back to the Speaker's office," Philip concluded. "I guess I'm getting tired of yelling fire, only to have the cold water poured on me." He reached across the table and put his hand on his father's arm. "I hope you're going to stay the night."

"No, no. I'm taking the two o'clock train to Annapolis." Gus offered no explanation of why he had to be in Maryland's capital that evening.

"Maybe I'll come up for the weekend," Philip said.

"Always pleased to see you." Gus sipped coffee and decided to forgo being diplomatically silent about Leah. "What's wrong between you and Leah?"

Philip looked away for a moment, then turned back. "Dad, I'm not quite sure."

"Serious, or just a lover's spat?"

Philip hesitated, then seemed relieved to be able to talk about it. "Well, I guess you could call it serious. She won't see me, and she says she never loved me." He tried to smile, but the result didn't fool Gus for a moment. "So no grandchild for a while yet, Dad. Sorry."

Gus, reading between the lines, figured that it was not the proper time to question Philip further. He leaned forward and patted Philip's shoulder. "She's worth fighting for."

"Well, there comes a time when you know that it's futile to fight anymore."

"And that time has come?"

"Yes," Philip answered. "I'd been reluctant to admit that, even to myself." He fell silent, and Gus could see that his son's admission was a heavy weight in his heart.

* * *

That night two meetings—one consisting of the movers and shakers of the Maryland Republican party in Annapolis, the other an encounter between two former friends in Washington—were to affect Philip Trent's life. The preliminaries to the political meeting were already under way when Gus Trent arrived at the governor's mansion. It was the type of meeting that was never called to order, nor were any minutes kept. It was a continuous interaction among the governor, the Republican senator, members of the House of Representatives, a couple of judges, members of the state legislature, and a few of the type of men without whom a political party is unproductive—men with abundant liquid assets and a desire to influence governmental affairs from behind the scenes. When the time came for all the players to congregate in one room, only nineteen men were there; yet they represented the power structure of a sovereign state.

At stake was a seat in the United States House of Representatives, for the purpose of the Annapolis meeting was to name a man to serve out the unexpired term of Congressman J. T. Moverly. The man who was appointed by the governor would have a very good chance of being elected to a full term of his own if he so desired in the fall of 1868. There were, of course, quite a number of worthy men who would welcome the appointment, a plum to be had without having to run for election. Many of them were especially deserving, having served the party well. The battle had raged for some hours, but the issue was still undecided.

There were many considerations. First, the appointee would have to be a credit to the Republican party. Second, he had to be electable, for the last thing the party wheelhorses wanted was a free-for-all scramble for the office in 1868. Hotly contested primaries tended to weaken the party and divide allegiances so that some of the losers, embittered by the fight in the primary, voted against their own party in the general election.

During the one-on-one discussions leading up to the gathering in the smoke-filled room in the governor's mansion, two names had been mentioned most often; both were members of the state legislature, both young men on the rise. One of them was backed by the U.S. senator, the other by the governor. The two names were submitted. The gathering's vote was nine to nine. Gus Trent had sided with the governor's group. The governor, horrified by the deep split among his guests, said, "Gentlemen, you know that as chairman, I have the right to break the tie. But I'm not going to do so at this time. I'm going to call for the servants to bring in some refreshments, and then we'll see if we can't settle this matter in a way that won't leave anybody's feathers ruffled."

After the repast, however, the discussion was still heated. Groups of two to four men left the room in order to make offers and counteroffers in privacy. A second balloting was held and was again a disturbing stalemate. The governor had already let it be known that he intended to run for the U.S. Senate against a war Democrat incumbent, and he needed a united party to back him in the effort. If he voted to break the tie, he would alienate nine very influential men. It was a case of being damned if he voted for his own choice to fill the office, or being doubly damned if, in an effort to compromise, he deserted his own most loyal backers.

The tension in the room was almost as thick as the cigar smoke when Gus Trent rose and walked slowly to a position beside the governor's chair. "Gentlemen," he said, "I was reading a book the other day by a feller named Thomas Hughes. Englishman. Not a bad book, but maybe a little long-winded."

There was dead silence in the room, an indication of the respect that Gus Trent had earned over the years. He was just a state legislator, but he had an enviable knack for winning, which in the end came down to being able to influence people. To a person, the powerful and successful men in the room listened to Gus's every word, for they knew that here was a professional at work before their eyes.

"Among other things," Gus said, smiling, his eyes twinkling, "this Hughes feller says that life isn't all beer and skittles. Now, I had to look up the word to find out that a skittle is some sort of a game. I happened to know what beer was."

There were chuckles.

"So what he was saying, I guess, is that life isn't all pleasing your belly and playing at games, and I told myself, 'Gus, this Englishman has been there and back.' So I kept on reading, and this English feller started talking about compromise."

There was a stir among the listeners. The governor was wondering just what sort of compromise Gus was going to offer.

"The trouble with compromise, says this Thomas Hughes, is that the other feller says that he only wants what is right and fair; but when you get to the bottom of it, what he considers to be right and fair is what *he* wants, and that makes what *you* want wrong and unfair." He paused to take a puff on his cigar. "Now, in this matter before us we have two men put forward to fill an office that will only hold one man, and what would be fair to one group and give it everything it wants would give the other group nothing at all that it wants."

"Gus, if you're offering yourself as a compromise candidate, you've got my vote," said the senator.

"Hear! Hear!" several men agreed.

"Nope, not me," Gus said. "I've got my roots down too deep in Baltimore to leave it. Washington's a fine place to visit, but I wouldn't want to live there a good part of the year. No, I'm going to offer you a compromise that is a true compromise—one that won't give any of you anything that you want."

There was general laughter.

"Both of the candidates you've named for this job are good men. I claim both of them as friends, and I pray that they feel the same about me. So I want it understood that if it didn't mean alienating half the party, I'd vote for either one of them. But since I can't vote for both, I think it might be a good idea for us to think of looking for a new face to send down to Washington. Besides, what with an election every two years for a House member, our two worthy candidates will have other chances to run."

Gus was fully aware that he had now lost both men as friends. That was the trouble with politics sometimes. You had to choose, and sometimes the choice was difficult to make, and quite often in making your choices you made an enemy or, at best, lost a friend.

"Gentlemen," he continued, "there are hundreds of thousands of men in this country who fought a war to preserve our national traditions, and I think it's time we remembered them. I think that it would be not only a fine compromise to keep the Maryland Republican party intact, but excellent politics in general if the governor appointed a representative directly from this group of young war veterans."

"I think I'm about to find out that you have a young veteran in mind, Gus," the governor said.

"I do. He enlisted right after Sumter, and he fought in some of the biggest battles of the war. He is one of the most decorated young officers of the Army of the Republic. Among the awards he holds is the Congressional Medal of Honor. He's a loyal Republican. He is able, conscientious, and when he runs for a full term in sixty-eight, he'll be a very good representative of the party."

"Sounds so good, it might be the Second Coming," someone said. "What's his name, Gus?"

"I'm getting to that." Gus waved his hand. "First, I have this to say. I've been sitting in the state legislature for twenty-two years. I have delivered my home precincts in Baltimore in every election since 1850, and I've helped raise money for the campaigns of every man jack of you that holds elective office. Now, I'm going to put this appointment on a very personal level, my friends. I'm going to call in my markers, as the gamblers say. I'm going to tell you that Gus Trent *wants* this man to be in the House of Representatives. But just so I won't be misunderstood, let me state positively that I am making no threats if you say you don't give a damn what Gus Trent wants. I'm just telling you that I'm asking you for this. I'm good for just a couple of things, and working for the party is one of 'em, so nothing will change there if you vote against me. I'll still do my job and work for the party and deliver my precincts. It might just happen, though, that my *personal* feelings toward you might not be the same."

Gus glanced at the governor and saw that his old friend

was astonished. Gus could not blame him; he was in the process of using up a lot of political capital, assets built up over decades of dedication to the party. He'd given a diplomatically worded ultimatum to each man in the room, and men don't like to be cornered and given no choice, not even by an old friend. But Gus knew that he would get what he wanted. The governor and every other man in the room knew in advance that whatever name Gus Trent spoke would be the name of the next congressman from Maryland. But he was well aware that what he had just said was a two-edged sword. Personal feelings toward him would be different too.

"I am asking you to give your backing to Philip Trent, my son, as the appointee to serve out the term of our late friend, J. T. Moverly. Call it nepotism if you must, but that's what I'm asking."

The room was silent for several seconds as Gus's words took root. The senator broke the stillness by saying, "Gus, even though I don't know whether this young man could win an election, you have my backing."

There was a tone of resignation in the senator's voice, a tone that told Gus it would be a long time before he would be able to call on the senator for another favor.

"Well, gentlemen?" the governor asked. He stood and puffed on the cigar. "I've known Gus Trent for thirty years, and I've never seen him be wrong about the potential of a candidate yet." He grinned wryly. "But to name his own son—" He patted Gus on the back. "Maybe our old friend is going senile at an early age."

"Move that we request the governor to appoint Philip Trent," one of Gus's very good friends said into the laughter that followed the governor's tension-relieving facetiousness.

The motion was seconded. So well had Gus Trent served the party in Maryland, so much was he owed, that the motion passed unanimously.

The evening that the men in Annapolis were determining Philip Trent's fate was a pleasant one in Washington. The heat of summer had abated after a late afternoon shower, leaving the streets washed clean. Philip arrived at the door to the Miles apartment shortly after dark. It was Lloyd who opened the door.

"I want to talk with Leah," Philip requested.

"Sorry. She isn't in," Miles answered.

Philip stepped forward an inch. "I'll wait."

Miles shrugged. "Come in, by all means."

Surprised, Philip followed him to the sitting room and accepted a brandy.

"I saw you in action at the committee hearing," Miles remarked.

"Did you?"

"Impressive performance, Phil, but futile, wouldn't you say?"

"The committee will continue the investigation."

"Under John O'Brian?" Miles asked, smirking.

Philip shrugged.

"Trent, you're so damned naive about what makes the wheels turn in this country that you're dangerous. Idealism without common sense is a peril. There never was a chance that you'd halt or even seriously slow the completion of the transcontinental railroad. Thank God, the men who hold office in the country are realists, not starry-eyed dreamers."

"If I was never a threat to the Union Pacific," Philip asked, "why were attempts made on my life?"

Lloyd Miles appeared to be startled. "Nonsense," he blustered.

"If what I had learned was so unimportant, why was I attacked by thugs right here in Washington in an effort to prevent that information from reaching the committee?"

"You do have a vivid imagination," Miles said. "I was telling Leah just the other night that you are an inventive fellow."

"If thinking that murder is not permissible business practice, not even for men involved in the admittedly worthy cause of building a transcontinental railroad, then I admit to being both naive and inventive," Philip said. "Speaking of Leah, I have no idea what you've told her, Lloyd. I don't understand the enmity you have developed for me. I understand her even less, I must admit."

Anger was simmering just below the surface in both of them.

"Nothing to understand, old boy," Miles said. "She's simply seen the light, that's all."

"With your help."

Miles shrugged. "I would say that if you're too good to be associated with me, Trent, then you'd be lowering yourself to marry my sister. Wouldn't you say that?"

"Yes, I guess I would." Philip knew when he said it that it was juvenile, an unreasoned reaction to Miles's prodding. He had come to fight for Leah, to make one more attempt to penetrate the barriers she'd thrown up between them, and instead he'd let himself be goaded into anger by her brother. Now the situation was lost beyond retrieval. He got up and showed himself out.

Leah had been listening from her bedroom, twisting Philip's engagement ring on her finger. She rose from her slipper chair and started to run after him, but she knew that she would have to face Lloyd in the sitting room. She heard the front door slam behind Philip. There was a feeling of finality in the sound.

Lloyd Miles was a troubled man. Since his talk with Philip, he had been going over and over the events of the past few months. He had heard that there'd been a near-fatal blasting accident involving Philip, but the Union Pacific's publicity man, George Train, had also been endangered. Given that no one had any reason to try to kill Train, Lloyd decided the incident had to have been an accident. He had also read about the Indian attacks that had enlivened Philip's trip to the railhead, and he had noted that a railroad foreman named Ewell Sullivan had died fighting the Cheyenne. This had worried Lloyd—for Sullivan was the man to whom he'd sent orders to steal or destroy any papers that Philip was trying to take back to Washington.

The time between reading about Sullivan's death and the onset of the Moverly committee hearings had been tense for Lloyd, for he had not known whether Sullivan had accomplished what he'd been ordered to do. Lloyd could not breathe easy until after he attended the committee hearing, where Ames and O'Brian so successfully discredited Philip's unsubstantiated testimony. He knew nothing about attempts on Philip's life, nor of the attack on Philip in Washington.

Thomas Durant had been in New York for a few weeks. Upon Durant's return to Washington, Lloyd went to his employer's office immediately. Durant made a few comments on his trip to New York and asked a few questions. With small matters attended to, he sat down, crossed his legs, and called on a secretary to provide coffee for two.

"I haven't had an opportunity to commend you for handling the Philip Trent matter out west," Durant said.

"Thank you, sir. Too bad that the Indians killed our man."

"Worse if they'd killed him before he burned the papers," Durant said.

"True," Lloyd agreed. "I do have a question."

"Yes?"

"Trent swears that there have been attempts to kill him."

"Not by me," Durant said quickly, spreading his hands and smiling. "If you so ordered, I don't want to know."

"I did not."

Durant's wide-set eyes peered intently at Lloyd. "Trent told you that someone had tried to kill him?"

"Yes."

"If I were you, I'd put no credence in the claims of a loser," Durant said. He was silent for several seconds, and Lloyd had the distinct impression that Durant was sizing him up. "By the way, Miles, we're going to miss you around here."

Lloyd Miles stiffened. He'd seen Durant slip the knife into unsuspecting people before. It would be just like him to praise Lloyd highly and then tell him that he was no longer needed. Lloyd began to fidget in his chair.

"I'm lending you to the Washington office of Crédit Mobilier," Durant announced. "You'll be number two to Oliver Ames—or possibly number three, since Oakes takes a hand in things now and again. It's at the request of Oliver."

Lloyd felt a flood of relief wash over him. "He asked for me?"

"Not by name," Durant said. "He described the qualifications he wanted in an assistant, and they fit you quite well."

"Dr. Durant, I'm perfectly happy—"

"You'll be happier at Crédit Mobilier," Durant said. "And I'll have a loyal representative inside the company who can keep me up-to-date on what the Ames brothers are going to do next. There'll be a sizable increase in salary, of course, and you'll have a good opportunity to learn the financial end of the railroad business."

Lloyd Miles had several days in which to conclude his affairs at the Union Pacific office. He had the actual work done on the first day, and he used part of the remaining time to touch base with the members of his Breakfast Club. Harold Berman was extremely optimistic for Lloyd, since Crédit Mobilier was the most profitable corporation in operation.

"You'll have stock options, no doubt," Berman said. "I'm sure you'll take advantage of them."

Lloyd laughed. "The problem is that I won't be offered stocks at the low price paid by a few of the honorables on Capitol Hill. There's a good-sized raise in pay with the new job, though. I should be able to seize any opportunity that comes my way."

"Well, old friend," Berman said, "if, as it's beginning to look, you are the first to achieve a goal we all share, I do hope that you remember us."

"Now you're putting me on, Harold," Lloyd said affably. "The man who can jump into Jay Gould's hip pocket is probably going to be the first one to make a million."

Berman grinned and crossed his fingers. "As a matter of fact, there've been some distant rumblings of something big in the works for some time now."

"So, remember *your* old friends when things begin to get exciting," Lloyd said. He liked Berman, perhaps better than either of the other two members of his group, and he wished him well. When it came right down to it, though, he hoped that Berman was right—that the advance in his situation, his move to Crédit Mobilier, would put him ahead of the others.

"Harold, I'm going to need an assistant with me at Crédit Mobilier, sort of a right-hand man."

"Anyone particular in mind?"

"I was thinking of Paul Jennings."

Berman considered the idea. "Well, Paul hasn't seemed to feel too secure lately. He calls himself Andrew Carnegie's forgotten man in Washington. And I know for a fact that his bonus arrangements have deteriorated. He just might be interested. You can tell him that I think it would be a good move for him, unless he's gotten things straightened out with the Carnegie organization."

"Thanks, Harold, I appreciate it," Lloyd said.

Lloyd Miles found Jennings alone in the Carnegie office near the Treasury Building. To his surprise, his friend was less than enthusiastic about the offer.

"Lloyd, Crédit Mobilier is nothing more than a creation of the Union Pacific Railroad. It might be the hottest thing going right now, but what will happen to it once the railroad is finished?"

"It's what we can accomplish before the railroad is finished that will count," Lloyd explained. "I'm going to be assistant to Oliver Ames. The job comes with stock options, and I know that there's going to be a huge dividend payment sometime during this calendar year."

"I don't see where that will do me too much good," Jennings said. "The stock you sold the Breakfast Club is still under your control, and you will get half the dividends. Let me think this over for a few days, Lloyd."

Besides Paul there was one other person whom Miles wanted with him at Crédit Mobilier: Rosanna Pulliam. Lloyd led a busy life, and he had not taken time to make any arrangements for his private pursuits other than the time he stole with Rosanna . . . and her new position with Huntington often made her unavailable. While it was true that to date she had not learned anything of any significance either to him or to the Union Pacific, as Huntington's mistress she was indeed in a position to glean valuable information. A man was often quite informative in his conversation under such relaxed circumstances. But she was to prove no more enthusiastic about the offer than Jennings had been.

"You know, darling, that I'd like nothing better than to be able to spend more time with you," Rosanna Pulliam told Lloyd. They were in the apartment paid for by Collis Huntington, in a large bed covered in satin sheets. Her closets were filled with new dresses and coats and furs. "But aren't you being just a bit selfish? I don't think it would be wise for me to leave Mr. Huntington's employment just when I'm getting in a position to gather what could be interesting information."

"I admit my selfishness," Miles said good-naturedly. "I've been missing you."

"But it would be foolish for me to walk out on Huntington just when I'm gaining his confidence," she said.

"I don't give a damn about Huntington or anything he knows," Miles said, nibbling on her ear. "I need you in the office and—"

"And?"

"And I need you here," he said, patting her bare hip, caressing her from buttock to breast.

"Nice of you to say so," she said with some irony. She enjoyed being with Lloyd Miles now and again, but to think of giving up her little nest and the generous bank account supplied to her by Huntington in order to be Lloyd's secretary was neither good business nor good sense. So far as her own affairs were involved, nothing would be gained by moving into the Crédit Mobilier offices.

As for Lloyd, he was still her main source of information about the affairs of Dr. Thomas Durant. Rosanna knew that he was so confident of his manhood that it would never occur to him that she would want something contrary to his wishes, much less that she had collected certain interesting items of information that had been duly delivered—but not to him.

"Let's think about it for a few days," Rosanna said, although she knew that there was no possibility of her working for him in the Crédit Mobilier offices.

Thomas Durant sat with his legs crossed in a closed carriage on a country lane outside Washington. He had arrived a few minutes early. At the appointed hour he heard the approach of another vehicle and heard footsteps, followed by a knock on his carriage door.

In the glow cast by the carriage lamp Lafe Baker's round face was shadowed by a slouch-brimmed hat. Before a word was spoken, Durant put a hand inside his coat, withdrew an envelope filled with crisp, new bills, and handed it to Baker as he climbed into the carriage.

"You were right about Lloyd Miles," Durant said. "He still seems to have a soft spot for Philip Trent."

Baker nodded.

"He's a good man in some ways," Durant commented. "I'll probably have some odd jobs for him in the future, but he should be made of sterner stuff, like you. You don't shy away from getting your hands dirty when necessary."

"In that I am not alone, am I?" Baker asked, stuffing the envelope into his coat pocket.

"I suppose not." Durant paused to light a cigar. Baker coughed and opened a window curtain. "But you have allowed things to get just a bit untidy."

"Be specific," Baker said stiffly.

"Do you have any idea what you risked when you tried to have Trent killed in Wyoming?"

"Whoa," Baker said harshly. "I gave no such order. I simply alerted certain men to be on the lookout for him and to give him no more information than they'd give to a hostile newspaper writer."

"Of course," Durant said. The man was lying. Of course he would deny responsibility. Men like Baker, and to a certain degree Durant himself, operated on the rule that if accused, one always denied everything. But Durant knew that as much as fifty million dollars in immediate construction profits was at stake. No effort was too great to safeguard a personal gain of millions, and when one considered the future, with profits to be made from the railroad itself and from the sale of the Union Pacific, no threat against the transcontinental railroad was to be taken lightly.

"There must be other ways, short of killing, to handle this situation," Durant said.

"Your suggestions?" Baker asked.

Durant shook his head in frustration. "Since he brought back nothing damaging from the West, perhaps it will be best to let things ride. He has no base now. He hasn't even gone back to the Speaker's office as yet."

Baker looked out the window into the darkness. "As you say," he murmured, "there are other ways to handle him."

CHAPTER 19

Gus Trent returned to Washington on a late train, took a hansom cab to Philip's apartment, and was reprimanded by neighbors for making too much noise before he was able to awaken his son. Philip, noting the time, yawned and asked, "Are you running late or early?"

Gus wasn't feeling too kindly toward the world. He had a stiff neck from having taken a very uncomfortable nap on the train, and his eyes felt as if they were full of still burning cigar ashes. He pushed past Philip into the apartment and threw his case onto a chair. "Think you can rustle up some coffee?"

"I can probably manage that," Philip said. "Want to come in the kitchen and tell me what's going on?"

Gus grumbled under his breath but followed Philip into the small kitchen, where he sat on a tall stool while Philip lit the gas and prepared the coffeepot. Then he leaned against a cabinet, his arms crossed on his chest, and looked at his father expectantly.

"Have I ever pushed you too hard in trying to tell you what to do?" Gus asked.

Flames curled up around the bottom of the coffeepot. Before answering, Philip adjusted the jet. "I suppose when I was a boy, I may have felt—"

270

"No, no," Gus said impatiently. "I mean what to do with your life."

"No, Dad, you haven't."

Gus wiped his eyes with the back of his left hand and replaced his glasses. "Maybe a few times in my life I've gone off half-cocked. I've never done too much harm, but I have made it pretty hot for myself once or twice." He fell silent.

"All right, Dad, let's have it," Philip said, laughing. "Who's in trouble, you or me?"

Gus laughed too. "Maybe both." He stood and stretched. "Look, let's find a softer seat, and I'll try to begin to tell you how I've planned out the next few years for you."

"That would be very kind of you," Philip said with rich sarcasm.

Gus sank into a chair in the sitting room and sighed. "I remember telling you once that you had the right to be anything you were capable of being in this life."

"More than once."

"And did I ever suggest that you follow in the old man's footsteps and be a politician?"

"You never suggested it exactly," Philip allowed. "But I knew from things you said that you wouldn't be displeased if I did." Philip knew his father well enough to know that Gus was not going to be rushed. Whatever he had to say, he would say it in his own time, and no sooner.

"I realized on the train ride down here that I'd done something I had no business, no right, to do. I apologize in advance, Philip, but I'm going to have to ask you for a little more than a year of your life."

"Oh, is that all?" Philip said lightly. "I see no objection to that. Where do I serve my time?"

"In the House of Representatives," Gus said, watching for his son's reaction. "I pulled a lot of strings tonight—last night. I asked payment for more than twenty years of faithful service to the Republican party, and I got it."

"Good for you," Philip said, pounding Gus on the shoulders. "Good for you, Dad. I can't think of anyone I'd rather work for. By God, my father, the congressman!"

Gus was trying to stem Philip's mistaken enthusiasm with

gestures. Finally he yelled, "Hey, hold on just a dad-gummed minute!"

Philip stood back and looked at him questioningly.

"I'm not asking you to work for me. It's *not* me. Damn it, Philip, you're the congressman, not me."

Philip backed away. He sat down. The color drained from his face. "You're joking!"

"I'm not. If you don't like it, you don't have to run for a full term. You can just serve out J.T.'s term and call it quits."

"My God, Dad," Philip said, in a reaction that left Gus silent for a long time, "you have that kind of influence? You always told me that you were 'just' a state representative, a good ward-and-precinct worker."

Each man lived with his own thoughts for a time. When Philip heard the coffee boiling, he went to the kitchen and returned with two steaming cups. "Thank you for showing so much confidence in me," he said, handing one cup to Gus.

Gus waved a hand. "Just want to see you make something of yourself, that's all."

"Dad, why me?"

"Because I wanted it for you, and because I think the office needs you."

"But I'm a novice at politics."

"Seems to me you've been putting up a pretty good fight in a matter that is highly political," Gus said. "People will have to listen to you now. You may not be able to plow through all the obstacles that they'll throw before you, and you may not reform the world, starting with the transcontinental railroad; but at least you'll have a better shot at it."

Philip shook his head numbly. "Well, I can't help but feel that it should be you. I think Baltimore and the Maryland state legislature could manage to operate without you, and if you were in Congress I could finally feel confident that there was at least one honest man there."

Gus was touched. "I could have had the office. I could have moved on to the national level a long time ago. I didn't have to wait for someone to die so that I could be appointed. But when you learn a little more about politics, I think you'll agree that I'm more valuable doing just what I do. I believe the most critical area of government is at the front door of a man who lives in a small house in a town like Baltimore. That's where it all winds up—all of the actions of the legislative bodies, the agencies, the bureaucrats—right at a factory worker's front door, and that's as far as government should be allowed to go. So I'm down there at the street level, keeping an eye on things, making sure that if, somehow, some good Samaritan in the state house or in Washington manages to extend a tentacle of government through the keyhole, I can start yelling hard and loud. I know thousands of people by name, most of them by their first names. By now I've got three generations of voters looking to me to watch over their interests. If I should see something coming down from on high in the form of some highfalutin new state or federal law, all I have to do is point out the fallacies in the law to the people I know by name, and there's such an uprising of what is called public opinion that the lawmakers listen."

He held out his mug, and Philip got the pot and refilled it. Then Gus went on, "I told myself I was not going to try to tell you how to be a congressman, but you've just been treated to Gus Trent's one-minute course in government. Maybe I'm talking nonsense, since I've never been in Congress, but I'd imagine it's not much different from being a state representative." He winked. "It's just that there'll be more names you'll have to remember. But that's not too bad, because the bribes are bigger in Washington."

"Ah, at last my chance to be wealthy."

"If you need someone to talk with at any time, I'll be glad to listen. And you know I'm always happy to run off at the mouth."

"I'll need lots of help, Dad."

Gus grinned. "Don't become a pest."

Philip laughed. "I'd give a pretty penny to be able to see the faces of a few people in this town when the word gets out."

Dawn. Gus had gone yawningly off to the spare bedroom. Philip sat in the parlor, his empty coffee cup hanging on one thumb. His first sense of shock and disbelief had passed. He was truly surprised that Gus had enough standing in the Republican party in Maryland to secure such a political plum for an unknown, a man who had never run for public office. But by now his thoughts had soared past amazement to practicalities. He would have the power of a United States congressman! He would be only a first-term representative, and an appointed one at that, so he would not inherit J. T. Moverly's power base, which had been built up during two decades of service in the House; but he would be in an infinitely better position to continue his investigations than he had been as a private citizen—one without employment.

Gus had said that the announcement would not be made for a couple of days to give the party wheelhorses time to demonstrate their inside status by spreading the word themselves among the faithful. It always made a man feel good to know something before it was published in the papers. But it would be a headline soon, and as he'd told Gus, Philip wished he could see the faces of a few men when they read it —and one woman, Leah. For a moment his need for her was as intense as a toothache, and then he forced her from his mind. He had other things to consider.

First of all, what could be done about the Colombian government's request to extradite him? Could a congressman be extradited? Would he begin his appointed term in office with a scandal when those men who were his enemies made the Panamanian affair public? Whatever happened, he would make Gus proud of him, and perhaps even please those men in the party whom Gus had squeezed into agreement to appoint Philip Trent to the office. He looked forward to the first time he could stand face to face with John O'Brian and Oakes Ames and tell them that it was evident that not everyone believed their implied condemnation of him during the Moverly committee hearings. He had been reprieved, and now he was equal in power to them under the law, if not in fact. He was a member of the United States House of Representatives.

Pride—and pain when he once again thought of Leah— raced through him. This time he thought the sorrow through, trying to come to terms with it. She had made the choice, not he. He wanted her at his side; he would have been thrilled to be able to tell her the news in person and to hear her say, "That is so wonderful, Philip. I am so proud of you."

But such a miracle was not forthcoming. He began his new life with a resolution that would be kept, regardless of the pain it caused him. He would forget Leah Miles.

Lloyd Miles read of Philip's appointment over breakfast. He swallowed wrong. Coughing and gasping for air, he waved his sister back into her chair. "I'm all right," he managed. Finally, his windpipe clear, he looked again, just to be sure that he'd read it right.

"What is it?" Leah asked.

"Nothing. Went down the wrong way, that's all."

"Is there something in the paper that upset you?"

He handed her the newspaper silently, tapping with his forefinger the article about Washington's newest congressman.

"Oh!" she said, blushing furiously. "Oh . . . my."

"Now the son of a bitch is really going to go after the railroads," Miles said.

Leah felt her eyes sting and, putting her napkin on the table, said, "Excuse me." She left him alone to wonder what Thomas Durant was going to have to say about this new development.

Rosanna Pulliam had heard about Philip Trent's appointment to the House from Collis Huntington, who thought it was a good joke on his competitors in the railroad business.

"I wish that I could have seen Thomas Durant's face when he heard the news," Huntington had said, chuckling.

Rosanna was not particularly interested in Durant's reaction to Philip's appointment, and it would be some time before she had the opportunity to satisfy her curiosity and, as a result, determine her own attitude toward Philip Trent as congressman. In the meantime, she learned quite quickly that Lloyd Miles and his employer were mightily displeased by events.

"I gathered from Lloyd Miles," she told Huntington, "that the good doctor was livid. He visited Crédit Mobilier to see Oakes Ames, and while he was there he stopped at Lloyd's office 'to rant and rave a bit,' as Lloyd put it. For some reason he seems to want to blame Lloyd for the whole thing."

Rosanna was dressed—some people would not have used that word to describe the way she looked—in a Paris negligee that seemed to consist of wisps of silk and a few feathers. Her apartment was comfortably warm and cozy. A tray containing the makings of Huntington's favorite drink was on a table beside her chair. Huntington was sprawled, legs wide, on the couch.

"If you're hungry," she said, "there's roasted beef on the warmer."

"Thank you, no," he said.

"Lloyd was once friendly with Philip Trent," Rosanna went on. "They were in college and in the army together. And Trent was once engaged to Lloyd's sister."

Huntington was listening with only half an ear. He was still bemused by the fact that they'd made Philip Trent a congressman.

"So I understand why Durant is tempted to vent his upset on Lloyd," Rosanna continued. "But it's really not his fault. Nor do I understand why they're so upset over at the Union Pacific. After all, Trent's charges against the railroads were proven to be groundless at the Moverly committee hearings."

"Trent is an idealist with no connection to the real world of business," Huntington said. "He couldn't hold down an honest job at the Central Pacific. Stanford had to fire him." He chuckled. "But if his appointment is causing a loss of sleep in certain quarters, more power to him."

"I take it, then, that you don't believe that any investigation initiated by Philip Trent could be a threat to the Central Pacific."

"There's only one Philip Trent," Huntington responded. "I can offset his minor influence with the power of two dozen men with far more seniority in government than he has."

Huntington was a man who believed in a set of adages as

old as business and politics. *Never miss a chance to have a square meal. Never miss a chance to rest, however briefly. Never miss a chance to relieve your bladder.* To those rules he had added an adage of his own: *Never waste an opportunity to enjoy a sweetly scented woman.* As far as he was concerned, the conversation was over.

There were many people in Washington who discussed Philip Trent's appointment. Some of the talk was idle gossip; some, mild-to-serious concern; but under a pale half-moon on a shadowy country lane, when two closed carriages came to a halt a few feet from each other, the words spoken were more intense.

Thomas Durant puffed on his cigar as he waited for Lafe Baker to join him in his carriage. "I know now why Andrew Johnson fired you," he said as Baker's weight caused the carriage body to shift on its springs.

"And a pleasant good evening to you, too, sir," Lafe said.

"*Goddammit,* Baker. You know why I'm here."

"I believe I do. I think that you have summoned me here to try to put the blame on me for the appointment of a certain young man to the Congress. That seems to be just about the measure of your mentality."

Durant sputtered for a moment.

"I've told you repeatedly, Dr. Durant, that it's dangerous for us to meet like this every time you get a feather up your ass—"

"Don't be crude."

"My, my, did I offend your delicate sensibilities?" Lafe laughed. "I've told you before, Durant, and now I'm going to tell you one more time: Philip Trent is no real threat to you."

"That's what you said when he was sent west by the Moverly committee. And if I hadn't pushed you into doing something, he'd have brought back some very damaging information."

"We can destroy Philip Trent's credibility anytime you give the go-ahead," Lafe said.

"Well, if it's so goddamned easy, why haven't you done it already?"

"There's been no need for it," Lafe calmly explained. "He wasn't a member of Congress then."

"I think, General Baker, that you may very well be a man whose worthwhile contributions have already been made."

"Don't tempt me to tell you what I really think of *you,* Durant," Lafe flared. "If you're thinking of discontinuing our association, that suits me perfectly." He opened the door and stepped down.

"Now, hold on," Durant said.

Lafe turned, a little smile on his lips. "Yes?"

"Don't go off half-cocked. You said that you could take care of Trent anytime I gave the word."

"Dr. Durant, the price for my services has just gone up. The fee, as of now, is exactly double—payable in gold."

Durant puffed furiously on the cigar.

"Do I take silence as consent?" Lafe asked.

"Yes, damn you, but only if you deliver this time."

Lafe Baker put one foot on the running board of the carriage and spoke in a low, even voice. "One year and some months ago Philip Trent was traveling to California across the Isthmus of Panama via the Panama Railroad. At a stop he intervened in a domestic dispute between a man and a woman and killed two men, two Colombian citizens. He was identified by fellow passengers at the Pacific terminal of the Panama Railroad, but he had already taken ship. Colombia has filed a request through our State Department to have Trent extradited to Panama to stand trial for murder."

Durant snorted. "That might have worked before he was appointed. The United States would never turn over a congressman to stand trial in the courts of a despotically run country."

"Perhaps not, but the scandal would kill any chance he might have of being elected to a full term in the Congress next year."

"And meanwhile? There's too much at stake to risk having him in office for over a year with the floor of the House as his soapbox."

Lafe grinned. "You fear him that much, do you?"

"It is not fear," Durant said angrily. "It is sensible precaution."

Lafe looked up at the moon and made a little humming sound in his throat. "You want him out of Congress one way or another. How far are you willing to go?"

"I hired you to do a job. We have just agreed to double your fee."

"All right, then."

Durant was silent for a few seconds and then seemed to tense. He said quickly, "Don't do anything stupid, Baker. We can't afford to have him become a martyr."

But Thomas Durant's last statement persuaded Lafe Baker that he was dealing with a man with a featherweight brain outside his field of talent, which was making money. More than ever Lafe was convinced that it was just about time to end his association with Thomas Durant and the Union Pacific Railroad. Despite Durant's words, the man had made it clear what he wanted Lafe to do. There had been a time when Lafe could have gotten away with murder—at the height of the war fever, when it looked as if Robert E. Lee's knack for running circles around a whole passel of Union generals would force the North to give up the war. But those times were long past. He had no intention of risking the hangman's noose just because Thomas Durant was afraid he might lose a dollar.

CHAPTER 20

J. T. Moverly had never been interested in building an empire of staff members in Washington. He had been content with a small suite of offices, with his wife as his right-hand adviser and one maiden lady named Mercy as secretary, file clerk, tea brewer, and all-around assistant.

When Philip Trent walked into the reception area for the first time after his appointment, the widow Moverly and Miss Mercy were packing personal items that had accumulated over the years of Jeb Moverly's service in the House. Agnes Moverly was a wrinkled, white-haired pixie of a lady. Moving with a graceful quickness, she put her arms around Philip after he had greeted her.

"I'm so pleased," she said, "—and I know that Jeb would be too—that you are the one who will take his place."

"Thank you, Mrs. Moverly. That does mean a lot to me," Philip said. "I don't want you to feel rushed. You're welcome to use the office just as long as you want."

Agnes Moverly wiped away one quick tear with a handkerchief. "Oh, no," she said. "For it's so empty, you see." Then she smiled wanly. "Actually, I'm eager to get back to Maryland." She sighed. "We had so looked forward to the time when we both could go home—time for the grandchildren, time to read all the books we didn't have time to read as long as we were working. Walking down by the duck pond . . ." She shook her head. "Well, this isn't getting it done, is it, Miss Mercy?"

"Then can I help in any way?" Philip asked.

"Thank you," Agnes said. "If you'd like to look at Jeb's files and see if you want to keep any of them—"

"At the moment I'm not sure whether I'd know enough to make an intelligent decision about what to keep," Philip admitted.

"Miss Mercy will help you," Agnes said.

"And speaking of you, Miss Mercy," Philip said, "may I inquire about your plans?"

"As a matter of fact," Agnes Moverly said quickly, "we were just discussing that. I've asked Mercy to come with me, to live with me as friend and companion. We all grew old together here in Washington, Jeb, Miss Mercy, and I."

"And?" Philip asked.

"Agnes Moverly," Miss Mercy said in a no-nonsense manner, "you're a lovely person, and I'm very grateful to you, but, after all, I'm much younger than you and not ready for retirement."

"Five months younger," Agnes said, winking at Philip.

"And I have my own little place here," Miss Mercy said. She and Agnes were a matched set, both well aged, silvered, a bit wizened, but bright and lively.

"I'd be very grateful, Miss Mercy, if you'd consider keeping your position here in the office," Philip said.

"Oh, that's so nice of you," she responded, "but . . ." She looked toward Agnes as if asking for help.

"Miss Mercy, you see," Agnes explained, "is concerned about the propriety of a maiden lady being alone in the office with an unmarried young man."

Philip nodded sagely, fighting to keep his face straight. "Rest easy, Miss Mercy," he assured her. "If you would consent to stay and be my right hand, as you were for Congressman and Mrs. Moverly, I hereby empower you to hire a helper for yourself, a person of your own choice to relieve you of some of the work and to serve as chaperone."

Miss Mercy blushed with pleasure. "I am very grateful," she said. "I'll be glad to stay."

"Good. That's settled then. Now," Philip added, "if you'd like to give me advice on which of J.T.'s files I should keep . . ."

"You just leave that to me, Mr. Philip," Miss Mercy said. "Don't fret yourself with it."

"I should have warned you," Agnes said, laughing. "She will not only take over your office, but she'll take over your life if you give her half a chance."

With Congress in recess, Philip had plenty of time to get settled in. He called in workmen and had the entire suite repainted, replaced the old carpeting, and had new gas jets installed to improve the lighting. He bought a new desk chair to replace the one that over the years had molded its leather to fit J. T. Moverly.

"Goodness, sir," Miss Mercy said when the workmen lit the jets, "you'll blind us all." She lifted a hand quickly to prevent comment and added, "But I'll grow accustomed to it."

A new desk had been placed in the outer office, but it was still unoccupied. Mercy had interviewed applicants, most of them male, for the job, but as yet had not advanced one person past her scrutiny to see the congressman, who had quickly learned to trust the woman's judgment and experience. Without her he would have been overwhelmed by a steady stream of lobbyists, petitioners, job seekers, and visiting constituents from the old home state who wanted to be able to tell the folks back in Maryland, "Well, I had a little chat with *my* congressman while I was in Washington."

Philip had thought that not much would be going on until Congress convened in December to take up the serious divisions that were tearing Washington apart, but he found himself to be extremely busy. He spent some time with Mercy as she familiarized him with several file cabinets full of material collected over the years by his predecessor. She was reluctant to discard anything but did so at Philip's insistence. He saw no reason to keep papers covering congressional actions or meetings with various people, personal items, or newspaper clippings that covered the long span of years from Moverly's first election to his death.

"After all, Miss Mercy," he said, "I'll have files of my own, you know, and the office is only so big."

Mercy had still not found a suitable assistant when Philip decided to follow his father's advice to spend some time walking the streets in Baltimore. He spent his nights in the Trent family home and his days dropping into places of business, to shake hands and listen to suggestions that ranged from eminently sensible to utterly foolish. He met with politicians in groups ranging from one to several. He wasn't quite sure he'd want to run for a full term of his own in 1868, but he was doing the things that Gus called the basics, just in case.

At first he found politicking to be a chore, an unnatural state of being; but before he was ready to go back to Washington, he had begun to feel that it was both interesting and informative to talk to the hansom-cab drivers, the small businessmen, the neighborhood iceman, the doctors, lawyers, and laborers of his district. It became second nature for him to stick out his hand, smile, and say, "Hello. I'm Philip Trent, congressman from this district."

He returned to Washington on an early autumn day that had started off beautifully in Baltimore but, during the train ride, had darkened. By the time he reached his apartment, a fine, warm rain was being blown in sheets by gusting winds.

The apartment, which was musty from having been closed, had stored the heat of the day. He opened the windows away from the wind so that the rain wouldn't blow in, then went through the mail that had accumulated in his absence. As he shuffled quickly through the stack he realized that he was hoping to see Leah's handwriting and tossed the stack aside to peruse later. There was a pleasant smell of rain coming into the room, freshening it. He went to an open window and watched nature wash the streets below.

He could remember vividly every lovely moment that he had spent with Leah. But now the time had passed when remembering was exquisite torture. Philip Trent wanted to be a good congressman, and this desire to do his duty helped to

numb the feeling of loss. He watched the blowing rain and
thought of Leah as she'd looked in white the last time they
had walked along the Potomac, remembering how she'd
smiled up at him from under the brim of a large and rather
silly hat. It was, after all, a pleasant memory of something
that had once been a part of his life . . . but was no longer.

The scab that had formed over his wound was itself beginning to heal.

Philip was whistling when he entered the anteroom of his
office the next morning. Hanging his hat on the rack, he
noted that Miss Mercy had brought in a bouquet of fresh
flowers. The desk that she had ordered for the assistant was
still unoccupied. He heard movement in Mercy's office.

"Good morning," he sang out, striding past the vacant
desk and around the corner of the partition to collide with
something soft, warm, feminine, and very much alive.

"I beg your pardon," he said, stepping back to look down
into a pair of startled, blue-green eyes that sparkled like a
summer sea. Long, dark lashes blinked.

"Excuse me," she said. She wore a sensible tan dress, and
her dark hair was full of highlights that ranged from reflected
gaslight to deep auburn. "You'll have to wait outside, sir. The
congressman is not in."

"He is now," Miss Mercy said from behind the petite
woman, whose face promptly darkened with embarrassment.
"Welcome back, sir. As you can see, I have hired an assistant."

Philip could see quite well. Small of waist and slim of neck,
she was of a height that put her brow at the level of his
mouth. Her smile was just a bit shy. Above a delicate nose
were the lively, summer-sea eyes.

"This is Mrs. Julia Stuart Grey," Mercy said. "She comes
to us highly recommended. I'm sure you're going to find her
to be satisfactory."

Philip smiled at her. "I'm sure I will."

"Forgive me for not recognizing you," Julia Grey said.
Her voice was soft with the inflections of Virginia.

"You are forgiven."

"We didn't know when to expect you back," she said.

"Well, Miss Mercy," Philip said, "what's the news?"

"Same old routine," Mercy answered. "You'll find a list of callers on your desk, along with a few communiqués from the House leadership. They're beginning to make their preparations for the December session. Nothing urgent."

"Thank you," Philip said. "And, Mrs. Grey, welcome aboard."

"Thank you," Julia responded. "I am very grateful to Miss Mercy and to you, sir, for giving me an opportunity at this position."

"Miss Mercy's doing," Philip remarked. He was still staring at the newcomer. She was a vivid picture. But his gaze must have made her uncomfortable, for she brushed past him and took her seat behind the reception desk.

Philip looked at Miss Mercy and winked. She nodded severely and followed him into his office. A window was open. The room smelled fresh, and more flowers sat on the corner of his desk.

"Have we bought interest in a flower shop?" he asked.

"Mrs. Grey brings them," Mercy said. "Her husband, it seems, is a great gardener." She shook her head and spoke in a hushed tone. "That's about all he can do, poor thing."

Philip looked at her, waiting for her to go on.

"Lieutenant Grey lost his legs during the last months of the war. Now, mind you, that's not why I hired Mrs. Grey. She's quite a competent secretary. I know, I know, women in the workplace are frowned upon; but I've been working in this office for two decades, and I've yet to find a man who could hold a candle to me. Things are changing, Congressman. Why, women are now even being admitted to professional schools, such as law school and medical school."

"Miss Mercy," Philip said, smiling, "I accept without question your evaluation of Mrs. Grey. I'm sure that she'll be just dandy."

John O'Brian had become chairman of the special investigating committee that had been headed by J. T. Moverly before his death. O'Brian had spent most of the summer in his home district, shaking hands and assessing his chances for reelection, which looked good since his own party was behind him and the opposition had not come up with a candidate strong enough to cause him any concern. He went back to Washington early and began to dismantle the Moverly committee by discharging staff members. In this decision he had the support of Oakes Ames. When his secretary announced that Congressman Philip Trent was in the outer office, he was in the process of discarding most of the paperwork that the Moverly committee had accumulated. He told the secretary to show Trent in and met him at the door, his hand extended.

"Well, Trent, congratulations. When we were giving you a bad time before the committee, I had no idea that you would soon be a member of the club."

"No more than I did, I would imagine," Philip said.

"You're going to find that it's an exciting thing, being a member of the House. Perhaps you'll be different, but when I was a freshman, I felt a bit intimidated. Some of the old codgers had been in the House forever and knew all the ropes, and I knew nothing; but I'm sure that you're much better prepared for the job than I was."

"I don't know about that. But I do know what you mean by feeling intimidated."

"Well, don't let the old boys keep you from doing what you think is right," O'Brian urged. "They can kill you, but they can't eat you. It's against the law."

Philip laughed. "I came to ask you what you're going to do about the investigation of the transcontinental," he explained.

O'Brian spread his hands. "What is there to be done? We heard all the evidence. We might not have been overly polite to you, but we heard what you had to say. You'll have to admit, Trent, that you gave pretty feeble justification for your accusations against the railroads."

"I have asked the leadership to name me to the committee," Philip informed him.

O'Brian led Philip to a chair. "I'm going to give you a word of advice, Trent, whether or not you want it. Don't make an ass of yourself by accusing good men of criminal activities unless you've got proof that will stand up in a court of law."

"To the degree that you heard me," Philip said, "I hear your advice."

O'Brian sat down and shrugged.

"I've been talking with several members of both the House and the Senate," Philip said. "I am not the only one who is concerned about the overruns in building the railroad. I have been assured by Speaker Colfax and by others that I will be named to the investigating committee. I came here to ask for your help in a line of investigation that I can't manage alone."

"I will not be a part of a witch-hunt against the railroads," O'Brian stated emphatically.

"I only want an official congressional subpoena for the records of stock ownership from Crédit Mobilier," Philip said.

O'Brian's lips compressed. "You're talking about an action that would have serious consequences."

"Yes," Philip agreed, "especially if, as it is quietly rumored around Capitol Hill, there are several members of both the House and the Senate who own sizable blocks of Crédit Mobilier stock."

"I don't think it would be a good idea to insult openly a corporation as vital to the nation as Crédit Mobilier," O'Brian said. "Damn it, Trent, I don't know what your motives are, but I, for one, am sick and tired of your attack on something that is going to benefit this nation more than anything since the Louisiana Purchase. It was one thing to throw libelous statements around when you were just a greenhorn, a hired hand. But now, although you have not yet earned it, you hold the title of representative, and when you drag that honorable title in the dirt with your personal vendetta against the transcontinental . . ." O'Brian seemed to have run out of words.

"I was told that the authority I ask for should come from the chairman of my committee," Philip said stiffly. "As I understand it, however, I have recourse to other sources if my chairman refuses to grant my request."

"Then you'll have to avail yourself of those sources," O'Brian said, standing. "I bid you good day."

O'Brian did not see Philip to the door. After the door was closed, he continued to stand. When he raised a hand to his brow, he found he was sweating, although the office was pleasantly cool. He summoned his secretary. "I'll be out for the rest of the day," he said. "Summon a messenger and send him to Mr. Lloyd Miles, at the Crédit Mobilier office." He scribbled a note, put it into an envelope, sealed it, and handed it to the secretary.

Lloyd Miles met him at the designated place, a coffee-house, two hours later. O'Brian did not rise when Miles walked in. "I want to talk with Durant," O'Brian said by way of greeting as Miles seated himself across the table.

"I'm sure he'd be pleased to see you," Miles said, "but is it wise?" He caught the strong aroma of whiskey on the portly man's breath.

"Wise or not, I want to see him."

"Perhaps there's something I can do," Miles said. "What's the problem, John?"

O'Brian looked away and seemed to be thinking. Then he looked back and said, "The new congressman from Maryland is going to be appointed to the investigating committee."

"So? You're chairman. Oakes Ames has thoroughly discredited the investigation. All you have to do is say that the committee's work is complete."

"He wants the committee to subpoena the ownership list of stockholders in Crédit Mobilier," O'Brian said.

Miles frowned, concerned. After summoning a waiter and ordering coffee with cream, he asked, "Can't you simply refuse?"

"Yes, but Trent can get the subpoena from the Speaker," O'Brian explained.

Miles nodded. Then his face brightened. "No problem, John. I'll just tell Oakes Ames that any sensitive names have to be removed from the ownership list. I don't think we need

to bother Durant with this at all. It's simple." He leaned
forward. "Look, I'll guarantee that neither your name nor
that of any other member of Congress will appear on the list
of owners if and when Trent gets his little subpoena."

"You'd better make damned sure," O'Brian grumbled. "If
I go down, Miles, I won't go down by myself."

"Don't worry," Miles said. "Don't worry."

"That's easy for you to say, Miles. And I'm sure that
Oakes would say the same thing. But I'm not a millionaire
like Oakes. And I'm not just someone's employee like you. I
like being a congressman. I'd like for the pay to be a little
higher, but I like the job. I don't intend to give it up lightly.
I'm up for reelection next fall, and I don't think my constituents would appreciate it if it looked as if I was on the take
from the Union Pacific. And they damned sure wouldn't like
it if it came out that I sold stock to other congressmen at a
price so low that you might as well say I gave it to them. So
you'd better talk to someone and make damned sure that it
doesn't get out. Because if my name is soiled with scandal, it
won't be the biggest name to be involved."

Miles left O'Brian to finish his coffee and returned directly
to Crédit Mobilier. He had noted that as O'Brian spoke his
impassioned threat, his hands were shaking. This made him
wonder if the congressman drank during the day every day,
or if he'd merely had a drink or two to settle himself after
Philip's visit to his office.

Lloyd found the Ames brothers at Crédit Mobilier. Oakes,
who considered himself a sure bet for reelection, had spent
only a few days in his home district. The rest of the summer
and early fall he had stayed in the office kept for him at
Crédit Mobilier. When Lloyd was ushered in after asking to
see Oakes, Oliver, also in the office, did not leave his chair.

Oakes greeted their visitor for both of them, and as Miles
told them of his meeting with O'Brian, the congressman nodded, leaned back in his chair, and locked his hands over his
belly. "Never did understand, Miles, why you thought it necessary to involve O'Brian in the stock distribution."

"He was all I had to work with at the time," Miles explained. "I didn't realize you were going to take a direct part in it."

"He's a weak sister," Oakes said, "but I don't think there's anything to be concerned about. Let young Trent get his subpoena. We'll have no problem removing sensitive names from the list, will we, Oliver?"

"What sensitive names?" Oliver Ames asked innocently. "It is well-known that my brother owns Crédit Mobilier stock. As for any other members of either the House or the Senate, no. There are no congressional names on the list of Crédit Mobilier stock owners."

"Thank you, Oliver," Oakes said. He turned to Miles. "Questions, Miles?"

"None, sir."

That evening, Thomas Durant was visited at home by Lloyd Miles, who briefed him on the events of the day, explaining that he was giving Durant the information not because there was any further concern about the matter but so that Durant would be aware of it.

"It sounds as if the Ames brothers have it under control," Durant said.

But as Miles's cab was turning from his driveway into the street, Durant called his valet and ordered his carriage to be readied.

Lafe Baker was not a man who required a complete set of instructions in order to piece together a puzzle. The irritation that had come with still another panicky summons from Thomas Durant the night before had faded quickly, for this time Durant had given him something to chew on, a hint of some pretty interesting information.

Durant hadn't told all, of course. First, he'd ordered Lafe to tell the newspapers about Philip Trent's trouble in Panama. Then he'd asked Lafe to keep a close eye on John O'Brian to see if the congressman from Indiana was acting oddly or drinking too much.

It was obvious to Lafe that Durant was trying to involve Trent in a scandal, with the hope that the House would refuse to seat the new congressman when it convened in December. O'Brian was another matter.

"What information does O'Brian have that could be damaging to you?" he'd asked Durant, and the railroad baron had sputtered for a moment, trying to deny that he had anything but friendly concern for a congressman who was favorable to the railroad.

"I can't do a job for you," Lafe had told Durant, "if you play coy with me and hold back information. If you're afraid that O'Brian is going to open his big mouth and spill something he shouldn't be talking about, I need to know. Sometimes the best way to keep a man quiet is to give him something more to fear than whatever it is that is tempting him to confess his sins."

Still Durant had been reluctant to speak. But he did not know Lafe Baker very well. To Lafe, knowledge was power. On that very evening, he had spent a half hour with a reporter talking about Philip Trent. The next morning he went to John O'Brian's home.

O'Brian was one of many members of Congress who chose to leave his family in the home state while Congress was in session. Lafe was pleased to find O'Brian alone in his flat. They'd never had occassion to talk, but Lafe saw that the congressman recognized him immediately.

"I thought you'd left Washington," O'Brian said.

"Only temporarily," Lafe replied. He pushed past O'Brian without waiting for an invitation, turned, and waited for the portly man to close the door. In that brief moment he saw that doubt and questioning were beginning to build in O'Brian.

"We're a little bit worried about you, John," he said softly.

O'Brian flushed with quick anger. "You have me at a disadvantage, General Baker. I simply do not know what the hell you're talking about."

"John, John," Lafe said benignly, "don't be hostile. We have the same associates, you and I, and we should work together, shouldn't we?" He took O'Brian's arm and, when O'Brian tried to pull it away, held it in an iron grip. "Come and sit down, John. Let's talk this over."

O'Brian sat down. Lafe sat opposite him and crossed his legs, smiling. "Now," he said, "Dr. Durant wants to know what's making you nervous."

"You're working for Durant?" O'Brian asked.

"Of course," Lafe explained. "And Dr. Durant asked me to talk with you, to assure you that there's nothing to worry about."

"Philip Trent came to see me," O'Brian said, rubbing his hands. "He's going to get a subpoena for the Crédit Mobilier stock ownership list."

Ah ha, Lafe thought. "Yes, we know," he said. "Now is that any reason to get upset?" Little bells were ringing. If Durant and O'Brian were worried about disclosure of the names of people who owned a certain stock, that meant that a lot of people who shouldn't did. "John, that will be taken care of, and you'll be taken care of, you see."

"I told Lloyd Miles to tell Durant that if my name is linked with the stocks, it won't be the only one," O'Brian said. "I've got a list of every man on Capitol Hill who was given stock."

" 'Given'?" Lafe asked.

"Well, sold, if you want to call it that. But sold for a fraction of its worth." O'Brian pushed back his hair with a shaky hand. "Miles said that it would be a simple matter to remove the names of members of the Congress, and, by God, it had better be done, or—" He looked at Lafe Baker's scowling face and stopped.

"John, don't make threats," Lafe said softly. "Threats make me nervous. Dr. Durant doesn't like threats, either." He rose. "I think you'd better give me your list of names, John, and then wipe your memory of it."

"No, I won't," O'Brian said, sounding somewhat like a petulant child. "And don't think you can find it. It's not here."

"Why, John," Lafe whispered, "I wouldn't try to make you do anything you didn't want to do, would I?" He towered over the seated O'Brian. "But you worry me, John. You're sweating, and your hands are shaking. I'd hate to think that you're in such a bad way that your judgment might be impaired. I'd sure hate to think that you might be on the verge of doing something foolish."

"No, no," O'Brian said quickly. "I won't do anything foolish. Just tell them to be damned sure that they've cleaned up that list before Trent gets his hands on it."

In Lafe's opinion, Philip Trent had essentially been removed from the arena. Once the reporter did his work per Lafe's instructions, the House would hardly allow a murderer to take his seat. As for O'Brian, he was certainly a risk, but a nervous man made a good source of information.

He took O'Brian's hand and shook it. "Look, John, I know how you feel. And let me assure you that you have friends. We're on your side, John. If you get concerned or if you just want to talk . . ." He gave O'Brian a card with a fictitious name and a post office box number. "Drop a note in the pickup at the main post office. It'll get to my box the same day."

O'Brian, looking visibly relieved, walked Lafe to the door. Lafe patted him on the shoulder and said, "Now, stop worrying."

Thomas Durant looked up when his butler entered the large, luxurious parlor where Durant was entertaining the new secretary of war, General U. S. Grant.

"There's a gentleman at the front door, sir."

Durant frowned. His man was well trained and knew not to interrupt his chat with General Grant unless it was important. "General," he said, "would you excuse me for just a moment, sir?"

"Go right ahead," Grant said.

"Evans will freshen your drink while I'm gone," Durant said.

"I'll do it myself," Grant said, lifting his glass.

Lafe Baker was standing in the hallway just inside the front door.

"This had better be damned important, your coming here," Durant warned.

"Oh, I don't know," Lafe said musingly. "Depends on

how you look at it. Would it be important if John O'Brian got
so nervous, he spilled his guts?"

"Not so loud, man," Durant said in a hoarse whisper. He
moved closer. "You've talked with O'Brian?"

"I'd advise you to get your house in order. I'd advise you
especially to get the names of the representatives and senators off the Crédit Mobilier list, and quickly."

"That has already been done," Durant said, but he felt a
little surge of worry. The only way Lafe Baker could have
known about the Crédit Mobilier stock was from O'Brian,
and if O'Brian had talked so easily and so quickly to Baker,
the man was a menace. "What in hell has gotten into
O'Brian?"

"A lot of whiskey and a lot of fear," Lafe said. "Look, if I
were you, I'd have a little talk with him. He's facing an
election campaign. He's not a rich man."

"Money." Durant nodded. "Would more money make him
feel secure?"

"Well, in my experience it never hurt to have money," Lafe
said. "And speaking of money, anything *extra* you want me
to do?"

"No. Not at the moment," Durant said. "You'd better go
now."

A gentle autumn rain made the cobblestones glisten, washing manure-stained streams into the gutters and making the
fall flowers on the White House lawn look new and fresh.
Miss Mercy and Julia Grey had walked down the stairs with
Philip after closing the office at noon on a Saturday. The
skies were soft gray, looking as if the sun might emerge any
minute in spite of the light rain. They stood under an overhang while Philip whistled up a hansom cab. He insisted on
dropping Mercy off at her little flat. Julia Grey lived farther
afield, south toward the river.

"Please," she said, "I rather enjoy walking in the rain. You
don't have to take me all the way home."

"My pleasure," he said. The woman had proved to be an
excellent secretary. She handled his correspondence with
skilled ease, kept order in the outer office, even when it was

filled, and was developing a knack for weeding out pests and lunatics from among the petitioners. "I thought perhaps I might get to meet your husband."

"Thank you. I'm sure Adam would like that." She nodded. "Yes, then." She leaned forward and gave crisp directions to the driver.

The Grey house was not actually in a shantytown, but it was close enough for the stench of the poverty-stricken areas that were the shame of Washington to waft occasionally into the garden in front of the three-room clapboard cottage. In the spendidly kept little garden asters and chrysanthemums lined the graveled walkway leading to a low stoop and the front door. Beds of perennials were shaped with obvious artistic intent. Around all of the beds and plantings ran a little path of smoothed dirt about three feet wide.

Philip, after asking the driver to wait, helped Julia down from the cab and followed her up the walk. The rain had stopped, and a watery sun, breaking through the overcast, provided enough light to allow him to see that her otherwise smart gown was a bit rump sprung and that the nap had worn off the fabric on the seat.

She opened the door and called, "Adam, we have company."

He heard a scuffling sound from inside as he followed her into the room. There was a rather delicious aroma, of cooking cabbage and corned beef.

"My dear," she was saying, "Congressman Trent was kind enough to give me a ride home."

Philip was looking past Julia's shoulder, his eyes not yet accustomed to the semidarkness of the little room.

"Mr. Trent," she said, "this is my husband, Adam."

Philip saw Adam Grey then, a tousled head at the level of his waist, a broad-shouldered, squat form with muscular arms. Grey extended one big paw upward and clasped Philip's hand with a firm grip.

Philip's face was red. He was thankful for the lack of light in the room, for he had just realized that Adam Grey was sitting on a wheeled dolly, the stumps of his thighs sticking out in front of him. His legs had been amputated not more than six inches below his groin.

"Nice of you, Mr. Trent," he said. "I'm doubly grateful, for your having given Julia a ride and for bringing her home to me early."

"My pleasure," Philip said. "We have come to value Mrs. Grey very highly, Miss Mercy and I."

Julia was bustling around. A lamp glowed, and in the reddish light Philip saw Adam Grey's face. The man was only in his twenties, but ancient eyes showed the darkness of pain in half-moon circles—the eyes were, Philip realized with a shock, so devoid of life as to be almost frightening in their pale-gray sunken dullness.

Grey's voice and manner belied his agonized eyes. "Mr. Trent, if you've a hankering for some wholesome nourishment, I invite you to partake with us."

"It smells delicious," Philip said. "But—"

"That's settled, then," Adam Grey said. He flattened his palms on the floor and pushed himself toward the door. The hardwood floor of the room was spotless. "Julia, my dear, would you set another place at the table while I see to the last-minute culinary details?"

Adam scuttled through the bedroom and out of sight. Julia had removed her jacket. She stood with the light of the lamp below the level of her face, her mouth and eyes in shadow.

"That's Adam," she said appreciatively. "He has meals ready for me when I come home. He keeps the house clean. He works in the garden."

"Remarkable man," Philip said.

"I think so," she said, her smile showing him that she meant exactly what she said. "Please come on out to the kitchen. We eat there."

The house consisted of the sitting room, the bedroom, and the kitchen-dining area, all in a row. After telling the cabbie he was no longer needed, Philip made his way through to the other end of the house, where he was directed to a shed adjoining the kitchen. In it was a shelf, a hand-powered water pump, a water bucket and dipper, a pitcher and washbasin, and a modest slop jar, protruding only slightly from a fabric skirt at the bottom of the washstand.

"Wash up, Mr. Trent," Adam called out. "Luncheon will be served momentarily."

Adam had constructed an ingenious scaffolding at the work areas in the kitchen. He was perched on a ledge raised to a height to allow him to work on the small wood-burning cookstove that filled the little room with just a bit too much heat. Other ledges gave Adam access to the enameled sink and drying board and a kitchen cabinet that showed a sprinkling of flour.

Philip washed up, dried his hands on a fresh towel, and reentered the kitchen, where he watched as Adam deftly clambered down onto his wheeled dolly and then reached up for a covered dish into which he'd just dipped steaming food. The man rolled back and forth with the energy of a two-year-old, and soon there were corned beef and cabbage, fresh corn, just-baked sourdough bread, and sweet butter on Philip's plate, and he was eating with an appetite that he hadn't known for some weeks.

"A fine meal, Mr. Grey," he said, his mouth half full.

"I'll make someone a good wife someday," Adam said.

Philip looked up quickly in an effort to see if the tone of Adam Grey's words had been as bitter as he had imagined.

Adam laughed. "It's a matter of training and necessity, Mr. Trent. I have a small income. Very small indeed. I am forced to agree to have my wife take my place in the labor market, to go to work each day to earn our daily bread. But I am not content to sit on my stumps and mourn my fate."

"Adam, pass the corn," Julia said.

Adam laughed. "It's all right, my dear. I will not embarrass you further."

"I'm really very interested," Philip said. "I would say that you do a remarkable job. When Mrs. Grey told me that the flowers she brings to the office were grown by her husband, I had no idea—" He paused, having talked himself into a corner.

"That I was a legless wonder?" Adam asked with a chuckle.

"I do think it's remarkable that you can care for the garden and do the other things you do," Philip said.

"Oh, the woman's work is really rather enjoyable," he said. "I've always been quite the trencherman. I can cook exactly what I want to eat, and my dear Julia pretends—no matter what it is or how horrid it tastes—that it is pure nectar and exactly what she wants."

"Your dear Julia," she said, inclining her head, "thanks you for preparing her favorite meal. It is delicious." She looked at Philip. "You may have noticed that Adam is eating very little. His wounds left him with digestive problems. He makes the sacrifice of cooking my favorite meal now and then even though I try to dissuade him."

"If it gives you pleasure, my dear—"

"It does," she said. She lifted the covered dish and passed it to Philip. "Your plate is empty, Mr. Trent."

"Why, so it is," he said.

"Julia tells me you were an engineer captain in the army," Adam said.

"Guilty," Philip said around a mouthful.

"Odd. There was a Captain Philip Trent who was awarded the Congressional Medal. Surely not an engineer captain?"

"I'm afraid so," Philip said. "And you? Army?"

"Heaven forbid," Julia said. "Generations of Greys would have rattled their bones in their graves if Adam had entered the army."

"Navy way back," Adam said. "I graduated from the academy too late to get in on the real action, like chasing down the *Alabama* or taking the Mississippi forts. I was assigned as a brand-new ensign to William Cushing's *Monticello* blockading Wilmington."

"Now, there's a man who deserved medals," Philip said. "What sort of fellow was he?"

"Sometimes just a wild kid," Adam said. "Sometimes as old as old."

"Adam landed on the beach with Cushing when General Terry took Fort Fisher," Julia said.

"Odd," Philip said. "I was in a reb hospital in Wilmington when Fort Fisher fell."

"That is a coincidence," Adam said. "I say, I remember it now. You were with Lloyd Miles in that fool attempt to cut the Wilmington and Weldon Railroad."

Philip nodded. It was easy to talk with Adam Grey. "They didn't hang me as a spy because I was shot in both legs and couldn't walk to the gallows."

"The rebs exploded a mine almost directly under me when we first hit the beach," Adam said.

"I would think it was a pretty rough occasion down there at the fort," Philip said. "We could hear the bombardment."

"Rebs in that fort took it on the nose," Adam said. "Bill Cushing came to see me in the hospital and told me that when he finally got inside the gun mounds, there was a pile of arms and legs outside the reb hospital building five or six feet high." He laughed. "They were a bit more sanitary aboard the hospital ship. They threw my legs overboard. No fuss, no muss."

As Philip talked and listened, Adam had begun to eat, picking out bits of corned beef from the cabbage. Julia was looking at him with concern when he began to eat the cabbage as well.

"Adam," she said quietly, "should you?"

"My dear, it is quite good." He smiled at her, but his dead eyes remained distant, sunken.

"Incidentally," Adam said, "your friend Lloyd Miles is in Washington, but I suppose you know that."

"Yes," Philip said.

"He finally got his medal, too, as I remember. He wanted one badly enough. The poor fellow suffered the agonies of the damned when he went up the river with Bill Cushing to sink the *Albemarle* and couldn't even brag about it because the navy insisted that the presence of an army observer be kept secret."

Philip's hand had halted with a forkful of food halfway to his mouth. "What? Are you saying that Lloyd Miles went with Cushing on that mission?"

"One of three men to make it back to the fleet," Adam said. "Not all of them were killed. Some of them surrendered to the rebs. Some of *them* died in reb prison camps."

Philip wasn't listening. *Lloyd Miles had been with Cushing.* He would never have suspected. One of the most daring, dangerous feats of the war, and poor old Miles couldn't ever claim his share of the credit. No wonder he'd been so keen on organizing a showboat feat of his own. No wonder that a hint of frustration had emerged during one of their confrontations regarding Philip's Medal of Honor. If anyone had deserved the nation's highest military honor, it was the men on Cushing's mission, Miles included.

Philip's musing was interrupted by Adam's precipitous departure from the table. He lifted himself down onto his dolly and rolled frantically toward the open kitchen door, misjudged, hit the doorjamb, and pitched forward out the door. Philip leapt to his feet, but Julia managed to catch his arm. Adam crawled out of sight, and there came the sound of agonized retching.

"Should I go help him?" Philip asked.

"No, please." There were tears in her eyes. "He knew he shouldn't have eaten any. He's aware of what it does to his stomach."

"Internal injuries?"

"They said he was lucky to live through the first night. It's a miracle that he's alive now. He lives mainly on milk and soft bread."

"Nothing the doctors can do?"

"Just marvel that he's alive and tell him how lucky"—she sobbed suddenly, and her voice thickened—"how very *lucky* he is." She pressed the back of her hand to her cheek. "Excuse me. I can get very, very emotional where Adam is concerned."

"Did I hear someone use my name in vain?" Adam called from the doorway. His eyes looked even more sunken, and there was a sickly pallor to his face. He put his dolly inside, pulled himself in, and hopped onto the wheeled platform. "Sorry, Captain Trent, if I spoiled your appetite."

"Not at all."

"Adam, please go lie down," Julia urged. "I'll clear the table."

"I'd be very grateful," Adam said. He rolled out of sight.

The look that Julia sent after him raised pangs of memory in Philip, for once Leah had looked at him with the same love so vividly evident in her eyes.

"Mrs. Grey," he said, "it has been a splendid meal, and I have enjoyed the company."

"If you'll come again, Captain," Adam called from the bedroom, "I'll do southern hoecakes and broiled pork chops for you."

"Just name the day, Lieutenant," Philip said.

"Thank you for coming," Julia said as she let him out the kitchen door. He walked a narrow dirt path between healthy shrubs that would be filled with flowers in the spring. The packed earth showed the tracks of the wheels on Adam Grey's dolly. He turned toward the house and threw a quick salute. "You're more man than I am, Lieutenant," he whispered.

The well-dressed woman who was shown to a corner table in the unassuming little restaurant on Washington's north side was obviously out of place. But she showed no discomfort as the proprietor, fawning and bowing, brushed cigar ashes from the soiled tablecloth and held a chair for her to be seated.

"What may I bring the lady?" the man asked.

"Only tea, if you please," said Rosanna Pulliam. She placed her handbag in a chair and looked out the dingy window at a street lined with various small businesses. The sky had been threatening rain when she left her apartment, so she had also carried her umbrella. She placed it atop the handbag and consulted the large clock on the wall above the front entrance. She had chosen a table with a window view, but one that was effectively separated from the rest of the restaurant by a rather attractive area of plantings in wooden buckets.

After her tea had been delivered, she poured milk, added sugar, and sipped, nodding in satisfaction. Once again she checked the clock. She had been a quarter hour late when she arrived, and already another ten minutes had passed.

Rosanna hated to be kept waiting. Under normal circumstances she never would have tolerated such a slight, for she was demanding of others and always insisted that they meet her on her terms. Ordinarily the idea of waiting more than ten minutes for someone was out of the question. But the person she was waiting for was no ordinary man.

She sighed, looked out the window, and immediately lifted one hand to cover her face. Directly across the street a familiar carriage had pulled to a stop. Quickly she rose and moved to another chair, so that she would not be sitting directly by the window. Peeking at the carriage from her new position, she watched as Collis P. Huntington emerged from it on the side facing her, walked in front of the horses, and disappeared into a men's haberdashery. She could not imagine why Huntington was in such an isolated commercial district until she looked at the sign: J. WELLS AND SON. She had seen the same words on a silken label inside the tall silk hats favored by Huntington.

She cursed her slackness. She should have checked the locale more thoroughly before naming the little restaurant as a meeting place. But it was too late now, for even as Huntington went into the shop across the street, the front door of the restaurant opened—and Oliver Ames walked in.

Rosanna smiled at the inadvertent irony of the situation. She wondered what Huntington would think if he happened to look in the window and recognize one of his business competitors in a workingman's café. It could be, she thought, quite amusing—provided that Huntington did not recognize *her* as well.

Oliver Ames spoke to the proprietor, nodded, and came toward her table. He removed his hat, placed it on a chair, and took the seat opposite her in front of the window. Their eyes locked, but they remained silent, each waiting for the other to speak first.

John O'Brian had not been sleeping well. He would awaken in a cold sweat after dreaming that he had lost the election. Before becoming a congressman, he had owned a general store in a rural community; but he'd sold the store when he went to Washington, and the money had long since been spent, for it was expensive keeping up two places of residence. In his dream he was no longer a congressman; he was broke. He was disgraced for having accepted bribes from the railroad, and he faced losing his wife, for it had been disclosed that he had let a woman drown, a woman with whom he was having an assignation.

After Lafe Baker had left, O'Brian, hoping to relax, sedated himself with four slowly sipped drinks. Since then he had been drinking to keep the dreams away. He was sleeping soundly when he was awakened by a harsh weight on his face. He tried to shout, tried to kick away the covers, but a terrible lethargy was coming over him.

He awoke not in the middle of the night but with the sun coming in his window. He had a vile headache, and an odd smell lingered in the room. He sat up and looked around, disoriented, for nothing was in its place. Books were on the floor, and drawers were open, their contents spilled out. *The smell* . . . it was familiar.

"Ether," he whispered, and his insides coiled in fear as he remembered the feeling of not being able to breathe, of a weight on his face. He got up slowly from the bed and staggered to his desk in the next room. It had been thoroughly rifled. Jerking out the lower right-hand drawer, he fell to his knees, thrust his hand into the well of the drawer, and cursed as he felt all around. *The list of men to whom Oakes Ames and he had sold Crédit Mobilier stock was gone.*

"Baker," he whispered. It had to have been Baker. He got to his feet, cursing himself for having kept the list of names. It had seemed to be a good idea at the time, a form of insurance, but now he knew that he should have relied solely on his memory. Still in his nightdress, he sat down at the desk and began to write. Yes, he could reproduce the list within minutes. He knew most of the men, knew them quite well.

He turned his head and sniffed. It seemed that he could still smell the ether, and he had a bitter taste in his mouth; but another aroma lingered there in his study. For a moment he could not identify it, but then it came to him. Lilacs. There was a smell of lilacs in the room. He tried to remember if Baker had used a lilac scent. But when Baker had called on him, O'Brian had been too upset to notice. Still, it had to have been Baker who had crept into his bedroom in the middle of the night, pressed an ether-soaked sponge to his face, and then ransacked his flat before finding the list.

Given that it was Baker, what then? He wrote again, hurriedly. The note was not addressed by name. He would make no mistakes this time. It read simply, *I know you had your man take the list. I have reproduced it from memory. Don't intrude into my life again.*

He sealed the note and, later, after he had dressed, took it to a messenger service and sent it along to Dr. Thomas Durant.

CHAPTER 21

Philip had the habit of breakfasting at a small restaurant between his apartment and the office that he still thought of as Jeb Moverly's. On a crisp and lovely autumn morning he arrived at the café after a brisk walk that had the blood singing through his veins. Flipping a coin to the small boy who sold newspapers on the corner, he tucked a newspaper under his arm and opened the door to the smell of cooking hoecakes and brewing coffee. He called out a cheery good morning to the counterman and nodded to the waitress who came to stand beside his table even before he reached it.

"The usual, Mr. Trent?" the matronly woman asked.

"No," he said, "I'm a bit more hungry this morning, Marge. I think I'll have an extra egg or two and some of those hoecakes. They do smell good."

Marge scribbled hurriedly. "I see you have your paper," she said.

The woman, Philip thought, was looking at him rather oddly. "Something in the paper, Marge?"

"You'd better see for yourself, Mr. Trent."

He felt a chill when he saw his name glaring out from the banner headline: NEW CONGRESSMAN WANTED FOR MURDER IN PANAMA. Under the headline beside the two-column story was a reproduction of the request for extradition of Philip Trent from the Colombian government.

305

"We here all say it's a lie, Mr. Trent," the waitress said.

"Thank you, Marge," he said numbly as he read the story.

A moment later he was moving swiftly toward the café's door and heading directly for the offices of the Speaker of the House, for he was certain that it was Archibald Edwards who had given the press the information about that unfortunate incident in Panama. He wanted a word with Edwards—perhaps more than words—but as he walked, reason replaced anger. It didn't really matter who had been the source of the information; the question now was what the government would do about it.

He berated himself for having let the matter ride. It had been too long since Archibald Edwards had threatened him with the Panama affair, and he'd been too busy worrying about Leah, about graft on the transcontinental railroad—and about half a dozen other things that now seemed inconsequential—to look into the matter. How long had the Colombian request for his extradition been floating around Washington? Why hadn't the State Department contacted him?

He knew that he was not a cold-blooded murderer; he had shot only in self-defense. He should have gone to the authorities the minute Edwards had shown him the request for extradition. Perhaps then he would have been able to settle the matter without publicity.

It was obvious why the information had been released now: previously, he'd been only a congressional staffer, a nobody. Now he was a member of the United States House of Representatives. Now he was in a position to use true power in his investigation of the railroads. It seemed clear to him that his suspicions had been correct. At best, Archibald Edwards was in the pay of the Union Pacific; at worst, Schuyler Colfax—Speaker of the House, leader of Philip's political party, possible vice-presidential candidate on the ticket with General Grant—was also taking money from Durant, and conceivably from Collis Huntington of the Central Pacific as well. For what other reason could anyone have given the extradition papers to the press than to blunt Philip's effectiveness in trying to expose the grand larceny of the railroad barons?

Once he was at the receptionist's desk in the Speaker's office, Philip said, "I want to see Edwards."

The door to the Speaker's inner office flew open. "That you, Trent?" Schuyler Colfax roared as he appeared in the doorway. "Come in here. I want to talk to you."

Philip went into the office. Colfax slammed the door behind them, picked up a newspaper from his desk, and thrust it into Philip's face. "What in the name of Beelzebub is the meaning of this?"

"I think you might ask Archibald Edwards that," Philip said.

"Now, just what in the hell do you mean by that?" Colfax thundered. "I don't see Archibald's name mentioned here anywhere. I see your name. I see it in black headlines. I see you identified as a member of the Republican party. A member of *my* political party, and I want to know why you didn't tell us before we soiled the reputation of the House of Representatives by making you a member!"

"I wasn't aware that you had any part in my appointment," Philip said, bristling.

"Horse manure!" Colfax shouted. "Your governor came to me and asked about you, and I told him I thought you'd make a good congressman, more's the pity."

Philip felt suddenly tired. He sat down and let his hands rest limply in his lap. "Mr. Speaker," he said, "I'll tender my resignation immediately."

"Resignation? Not on your dad-blamed life. That would be too embarrassing to the party, your father, yourself—no, you'll stay on if it can be managed." Colfax turned, marched to sit behind his desk, and shook his head. "All right, tell me all about it."

When Philip was finished, Colfax asked, "No witnesses other than Panamanians?"

"None."

"None of the American passengers on the train?"

"Not to my knowledge."

"But the paper says that you were identified as the killer

by fellow passengers after you'd boarded your ship to California."

"I don't know," Philip said helplessly. "I shouldn't have gotten involved. Don't you think I've suffered, knowing that one of the men I killed was probably that woman's husband? Don't you think I'd give anything to have a chance to do it over?"

"But the man shot at you first?"

"Yes. And if I hadn't shot the second man, the one with the shotgun, I'd be dead."

Colfax nodded. "Why did you tell me to ask Edwards about this?"

"He knew about it several months ago."

"The devil you say," Colfax said with a jerk of his head.

"I came here this morning because I felt certain that it was Edwards who gave the story to the press."

Colfax was clearly at a loss. He rose, went to the door, and bellowed, "Get Edwards in here!"

"He's not in the office yet," the receptionist said.

Colfax closed the door. "You say that Edwards knew months ago?"

Philip nodded. "Mr. Speaker, do you know a man named Victor Flanagan?"

"No, why?"

"Have you any association with General B. F. Butler?"

"I don't think you're in a position to be asking questions, Trent," Colfax said, "but I'm interested in your reasons. Butler is a buffoon—a disgrace to the uniform of the Union and a disgrace to the House of Representatives. Now perhaps you'll tell me what's going on."

Colfax listened incredulously as Philip related his meetings with Flanagan and the association between Butler and Edwards. "Archibald Edwards tried to recruit you into some organization gathering information about crooked congressmen?"

"Yes," Philip said.

"And he threatened you with this Panama thing if you didn't cooperate?"

"He did."

"Son, you'd better not be lying to me."

"Why would I lie, knowing that all you'd have to do is ask Edwards?"

"I'll ask him, you can bet your ass on that." Again Colfax went to the door and yelled, "Is Edwards in yet?"

"No, sir," the receptionist said.

"Well, I'll take care of Edwards later," Colfax said. "Let's go."

"Where?"

"Just get off your butt and come with me."

Colfax made Philip go over the entire story again during a cab ride to the War Department. They were admitted to the office of the secretary of war immediately. General Grant rose from his desk to greet Colfax and to look at Philip with curiosity.

"This is Congressman Philip Trent," Colfax said.

Grant, a broad and stumpy man, grimly nodded his bearded head. "I know the name. I know the name of every winner of the Congressional Medal of Honor, living and dead. And I did not enjoy seeing that great and honorable award mentioned in the morning paper in a story about a double murder in Panama." He motioned the men to sit down. "I suppose, Schuyler, that you've brought this young man to me expecting me to do something about the trouble he's in."

"I thought maybe you'd be interested, General," Colfax said.

"I would think that this is a matter for the attorney general," Grant said, "not the War Department."

"Maybe, maybe not," Colfax replied. "I think this boy's war record entitles him to your help, General. And if you don't think so, then I call on you as the man who, after the next presidential election, will be the undisputed leader of the Republican party. Someone is out to get Philip Trent, probably because he's been raising a stink about overruns on the transcontinental railroad, or maybe just because he's been appointed a Republican member of the House. At any rate, he deserves better."

Grant was silent for a moment. "Tell me what's going on."

Once again Philip was called upon to tell the story of his misplaced chivalry in Panama. Grant listened with intense concentration. When Philip finished, the secretary looked at Colfax. "You believe this boy, Schuyler?"

"I do," Colfax confirmed.

Grant growled in his throat. "Well, I believe you, too, Trent. Damned fool thing to do, but I guess it was in character. Couldn't expect anything else from a man with your decorations." He stood with his head down, just as Philip had seen him do once after a battle. "All right," he said, a brooding expression on his face. "Let me run with this, Schuyler." He rang a bell, and a young man popped into the office. "Jimmy," he said, "go out and round me up a few newspapermen. Get Flemming of the *Post* especially." The young man nodded and disappeared.

Grant turned to Colfax. "Schuyler, you might do a little talking on your end too. By the time I finish with Flemming and the others, they'll write stories that will make this young man look like a modern knight in armor, daring death to protect a beautiful dusky-skinned Panamanian maiden. Maybe you can come at it from the angle that it's all a Colombian lie to try to discredit the United States Congress."

Colfax nodded.

"Now you two git," Grant said. "I have things to do."

On the way back to Colfax's office Philip said, "I appreciate this, Mr. Speaker. What can I do to help?"

Colfax grunted. "Go home. Lock the door. Keep your mouth shut. Don't talk to any newspapermen."

"I'd like to talk to Edwards," Philip said.

"You leave Edwards to me," Colfax ordered. "If that gentleman has had something going on the side, using the power of my office, I'll take care of it."

Gus Trent sat in Philip's apartment sipping hot tea. The Philip Trent story had been news for several days. The headlines thundered: WAR HERO SAVES THREATENED WOMAN IN PANAMA, CONGRESSIONAL LEADERS DEFEND FALSELY ACCUSED CONGRESSMAN, GEN. GRANT ASKS STATE DEPART-

MENT TO PROTEST FALSE ACCUSATION AGAINST MEDAL OF HONOR WINNER.

"Well," Gus said, "you came out of this one smelling like a rose." He had heard the story straight from Philip's mouth. "How'd you get to be so quick with a handgun?"

"There were times when that's all I carried, a pistol and sword." He shrugged. "I liked the new .44. It's a fine weapon. Well balanced, accurate. I had a lot of time on my hands here and there, and I did some practicing with it."

"Lucky you did." Gus laughed. "I hope you don't carry it here in Washington—even though a man sometimes needs a gun in this town."

Philip shook his head. "No, I keep it in the desk, there. In the drawer with the lock."

"I wish you'd told me about all this right after you got home. We could have started some damage control right then."

"I guess I was ashamed of it, Dad. I stuck my nose into someone else's business and—"

"And you could have gotten it shot off," Gus said. "I'm not blaming you for doing what you thought was right. Damned sad thing to have a man beat a woman."

"I'm sorry to be an embarrassment to you." Philip shook his head ruefully. "I told you it should have been you taking J.T.'s place in the House."

"I'll have none of that," Gus objected. "It's all come out for the best, anyhow. You're the most famous congressman in Washington at the moment. And having General Grant on your side will assure that you'll be elected to a full term next year." He paused. "That is, if that's what you decide you want."

Philip laughed. "I haven't even sat in one session of the House yet. But I have to admit that I'm growing accustomed to being recognized and treated with respect. I could do without the attentions of the lobbyists, but I know that's a part of the job. Right now I'd say that if you and the others think I should run for election next year, I will."

"Good, good. Glad to hear it." Gus rubbed his chin.

"Now, who do you think it was that released the story and why?"

"I think it was Archibald Edwards," Philip said without hesitation. "Why? Damned if I know, unless he's in the pay of the railroads. That's the only reason I can think of that anyone would want to discredit me, maybe have the House refuse to seat me when it convenes."

"It backfired on 'em," Gus said. He was thoughtful for a while. "I'd guess that they're scared of you. They must think that you know something that can be damaging to them. The question is, what will they do next?"

"What can they do?" Philip asked.

The answer to that question was to come to him with brutal clarity in the near future.

For John O'Brian, things started to go bump in the night. Even after liberal quantities of alcohol to deaden his senses, sleep shunned him. He would close his eyes, and his imagination would hear the soft footfall, the creak of the stairs, the rustle of clothing, as a feral thing of the blackness crept toward his bed to lay a heavy hand over his mouth. The memory of the smell and taste of ether stayed with him in the quiet, chill hours before dawn. To know that someone had entered his flat, had penetrated to his very bed, was a horror that eroded his confidence more and more as the days passed.

He had given most of his office staff time off to visit their homes. Only one new woman was left to take the names of visitors and to announce them to O'Brian when he was there. No one who knew O'Brian well was around to witness his disintegration; the new employee simply believed that her boss had always been a heavy drinker, rather vague in his speech, and often in something akin to a trance, with his eyes wide and staring and a haunted expression on his face.

O'Brian was like a man on the scaffold with the rope around his neck, waiting for the trapdoor to open beneath him, anticipating that terrible, short, quick fall. Day after day he expected to see headlines announcing his guilt or to be visited by some grim-faced law enforcer. When nothing happened, he concluded that his persecutors were waiting for

Congress to convene before dropping the bombshell that would expose John O'Brian and ruin his life.

Twice he tried to see Oakes Ames, and each time he was told that Congressman Ames was not in his office. Twice he went to the Union Pacific office in Washington and asked for Thomas Durant; twice he was told that Dr. Durant was out of town, the second time by Lloyd Miles, who looked at O'Brian's rumpled clothing and bloodshot eyes and said, "John, you've got to get hold of yourself."

December came, bringing with it dreary days, a light snow, and freezing winds that cut through the thickest overcoat. O'Brian was sure that he was being followed. He could never quite catch the spy at it, but he often had the feeling that eyes were on the back of his neck. Once, when he turned suddenly, he saw a bearded man, his hat pulled low to shadow his features. The man turned aside quickly and looked into a store window. Though O'Brian never saw that man again, his feeling of discomfort grew.

Ten days before Congress was to begin the 1867–68 winter session, O'Brian reached the end of his rope. He was existing in a haze of half-drunkenness and near exhaustion. Unable to sleep for more than a few minutes at a time, he sought desperately for a way out of his torment, and the answer came to him in a thunderclap of revelation. He inadvertently got a glimpse of himself in the mirror, and his shock at his appearance prompted him to reach for a bottle. He caught himself in the act of tilting it to his mouth; in disgust, he smashed the bottle against the wall. Afterward he bathed, found fresh clothing, and visited a barber for a trim and a shave. He felt fresh and clean but a bit shaky on the inside when he arrived at the office of Philip Trent.

He was greeted cordially by Trent, but he could see the question in the young man's face. "I guess you're wondering why I'm here."

"Well, it's always nice to see you, John," Philip said.

"Odd that you should feel that way, in view of what you think of me," O'Brian said.

"What can I do for you, John?"

"You think you're so all-fired holy," O'Brian heard himself

saying accusingly. He shook his head. "Sorry. Didn't mean that. Actually I'm here to help you, Trent."

"In what way?" Philip asked.

O'Brian sat down and felt better, felt his confidence growing. "Trent, I did you wrong during the Moverly committee hearing, but I plead ignorance, maybe stupidity. You see, Trent, I sincerely believe that the transcontinental railroad is going to be a boon to this country, and I couldn't believe that men would take advantage of this great, patriotic endeavor to line their own pockets. I'm afraid that I let myself be used."

Philip Trent remained silent.

"You're not making it any easier for me," O'Brian complained.

"Sorry, John. I'm very interested in what you're saying."

"They trapped me," O'Brian said. For a dizzying moment he considered telling Trent everything—the woman, the dark, frigid waters of the creek . . . it all came back to him with a force that silenced him for a few moments. But the next thing he said was "I can give you names, Trent, of senators and members of the House—all of them sharing in the profits of railroad construction."

Philip was leaning forward, hanging on O'Brian's every word. "John, we can do this country a great service by stopping the graft on the railroad. Give me the names. Let's take them to Schuyler Colfax—"

"No!" O'Brian said forcefully. "Not so fast. We have to have an understanding. I'll blow the whistle on everyone who owns Crédit Mobilier stock only if my name is taken off the list and not mentioned in the investigation."

"But your name is on the list?" Philip asked.

"I didn't want their damned stock, Trent," O'Brian said. "You've got to believe me."

"All right," Philip said. "I'll do all that I can to keep your name out of it, John."

A disturbing thought made O'Brian want to weep. "But they'll tell," he muttered. "They'll bring me into it when they realize that it was I who opened up."

"John, I don't know what to say. I'm not fully informed

about how Congress handles a situation like this. Let me talk to a few people. Maybe something can be worked out."

O'Brian brightened. "I can say that I played along with them just to get the goods on the ones who were being paid off." He slapped his thigh. "Yes, that's it. All the time I was working with you, and I pretended to take the stock just to get on the inside."

Philip, shocked and saddened by O'Brian's condition—his hands shaking, a tremor in his chin, his eyes red and sunken —knew that he didn't sound convincing when he said, "Yes, that might work, John. Have you got the list of names with you?"

O'Brian laughed. "Think I'm crazy? Think I'd carry a thing like that around with me?" He struggled to his feet, swaying. "Come to think of it, Trent, I'm not so sure it was a good idea coming here. If they saw me talking to you . . ."

He remembered how the bearded man had turned so quickly to put his hands behind his back and look into a store window, and he shivered as he remembered how it felt to be followed. "Maybe I'll be in touch," he said, but his voice held no conviction.

O'Brian had never replaced the surrey that had been lost in the creek. He had sold the horses after both of them had been found by a man hired by Lloyd Miles. Now he either walked or hired a cab. When he left Philip Trent's office, snow was falling again, the small flakes blown on an Arctic wind. He hailed a cab, and when he had given the driver his address, he sank back into the seat.

He felt miserable and cold. The clarity of mind that he had enjoyed on the way to see Trent was gone, replaced by an aching need for a drink. He ordered the driver to stop at a saloon, where he purchased bourbon.

When he stepped down from the cab in front of his building, he clutched a whiskey bottle to his breast and ran through the frigid wind and snow to the entrance. It was an old three-story building that sat on a corner, its dark, heavy brick surrounded by a wrought-iron fence as high as a man's head. He grasped two of the decorative spears that topped the fence and pulled the gate securely closed.

At the door O'Brian stopped to look back into the blowing snow. The cab that had delivered him was rolling smartly down the street; nothing else moved. Still he had the feeling of eyes on him. In his room, before he lit the gas jets, he peered out the window. That street was empty. Two floors below him, snow was being blown into a drift against the side of the building. The wrought-iron fence, quite close on that side of the building, made a startlingly black line against the snow.

It was growing dark. He lit lamps, opened the bottle, and after some hefty pulls on the neck began to feel better. Perhaps things were not so bad after all, he decided as the whiskey warmed his throat. Philip Trent had seemed eager and willing to help. Perhaps his idea of saying that he'd accepted Crédit Mobilier stock and distributed it in order to expose congressmen and senators willing to be bribed by the railroads was the answer.

After thinking about it for a while, O'Brian was sure. He sat at his desk and wrote a copy of the list of the men to whom Ames and he had sold stock. Leaving it on the desk, he went to bed, thinking that now, at last, he'd be able to sleep.

He heard his name being called as if from a great distance. He had to struggle up from a deep sleep to open his eyes. He'd left one gas jet burning in the sitting room to dispel the terrors of the dark, and its light came dimly into his bedroom.

"John, John . . ." a voice was whispering. A woman's voice, plaintive and sad. "Help me, John."

He lifted his head. There was a stir at the foot of his bed . . . pale flesh . . . movement.

"John, help me. Don't let me drown."

He tried to scream but managed only a strangled croak, for *she* was moving around the footboard of his bed. Her blond hair was hanging lankly to her bare shoulders. Her face was white, a ghastly white, and her eyes as dark and sunken as the coals in a snowman's face.

"I'm dying, John. Help me." Her eerie, raspy voice was echoing in his mind. And the stench of her . . . the pungent, piercing stink of the long dead cut into his senses. He was gagging and strangling in his effort to scream out his protest.

She stood only feet away now, and she was moving toward him, gliding as if her feet did not touch the floor.

"Hold me, John. Kiss me. Love me and I won't die."

"God, no," he whispered, leaping from the bed. His feet tangled in his nightdress, and he fell heavily, quickly rolling to his hands and knees, for *she* was moving toward him.

"Help me, John. Help me. Come to me."

Her arms were spread wide. He could see the white glow of her breasts, and the stench of her was overpowering.

"You can't get away from me, John," she said as he scrambled on all fours like an animal toward the bedroom door. She moved between him and the light. Her eerily white face and the black, sunken eyes bent toward him. "Kiss me, John, and you will join me. Kiss me. Hold me, and you will be with me."

The scent of the grave, the whiteness of her, and the sunken eyes sent him to his feet. She moved toward him rapidly, and he managed one dreadful, throat-tearing scream as he ran full tilt and smashed into the glass of the tall, big-paned window overlooking the snow-covered street. His weight carried him through glass and window frame, sending him outward on a descending arc. He screamed all the way down, kicking his feet and turning in the air to land lengthwise on the upright spears of the wrought-iron fence, the cold, rusting points penetrating from throat to groin at intervals of ten inches.

In the open window of the flat above, a white, eerie face appeared briefly. She ran from the bedroom, pulled on a heavy coat with a hood, and hid the white face in its shadows, moving swiftly and silently to fold the list of names that O'Brian had left on his desk, thrusting it into her coat pocket. There was no time to conduct a thorough search of the flat. She gathered newspapers, crumpled them, and placed them below the draperies beside the window through which the chill breath of the snowstorm was blowing.

She used one newspaper as a torch, rolling it and igniting it with the gas jet in the sitting room. She waited until the drapes had started to blaze. Closing the door to O'Brian's flat behind her, she walked calmly to the stairs. Behind her the wind sucked at the flames, snuffed them, and soon the smoke had dissipated. At the front entrance she looked both ways. The snow had thickened, and the streets were empty. She faded quickly into the night.

Only when she was a safe distance from O'Brian's flat did she discard the dead, decomposing rat, wrapped in cheese-cloth, that dangled at her waist.

CHAPTER 22

The death of Congressman John O'Brian made the front page of the newspapers, but the investigation, conducted by Lieutenant Tom Jensen of the Metropolitan Police, was pushed to the back pages by larger events. President Andrew Johnson appeared before the Senate to defend his dismissal of Edwin Stanton as secretary of war. Johnson's appeal for Senate approval of his decision fell largely on deaf ears, for the vote to disapprove the President's action under the Tenure of Office Act was overwhelmingly against him. As a result, Ulysses S. Grant resigned as secretary of war, and Stanton was quickly back in his old office. The fires of hatred for Andrew Johnson burned brighter than ever in Stanton's breast.

One of the first visitors to Stanton's office after his reinstatement was Lafe Baker. The secretary of war looked at him questioningly.

"I just wanted to congratulate you on your victory, Mr. Secretary," Lafe said.

"I've won a battle," Stanton contended. "The war continues."

"But I hear rumblings, Mr. Secretary. I hear that the House of Representatives is going to impeach Johnson within the next few weeks."

319

"They will begin discussion of a resolution of impeachment," Stanton confirmed.

"I'd say, Mr. Secretary, that in a battle against the most powerful man in the United States, the President, you need all the help you can get. As it happens, I'm available."

"Thank you, Lafe," Stanton said without enthusiasm. "But it seems to me that we've traveled that route before."

"Well, Mr. Secretary, I did hand you some pretty incriminating evidence against the man."

"Lafe," Stanton said, "if adultery were an impeachable offense, we'd have a devil of a time staffing the government."

"I understand that Johnson is to be charged with several counts of violating the Constitution, with spending public funds unlawfully, and with violation of the Tenure of Office Act. Now, I still have contacts in Washington, Mr. Secretary. I can help you to document some of the charges."

"Thank you, Lafe," Stanton responded. "I appreciate the offer. But I think it's time you realized that you have become more of a liability than an asset to any man in public life."

Lafe stood up. "Well, thanks a hell of a lot!" He gave Stanton a slight salute. "I'll remember you in my memoirs, Mr. Secretary."

As Lafe left the War Department, he realized that he'd entered that building for what was probably the last time. Oddly enough, he felt as if a load had been lifted from his shoulders. His mind was made up. He had a few loose ends to tie up, and then he was going to contact Phineas Headley, the newspaperman who was going to help him write his book, and tell him that it was time to get started.

He did not want to leave any unexploded mines on his back trail in Washington. The first item on his agenda was to find out why Archibald Edwards had been fired so suddenly by Schuyler Colfax. Lafe had gained that information from a clerk in the Colfax offices when he had tried to contact Edwards just before making one last attempt to secure honorable employment in Washington under Stanton, a man who could give him the protection he needed to ply his trade. Now that he'd been turned down, it was time to erase his tracks.

He found Edwards working in the office of Congressman Benjamin Butler. When Lafe entered, Edwards looked up from his desk and nodded coldly, and Butler, who was standing over Edwards, fixed Lafe with one crossed eye and looked grim.

"Your welcome overwhelms me," Lafe said with a grin.

"You cost me my job," Edwards accused.

"But you have another here with General Butler," Lafe said, spreading his hands.

Edwards opened his mouth to reply but quickly looked up at Butler and fell silent.

Lafe continued, "Admittedly, with General Butler you are a bit removed from the center of power, but there are still plenty of opportunities for an ambitious man."

"What do you want here, Baker?" Butler demanded, coming around the desk.

"Just touching base with my friends."

"It has been demonstrated that you are incapable of protecting your friends," Butler maintained. "You said all along that Philip Trent was no threat. You instructed Mr. Edwards to threaten Trent with exposure of the Panama affair, and you badly misjudged the effect of such an action. You made Trent a hero and cost Mr. Edwards his position."

"Well," Lafe said lightly, "some you win, some you lose."

"You may consider our association at an end, Mr. Baker," Butler stated coldly. He turned away from Lafe.

"Oh? Are you going to gather your own blackmail material now?" Lafe asked acidly. "Or do you expect Edwards to do it for you?"

Butler's face puffed up and turned red. He cleared his throat. "Good day, Mr. Baker."

Lafe Baker tipped his hat to Butler, nodded to Edwards, and sought the street.

Well, he thought once his lungs were filled with fresh air, *since good things don't last forever, isn't it marvelously convenient that irritating things come to an end too?* Part of the fun of the whole enterprise had been playing Butler for the fool. And Edwards? He was just a small cog in the little information machine that Lafe had put together for Durant. If he needed an errand boy, he still had the good sergeant Victor Flanagan. Despite his scheme to embarrass Philip Trent having backfired rather badly, he still might be able to squeeze a golden eagle or two out of Thomas Durant.

It was, after all, going to be difficult to leave Washington when such exciting things were happening. The upcoming impeachment hearings would be interesting. And Lafe had been greatly intrigued by the grisly death of Congressman John O'Brian. He would have bet his watch and chain that O'Brian's demise was tied in with the matter of Crédit Mobilier stock ownership in Congress. O'Brian had been known as a railroad congressman. His death had been called suicide. But Lafe thought it odd that a man dressed only in a nightshirt would dive through an unopened window with enough force to smash glass and pane frames. Somewhere, he feared, he was missing an opportunity, but for the life of him he couldn't get a handle on it.

He decided to stay in Washington for a few more days, even though his morning mail brought a note from Thomas Durant telling him curtly that his services were no longer required. The coin of the realm was flowing into the pockets of everyone in Washington, it seemed—everyone but the very deserving Lafe Baker.

He began to feel put upon. First he'd been deserted by Stanton in a time of crisis; then two fools, Edwards and Butler, had turned insultingly against him; and now Thomas Durant had fired him. It was time to find either a new employer or a new opportunity. He decided to seek the latter.

Lafe knew Lieutenant Tom Jensen of the Metropolitan Police from the war years. He caught Jensen coming out of Police Headquarters and walked a way with him, reminding the lieutenant of old times before asking about the bizarre death of John O'Brian.

"What's your interest in this, Lafe?" Jensen asked.

"Curiosity, just professional curiosity," Lafe answered. "From the outside, Tom, it just doesn't look like suicide to me."

Jensen came down with a fit of coughing.

"You neither?" Lafe asked.

"Well, you've got to do something to close the file when it's a congressman involved," Jensen contended.

"So you're going to call it suicide and let it go at that?"

"I'm going to keep it open as long as I have to," Jensen said. "Although a couple of things about it bother me."

"Such as?"

"I notice smells, Lafe. I guess I've got a more sensitive nose than most folks. And up there in the flat, even with the bedroom window open, I smelled something, especially in the other rooms, where the wind wasn't blowing in. Something dead—dead a long time."

"Well, the newspapers said there'd been a small fire," Lafe offered.

"Only in the bedroom. Looked as if someone had made an attempt to set the place on fire. There were curled paper ashes under the draperies. The material had burned about halfway up, then, I guess, the wind blew out the flames. So there was a little bit of a burned-cloth smell in the bedroom, but not much because the wind was whistling right in through the broken window. There was snow blown all the way across the room to the bed."

"Any footprints in the snow?"

"Nope. So it had to have blown in after he went through the window."

"Something dead . . ." Lafe mused. "Dead mouse in a trap? Leftover food?"

"You ever go onto a battlefield in the hot summertime about four or five days after, before they had a chance to bury all the bodies?"

"Yep," Lafe said, wincing at the memory.

"Like that. And you'd think that that smell would overpower everything else, but in O'Brian's study, around his desk, there was a faint hint of lilacs."

"Scented hair tonic?"

"Nope. I checked O'Brian's stuff. He had some rose water. Nothing scented with lilacs."

"No sign of a struggle, maybe like someone threw him through the window?" Lafe asked.

"No. Everything was in order except the bed. The covers

were thrown all the way off, as if he'd gotten up in a hurry."
Jensen halted. "Here's where I'm headed, Lafe," he said.
"How long you gonna be in Washington?"

"For a while," Lafe said.

"I don't have to remind you that you have no official
status, do I?"

"I know my place, Tom," Lafe said. "I won't go messing
around in your business. As I said, I was just curious. I never
heard of anyone diving onto four wrought-iron fence spears
before. By the way, how'd you get him off?"

"Had to saw off the barbs on the tips of the spears with a
hacksaw," Jensen explained, grimacing. "And it was colder'n
a witch's tit. Then we got four ladders and climbed up above
him, and four of us lifted at the same time."

After being sworn in as a member of the House of Representatives, Philip Trent was assigned a back-row desk on the
right side of the center aisle. He was given five minutes on the
floor in which to introduce himself, and it seemed that all he
did for the first few days was shake hands and try to remember the names and faces of his fellow congressmen. There
were several bits of housekeeping legislation to be handled,
and Philip followed the lead of Speaker Colfax in his votes on
the purely internal matters. He was inundated with paper. It
seemed that everyone in the house had a pet bill he wanted to
introduce during the session, and it seemed to take a ream of
paper to explain every one of them, so that Philip was doing
more reading than he really wanted to do.

When Andrew Johnson fired Edwin Stanton that February
for the second time and nominated General Lorenzo Thomas
in his place, the long-awaited explosion came at last. The
House of Representatives voted a resolution of impeachment,
with a freshman congressman from Maryland going against
the majority to vote nay. The resolution cited eleven charges,
including a very general one that Johnson had tried to
disgrace Congress with his inflammatory and scandalous
harangues. Trial was set in the Senate to begin on March
thirteenth, and Congressman Benjamin Butler was named as
one of the prosecutors.

With attentions being absorbed by the upcoming drama in the Senate, the House leadership refused to call up any important legislation, and absenteeism was high. Sometimes half the chairs on the right side of the aisle were vacant. Philip asked the leadership for floor time, and on an afternoon when half the House membership was in the Senate galleries watching the big show, he held the floor for over an hour, detailing his charges against the two Pacific Railroad builders. He was flattered when, after adjournment, half a dozen of his peers in the House approached him, questioning the sources of his charges and agreeing that something should be done to curb the arrogant raid on the Treasury.

It was a good feeling to be praised by other congressmen. He felt that he'd expressed himself well with his speech on the House floor, and he left Capitol Hill in good spirits—which evaporated as soon as he entered his cold, empty, gloomy apartment.

He stopped in the middle of the parlor and listened to the silence. True, he was recovering from the hurt that the loss of Leah had caused, but now and again the old pain returned, as fierce and as potent as ever.

He poured a measure of brandy from a bottle of ancient vintage that Gus had given him as a congratulatory gift after he had been sworn in. He was hoarding it, allowing himself only a few sips each evening. There was some reading he had to catch up on. Positioning himself on a sofa near a gaslight, he loosened his collar, slumped onto his tailbone, and lifted a sheaf of paper, which outlined some other congressman's idea of a desirable law. He'd read only a few lines when his eyes became heavy, and the words blurred and ran together. He let his eyes close, only to be startled into instant wakefulness by a knock on the door. A messenger handed him a note. He tipped the boy with a silver coin and walked back to open the message under the lamp.

The note was brief: *Trent: Come to my home immediately if you want a certain list of names.* The message ended with an address and a scrawled signature—*Victor Flanagan.*

Philip left his apartment with haste, taking a cab toward the northern outskirts of the city into a section of small cottages mixed in with the lean-tos and shanties of the horde of unemployed veterans, freed slaves, and riffraff that had descended on Washington during and after the war. Flanagan's house showed scaling paint, loose shingles, and general neglect.

After Philip had climbed out, the cab with its smart team of horses sped away down the muddy, rutted street. Lamplight glowed from the windows of some of the houses. He opened a weakly hinged gate in a picket fence, walked to the front door, and knocked. There was no answer. He knocked harder, causing the door to swing ajar with a creak of hinges.

"Flanagan?" Philip called. He pushed the door open farther. One oil lamp was burning on a desk in front of Victor Flanagan, who was sitting with his back to the door, slumped over the battered desk. "Hey, Flanagan," Philip called. He entered the room, closing the door behind him.

As he moved toward Flanagan his toe contacted something on the floor, and he looked down. A New Model Army Revolver, a Colt .44, skittered to a stop. Philip bent, picked it up, and froze, for etched into the metal just in front of the trigger guard was his own name, Captain Philip Trent. He'd been given the Colt .44 by the men of his company after Gettysburg, while he was still in the hospital, and they had had the weapon engraved with his name.

His heart pounding, Philip moved to the desk and looked into the dead face of Victor Flanagan. He had been shot in the heart. His blood soaked his clothing and ran down between his legs onto the littered board floor.

Philip looked around quickly. The house was built on the same pattern as Julia Grey's—three rooms in a line. The bedroom was rank with the musty smell of unwashed linens. The kitchen smelled of long-since-eaten cabbage and onions.

He came back to the front room, his .44 still in his hand. He lifted the gun and sniffed at the barrel. It had been fired recently. Victor Flanagan's flesh was cold; but when Philip lifted one hand, there was a limp flexibility to the arm. The touch of the dead man's flesh penetrated the shock that had insulated Philip from the realization that someone had gone to great lengths to make it look as if he had killed Flanagan.

He looked at the .44. The last time he'd seen it was when he'd put it away in the locked drawer of his desk. That it was his was beyond doubt.

He thrust the gun under his coat into his belt and turned toward the front door. He needed to get out of Flanagan's house and find a place where he could think. He had taken only one step when the door burst open, and he was looking down the barrel of a pistol.

"Stop where you are!" a hard voice grated.

It took Philip a moment to put a name to a face that was quite familiar. "Ah," he said after a long pause, during which the gun pointed at his nose did not waver, "Lieutenant Jensen." Jensen, he recalled, had talked with him after his encounter with the two thugs who were after his notes on the operations of the Union Pacific.

"Mr. Trent," Tom Jensen said, "I want you to use your left hand. Reach under your coat and very slowly remove your gun, using just your fingertips."

Philip did as he was told.

"Now bend over and put it on the floor."

Philip straightened after obeying the order.

"Now back up and put your shoulders against the wall, there."

Jensen moved to the desk and took a quick look at the dead man, but the muzzle of his pistol remained pointed at Philip's nose.

"Lieutenant Jensen," Philip said, "if you'll allow me, I have in my pocket the note that brought me here."

"Slowly," Jensen said.

Removing the note from his inside coat pocket, Philip held it out. Jensen reached for it gingerly and then opened it. He bent, picked up Philip's gun, sniffed at the barrel, turned it in his hand, and lifted his eyebrows when he saw Philip's name engraved on the metal.

A uniformed policeman came into the room. "All clear outside, Lieutenant," he said.

"Right," Jensen said. "I want you to call on the neighbors, Murphy. Ask if any of them heard a gunshot and, if so, at what time. See if you can find out who reported the murder."

"I wish you'd put that gun away," Philip said. "It makes me nervous."

"It makes me feel right secure," Jensen said, but he let the muzzle drop so that it no longer pointed toward Philip. "All right, Mr. Trent, maybe you'd better talk to me."

"I went directly to my apartment after the House adjourned for the day," Philip explained. "I was the last speaker. I finished just before five. I went home, sat down to read, and fell asleep. I was awakened by a messenger with that note you just read."

"What time was that?"

"Ten minutes of seven. I know because I looked at my watch. I found a cab and came here. My pistol was lying on the floor between Flanagan and the front door."

"You admit that it's your pistol?"

"Of that there can be no doubt," he said. "It's possible that someone could have had my name engraved into the metal; but it would have been impossible, without having my pistol as a model, to duplicate certain dents on the grip."

"How would you explain its being here?" Jensen asked.

"I'm sure that it was stolen," Philip asserted.

"Convenient," Jensen muttered. "Do you know this man?"

"Yes. His name is Victor Flanagan. He worked for General Ben Butler."

"The Beast?"

"Yes."

"How do you know that?"

"This man approached me on behalf of Butler, asking me to join Butler in an effort to ferret out wrongdoings by members of Congress."

Jensen frowned. "So you are working with him?"

"No, I am not. I listened to him because it seemed at first that General Butler and I shared the same interests."

"Which were?"

"Stopping the overruns on construction costs on the transcontinental railroad."

"Mr. Trent, you will have to admit that it looks pretty bad. Here's a dead man, and here you are with a gun that's been recently fired. And you admit knowing him, admit that you've been associated with him."

"Lieutenant, I was brought here by the note you have in your hand. Flanagan was dead when I arrived, and my pistol was lying on the floor. It's quite obvious that someone has taken a great deal of trouble to make it look as if I killed Flanagan."

Jensen stuck Philip's pistol in his belt. "All right, Mr. Trent, stand easy." He holstered his own gun and walked into the bedroom. "Mr. Trent, would you bring that lamp in here?"

Philip carried the lamp and watched as Jensen examined the room, then gave the kitchen the same treatment. Back in the living room he stood in front of the desk and sniffed the air. "Mr. Trent, do you use something that is scented with lilacs? A hair tonic or skin tonic of some kind?"

"No. Why do you ask?"

"You don't smell it?"

Philip smelled only the rankness of Flanagan's house and the rich, sickening stench of drying blood. "No, I don't."

The uniformed policeman was back. "Everyone in that closest house is dead drunk, Lieutenant. They wouldn't have been able to hear it thunder. Folks in the other houses didn't hear anything either. None of them reported the murder."

"Thank you, Sergeant," Jensen said.

"Shall I put the cuffs on this one, sir?" Murphy asked.

"No, that won't be necessary, will it, Mr. Trent?"

"I hope not," Philip said.

"You understand that it's going to be necessary for me to take you in," Jensen added.

"I see why you might think it's necessary," Philip replied, "but I assure you that you're making a mistake."

"If you think I'm pleased with the idea of arresting a congressman, you've got another think coming," Jensen said. "I don't like this at all. One way or the other it's going to be trouble. If I didn't arrest you, it might cost me my job. Look at it my way, Mr. Trent. If you were in my position, what would you do?"

Philip was silent.

"On the other hand, if I arrest you and you can prove you didn't kill this fellow, you, as a congressman, could cause me to lose my job."

Philip was angry, but he found that he could not direct that anger toward Jensen. He walked with the policeman to a surrey. Neither of them spoke during the long ride to the police station.

The entire situation seemed unreal to Philip until he walked into the warmth of the station to see a busy swirl of blue uniforms. He stood before a uniformed sergeant and heard Tom Jensen say, "We're going to have to charge Mr. Philip Trent with the murder of one Victor Flanagan."

The words seemed to hang in the air like a noxious gas.

"I don't want him put in the tank with the lowlifes," Jensen said. "He is a member of the Congress."

The uniformed sergeant raised his eyebrows in surprise and looked at Philip with new interest. "All's we got is the isolation cell, then."

"I think Mr. Trent would prefer that," Jensen said. He turned to Philip, who nodded his concurrence. "I imagine you'll want to contact your lawyer."

Philip hadn't thought of that. "Well, I don't have one," he said. "What you can do for me, Lieutenant Jensen, is get a message to the Speaker of the House, Mr. Colfax, and ask him to send an attorney. And I'd appreciate it if you'd also ask Mr. Colfax to contact my father. He'll know where."

"Be glad to do it, Mr. Trent," Jensen said. He shuffled his feet, looked away, and added, "Mr. Trent, that was a damned fool thing to do, going into a neighborhood like that all alone. If you had only taken someone with you, someone to verify that Flanagan was dead when you arrived."

"Thank you," Philip said. "I appreciate your concern."

He was taken to a small cell, which contained only a cot, a straight-backed chair, and a slop bucket that reeked of past use. He sat down on the cot. He'd slept in worse places during the war and with more assurance that the bedding was populated. He had no idea how long it would take for Schuyler Colfax to send someone to his aid if, indeed, the Speaker didn't decide to wash his hands of a freshman congressman who couldn't stay out of trouble.

He removed his coat, loosened his collar, hung the coat on the back of the chair, and lay down, his hands under his head. He knew that he was in a tight spot. There would be only his word that he was not the killer, for he had seen no one after leaving Capitol Hill, other than the messenger boy, until Jensen had walked into Victor Flanagan's house. It looked as if they had him this time, "they" being the railroad barons, for there could be no other reason for the deliberate frame-up. No one other than the railroad barons would have any reason to remove so effectively a troublesome congressman from public life.

He asked himself who would have known that he'd had any association with Victor Flanagan. Butler and Edwards, of course. And he'd mentioned Flanagan to Schuyler Colfax. Perhaps that shadowy figure, the former head of what he had liked to call the secret service, General Lafe Baker, was behind this. Neither Flanagan nor Butler had an overt connection with the railroads, but the power of railroad money was not to be underestimated. The millions of dollars at stake in overrun profits was enough to corrupt a thousand Butlers and Flanagans.

"Well," he said to himself, "there's not a blessed thing you can do now."

He shook out a blanket, threw it over his legs, and went to sleep.

CHAPTER 23

Lloyd Miles was very concerned about his sister. She was no longer the vital, vibrant, vivid young woman she had always been. She had lost weight; she had never been fashionably plump, but now her cheekbones were quite prominent. Though she kept the apartment spotless, had meals ready on time, and was polite, Miles missed the conversations and spontaneity that had once been theirs.

He blamed Philip Trent for Leah's condition. Once or twice he had tried to talk to her about Trent, to tell her that she was being childish to moon over a man who had obviously forgotten her. But Leah would not discuss Philip. At the mention of his name she would leave the room. As for Miles's contention that Philip had forgotten her, he knew that to be untrue; he had found tucked away in the bottom of a drawer in her bedroom several letters from Philip. He had continued to write for several weeks.

Along with the letters, Lloyd came upon clippings that Leah had cut from newspapers. There the saga of Philip's Panama adventure was documented, along with the brief story that told of his appointment to the House.

And with her jewelry Lloyd found the engagement ring that Philip had given her. Lloyd found it interesting that Philip had not requested its return, as he himself would have done under similar circumstances. That Leah had not returned it of her own volition did not surprise him; she would cherish the ring with the same intensity she afforded the memories of their failed relationship.

Each day he watched her scan the newspaper thoroughly, searching for Philip's name. On the morning after the murder of Victor Flanagan, Miles came out of his bedroom expecting, as usual, to walk into a kitchen filled with cooking and coffee aromas. But instead Leah was in front of the hall mirror, pinning her hat to her hastily arranged hair.

"What are you doing?" he asked.

She turned, looked at him blankly, reached for her coat, and pulled it on. He caught her at the door. "Leah, what in the world . . . ?"

"Leave me alone," she said.

"What is it? What's happened?"

She tried to pull away from him, but he held fast to her arm.

"I must go to him," she said.

"Trent," he whispered, for she could have meant no other.

"He's in trouble," Leah said.

"Come," Miles said, pulling her toward the kitchen. "Come and sit down and tell me about it."

She allowed him to guide her to a chair. When he was seated, she pointed wordlessly at the morning paper. He scanned it quickly. Philip's name was once again emblazoned in headlines on the front page.

"He would not commit murder," she said. "I must go to him."

"You can't know that," Miles said. "You can't know the true circumstances. From the paper the authorities seem quite certain that he did indeed kill this Victor Flanagan." Miles's heart was pounding. Something unnerving was going on. First the odd death of John O'Brian, and now Philip Trent connected with the death of a man of whom Miles had never heard. On the surface, as far as he was concerned, there was no connection between the two events—except that both O'Brian and Philip had been involved in their own ways with the railroads.

"I know that Philip would not commit murder."

"Leah, there's nothing you can do. You'd just be involving us in a nasty situation."

She started to rise, but he leapt to his feet and pushed her back into the chair. "I'm not going to let you bring us down to his level, do you understand? You will not go to him. If he is innocent, then he will be released. My God, girl, isn't it evident to you yet what sort of man Trent is? Tell me, has he made any attempt to see you in recent months? Has he tried to contact you?"

She was silent. She wanted to deny his words, but they were true.

"So much for his undying love for you." He rose and began to pace, his hands clasped behind his back. "Look, Sis, I'm going up to New York on business with Geoffrey Lancaster. His wife is going to meet him there, and then they're going to sail for Europe. I think Mrs. Lancaster would love to have you join them, to give her a hand with her two children and to keep her company while Geoffrey is involved in business dealings."

"No," Leah said softly, shaking her head.

Miles's voice was harsh. "I want you to pack a few things now. Just for two or three days. We'll do some shopping for you in New York. Would you like that?"

"Lloyd, I want to see Philip. I want to talk with him, to tell him that he is not alone in his hour of trouble."

Miles's face darkened. "All right, then," he said angrily. "Go."

She rose to her feet.

"But take your things with you," he grated, "because if you walk out this door to go to Philip Trent, you will not come back."

Leah was silent for a moment before she whispered, "You can't mean that."

"I never meant anything more."

She wavered, and as if a kind nature took pity on her, the blood rushed from her face, and she crumpled to the floor. . . .

When she awoke, she was lying on her bed. Miles was putting things into a carpetbag.

"Are you all right?" he asked.

"Yes," she said.

"You might want to check this, to see if I've packed everything you'll need for a couple of days."

She stood, still a bit light-headed. The faint had drained her of all resistance. She rearranged the things in the bag, added more, and packed another. Before noon she was seated at Miles's side as a train clacked its way northward to New York. She did not have the strength to fight him anymore.

In New York she tagged along dutifully as Lloyd selected lovely gowns, accessories, and new luggage, and, to her continued indifference, purchased steamship tickets for one to London and Calais.

"Just what you need, Leah," he told her, chucking her under the chin as he'd done when she was a child. "A few weeks in Londontown and gay Paree. I'm sending along a liberal amount of money so that you can do some shopping." He laughed. "You might bring me one of those Shetland-wool sweaters that's heavy enough to keep a man warm at the North Pole."

Miles's eyes were damp as he stood on the pier and waved good-bye to her. She stood beside Geoffrey's wife at the rail, pale and so pretty that he was filled with both pride and loneliness. She smiled at him, but her smile was unconvincing, her eyes sunken. Geoffrey's two-year-old daughter clung to Leah's hand, having very quickly accepted her as Aunt Leah.

He'd planned to use the money he'd spent on her to buy into a promising new stock issue that was being supported by Jay Gould, but the welfare of his sister was more important than any opportunity to make a quick profit. There'd be other opportunities to make money. There was only one Leah.

True to his word, Lieutenant Tom Jensen visited Schuyler Colfax after having deposited Philip in a cell. The Speaker was just finishing dinner when Jensen was announced by the one maid Colfax employed at his Georgetown house.

When Jensen came into the room, the Speaker remained seated. His wife asked the lieutenant if he'd like a cup of tea. Jensen declined.

"If I may have a word with you, Mr. Speaker?" he said.

"You may speak," Colfax said.

"It's a rather delicate matter," Jensen said.

"Confound it, man, I'm waiting for my dessert," Colfax said. "Speak up."

Colfax listened with growing anger as Jensen explained briefly why he had interrupted the Speaker's evening meal.

"By God," Colfax thundered, jerking his napkin from under his chin and throwing it violently on the table. "Can't that boy stay out of trouble?" He glared at Jensen. "And just what in blazes am I expected to do?"

"Mr. Trent thought that you could find an attorney to represent him," Jensen explained.

"I'm damned if I will have anything to do with this affair!" Colfax shouted.

"Now, Schuyler," Mrs. Colfax said softly, laying a hand on his arm, "remember that he's a member of your party. And he seems to be such a nice young man."

"Yes, yes," Colfax said, making a concerted effort to relax. "You're right, my dear." Calmer, he looked back at Jensen. "Well, there's blamed well nothing I can do until morning, is there?"

"No, sir," Jensen agreed. "Once again I apologize for intruding."

"Not at all," Colfax said, resigned. "Did Trent kill this Flanagan beggar?"

Jensen coughed once or twice and rocked back on his heels. "Well, sir, that remains to be seen."

"What do you think?"

Jensen frowned. "It looks quite bad for him, sir, but I don't think he did it." He turned to leave but halted after a few steps. "By the way, Mr. Speaker, young Trent asked me to request that you notify his father in Baltimore."

"Thank you, Lieutenant," Colfax said. "I'll take care of that."

* * *

Tom Jensen was an early arrival at the station the next morning. He wanted to be very careful in writing his report about the previous evening's events. He had just composed himself to begin the task, pen in hand, when the desk sergeant came into his office.

"Lieutenant, there's a lady outside who wants to see the congressman. I told her that it was too early for visitors, but she won't take no for an answer."

Jensen followed the sergeant to the desk and saw a vividly attractive, dark-haired young woman whose eyes were the color of a sunny summer sea. "Are you the lady who wants to see Philip Trent?" he asked.

"I am. I am Mrs. Julia Stuart Grey. I work in Congressman Trent's office."

"Mrs. Grey, it's a little early yet." He mused for a few moments, then turned and told the desk sergeant, "Bring Trent to the interrogation room."

"Lieutenant, they're trying to serve breakfast back there, and then it'll be time to clean up the cells."

"I know, Sergeant," Jensen said patiently. "Just bring Trent to the interrogation room, please." He took Julia's arm and steered her into the poorly lighted little room. He had hoped to detect the scent of lilacs, but he was disappointed. "Please, be seated," he said. "I'll be just outside if you need me."

Philip had been awakened by the clanging of tin trays, the slamming of cell doors, and the muted, sullen morning talk of the prisoners in the common cells down the corridor from him. He rinsed his hands and face in a tin basin, combed back his hair with his fingers, and arranged his clothing as best he could after having slept in his trousers and shirt. When he heard footsteps, he looked up, expecting to see his breakfast being brought to him. With his healthy appetite he suspected that he could eat even jailhouse food. Instead, a policeman ran his billy across the bars and said, "Up and at 'em, Trent. You got company."

"That's quick work," Philip said, thinking that Colfax had sent a lawyer.

He halted in midstride as he walked into the interrogation room. "Mrs. Grey," he said with surprise.

"Adam and I read the news in the morning paper," she said, rising from the chair. "He agreed that I must come to see you immediately. Have you had a chance to arrange for an attorney?"

"I think it's being arranged for me," he said.

"By whom, please?" she asked, all business.

"Lieutenant Jensen went to see Schuyler Colfax."

"Oh, good. Well, I'll just check with Speaker Colfax to be sure he's contacted a good man. Now, how long will they be holding you?"

"Mrs. Grey, I have no idea."

"You'll need clothing and toilet articles. If you'll give me the key to your apartment, I'll take care of all that."

He grinned. Mrs. Efficiency was at work.

"Has your father been notified?" she asked.

"I asked Colfax to contact him."

"Do you know of anyone you'd like to have as your attorney?"

"The only lawyer I know is Ben Butler. Even if he weren't busy with the impeachment, I sure wouldn't want him." Butler was acting as one of the prosecutors in President Johnson's trial before the Senate.

She smiled. "Well, I guess we'll leave that choice up to Mr. Colfax. Don't worry. We know you didn't do it."

He was touched.

"Adam was about ready to come down here to take on the whole Washington police department," she said with a tinkly little laugh.

"Thank him for me for his concern, and thank you both for your faith in me."

"Good jobs for women are hard to find, Congressman," she said, her eyes twinkling. "Let me be off now. You're in need of a shave—"

His hand went to his bristly cheek, and he grinned ruefully.

"—and a change of clothing is in order. I'll be back before you know it."

She was back, in fact, in less than a minute, sticking her head around the door to say, "Mr. Trent, there's a very impressive-looking gentleman of the law profession out here demanding to be given immediate access to his falsely accused client."

Elias Younger was a reedy, sharp-nosed aberration in an age of well-fed men. While others wore uniformly somber garb, he favored light-colored suits; while most men wore beards, he was beardless. He carried an old .54-caliber Johnson Army Model percussion pistol in his belt. The polished, gracefully curving grip was clearly visible because he almost never buttoned his coat. The only time he was without his weapon was when he was in court, and this was often, since he was much in demand in both civil and criminal cases in the District of Columbia and adjoining Maryland.

When the desk sergeant refused to allow Younger to see Philip Trent without the attorney first surrendering his pistol, Younger's voice rose from its usual baritone to a rich, reverberating alto that carried so well that Tom Jensen came hurrying out of his office.

"Now, Elias," Tom said soothingly, "you know you can't go walking around in a police station with a gun in your belt."

"Are you going to take it away from me?" Younger challenged belligerently.

"No," Jensen said quietly. "But if you want to stay in my station house, you'll give that weapon to the sergeant for safekeeping."

Suddenly Younger's pinched, thin face relaxed. He laughed, and his voice lowered. "So, Tom," he said, pulling the pistol from his waist and extending it, barrel first, toward the desk sergeant, "what have you got on my client, Congressman Philip Trent?"

"A smoking gun," Jensen said. "Apprehended at the scene of the crime with the murder weapon in his possession."

"Dear me," Younger said, "I guess I might as well go home then, since you already have the boy convicted."

"With you on the case, Elias?" Jensen asked.

Younger laughed again. "Well, let's begin, shall we?"

In spite of the fact he was charged with murder, Philip was allowed to walk out of the police station at Elias Younger's side just before eleven o'clock that morning. The fact that he was a congressman certainly did not act against him, for Lieutenant Jensen felt certain that Philip would neither flee nor present a danger to society. More important, however, was Jensen's own background. He had dealt with enough murderers in his time to know that Philip was framed. The stranger who had notified the police of the murder had conveniently disappeared before a statement could be taken. Furthermore, the exquisite timing of Philip's and the police's appearance—not to mention the lilac scent—left too many questions unanswered. Catching a murderer was never this easy.

On the sidewalk the tall attorney took Philip's arm and pulled him to a halt. "I want you to go home and stay there," he instructed. "You've got a lot of people very upset. Here we are, in the middle of a presidential impeachment trial, one of the most exciting events in our history, and you're forcing men like Schuyler Colfax to divert their attention to helping you."

"I am just as sorry as I can be about that," Philip said testily.

"If you were just plain John Doe," Younger said, "you'd be back there in jail, and not in a private cell, either. You're on the street because some pretty good men went to bat for you. Colfax himself has guaranteed that you won't cut and run, and your father has put up a sizable bond." He looked at Philip piercingly. They were of a height, eye to eye. "You're not going to run, are you?"

"What do you think?"

"I think it's damned foolish of you to be short-tempered with the one lawyer who just might be able to save your dumb ass from being hanged."

Philip wiped his forehead wearily with the palm of his

hand. He felt dirty, soiled. "Mr. Younger, I am truly sorry. It's just that—"

"Yep, I know," Younger interrupted. "You feel right put-upon. That's always the case. If a man is innocent, he's insulted because he's being falsely accused. If he's as guilty as sin, he's angry because he got caught. Just go home, Trent. Don't talk to anyone from the press. Let me determine what gets into the papers."

"I am grateful," Philip declared by way of apology.

Younger turned and started to walk away, then turned again. "And by the way, Trent, no heroics. Don't go looking for the murderer. Leave that to the professionals."

Philip met Julia Grey, a small carpetbag in her hand, coming out of his apartment building. "Hello!" she said. "So he *is* a good lawyer."

"At least a very confident one," Philip concurred. "I'm sorry that you went to so much trouble for nothing, Mrs. Grey."

"Not at all," she said. "I'll just go up and put it back where it was."

They mounted the stairs to his apartment, and she quickly unpacked the bag. While Philip put on a pot of coffee to brew, she began to attack an accumulation of dust and bachelor untidiness. He walked out of the kitchen to find her working busily. "I didn't hire you as a housekeeper, Mrs. Grey."

"You men," she said with mock dismay, continuing to straighten and dust.

Five minutes later Gus Trent came into the flat without knocking and stomped into the living room, thundering Philip's name. He was halted in his tracks when he came face to face with Julia.

"I'm not the maid," she said, suddenly realizing that she was a married woman in the apartment of a single man.

"No, I don't expect you are," Gus said.

Philip came into the room.

"The jailbird," Gus declared. "In the flesh."

"Sorry," Philip muttered.

"He did not do it," Julia said.

"Dad, this is Mrs. Julia Grey. She works in my office."

"But not as your maid," Gus said.

"No," Julia and Philip said together.

"I'll be going, Mr. Trent," Julia announced.

Philip grinned. "Thank you very much, Mrs. Grey."

He started to explain Julia's presence to Gus, going into detail about how Adam Grey had insisted that she come to the jail, adding how so very, very efficient Julia was. But Gus held up his hand and said, "Enough."

"I just don't want you to get the wrong idea about Mrs. Grey."

"I'll try not to. But at the moment I'm interested in just what in the holy hell you were doing to end up in jail."

Gus listened quietly, asking only a few questions.

"Does it sound that bad?" Philip asked, because his father's look was gloomy.

"Bad enough," Gus answered. "But we won't quit. Not just yet. I'll want to talk with your lawyer, this Elias Younger. I've heard that he's the best defense man around. And there are a few other people I'll want to see."

"Dad, you don't have to pull strings in this matter. I am innocent, you know."

Gus looked squarely at his son for a long moment before saying, "Let's just hope that we can prove it, and prove it quickly."

Archibald Edwards was a bachelor with a fetish for neatness. He spent several hours each week straightening and cleaning his three-room apartment, which was composed of a bedroom, a sitting room, and a combined kitchen-dining area. Of late he had developed a new interest. He had become fascinated with the Sholes typewriter and spent many hours working at it, experimenting with various ways of striking the keys. He had developed a technique that enabled him to turn out a neat-looking letter in a relatively short period of time.

He had finished his nightly chores, had taken his bath, and, dressed only in his nightshirt, was preparing for his evening session with the typewriter when he heard a knock. Pulling on his robe, he padded in his bare feet to answer the door.

"Oh, I beg your pardon," he said, flushing with modesty when he saw the tall, attractive woman. She wore black, with a black fur jacket open to the waist to show that her gown was cut enticingly low. Her dark reddish-brown hair was a smooth mass atop her head. In one hand she held a small black purse.

Edwards closed the door to leave only a space large enough for his head, hiding his improperly dressed body. "How may I help you, miss?" he asked.

She smiled, showing dainty, even white teeth. "You can start by inviting me in."

"Uh, perhaps you have made a mistake. You see—"

"No mistake, Mr. Edwards." She pushed on the door.

Edwards stepped back. Women always made him feel uneasy, and this one was in the room, closing the door behind her. Without being asked she shrugged out of her fur and deposited it over the back of a chair. She was shapely, tall, and elegant . . . and he was in his nightshirt. He tucked the collar of the robe more tightly under his neck.

"Please, relax, Mr. Edwards," she advised. "I would accept a drink if you'd offer it."

"Now, see here, miss," Edwards protested. "There *has* been some mistake."

"We have friends in common, Mr. Edwards." She sat down on the couch and smiled up at him. "I will not mention any names, but our mutual friends have a common desire to prevent any embarrassment to the railroads."

"Oh," Edwards said.

"Our friends are quite generous with those who support them."

"I have always been a supporter of the transcontinental," Edwards said, thinking that at last he was going to be given a chance to earn his share of the railroad money that poured into Washington in seemingly limitless amounts. "How can I be of service to—our friends?"

"They're a little concerned," she explained, "about your

connection to this Victor Flanagan, the man who was murdered."

"I had no real connection with Flanagan," Edwards said quickly.

The woman's eyes hardened. "You passed information through him to Lafe Baker."

"I thought that Baker was working for—"

"No names," she said.

"—for our friends," he said.

"You talked with Philip Trent often," she continued. "Our friends are interested in the subject of your conversations with him."

"Actually, other than the everyday small talk that goes on around an office, I had little contact with Trent. Occasionally he would come to me to ask when Colfax was going to meet with him to discuss the report he had compiled on the Central Pacific."

"I understand that you were the bookkeeper in the Colfax office."

"Yes."

"It would seem to me that when your job with Colfax was terminated so suddenly, you would have been unhappy."

Edwards nodded. "It seemed poor repayment for the years of service that I gave to Schuyler."

"And were you unhappy enough to think of getting even someday?"

"I am not a vengeful man," Edwards insisted.

"I think that had I been in your place, I would have copied certain entries in the books—just in case I should find a use for them in the future."

"No, no," Edwards denied.

"Too bad," she said. "Our friends had hoped—"

"But I have an excellent memory for figures and dates," he broke in. "If there's anything in particular that our friends want to know . . ."

She rose and ambled to a window, the movement and the style of her gown emphasizing her derriere. After a long pause she turned. "There is a good possibility that Philip

Trent will have you called as a witness during his trial for the murder of Victor Flanagan."

Edwards's brow furrowed. "I can't imagine why."

"Because you tried to get him to work for you, or for Lafe Baker."

"I would think that my testimony would do nothing to help Trent," he said.

"And if they should ask you about contributions to Schuyler Colfax and his so-called campaign fund?"

"I—I would say nothing to embarrass our friends. In fact, I would deny that I had ever worked with Victor Flanagan or that I had tried to get Trent to do so. After all, it would be my word against that of a murderer."

"An accused murderer," she corrected. She moved toward Edwards. "I'm afraid, Mr. Edwards," she purred, "that you wouldn't make a very convincing liar. At any rate, that's a risk that our friends are not willing to take."

"What do you mean?" he asked, puzzled.

When her hand came out of the little black purse that she carried, Edwards felt no threat. She was a pretty young woman, and he was sure he could make Thomas Durant understand that he could handle any questions that might be asked of him, that he would be a valuable asset to the Union Pacific. After all, he was a veteran of the political circus that was the nation's capital. He was the right-hand man of a congressman who would be very close to General Grant once Grant was elected President.

He opened his mouth to say as much as the woman's hand reached for his face, and he thought for a moment that she was going to touch him. She wore a peculiar expression, the sort of look he'd seen only a few times in his life when, during the war when he was younger, he had consorted briefly and not too satisfactorily with one of the young women who had followed the armies, one of the type that had at first been called Hooker's girls. He was thinking, *No, young lady, I am no longer interested in such things,* when he saw the gleam of metal in her gloved hand.

She pulled both triggers of the tiny derringer at once. As his body lost its muscle tone, became flaccid, and began to crumple, she guided him into a sitting position in a chair. Blood oozed from the wound in his temple. She positioned his hand on the arm of the chair, put the derringer in it, and curled his fingers to hold it.

Then she stood still, listening. She heard nothing—no shouts of alarm, no pounding footsteps. The discharge of the tiny gun had been nothing more than a quick bark of sound. She went to the table where Edwards had the typewriter set up. Using it took her a long time, for she had to search for each letter, and she wanted the note to be as neat and as professional-looking as the sample letters on the table. When she had finished at last, she placed the note on the table and carefully copied Edwards's signature. To make it more difficult to see that the signature was a forgery, she smeared blood onto the paper and left the typewritten note in Edwards's left hand.

After a thorough check to be sure that she had left nothing behind to place her in the apartment, she pulled the fur around her and closed the door quietly behind her.

She had one more call to make.

Lafe Baker opened the door to see the woman in black, her fur open and the black purse clutched in one gloved hand. "Well, by God," he said. "Rose. Come in, come in."

"Hello, Lafe," Rosanna Pulliam said.

"Rose, it's a true pleasure to see you," Lafe said. He kissed her on the forehead. "My little Confederate Rose, best undercover agent of all, regardless of which side, and I mean undercover in a couple of ways, don't I?"

Rosanna laughed. "You always did have a delicate way of putting things."

"Well, hell," he said, "have a seat. Let me get you a drink. Still favor southern bourbon?"

"Thank you," she said demurely. She let her fur slide from her shoulders and hung it carelessly on the back of a chair.

He kept talking from the kitchen as he poured drinks. "I was looking forward to seeing you after the surrender."

"I wasn't quite ready to come back north."

He returned, and she accepted a glass from his hand.

Lifting his glass, he declared, "Well, here's to Rose, who thumbed her nose at the entire Confederate nation and kept a flow of information coming out of Richmond throughout the war."

"To old times, Lafe," she said, raising her glass.

He drank and then sat down in a chair opposite hers, looking at her with new eyes. Lord, she was beautiful, even more beautiful than she'd been as a young actress, when he'd first courted her and then, having discovered what he considered to be fascinating attitudes toward life, recruited her into what he had promised her would be *the* Union secret service in the war that was brewing.

"That young man you married," he said. "The major. Too bad about him."

"Yes."

"A lot of good men died in the war," he said. "Good men on both sides."

"The war didn't kill my rebel husband," she stated matter-of-factly. "It only wounded him."

"The hell you say . . ." He shivered. She'd made the statement so calmly. He was not a stranger to death, having seen plenty of it during the war, but to hear such a beautiful woman speak of it so calmly had an unsettling effect on him. "Why?"

"He was badly wounded but was recovering. I didn't think he had the strength to get out of bed. I was careless—I had left one of my letters lying on my desk. He came looking for me when I was out in the garden, and he found the letter and opened it. He was more hurt than angry to find out that I was reporting troop dispositions and defensive construction to you."

"How?" he asked.

"A pillow over his face when I got him back to his bed. The exertion of getting up had weakened him. I think when he realized what I was doing, he just gave up. He gave me no struggle at all. It appeared that he had died in his bed of his wounds."

Lafe shook his head. She'd lived with her husband for four

years. There was more steel to this little Rose than appeared on the soft surface.

"Another little sip or two?" he asked. She'd finished her bourbon rather quickly, drinking as a man would drink, in gulps.

"No, I haven't the time, Lafe. I'm on a job."

"Are you still working for the Old Man?" he asked, referring to Stanton.

"No."

"Well, maybe there's something in it for me," he suggested. "I'm going to be fresh out of work soon."

"Let's not talk about work," she said, smiling at him. Rising, she walked to his chair and took his hands. He stood and gathered her into his arms, and the memories came flooding back. She'd been the most exciting woman he'd ever known —vibrant, eager, seeking her pleasure with the openness of a man.

"So you're not in that big a hurry," Lafe whispered as he tasted her lips and smelled the fresh lilac scent of her.

"For old time's sake," she whispered as he led her to his bedroom. . . .

As they made love, she was satin and silk, heats and dampnesses, clinging arms and strong, lithe legs. "Rose," he said, when the first energetic merging ended in mutual depletion, "I'm in love with you all over again. Tell me you don't have to leave, not just yet."

"Not just yet," she agreed.

He knew a lingering, all-pervading, bittersweet pleasure as, this time, they had the desire and the patience for mutual explorations. And then she wept. Intense pleasure sometimes did that to her, Lafe recalled, as if filling her with a kind of painful joy.

"It should have been different with us," she whispered.

"Maybe, if the war hadn't come along."

"I have to go now," she said.

"When will I see you again?"

She laughed. "In hell, I guess, Lafe."

He laughed with her, slapped her bare haunch playfully as she got off the bed and began to dress. He pulled the covers to his waist, put his hands under his head, and watched with genuine regret as her charms were covered by layers of clothing. She used his bath, then came out with her hair back in place, looking as if she'd just stepped from her toilette, prepared for an evening on the town. She came to stand beside the bed, bent to kiss him, and placed the derringer at his temple.

"Ah, Rose," he said. He lay very still. He had seen the flash of blue metal and had recognized the feel of the little weapon that she pressed against his head. It was small but, at such close quarters, deadly. He felt a heavy weight of sadness. There'd been a time when not even Rose could have caught him so flat-footed. "Will you tell me why?" he asked, for she was not one to play games. She would not have pressed the derringer to his temple unless she had every intention of using it.

"Yes," she said. "It's all gotten too messy, Lafe. Too many people have been allowed to get into positions where they might be able to make some damaging guesses. Durant was too skittish. He spread too much Union Pacific money around."

"That doesn't sound as if you're working for the Old Man."

"Stanton? No."

"Durant?"

"Twenty questions, Lafe?"

"I'd just like to know."

She gave him a sardonic smile. "You were too good at your job. In time you would have to start inquiring about a certain fatal event."

"I'll be damned." He chuckled. "How'd you convince him to dive through the window?"

"Sorry," she said. "The story is too long and too involved."

It was ironic that after all he'd been through, he was to die because he'd involved himself with amateurs, with rich men playing at the world's most deadly game. "I am grateful to you, Rose, for making my last hour so pleasant."

She sensed that he was tensing himself for one last desperate effort to beat the quick movement of her finger on the twin triggers of the derringer. "Don't try it, Lafe," she warned.

"I was thinking that I had nothing much to lose."

She seemed reluctant to pull the triggers. Then she said, "Flanagan and Edwards are dead."

He shivered and took a deep breath.

"And, damn it, Lafe," she said angrily, "it's your fault. You brought all of the beginners into it. It got too messy because they didn't know what they were doing."

"Who'd it get too messy for?" Lafe asked.

"For Durant. He was so damned clumsy, so inept about it all. With so many people knowing that he was paying off members of the Congress, sooner or later someone would get fidgety and lead Trent or some other investigator into areas that could be damaging—not just to Durant but to everyone."

Lafe was wondering why she was still talking. It was very unprofessional of her. "It would be interesting to some members of Congress to know that several of their peers had been given large blocks of Crédit Mobilier stock," he affirmed.

"Exactly. You see why we had to clean up a bit."

"I can see where someone might think it desirable," he said. "But it wasn't Durant?"

"No," she admitted.

"Just out of curiosity, was John O'Brian's death a part of your cleaning things up?"

She nodded.

"Then why not Butler? Why is he still alive?"

"We're not dealing with professionals, Lafe," she said. "I asked the same thing. I was told that Butler was too important, that the investigation into his death would be a bigger risk than the risk of his talking." She sighed. "Actually, I'd rather kill Butler than most anyone I can think of."

"Including Lafe Baker? I'm glad you care, Rose. Your people seem to believe that the world would not give a damn if Lafe Baker shuffled off this mortal coil."

She sighed. "Damn, Lafe."

He was beginning to hope. The derringer was still pressed

to his temple, but for some reason she had not pulled the triggers. "Honey, I am flattered," he said softly. "I think you sort of like old Lafe. Maybe we can work something out, you and I."

"You always kept your word to me, Lafe."

"Yes, and you to me."

"I fear that what I'm about to do will cost me dearly in the future."

"You'll have no price to pay to me, Rose." He held his breath. "You will have only my eternal gratitude."

"I'm going to give you a farewell gift," she decided.

"I appreciate it."

"I'm going to give you to you."

"Who is leaving, you or me?"

"You. I'm going to ask you to give me your word that you'll forget what you know, that you'll leave Washington, and that you'll lie low for a few months." She put a bit more pressure on the derringer.

His heart pounded. He felt dizzy. Had she been toying with him? Was death about to tear into his soft brain in the form of two lead pellets?

"I'm taking a big risk, Lafe."

"You have my solemn word that I will do as you ask. I'm fresh out of work here in Washington anyhow. I've got a friend up in Lansing, Michigan, who wants me to go into the hotel business with him. I think a town like Lansing would be a good place for me to get started on that book."

"Still going to write *the* book . . ." she mused.

"I want to tell them about what we did during the war."

"Don't use my name, Lafe."

He held up one hand. "Don't worry. No names if I put in something about my best agent. I just want the world to know how it was."

She stepped back. The little gun disappeared into her purse, although she remained tensed for action.

"Rose, come with me. We're damned good together. You might like the hotel business."

She laughed. "Would I be on call for lonely commercial travelers?"

"Only for me," he said. "And the two of us can take care of anyone who might be unhappy about us leaving together."

She smiled. "I'm tempted, but not now, Lafe."

He shrugged and swung his legs off the bed.

"Don't make me sorry about this, Lafe."

"No, I won't."

She leaned over and kissed him. "Maybe I'll want to visit Lansing someday."

"I'll have one room of my hotel decorated especially for you, and I'll plant lilacs all over the place, so that when you visit, I can fill the room with their flowers."

She turned at the doorway, kissed the tips of her fingers, and threw him a kiss and a smile.

He had been able to control his trembling until then. Alone, he felt his shoulders begin to shake, as if with extreme cold. He had never been closer to death. He padded across the room, poured himself a drink, and gulped it down. It would be interesting to know who had sent his deadly little Rose, a woman he himself had trained, to "clean up" Lafe Baker.

He sighed. He had given his word, and he would keep it. Meanwhile, he was damned glad to be alive. If there hadn't been something between Rosanna and him, something that had lasted through the war years and the glory times, he would now be lying in his own blood, a large hole in the side of his head.

Yes, the good days were gone. Damn, hadn't it been fun? All of it. The satisfaction of fooling the whole damned Confederacy during that tour through Virginia . . . the look on old Jeff Davis's face while the master spy of the Union was interviewing him in Richmond . . . all of it. The people, the women, and Rose. He'd done a job then, and now he was about as useful as tits on a boar.

He had another drink, then went to the washstand. It took a while to wash away the lilac scent and womanish smells of Rosanna Pulliam. He slept well that night, woke early the next morning, and after packing his few belongings, caught the early train heading west.

CHAPTER 24

Lieutenant Tom Jensen had sent his uniformed helpers out into the neighborhood talking with the residents to see how many of them had heard the gunshot that left a sizable hole in the temple of Archibald Edwards. The lieutenant was on the scene early, and the blood had not completely clotted in the entry wound. The smell of lilacs was strong in the room, leading Jensen to conclude that Edwards and Victor Flanagan had been killed by the same person. A suicide note lying beside Edwards's chair tried to implicate Philip Trent in the sordid mess, but Jensen was convinced otherwise.

The note had been typed on the newfangled invention sitting on a table in Edwards's living room, and the style matched the other letters that had been written on the same machine. But it just didn't ring true . . . and there was that smell of lilacs.

The note was a confession by Archibald Edwards that he had entered into a conspiracy with Victor Flanagan and Philip Trent to generate false and damaging information about the construction practices and political actions of the builders of the transcontinental railroad. The intent was, the note said, blackmail of the railroad. It went on to say that Philip Trent had killed Victor Flanagan when Flanagan had threatened to expose the scheme, and that he, Edwards, was killing himself because he knew that Trent would expose his part in the conspiracy at the trial.

Two things came to Tom Jensen's attention quickly as he walked around the neatly kept room and examined the evidence. First, Archibald Edwards could not possibly have pulled both triggers of the small gun at one time. His stumpy, thick fingers simply would not fit in front of two triggers at once. It was hardly likely that Edwards had fired first one barrel of the derringer into his temple and then lived long enough to discharge the other. Secondly, even though he was not an accredited handwriting expert, Jensen was observant enough to see subtle differences in the hand that had signed the "suicide note" and the hand that had signed the letters on the table. The fact that he had smelled lilacs at the scene of three violent deaths would not be sufficient evidence in a court of law to prove that the same person or persons had killed Flanagan, O'Brian, and Edwards, but it was proof enough for Jensen to know that Philip Trent was not guilty of any of the deaths.

The lieutenant made his detailed report, which stated without equivocation that the same person had committed three murders, that the person had not been Philip Trent, and that the perpetrator had been either a woman or a delicately boned man with slender fingers. There were sighs of relief all the way to the police commissioner's office and, indeed, throughout Washington. No one wanted to see a member of the Congress dragged into court on a murder charge. The office of public prosecution agreed with alacrity to drop all charges against Congressman Philip Trent and to publish an apology for having inadvertently involved the honorable Philip Trent in a crime investigation. Police authorities made a statement to reporters that the department's finest detectives were working on the three deaths and that developments were expected shortly.

For days Tom Jensen worked only on what he had come to think of as the Lilac Murders. When he did not turn up a shred of evidence, he realized that he was pitted against a professional assassin or an extraordinarily adept amateur.

When Jensen received a note from Congressman Oakes

Ames asking him to call at the office of Crédit Mobilier, he welcomed the diversion, for he was becoming very frustrated. He was stunned when Oakes Ames offered him a position with the Union Pacific Railroad as chief of security at a salary that would have made even the police commissioner envious. Jensen thought of what the princely sum would mean in connection with a better life for his family and accepted Ames's offer on the spot.

In his absence the investigations into the deaths of Congressman John O'Brian, army veteran Victor Flanagan, and congressional aide Archibald Edwards withered and were gradually relegated permanently into the files of unsolved crime.

Philip Trent slathered freshly churned butter onto a stack of southern-style hoecakes, poured on honey, and filled his mouth, saying, "Ummm." Julia Grey passed a plate of thick, fresh pork chops that Adam had broiled in the oven.

"Julia," Philip said after he had swallowed, "if you ever get tired of Adam and kick him out, I'll adopt him."

"Him's happy just where him is," Adam said.

"Thank you," Julia said, reaching across to touch Adam's hand. There was concern in her look. Adam's pale gray eyes were more sunken than usual, his pallor even more unhealthy.

"No desire to better yourself by seeking honest employment?" Philip asked.

"Well, my current boss doesn't pay me much," Adam said, "but the benefits of the job would be impossible for you to match, old boy."

"I think I know what you mean," Philip said.

"Hush," Julia said.

Philip had become a regular guest at the Grey table, and after an initial protest when he brought a basket of provisions with him, that, too, had become habit. Adam's cooking was worth accepting weekly invitations, but that was only a pleasant bonus to the genuine satisfaction he got from talking with Adam and Julia Grey. The pair had become a sort of unofficial sounding board for him. At the table and afterward, when both Philip and Julia would pitch in to clear away the dishes and clean the kitchen, the events of the recent past were rehashed and Washington gossip was reviewed.

By the time Andrew Johnson's impeachment trial in the Senate had ended in disappointment for the radicals, Philip would have said that Adam Grey was his best friend.

"There wasn't a shred of proof offered that the President had violated the laws of the land," Julia said, talking about the trial. "He could not even be called into question for violating the Tenure of Office Act, since that law applies only to the removal of officials who have been appointed by the incumbent in the White House. Stanton was Lincoln's appointee. Johnson had the right to fire him at any time."

"It takes a lawyer as brilliant as Ben Butler to ignore such an obvious fact," Adam said sarcastically.

Stanton relinquished his office at last. The radicals in Congress tried to hide their chagrin at having failed to unseat Johnson by engaging in a frenzy of plunderings in the defeated South. Carpetbaggers, scalawags, and black puppets put into office by the victorious North raided state tax revenues for such extravagant personal possessions as sixty-dollar imported spittoons.

"What sort of spittoons?" Julia, incredulous, asked when Philip told the Greys about the purchase. "Hand-carved gold?"

"One black state senator in Georgia managed to bill the state for a six-hundred-fifty-dollar chandelier for his home, not to mention feather beds, hams, perfume, and whiskey."

"How does it feel, my friend," Adam asked, "to be one of the few voices of sanity in a town gone mad?"

"Lonely," Philip said, laughing. He had brought a bottle of good after-dinner port. He lifted his glass. "I want to thank you two for being so patient with me, for allowing me to seek moments of peace by intruding on you."

"Nonsense," Julia said.

"We put up with you only because you are a good judge of wine," Adam said, lifting his own glass.

"Philip, what can good people do?" Julia asked seriously. "What can *we* do?"

"Just continue to fight, I suppose," Philip said.

"You're coming up for election," Adam noted. "Are you going to take the stories of graft and corruption to the people of your district?"

Philip nodded. "They advise me against it," he said. "They tell me—"

"Who?" Adam asked.

"The professional politicians. They say, 'Don't stir the pot, boy.' "

"And what does Philip Trent say?" Julia asked.

"I took this job for one reason," he explained, "—to try to put a stop to the continuing raid on public funds by the builders of the railroad. I didn't start the fight, but then I've never quit a fight until it was over."

"Hear, hear," Adam approved.

Philip was away from Washington frequently during his campaign for office in the summer and fall of 1868 and continuously in the last weeks before the election. He was facing strong opposition from a radical who tried to revive the failed Panama scandal by pointing out that Philip had been arrested as a suspect in the murder of a man in Washington. But ultimately the man's accusations fell flat, and Philip won with a majority almost identical to that of presidential candidate Ulysses S. Grant, fifty-two percent of the popular vote. Grant went on to score a resounding victory in the electoral college.

Philip's victory earned him a seat on the Railroad Committee. One of the first men to seek him out when he returned to Washington was Congressman James Garfield, who offered perfunctory congratulations before saying, "Trent, the transcontinental railroad is too important to the needs of this expanding nation to be badgered any further about what are, in reality, very insignificant matters."

"Mr. Garfield," Philip countered, "I question your reasoning and your choice of words. Are there different degrees of graft? What is the moral difference between stealing a few hundred dollars and a few million?"

Garfield's face was stony when he replied, "As for the question of morality, where in the ethical equation would you place betting on a fixed horse race?"

Philip was grateful for the opportunity to deny the charge. "I had been asked, sir, to place a bet for a friend who gave me no indication beforehand that anything about the race was irregular. Furthermore, I returned his winnings immediately after the one horse died, when I realized something might be amiss. Do not, Mr. Garfield, question my integrity again."

Some days later Philip received a message asking him to call on Vice-President Schuyler Colfax. When Philip was shown into the former Speaker's office, Colfax was on his feet quickly, his hand outstretched, full of congratulations on Philip's election victory. Soon, after Philip and Colfax were seated facing each other in comfortable leather chairs, the purpose of Colfax's summons became clear.

"I think you're showing good political sense in backing off from your accusations against the railroad," Colfax remarked. "Of course, we're all interested in seeing that the most efficient use is made of federal funds, but I can't over-emphasize the importance of getting this job done, Philip. The economic health of this country depends on a swift completion of the transcontinental railroad. I think that it might be justified to ignore tiny and insignificant incidents of waste. I have never been convinced that there has been outright fraud. After all, the men are entitled to a fair profit—they contracted to drive the rails through country where their lives are endangered by Indian savages."

Philip started to speak, but Colfax held up one hand to stop him.

"Yes, yes, there's been greed," he continued, "but I submit to you, Philip, that that is, unfortunately, the nature of doing business in a booming country."

"Mr. Vice-President," Philip said when it was clear that

Colfax was finished, "you're not the first to advise me to stop my investigation of the railroad."

"Nor will I be the last, I'd imagine," Colfax interjected. "Look, my boy, we're living in an exciting time. Those of us who have had a hand in seeing that this railroad gets built will go down in history."

Philip was silent. He had never believed that Schuyler Colfax had taken money from the railroad, nor could he believe it now. But he was, he had to admit, having his doubts. Was he the shortsighted one? Was he wrong to think that honesty and honor should be demanded from the men who were taking federal money? Was the railroad of such importance to the nation that any means were justified, just so long as the job was completed? No, Philip decided, Colfax was too moral a man to accept a bribe. Taking bribes was for little men, men like Beast Butler, who at that moment was leading a drive in Congress to vote a retroactive pay hike, which would amount to a neat little five-thousand-dollar bonus for each member.

Schuyler Colfax was Vice-President of the United States. He could, quite possibly, become President after Grant. No, a man so respected, so powerful, would not allow corruption to touch him.

"I hope that I'm making sense, Philip," Colfax said.

"I understand what you're saying, Mr. Vice-President."

"But?"

"I agree with you about the importance of the railroad, but I just can't agree that the need for it justifies a one-hundred-percent overrun in costs."

"Well, I'm sure you'll be reasonable about it," Colfax said, smiling. He stood and put out his hand. "If there's anything I can do to help down there in the House, just let me know. About all I do these days is preside in the Senate, and I'll have to admit that it's not quite as lively as the House. I miss it."

Quickly, with a practiced smoothness that he'd demonstrated before, Colfax walked Philip out of the office, a hand on his shoulder and friendly words in his ear.

* * *

Lloyd Miles was not really surprised when he was called in to Oakes Ames's private office to find the Ames brothers together, their faces uniformly grim. Over the months Miles's duties at Crédit Mobilier had been reduced to the point where about all he did during the day was sharpen his pencils.

"Mr. Miles," Oakes Ames said as an opener, "you don't seem to be very happy here with us."

"On the contrary, I—" Miles began, but before he could continue, Oakes cut him off.

"You came to us highly recommended from the Union Pacific. I'm truly sorry that it hasn't worked out better, but we're going to send you back to Dr. Durant. I'm sure he'll have a place for you."

Miles was not so sure, especially when, after several days of trying, he was unable to see Thomas Durant. Finally he went to the rear entrance of Durant's offices and, using a key that he'd never given up, walked confidently down a series of corridors to Thomas Durant's door. He let himself in without knocking.

Durant was busily writing, and when he looked up, he dropped his pen. "Miles."

"I seem to be having difficulty getting to see you, Dr. Durant."

"I'm sorry," Durant said. "I've been very busy."

"I've been sent back to you," Miles explained. "It seems that the brothers Ames have no further use for me at Crédit Mobilier."

"Too bad," Durant sympathized. "Things are tight now, Miles. Can you come back and see me in, oh, two weeks?"

"All I want, Dr. Durant, is my old job back."

Durant's face hardened. "Miles, I don't expect the men who work for me to dedicate their entire lives to me, but I do expect loyalty."

"Are you saying you didn't get that from me?"

"You tell me," Durant answered. "You tell me how the man who was engaged to your sister obtained information that would have had to come from someone inside the Union Pacific."

Miles burned inside. He'd been willing to bend the law severely for this man, to risk criminal charges. And now he was being accused of disloyalty.

Durant picked up his pen. "But I'm not one to hold grudges, Miles. It's just that I'm busy. Come back and see me in a couple of weeks. Maybe we can find something for you."

"Thank you, no," he said, and for the first time in years, Miles felt the heady freedom of being his own man, of standing on his own two feet to tell the world, if necessary, to go to hell. "Loyalty has to go both ways, Durant, and I don't think I ever had it from you."

Durant leapt to his feet, and his face went dark with outrage. "Just whom do you think you're talking to?"

"Durant, I had jobs before I met you, and I'll warrant I'll have jobs after I walk out the door."

"Not with any man I know," Durant vowed. "And, Miles, if you get any idea of talking about anything, *anything* that happened when you were employed by this office, I want you to keep in mind that bribing a congressman is a more serious crime than the congressman's accepting that bribe. If you get any smart ideas, remember that you'd have more than a few years in a federal prison to savor your revenge."

"Good-bye, Dr. Durant," Miles said, opening the door. He turned. "No, you don't have to worry about my blowing the whistle." He grinned. "I still have a few shares of stock in Crédit Mobilier, and since I'm out of a job, I'll be vitally interested in the financial health of the company."

After leaving Durant, Lloyd Miles headed for the Gould offices, where he found Harold Berman preparing to go to lunch. Miles joined him. Halfway through a fine meal Miles told Berman that he was currently unemployed.

"But that's great," Berman enthused. "We are about to embark quickly on a project that will knock your socks off when you hear about it, and I'm going to need a lot of help here in Washington. Tell me what you were making with Durant, and I'll at least match it."

"I appreciate the offer, Harold, but I'd have to know more about what kind of project you're going to start."

"Hush-hush right how," Berman said.

"Give me a hint."

"You're a personable fellow, Lloyd. You're very good with people. I'm going to need someone to act as a contact man between the office and certain members of the government. That's all I can say right now." He grinned foxily. "Except that it's going to involve a certain heavy yellow metal of which I happen to know you are quite fond."

"Gold," Miles said.

"Hush," Berman whispered. "Come on in with me, Lloyd. You won't be sorry."

Lloyd Miles grinned back at Berman. "You talked me into it, you golden-tongued bastard."

Leah Miles spent her evenings alone. More and more often her brother was coming home late, though she was indifferent to his absence. Many nights she went to bed before Lloyd returned to the apartment. Several times he had awakened her to tell her in a low, excited voice of financial coups, of lucrative market transactions, of the buying or selling of gold futures.

She had lost weight since returning from the European tour with Geoffrey Lancaster, his wife, and the two Lancaster children. If Lloyd intended to be at home for dinner, she cooked; but even when she placed a well-rounded meal on the table, she ate little.

She subscribed to three newspapers and passed the days reading. For a while it seemed that Philip Trent's name was in almost every edition, but she no longer clipped articles telling of his congressional activities. In the afternoons she napped and sometimes walked along the Potomac, but only rarely, for there were too many memories there.

Just after Christmas of 1868, Lloyd announced that he had purchased a house for them. The move was handled by a hired firm. Leah directed the placement of furniture in the magnificent three-story town house in Georgetown and joined Lloyd on a shopping spree to add new items to the furniture from their apartment, which seemed lost in the big house. The move and the pleasure of furnishing and decorating their new home put a sparkle back into her eyes; but when she went to bed at night, she had the same dream, a recurring nightmare that had begun to visit her in France, when Geoffrey Lancaster's wife took ill briefly and left "Aunt" Leah to care for the two children, aged two and five.

In the dream Leah, prim and severe, was dressed in an old woman's black dress. Her hair was pulled into a tight bun. Her face was pale, washed out, and old, and around her were children—children weeping, children wanting their clothing changed, children fighting among themselves. She would awake with the weight of ages pressing her down into her bed, for not one of the children in the dream was hers, and even when she was fully awake, she seemed to be able to hear the voices of children, many children . . . the children of other women.

Aunt Leah, Aunt Leah.

CHAPTER 25

The sea was still cold in July. Rosanna Pulliam swam with strong, sure strokes to catch the freight-train speed of a cresting wave and let the force of the wave carry her toward the strand. She felt shifting sand under her feet and ran from the water, tall, lithe, and nude. She briskly toweled her skin, made pink by the chill of the water, donned a heavy robe, and made her way toward the top of a towering dune. The sands extended away on either side, providing the isolation that, on the sandy fishhook that was Cape Cod, represented wealth. The house, a cottage in name only, was nestled among high dunes, which protected it from the wind. It was solidly and expensively built. Hardwoods had been allowed to weather with the elements, graying to match the surroundings. The cedar-shake roof was grown over with moss, and the windows were hazed by salt spray; but inside the furnishings spoke of luxury.

The house was staffed year-round. No fewer than three maids cleaned and dusted and battled the dampness that came from the sea. The excellent chef could have found employment anywhere in the world. Near the cottage the stables housed a closed carriage and a little gig for traveling the sandy roads of the narrow peninsula. Well-trained riding horses were there for the pleasure of the one guest of the house.

Rosanna had always been partial to silks and satins. She liked the sensuous slide of silk against her skin and luxuriated in a huge bed fitted with satin sheets. In the bedroom that she'd chosen for this visit was a large rosewood wardrobe in which the maid had hung her clothing, some of it newly purchased in New York. There was no need for furs in July, but they were there, along with the latest gowns imported from Paris.

She enjoyed lunch shaded by a canopy on a wooden deck built high on a dune. The garden salad was so crisp and delicious that she lingered over it, neglecting the fresh fillet of flounder that the chef had prepared so lovingly and displayed so attractively with a topping of paprika and surrounding greenness of spinach leaves. She topped off the meal with a glass of splendid white wine, then lounged there on the wooden deck to let the quiet of the summer afternoon lull her into sleep. Later in the day she rode the bridle paths among the dunes, then cantered along the strand with the horse splashing cool salt water into her face.

For a week she reveled in the solitude. Then she began to count the days. She was a city girl, after all. While the bucolic and salty pleasures of the isolated estate on Cape Cod had pleased her for a short time—had been, as a matter of fact, quite restful and restoring—she was more than ready when, late on a Saturday evening, she heard activity at the stables. She walked out onto the veranda and saw the familiar slim form walking toward the house, recognizing him even in the growing dusk.

She waited for him in the grand parlor. Her hair had been rinsed to its natural color, the hue of bleached ash, pale and silvery. She had chosen to wear a clinging blue gown without the usual bulky undergarments.

Oliver Ames halted just inside the door, obviously mesmerized by her beauty. "Ah, my dear," he said, and moved to her rapidly.

He smelled of horse and male sweat from his journey. She accepted his embrace and returned his kiss, but when he swiftly became more amorous, she pushed him away. "Darling," she said, "perhaps you'd feel better if you had a bath and then something to eat."

He clutched at her, but she skillfully avoided his grasp and moved away.

"Yes, you're right," he said. "It was a long, hot trip."

"Shall I do your back?" she asked, looking at him through her long dark lashes, a vivid contrast with her ash-blond hair.

"My dear . . ."

He didn't eat until much later. By then he had sent the servants off to their quarters. The chef, having anticipated his hunger, had readied a platter of cold turkey and freshly shucked oysters.

Rosanna sat opposite Oliver at the kitchen table. She had slipped a silk wrapper over her shoulders. She sat carelessly, allowing the wrap to gape open over her firm, full breasts. "How did you leave things in Washington?"

"Well in hand," Oliver said. "Tom Jensen is working west of Omaha. Without him the police are no longer actively investigating the Lilac Murders. You have no need for further concern."

Rosanna nodded, satisfied. She lifted her glass and sipped the delicate, vintage white wine.

"I trust," Oliver said, "that you have found the facilities here to be adequate."

"Very nice," she replied. "A bit lonely, though."

"I shall visit you here at every opportunity."

"I won't be staying," she announced.

He suspended a bit of turkey on the way to his mouth. "But we agreed that it would be advisable for you to stay out of sight for some time."

"I have been here for some time," she said. "It's beginning to feel as if I've been here forever."

He chewed thoughtfully. "You'll have to stay. That's all there is to it."

"How long will you be here?"

"I'll be leaving day after tomorrow."

"Then that's when I'll be leaving."

Oliver touched his lips with his napkin, chewed, and swal-

lowed. He put down his napkin, rose, leaned over the table—
and slapped her resoundingly. Afterward he sat down. "You
will do as I order you to do."

Rosanna's eyes were fixed on the knife holder hanging on
the side of a kitchen cabinet. She rose and nonchalantly
walked around the table. Oliver was eating again, unaware
that he might be moments away from death. She stood near
the knife rack, looking at the back of his head. . . .

Ames had just filled his mouth with a plump oyster when
he felt her fingers clench in his hair. His head was jerked
back, and he felt a stinging at his exposed throat as the razor-
sharp blade of the chef's fillet knife pressed there, bringing
up a tiny line of blood as it penetrated the two layers of skin.

"No man strikes me," Rosanna said softly. "No one. Do
you understand?"

"Put the knife away, Rosanna," he told her.

The pressure on the knife blade eased. He chewed, swallowed, lifted his napkin, and touched his throat, examining
the bloodstain on the damask. "You must learn more self-
control, my dear."

He was jolted to the core as a skillet slammed against the
side of his head. He caught himself before he hit the floor,
but the chair overturned with a crash. He sat down weakly
and put a hand to his head.

"You will never, *never* lay a hand on me in violence again,"
Rosanna said. She held the iron skillet at the ready.

Ames shook his head and struggled to his feet. "You have
made your point," he said.

"I will be leaving here in the morning."

"Perhaps that would be best."

She put the skillet down and turned to walk away. He hit
her in the back of the neck with his fist. In a few seconds she
had crumpled onto the floor, and he was kneeling astride her,
his fists pounding into her face, into her stomach, into her
soft breasts. She tried to reach for his eyes with her long
nails, but he had no difficulty evading them, and then she lost
consciousness.

* * *

Breathing heavily, Oliver Ames stood over the fallen woman. His face was flushed, his heart pounding from the exertion. His head hurt, but his pride was hurt worse; if she had hit him just a bit harder with the iron skillet, he would have lost a fight to a woman—a woman who had first risked his anger by disobeying him in the matter of Lafe Baker. Worse than sparing Baker's life, she then had the effrontery to defy him to his face.

She would never know how close she came to death as he stood over her, his fists still clenched, his blood up. All the tension of the past few months flooded over him. He seethed with the knowledge that he had almost lost the home company, the firm to which he had been apprenticed at an early age, the source of the Ames brothers' heavy investment in Crédit Mobilier and the Union Pacific. He'd been so busy looking after his brother Oakes's business that he'd almost lost Oliver Ames & Sons. By the time he had come to his senses, the vultures were gathering eagerly to pick the bones of the company that had been founded by his father. And although the shovel works could show assets of fully fifteen million dollars against debts of only eight million, it had been touch and go. That was why he had ordered Rosanna Pulliam to go on a cleanup campaign. That was why, in retrospect, he felt like killing her—for letting Lafe Baker live with the knowledge that Oakes had bribed members of Congress.

Slowly, slowly, sanity came back to him. He had stopped the spasms of bankruptcy and had stanched the outflow of the company's lifeblood. All was well. Money from the profits of Crédit Mobilier had been directed back into Oliver Ames & Sons. He was secure.

He had no need to kill Rosanna.

She was in bed on satin sheets. She hurt. Her face hurt, and her stomach hurt, and her chest hurt. It hurt to breathe. She feared that one or more of her ribs was broken. She had to force one eye to open, just a slit. Next to her on the bed was Oliver Ames.

"Ah, so you're with us again. . . ."

"You son of a bitch," she whispered through her swollen, battered lips.

"I won't kill you," he said. "You're much too decorative and much too useful to kill."

Rosanna was silent. She was not going to make him the same promise. He was a dead man. He was a walking dead man unless he did kill her before she could get to her feet and catch him unawares.

"Perhaps now you'll listen to reason," Ames challenged her. "I want you to stay here at least through the summer."

"I want a doctor," Rosanna said, and the effort brought pain to her ribs.

"I'm afraid that will be impossible," he replied. "In fact, before the staff see you in this unfortunate condition, I'm going to send them away for an extended holiday."

She slept. He brought her food the next morning and sat beside the bed as she ate.

"I'll be going in an hour or so," he informed her. He stood and began to remove his clothes.

Realizing his intention, she tried to pull herself away to the other side of the bed, but he seized her by the arm and jerked her toward him. The resulting pain in her chest caused her to scream.

He was on her then, his weight causing terrible pain, though she did not cry out again. She had to fight for breath. He was finished quickly.

"You'll have to manage for yourself, my dear," he said as he dressed afterward. "I'll send the servants back in a month or so, after you've had time to heal. We wouldn't want them to see you in this condition, would we?"

Again she slept. This time when she awoke, the house was deathly quiet, and darkness was coming. She felt a great need to relieve herself. Movement was agony, but while she was out of bed, she made her way slowly and painfully to the kitchen. She drank a glass of water and tried to eat, but was prevented from it by the pain in her stomach.

For days she burned, but with each day the hurt receded. Her face had gone livid, with colorful blues, reds, and purples, but the swelling in her eyes had gone down a bit, enabling her to see. She was able to breathe without the sharp, piercing stabs of pain. She was eating again, and soon she was taking short walks outside, then making it as far as the strand. The salt water seemed to help her aches and pains.

When she was able to walk without stooping, when a heavy veil could conceal the yellowing bruises on her face, she packed her things. All of the horses had been removed from the stables, so she walked northward to the nearest house and arranged for a local man to come in a buggy for her and her belongings. Soon she was on a train heading for Boston and then New York.

She had decided not to kill Oliver Ames. A swift death was too merciful. She had decided that before she reached New York City and disappeared into its masses, she would hit Mr. Oliver Ames where it would hurt him most: in the pocketbook and in his position of power.

She had learned a lot about Oliver Ames when he had panicked and ordered the deaths of three men whom he perceived to be a threat to his wealth and position. She knew what meant most to him in life, and she had the ammunition to hurt him—and his brother—badly. She had learned during the war years never to trust anyone, always to scout in advance a path of retreat, and always to gather incriminating information on one's so-called allies as well as on one's enemies. In spite of his money and his power, Oliver Ames was, in matters of intelligence gathering, an amateur.

Rosanna had had little difficulty obtaining a copy of Crédit Mobilier's list of congressional stockholders. John O'Brian had not done a very imaginative job of hiding it. She had tucked it away in her little Brooklyn hideaway since the night of O'Brian's murder.

After an extended visit to the home district, Philip Trent returned to his Washington office, where he found Miss Mercy alone. He interrupted her recital of events during his absence to ask, "Where's Mrs. Grey?"

"She is no longer with us, poor dear," Mercy said, shaking her head.

Philip felt a totally unexpected sense of loss. "And why is she no longer with us?"

"It's her husband, poor thing," Mercy explained. "He has been quite ill—he was even in the hospital for a while. She worked during that time, but after the doctors sent him home, she said that she had to be there to take care of him. I begged her to take only a few days off—or a few weeks if necessary—but she said that it just wouldn't work out. I got the idea that she was planning to leave Washington altogether."

Philip realized that he was already missing not only Julia but Adam as well. Mercy had picked up a stack of correspondence and was beginning to brief him on letters of importance. "Let it wait, Miss Mercy," he said.

"But, Congressman," Mercy wailed as he went out the door, "you just got back."

He breathed a sigh of relief when he saw that the windows were open in the Grey house. He walked rapidly up the pathway through blossoming flowers, then knocked on the door.

The door opened, and Julia was standing there, her eyes swollen from weeping. She wore a dark color, something between purple and black, which made her look slim and regal.

"I came as soon as I heard," he said. He took her hand, raising his other hand to her cheek to wipe away a stray tear.

"Don't mind me," she said. "I cry easily. Actually, he seems to be much, much better."

She removed her hand from Philip's and motioned him into the little sitting room. "He's sleeping now. I was hoping that you would get back to Washington before we left the city."

"But where are you going?" he asked.

She sat down, indicating that he should also make himself comfortable. "We're Virginians, you know."

"I know."

"We've talked many times about going home."

"Does Adam think it wise?"

"He had two brothers who died fighting for the Confederacy," she explained. "His father disowned him. When Adam chose to fight for the Union, his father wrote him that his 'treasonous act' had killed his mother. They're all dead now, all of our immediate families. My parents died during the war. But I imagine we'll encounter a relative or two when we go back."

"Then why go at all?" Philip asked. "It seems to me that I've heard Adam say he'd never go back."

"You're right," she admitted, nodding. "There will be many people who will remember that he left home and hearth to fight for the enemy. Adam said that he would never give them the chance to laugh at him . . . to tell him that he got what he deserved."

"What made him change his mind?"

She sighed. "He thinks he's going to die."

"No," Philip said quickly. "We won't let him."

Adam's voice came from the bedroom. "That's going a bit far, you know," he called weakly, "when you won't even let a man die when he's ready."

One of the wheels on Adam's dolly squeaked as he rolled into the room. His face was a death's-head, his skull covered by so thin a layer of flesh that the bone structure showed through. Philip leaned down and took Adam's hand.

"Give a man a lift," Adam said.

During past visits Philip had seen Adam pull himself from his dolly into his favorite chair with the strength of his arms; now Philip had to lift him. He weighed no more than a six-year-old child. Close up, there was a quality of parchment-like fragility in the skin of Adam's face and neck.

"I'm glad I didn't miss you," Philip said, taking his usual chair across from Adam's.

"I haven't even started packing yet," Julia said.

"Must you go?" Philip asked, looking at Adam.

Adam shrugged his thin shoulders. "Perhaps I just want to show them at home that I can stand up to their hatred."

"Adam, won't you be fighting the wrong enemy if you go back to Virginia?" Philip asked seriously. "The South is defeated. The radicals are rubbing her nose in the mud and mire. I don't think you'd enjoy seeing that."

"I didn't fight to punish anyone," Adam said.

"So let it be as it is," Philip beseeched him. "If you feel you have to fight something or someone, join me in my fight. God knows I need all the help I can get. I think you'll find that corruption in government and business is a worthy adversary. You've told me several times, Adam, that I shouldn't give up, no matter what." He sighed. "I think I understand why you want to go home, and I can't say positively that you're wrong. I guess I'd want to go home to Maryland if . . ." He paused.

"So you're throwing my words back into my teeth," Adam said. "You're telling me that it's not time to quit, not time to go back to Virginia to seek the dubious comfort of being buried in the earth of my home state." He sighed. "Well, you may be right, my friend." He laughed. "At least it's nice to know that you care enough to ask me not to go."

"Actually," Philip said teasingly, "it's because I don't want to lose Julia at the office. Miss Mercy cringes away from me and tries to keep a desk between us when we're without a chaperone."

Julia laughed heartily.

"And all the time I thought it was my brilliant conversation," Adam said.

"And the way you cook hoecakes," Philip put in. "Let's not forget that."

"I'm afraid you'll have to cook your own for a while," Adam said.

"For a while?" Philip echoed. "Does that mean you're not going to take my number-one office worker away from me?"

"Since you have begged so nicely," Adam said.

"Adam—" Julia began.

But Adam lifted a hand to hush her. "I apologize to both of you for upsetting you. I suppose it was my being in the hospital." He shuddered. "Melancholy place. Actually, I began to feel better the minute I came back home." He shifted in the chair and tried to hide the spasm of pain that obviously came to him with the movement.

Julia hurried to his side.

"I think I'll rest a bit," he said weakly.

Over his protests Philip carried him to the bed and placed

him down gently. Adam slept all afternoon and through the evening.

As darkness came Philip lit the lamps while Julia prepared an omelet, which they shared. During the meal she talked about Adam, about how they had been children together, how their families had been close friends. Adam and she had been childhood sweethearts, and neither of them ever had the slightest doubt that they would be married when they were of age. Julia was in her teens when she married Adam—a brand-new graduate of the United States Naval Academy—when he was on his way to join his ship in southern waters. When the war came, she took herself into exile, for Adam chose to stay with his ship. She had come alone to Washington, had found the little house and a job, and had waited for the war to end.

She talked for over an hour, and Philip listened intently until she was talked out. "My goodness," she said as she rose and began clearing the table. "It's nine o'clock."

"Yes," he said.

She came to him and took his hands. "Thank you, Philip," she said. "I needed someone to listen. And thank you for convincing Adam to stay. I will do whatever he wishes, of course, but I was not at all sure that it was wise for us to go back to Virginia."

Yet, as it happened, the three of them went to Virginia only ten days later. Adam had rallied extremely well, looking less like a living skeleton. The trip, which was his idea, was made in a rented surrey, with Adam tucked between Philip and Julia, a padding of thick cushions under him. Their destination was an area that had been appropriated by Edwin Stanton, secretary of war, in 1864, when Union casualty lists were at a bloody peak, to be used as a military cemetery. The two-hundred-ten-acre site was on the grounds of a house that had been built by George Washington Parke Custis, the adopted son of George Washington. In the mansion house Lieutenant Robert E. Lee had been united in marriage with Mary Anna Randolph Custis in 1831; and the house had served as a departure point for General Robert E. Lee when he started south to take command of the Virginia troops at the beginning of the war.

They stood on a little rise, looking down at neat rows of simple headstones. "What do you think of it?" Adam asked his wife.

"It's a beautiful place," Julia said.

"It's in Virginia," Adam said. "It finally occurred to me that I didn't have to go all the way home. A simple request in writing, that's all, and any man who fought for the Union can have his resting place here."

Philip cleared his throat. It was a bit unnerving to hear Adam talk so calmly of being buried in the Arlington Cemetery, but he made no comment.

Philip entered his office one morning to find Julia at her desk, smiling at him from behind a large vase of fresh flowers. "Are we keeping banker's hours these days, sir?" she asked.

"Good morning, Mrs. Grey," he said with genuine pleasure.

"The mail, sir," she said.

"Sort it for me, please."

"I have done so." She held out one envelope. "Now here's an interesting one. It smells of lilacs, and isn't that a lovely lavender?" She smiled, cocking one eyebrow suggestively.

Philip sniffed the envelope and checked the postmark. It had been mailed in New York. It was addressed in block letters. He opened it to read, also in block letters: ASK OAKES AMES HOW MANY SHARES OF CRÉDIT MOBILIER STOCK HE GAVE TO JAMES BROOKS.

James Brooks was the Democratic floor leader in the House, and he was known as a railroad congressman.

Two days later another lavender lilac-scented letter arrived. It read: ASK OAKES AMES HOW MANY SHARES OF CRÉDIT MOBILIER HE GAVE TO HENRY WILSON.

Oakes Ames and Philip Trent shared seats on the Railroad Committee, which had become nothing more than a debating group. Since no favorable legislation was needed—the transcontinental was being rushed toward estimated completion in 1869—and since there were not enough votes on the committee to force investigation of Philip's constant charges of corruption and graft, nothing was done. The committee did, however, meet occasionally.

After one such meeting Philip, intrigued by the anonymous letters from New York, caught up with Oakes Ames in the hall and asked, "By the way, Oakes, how many shares of Crédit Mobilier did you sell to the Democratic floor leader?"

Oakes Ames's mouth fell open, but he recovered quickly. "I consider that an insulting question, Trent."

In Utah, a spasm of greed and competition brought destruction to the transcontinental railroad and death to its laborers. Each mile of track laid represented huge amounts of money. Union Pacific crews stole dirt from the Central Pacific's embankments; Central Pacific men stole the dirt back. The two companies blasted out parallel cuts from the hard rock, past the point where the tracks extended from the west and the east could have met. Neither company gave the other any warning before setting off the dynamite. The Irishmen of the Union Pacific took pleasure in sending the blue-clad Chinamen scrambling for safety with tons of loose rock tumbling toward them. The Chinese retaliated, sending down a mountainside on an Irish crew, to kill many of them.

It took action by President Grant to halt the railroad wars. He ordered General Grenville Dodge to stop the parallel construction and to bring the rails together at a place called Promontory Point, near Ogden, Utah. Congress concurred, quickly passing a law: . . . *the common terminal of the Union Pacific and the Central Pacific railroads shall be at or near Ogden; and the Union Pacific Railroad Company shall build, and the Central Pacific Railroad Company shall pay for and own, the railroad from the terminus aforesaid to Promontory Summit, at which point the rails shall meet and connect and form one continuous line.*

To the surprise of many and to Philip Trent's satisfaction,

the Senate of the United States added a few clauses to the new act, which proved quite disturbing to the railroad men in both houses of the Congress. Most importantly to Philip Trent and the few men who, as the months went by, had come to stand with him, the Senate called on the U.S. attorney general to investigate both companies to determine if any fraud had been committed.

"It's like locking the barn door after the horse has been stolen," Julia said.

"True," Philip agreed. "The money has been spent and will not be recovered; but I still think it is necessary to air the matter, to expose to the nation those who were involved."

It would take Philip Trent until 1872, three years after the rails met in Utah and the transcontinental railroad was opened, to compile a complete list of participants in the scandal. One by one, the anonymous letters continued to arrive, sometimes weeks apart. At first they came from New York, then from Washington, and finally from San Francisco. Each letter was similar; only the names were different: ASK OAKES AMES HOW MANY SHARES HE GAVE TO JOHN GARFIELD. ASK OAKES AMES HOW MANY SHARES HE GAVE TO SCHUYLER COLFAX. And on and on until—as Philip Trent exposed each new name to the congressman from Massachusetts and as pressure was mounted on Ames from the Justice Department—Oakes Ames broke.

The nation gasped and held its breath as Ames testified before the full House of Representatives.

Philip, who had won reelection overwhelmingly in 1870, felt no sense of victory, only sadness as Oakes Ames called the roll of dishonor that included a former Speaker of the House who was now Vice-President, the Democratic floor leader of the House, and several other senators and representatives, including a political "comer," Congressman James A. Garfield.

When Oakes Ames had completed his testimony, the Speaker gave the floor to the congressman from Maryland, Philip Trent.

"I have only a few things to say," Philip said, speaking so softly that those in the gallery had difficulty hearing him. "The men you have heard named before this great legislative body—the senators and representatives and the others who have been entrusted with the responsibility of governing this nation by the electorate—have shared in a profit of somewhere between thirty-three and fifty million dollars. But that is not the last of it. The profits that they pocketed represent only a portion of the cost to the taxpayers that resulted from the railroads' owning a certain number of legislators. The record shows that the men whose names you have heard successfully led the fight to set aside the Union Pacific's first mortgage—in effect forgiving, or canceling, a debt to the federal government amounting to twenty-seven million dollars. Not satisfied with that arrogant raid on the public assets, these same legislators, with only a few of us resisting their eloquent pleas, executed a second mortgage, once again using public money, in the same amount, twenty-seven million dollars. Both sums, or a total of fifty-four million dollars, went into the coffers of the Union Pacific holding company, the Crédit Mobilier."

And so, suddenly, morality was discovered by the radical Republican Congress. Man after man asked for time to shout his anger to the world and to demand that the guilty be drawn and quartered.

Philip Trent let the radicals do the talking. He had only one other thing to say, and that was in private, with only one other man present. He made a special trip to the office of Congressman James A. Garfield, who, along with Schuyler Colfax, was loudly denying any connection with the Union Pacific Railroad and calling a liar anyone who said that he owned Crédit Mobilier stock. Since the stock ownership list had disappeared from the records of the company by the time subpoenas were issued, it was the word of Garfield and Colfax against that of Oakes Ames.

Garfield did not offer to shake hands with Philip. He merely nodded to acknowledge Philip's entrance into his inner office and waited.

"You told me once, Mr. Garfield," Philip said, "that you never bet on fixed horse races. You questioned my morality, my ethics, without asking whether or not I had known that the race was fixed, and when you formed your opinion of me, you didn't take into account that I returned the winnings on a bet that, in the first place, had not been my own."

"That was a long time ago, Trent," Garfield said. "Perhaps I did get the wrong idea about you."

"You did indeed," Philip said. "I only wish, Mr. Garfield, that I could say the same about you at this moment."

Garfield flushed, then opened his mouth to speak but remained silent.

Philip nodded once and then gave Garfield his back.

Gus Trent walked into a crowded Washington restaurant at lunchtime on a steamy, early-summer day. A waiter bowed to him when he said, "Congressman Trent's table, please."

Philip came to his feet and took his father's hand as Gus approached. Gus nodded and smiled to Miss Mercy and Mrs. Julia Grey. "Who's tending the store?" he asked.

"It's locked, barred, and secure," Mercy said. "Don't begrudge us one little outing, Mr. Trent."

"In fact," Gus said, taking his seat, "I'm delighted to find that I won't be left solely to the devices of my son during lunch."

"We're having the fillet of sole," Mercy said, "it being Friday."

Gus nodded. "So we'll all be good Catholics today, even if my Methodist forebears haunt me afterwards."

Gus had never voiced his disappointment that Philip had not married Leah Miles. He knew that Lloyd Miles and his sister were still in Washington and that Lloyd was now working for Jay Gould. Leah, he had learned, was still unmarried. He had deduced the reasons for the breakup of what he had thought an ideal romance from little things that Philip said and from the Washington gossip that had told him of Lloyd Miles's being dismissed from Crédit Mobilier and the Union

Pacific. He thought it was all a damned foolish way to be deprived of the chance of having a grandchild. He liked the vivid little lady who worked in Philip's office, but she was married.

Philip ordered for all, and at the insistence of Gus—much to the eyebrow-raising disapproval of the waiter—coffee was served before the meal.

Gus asked, "Is this some sort of celebration?"

"Yes and no," Philip replied. "Perhaps a belated celebration."

"Because the guilty have been punished?" Gus asked.

"Ha," Julia Grey said.

"Do I detect editorial comment in that syllable?" Gus asked teasingly.

"Only because the railroad barons have their little empires of western land," Julia explained. "And the stockholders of Crédit Mobilier have banked their windfall profits."

"But Philip has been vindicated," Gus said. "He has been proven to be on the side of the angels. At least some of the guilty have been punished."

"I'm afraid I have to agree with Julia," Philip said. "Ha."

"Meaning?" Gus asked.

"Two men were censured by Congress, one of them more for having been a Democrat than for having taken the railroad's bribes."

"James Brooks?" Gus said.

Philip nodded. "Poor old Brooks got the smallest cut of the pie because he belonged to the wrong political party. They let him in on the Crédit Mobilier bonanza just so they could say that the 'other side' in the House had been taken care of, brought into the fold of the bribe takers."

"Well, he did take the bribe," Mercy said. "I can't feel any sympathy for him."

"I suspect that John O'Brian's punishment was the most severe of all," Philip said.

"You're still of the opinion that his death was not suicide?" Gus asked.

"For what it's worth, yes."

"Dead is, I suppose, a bit more serious than being reprimanded by Congress," Gus allowed, "especially if, like Oakes Ames, the fall from grace is cushioned by a profit of millions from Crédit Mobilier and the railroad."

"We did show the nation that there is moral turpitude in the Congress," Julia said.

Gus noted that she had said "we."

"And we're not finished," she went on. "Philip is gathering evidence to show that the railroads still lord it over the little towns along the right-of-way. And they set freight rates at whatever the traffic will bear in any given locality."

"I think we can be proud of our congressman," Mercy said.

Philip smiled wryly. "I don't know, Miss Mercy. The graft that was exposed was minor. The side effects of the scandal will be felt for decades. We knocked the artificial props out from under the top-heavy structure that the railroad builders had fashioned and set the whole financial edifice to rocking. We revealed to the nation that the builders had taken all of the profit from the whole enterprise in advance, during the construction phase. We've shown that the greed of the barons has put the railroads in debt for what might well be decades. We've proved that the owners of railroad stock will have to wait years before they receive any dividends from their investment. That doesn't hurt the barons; they already have their money. It's the little people who are hurt, the average man who felt a patriotic duty to invest his savings in railroad stock. Many people put everything they had into the transcontinental, and the scandal sent the price of railroad stock tumbling."

Philip took a sip of coffee. The others, realizing that he had not finished, remained silent.

"So, you see, I'm not proud of my part in this affair. Two congressmen got kicked out, and one is dead. Does that make up for the thousands of ordinary people who got hurt badly when the market panicked because of the Crédit Mobilier affair?"

"You can't blame yourself for that," Julia said quickly.

"You did what you had to do, Son," Gus consoled. "Regardless, I'm proud of you."

"And I," Julia and Mercy said together.

"All right, bless God," Philip said, managing a grateful smile. "I'll settle for that."

Author's Note

Although some of the great American fortunes had been established prior to the American Civil War—John Jacob Astor, for example, had amassed something over twenty million dollars prior to his death in 1848—the base of the wealth of many of the so-called Four Hundred families rested firmly on war profiteering and/or that great burst of westward expansion that began during the Civil War, fueled by the urgent need to link the mines of the West with a Union starved for raw materials. Thus it is generally agreed that the period of our history known as the Age of the Robber Barons began in 1860 and, although it can be said with some justification that it never ended, was at least moderated during the administration of the trust-busting President, Theodore Roosevelt.

In telling stories involving both real and fictional characters, a writer often finds it difficult to achieve the proper combination of fairness, interest, and suspense. I have endeavored, however, even while indulging in fictional speculation about the covert actions of certain "barons," to give at least a hint of both sides of the story; for there was in those charismatic men who seized opportunity and fortune while helping to expand this country more than mere greed, more than amorality or lack of ethics, and something other than sheer ruthlessness. The achievements of the robber barons required foresight along with a burning ambition powered by personal dreams, native shrewdness coupled with ingenuity, and liberal quantities of sheer courage.

From the viewpoint of the 1990s it might be difficult to understand why President Lincoln and those who followed him were eager to lend six pioneer western railroads a total of sixty-five million dollars and, in addition, give the railroads clear title to land grants valued at an additional one hundred thirty million dollars.

To balance out the one-hundred-percent overrun on the estimated cost of building the first transcontinental railroad, one should look at another set of figures.

When the original Railroad Act, which was partially written by Abraham Lincoln, expired in 1946, the federal government had been repaid one hundred sixty-seven million dollars in principal and interest on the original loans. Moreover, it has been estimated that because of favored-treatment clauses written into the Railroad Act, the government has saved over one billion dollars in freight costs since its passage.

It is evident, then, that in the long run it was good financial policy to subsidize the building of the first transcontinental railroad. Whether it is possible to excuse the graft and greed that involved a future President, a Vice-President, and many influential members of Congress is left to the reader to decide.

THE HISTORICAL CHARACTERS

PRESIDENT ULYSSES S. GRANT had the dubious honor of presiding over one of the more corrupt periods in the history of American government. In addition to the celebrated Crédit Mobilier scandal and Benjamin Butler's abortive raid on the Treasury in the matter of a retroactive salary increase for Congress, Grant's secretary of war, W. W. Belknap, resigned when threatened with impeachment for accepting bribes. Treasury officials conspired with the Midwest Whiskey Ring to defraud the government of hundreds of thousands of dollars each year. The Sanborn Contracts scandal involved payments of about one hundred thousand dollars to a tool of Benjamin Butler's for work that should have been handled by the Treasury Department. Grant's private secretary was involved in graft. Grant's brother-in-law gave inside information to Jay Gould when Gould and James Fisk tried to corner the market in gold, an affair that resulted in near financial panic on Black Friday, September 24, 1869.

There are historians, however, who think that Grant himself was guilty of the same crime committed by President Richard Nixon, namely overreliance on his aides and advisers. These writers also point out that corruption was epidemic, and not only in Washington. Senatorships were for sale in Kansas. In the cities corrupt politicians sold paving, sewage, garbage disposal, and other municipal contracts to themselves in the guise of contractors. Boss William Tweed rose to Tammany Hall leadership in New York City through bribery of officials and donations to the poor.

So, while it was true that Grant made mistakes, perhaps he has gotten a "bad rap" over the years, and the worst thing that can be said about him is that good generals seldom make good presidents. It is on record that Grant did not profit from the corruption surrounding his administration. In fact, after leaving the White House, he found his income to be short of proper support for his family. He mortgaged all his property and used the money to buy a partnership in a banking house, where his penchant for trusting unworthy people cost him dearly—when his partners perpetrated frauds that left the firm, and Grant, bankrupt and penniless at a time when the disease that would kill him, cancer of the throat, was beginning to cause him intense suffering.

In pain, he wrote his *Personal Memoirs,* the generous publication of which contributed to the bankruptcy of another man who had difficulty managing money, Mark Twain. However, the five hundred thousand dollars earned by Grant's book enabled him to die in dignity, four days after he had finished writing it, and left his family secure.

SCHUYLER COLFAX was not renominated for the vice-presidency in 1872 because of his implication in the Crédit Mobilier scandal. It was also proven that in 1868 he accepted a four-thousand-dollar bribe from a supplier of stationery while he was chairman of the House Post Office Committee. After his term as Vice-President he returned to private life and earned his living through lecturing. He died on January 13, 1885.

OAKES AMES died, in disgrace, on May 8, 1873.

JAMES BROOKS and HENRY WILSON were U.S. representatives implicated by Oakes Ames in the Crédit Mobilier affair. Only James Brooks was reprimanded by the Congress.

OLIVER AMES, a shadowy figure seldom mentioned in history other than in connection with his older brother, Oakes Ames, died in 1877.

ANDREW JOHNSON, after his term in the White House ended, went back to Tennessee, where he never ceased efforts to vindicate himself politically. After several unsuccessful campaigns for office in Tennessee he was elected to the Senate in 1875, but died on July 31, 1875, after sitting in one short session.

EDWIN McMASTERS STANTON surrendered the office of secretary of war on May 26, 1868, and returned to the practice of law. He died on December 24, 1869, four days after the Senate had confirmed his appointment by President Grant to the Supreme Court.

GEORGE FRANCIS TRAIN, that curious man who, by twice setting the world's record for circling the globe, became the model for Phineas Fogg in Jules Verne's *Around the World in Eighty Days,* continued his fight for women's rights, vegetarianism, and the railroads.

JAMES A. GARFIELD became the twentieth President of the United States after being named on the thirty-fifth ballot as a compromise candidate at the Republican convention of 1880, breaking a deadlock between supporters of U. S. Grant and James G. Blaine. On July 2, 1881, Garfield was shot at the Washington train station by a man who had wanted Chester A. Arthur, Garfield's running mate, to be

President. Garfield died on September 19, 1881, after only four months in office, during which time he was incapacitated for eighty days.

In the matter of Crédit Mobilier, Garfield stated that he had been offered a gift of stock in January of 1868 but had refused the offer—in 1870.

GENERAL BENJAMIN FRANKLIN BUTLER, the Beast of New Orleans, was elected governor of Massachusetts as a Democrat in 1882. He ran for the presidency in 1884 on the People's party ticket but failed to win one electoral vote. He died in Washington on January 11, 1893.

GENERAL LAFAYETTE C. (LAFE) BAKER, "one of the worst rapscallions of an age in which rapscality paid high dividends," "cruel and rapacious," "that most notorious character," "the American Fouché," "the youthful head of the secret service," was never involved with the Secret Service as we know it today, a division of the Treasury Department. While working for Stanton's War Department during the Civil War, Baker called his intelligence and counterespionage organization the National Detective Bureau. After being fired by President Andrew Johnson, Baker published a melodramatic account of his service, a book written with the help of a journalist named Phineas Headley. As in this story, Baker was involved in a hotel venture in Lansing, Michigan, but any other connection he might have had with events in Washington during the period covered by this work of fiction is pure imagination and literary license.

THE BARONS, Thomas Durant, Collis P. Huntington, Leland Stanford, Mark Hopkins, and Charles Crocker, were quite real, and their achievements as outlined herein were commendable, even if their methods of ensuring favorable treatment by the national legislature were not. Aside from isolated quotes taken from historical records, the conversations and many of the actions of the barons come from the imagination of the writer, who claims fictional license in a speculative effort to explain the events leading up to the exposure of Oakes Ames and the Crédit Mobilier scandal.

* * *

The author wishes to thank the hardworking editorial staff at Book Creations Inc.: Pamela Lappies and Laurie Rosin, editors; Elizabeth Tinsley and Marjie Weber, copyeditors; Betty Szeberenyi, researcher; Donna Marsh and Deborah Dobson, keyboardists.